REVELATION ON THE SEA ISLAND

NANCY FLINCHBAUGH

I dedicate this book to the Gullah people, the descendants of West African slaves who have suffered and triumphed, contributing so many gifts to our American lives.

I dedicate it particularly to these African American coworkers and friends who have taught me so much: Selena Singletary, Michael Crockett, Cheryl DeGroat Ayers, the late Winkie Mitchell, Mary Anna Robinson, Tiffany Wanzo, and Pastor Adam Banks.

Acknowledgments

I am grateful to the following people for helping me bring this story to life: Kathie Giorgio of AllWriters' Workplace and Workshop, who met with me weekly for several years through two drafts of this book; my husband, Steve Schlather, my traveling companion, guide and editor; and Deb Harris, All Things That Matter Press for believing in this project and for her painstaking editing.

In writing this book, my husband and I traveled to Georgia, North and South Carolina twice in my effort to learn about the Gullah culture. I want to acknowledge the wonderful travel guides, tourist sites, and tours that have been developed to teach the history of the South and particularly the African American and Gullah history, which included the following.

Savannah, Georgia: the Hop On/Hop Off tours; Harriet Beecher Stowe, Flannery O'Connor, and Andrew Low houses; Pin Point Heritage Museum; Journeys by Faith Savannah tour by Karen Wortham.

Hilton Head, South Carolina: Coastal Discovery Museum, Gullah Tours; Sunset Cruise.

Charleston, South Carolina: Angel Oak Tree, Gullah Tours, Boone Hall Plantation.

Monck's Corner, South Carolina: Cypress Gardens Nature Preserve. Myrtle Beach, South Carolina: Brookgreen Gardens, Huntington State Park.

Wilmington, North Carolina: City's Guide to Wilmington's African-American Heritage, Eagle Island Cruise.

CAST OF CHARACTERS

The Magnificent and Marvelous Book Club

Abigail Wesley – environmental activist
Jane Masters - entrepreneur
Katharine Long – retired religion professor
*Molly Mabra – retired government worker
*Priscilla Johnson – administrative assistant
Sallie Quisenberry – retired kindergarten teacher

Mabra Brothers

*Tom Mabra – wife of Molly Mabra
*George Mabra – Sun Power House coordinator
*Leo Mabra - attorney

Sun Power House Group Home Guys

*Marcus Welby Jones
*Antonio
*Max

Farming and Restoring with the MAMs Group Home Women

*Nancy Reagan Hunter Smith
*Zorastria
*Artemis

Priscilla's Ancestors

John – Son of a plantation owner
*Annie   former slave who birthed John's daughter, Moriya
*Moriya – daughter of John and Annie

Others

*Mr. and Mrs. Ronald Hunter Smith – Reagan's parents
*Sonia Jackson, "Mama Jack", anthropology professor and gourmet chef
Moses Sun – former boyfriend of Priscilla

*Grand Ma Ma – Welby's great-grandmother, a Spirit speaking from the other side
*Madame Biddy – Medicine Woman on Hilton Head
*Rita Mae Sheldon – Relative of Priscilla

*Denotes Gullah roots

PROLOGUE

John slowed Old Cotton, approaching the small dock nestled among the pines by the ocean. Grime from his night ride caked his face and riding garments. The crickets serenaded him as he secured his horse to a nearby tree. Coast clear, he slipped out of his shirt and britches and waded into the sea. On this warm August dawn, the water refreshed his sleep-deprived bones. He splashed out, then fell back into the waves, floating on the saltwater, letting it soothe and cleanse, rocking him back and forth in the gentle ebb and flow of the sea.

On the horizon to the east, brilliant colors dispersed fading night, reflecting bright orange and pink on the waters of dawn. He congratulated himself on perfect timing while he relaxed into the surf, watching the magnificent display. As much as he detested the weekly trek to the island to manage the plantation, he always loved this moment and the young woman, Annie, who would greet him soon.

"I'm makin' you into a man," his dad told him. Really? Or was that just an excuse to get John to do the dirty work? Next year, he planned an escape of his dad's orders, with college in the north. Right now, he could only be his father's child.

As the golden ball emerged from the great green sea, seagulls soared overhead and landed on the beach. Did the birds enjoy the sunrise, too? He caught a wave and body-surfed toward shore, then squatted and pushed up against the flow, wading. The birds scattered, taking flight, sweeping above, winging toward the heavens. He plodded along, his feet heavy in sand, preparing for his onerous responsibility.

CHAPTER ONE
INTRODUCTION TO GULLAH LAND

The MAMs Reconvene

Priscilla Johnson poured cider into a large cauldron on the Mabras' stove and turned on the burner. "I want to help you, Molly," she explained. "I feel guilty that you host the MAMs Book Club every month. You do all of this for us. I came early to help."

"Thanks," Molly said. "I appreciate you, and your cider and those caramel apples you brought." She smacked her lips. "It's been a long time since I enjoyed a caramel apple. Love them! You're the only one of us still working, so I'm glad I can do this for you. You deserve a break now and then."

"Bless your heart," Priscilla responded, feeling grateful for a friend like Molly. She watched her working quickly, knowing the rest of the group would arrive soon. She grabbed the Irish whiskey from their liquor cabinet, fixed a fresh pot of coffee, and heated water for tea.

"Hard to know what to prepare for the MAMs," Molly complained. "Most of you don't eat much, but Jane always wants wine. Tonight, I thought we could celebrate our recent trip to Ireland with some Irish whiskey." She pulled out a bottle of Merlot as well.

"Anything else I can do to help?" Priscilla asked.

"Here," Molly suggested, opening the silverware drawer and pulling some plates out of the cupboard. "Set the table."

Priscilla organized and arranged, lighting the Thanksgiving candle beside the cornucopia. Molly brought out a tray of cheese and crackers. Priscilla unfolded an orange napkin to provide some autumn color by the clear tray.

When the doorbell rang, Molly rushed to answer and Priscilla heard Sallie's familiar laugh as she greeted Molly. "Hello, dear! How are you tonight, Mol?"

"Still enjoying retirement, I'd say," Molly responded.

"Wonderful, isn't it?" Sallie replied. "Highly recommended, no?"

"I never would have retired, if not for the breast cancer, but now I'm wondering why I didn't do it earlier." Molly stood by Priscilla at the table.

"I know, I know," Sallie said. "Work is overrated."

"But we are some of the fortunate few these days with an actual pension, you know? Me with my state pension after working at the city, and you with your teacher retirement," Molly replied.

"Tell me about it," Priscilla responded. "I don't know if I'll ever get to retire. We laugh about being greeters at Wal-Mart, but it's really not funny at all."

"Righto, righto," Sallie agreed as the doorbell chimed again. This time, Sallie did the honors, leaving Molly and Priscilla to finish preparations in the kitchen.

When she finished, Priscilla slipped into the living room to greet Abigail, Jane and Katharine and take drink orders. Then she helped Molly serve everything up, before relaxing into the warm, familiar monthly circle.

Molly began, "It's great to be back home with all of you. And time to prepare for another adventure. Destination: North and South Carolina and Georgia!"

Priscilla scanned the room, enjoying the faces of her good friends of the MAMs Book Club, aka The Magnificent and Marvelous Book Club. They'd journeyed a long way since Molly first called them together to start a romance-reading book club many years back. She reminisced on all the fun they'd shared. First, as Romance Readers Anonymous, they'd enjoyed the predictable fare of strong women finding wonderful men in that delightful genre. But they branched out after a transformative moment while visiting the Butterfly House on the Canadian side at Niagara Falls, taking a leap into a variety of other genres. Forays into nonfiction and mysteries led to nonfiction pieces on the environment, criminal justice and more.

Priscilla had learned so much from these ladies. Because of them, she'd traveled to an archaeological dig in Turkey and, most recently, to Ireland to explore roots. What good fortune, although she didn't always agree with them, and wished they wouldn't drink so much wine. Truth be told, she really appreciated their friendship.

She focused on Molly, the only African American in the group. But, no, she remembered, so not true. She kept trying to process her recent news. The MAMs sent away their DNA for testing after studying genealogy, before their trip to the Emerald Isle. Priscilla learned her own blood contained African roots, and that therefore, Molly was her blood sister, a fact that still hadn't quite sunk in. She really admired Molly's career at River City in Community Development over the years. In retirement, Molly remained active, volunteering with the FARM and the Sun Power House, the re-entry and recovery group homes the MAMs birthed. Without Molly, there would be no book club. She couldn't ask for a better blood sister, really.

Molly interrupted Priscilla's thoughts. "Okay, ladies, welcome back.

I'm serving Irish coffee to celebrate our trip to the Emerald Isle. What a journey. And the timeline of our grant to take our group home residents traveling is ticking. We head south in February."

"Cheers!" Jane held up her glass. "To us! And now, could you serve me up a glass of wine, too? It wouldn't be a proper MAMs meeting without that red wine!"

Molly poured a glass of wine for Jane. "Anyone else?" she asked.

Priscilla watched the others turn down the wine, glad they weren't all drinking as much as Jane tonight. She didn't like that habit of the MAMs, but she felt so grateful for the grant Molly and Abigail wrote to help the group home members explore the lands of their DNA, not only because it helped the young ones in recovery, but also because it gave her an opportunity to travel. Her own budget didn't create much extra for such extravagance.

"Won't it still be snowing then?" Sallie asked. Sallie Quisenberry, a retired kindergarten teacher, never failed to make Priscilla laugh. And Sallie still focused on the children every time they discussed a book, even though she'd never married or had children of her own.

"Possibly," Jane said. "But you know I have a condo at Myrtle Beach and my experience is that February isn't too bad. Now, avoid January, but February? Almost spring, really. We're talking the South, warmer down there, you know!"

Priscilla nodded. Yes, Jane would know. The one millionaire in the group, she jet-setted about, occasionally springing for funds to let the MAMs travel with her. Jane had helped with the airfare for Ireland and financed their trip to Hawaii, as well. Priscilla also identified with Jane as the only other tried and true Republican in the bunch.

Molly announced, "So, now we're going to read about the Gullah people. We hope to visit some Gullah communities on our trip. The old villages are breaking up too quickly these days with all the development going on."

"Remind me again," Priscilla said. "Who are the Gullah?"

Molly gave her a look, like she'd said something wrong, then asked, "Didn't you read *Mama Day*? The story exposes aspects of the Gullah culture, but doesn't really come right out and say, 'This is Gullah.' Let me give you a little background.

"My ancestors— yours, too, Priscilla— were kidnapped from their homes in western Africa and brought to the United States as slaves, to make the Southern plantation owners rich. Some were brought because they were experts in growing rice. West Africa's coastal regions are very similar to our southeastern coast. The islands along the coasts of Florida, Georgia, South Carolina, and North Carolina are called the Sea Islands. The plantation owners relied on the slaves not only to do the back-breaking manual labor, but also to develop the rice paddies. They knew how to build channels and provide the flooding needed to nurture the rice crops.

"The Sea Islands were dangerous areas for the white plantation owners. They were subject to malaria and other diseases from the mosquitoes there. The African slaves were more resistant to those illnesses, having built up immunities, both from living in this environment and from their gene pool, although some also died — expendable to the owners. Because of this, the slaves experienced more autonomy on the islands and the culture they brought from Africa remained relatively intact. That culture is now referred to as Gullah and sometimes Gullah Geeche. We'll read more about this later in some other books."

"But what does that have to do with Cocoa and Mama Day?" Priscilla asked. "Were they Gullah?"

"Bingo!" Sallie laughed. "They lived on a Sea Island. Yes, that's the point."

"Oh," Priscilla said. "They were very superstitious then? I didn't like that about them. Are all the Gullah people that way?"

Molly smiled. "One of the books I've got for you to read is called *Blue Roots* and it explains all about the folk magic of the Gullah people."

Katharine added, "Most early cultures had folk medicine. Now it might seem rather strange to us, but when they do research about it, they often find that the herbs actually have medicinal value."

Abigail said, "Research also shows that the power of prayer affects illness. And the placebo effect is more powerful than many drugs. So what you believe is going to happen makes a big difference. We can't just dismiss all these folk remedies."

"But in this book, some of the remedies were pure evil. Look at what happened to George! Do you believe in Voodoo?" Priscilla said. "That's not Christian."

"Okay, okay," Molly said. "Now you're getting into the book. Let's take some time to talk about this book and how we responded."

Their discussion plunked them down into the heart of Gullah land on a fictitious island where the infamous matriarch gave the plantation owner seven children, then coaxed the deed to the island from him before she killed him. Gloria Naylor spun the story around the matriarch's descendants, which created a lively debate among the MAMs, as they prepared to explore the Gullah culture firsthand. The evening seemed to end before it began.

Priscilla's head swam, trying to sort out all the characters and the Gullah consciousness that wove its way through that very strange book. Were these people her ancestors, she wondered. They upset her sensibilities as a Bible-believing Christian who liked to pride herself on the straight and narrow.

"Whew," she said as the discussion came to a close. "That's a lot to process. You said we are going to just read some straight stuff explaining the Gullah, too, Molly?"

"Oh, yes, yes. I have many books for you." Molly pulled several off the bookshelf nearby, displaying them on the coffee table in front of the sofa.

"That's too many, Mol," Sallie said. "We'll never get through all those before February."

"Right, I realize that. How about we each pick one book and plan to do a book report next month? Create a summary sheet if you can, to enlighten us all."

Priscilla perused the possible books, worried about doing a book report for the MAMs. Usually, she didn't talk much at meetings. She needed a short book with basic information. *The Water Brought Us: the Story of the Gullah-Speaking People* by Muriel Miller Branch seemed basic—and rather thin.

Once home, she placed it on her nightstand and procrastinated. She didn't mean to avoid it, but she did cover it with her daily devotional book. She scheduled herself a whole Saturday to read the little book, before the next club meeting. Then unpleasant memories from high school history class flooded back, slave ships and plantations, yuck. Jesus wouldn't approve, she knew. Nothing could be glossed over from those days. She hated the plain evil of it all.

The chapter on religion swept her preconceptions away. The Gullah people were very Christian. Yes, they incorporated some African rituals into spiritual practice, but they believed in Jesus and God. They took baptism very seriously. Some dabbled in folk medicine— the only kind they could afford —but overall, they were a God-fearing people. At the end of the day, she wanted to meet some of these Gullah people, her ancestors.

***

When the MAMs convened for their December meeting, they each shared about their various books. Priscilla tried to calm her racing heart when her turn came. Her voice quivered as she read from her notes. But after a few minutes, she stopped reading and explained how the Gullah people maintained their African culture for years because they were left more alone on the Sea Islands than the other slaves on the mainland. She asked, "Did you know the Gullah people were Christians? They worshipped in churches and wanted all their children to be baptized.

Before they could accept the Lord as their Savior, they had to spend time seeking. An elder would talk with them and send them outdoors to pray and meditate." She found this so interesting, she forgot to be nervous.

"That sounds like a vision quest," Katharine said. "The Native Americans had a practice like that, as did the native people in Australia. The Africans must have done something similar."

"But isn't it so nice that they used it to help their children become Christian, instead of just doing it the old way?" Priscilla asked. "Only after the elder decided they were ready could they get baptized and become a full-fledged Christian. In the back of the church, they had a 'mourner's' bench for those still living in sin and not ready to take the step. And they did this thing called the 'Shout', where they praised God and danced after worship. Sort of like the holy rollers where I come from. Not to say some of them didn't keep their superstitious stuff going on, too. I read a chapter about their folk practices," Priscilla added. "I guess that was what Mama Day was talking about, but I'm glad most of them were actually Christian."

Molly nodded. "Most African Americans back in the day became Christians, that's true. The plantation owners required it, but they weren't about to worship with their slaves. Can you imagine trying to read the Bible verses about loving your neighbor when you're treating your slaves like cattle? No, so the Black church developed on its own and with a very strong religious tradition. God knows they needed it to carry themselves through years of slavery and discrimination. Very hard to face all that without God."

Priscilla felt divided. How could her heart sing and moan at the same time? On the one hand, knowing these people followed Jesus made her so happy. On the other hand, their suffering made her want to cry. She held both feelings within her as the MAMs shared other books.

Abigail taught them about *Blue Roots: African American Folk Magic of the Gullah People* by Roger Pinckney. Katharine explained *Gullah Culture in America* by Wilbur Cross. Molly picked a new book, *Making Gullah: A History of Sapelo Islanders, race and the American Imagination* by Melissa L. Cooper, that was a little more political, talking about what really happened to the Gullah people and how they continued to get pushed off the Sea Islands as the tourism industry gained a strong hold on the southeastern coast.

Jane talked on *Gullah Branches: West African Roots*, written by the creative director at Brookgreen Gardens, Ronald Daise, who starred on Nickelodeon's rendering of the Gullah back in the '90s. Jane heard him do a game show presentation when she stayed at her condo at Myrtle Beach last winter and visited the gardens. She wanted the MAMs to meet her friend Ron on their trip south.

Sallie picked a different sort of book by Barbara Holmes called *Joy Unspeakable.* "You know," Sallie said, "there's a very deep thread of spirituality running through the Black experience in America. They say that persecution stokes the spiritual fervor of a people. Barbara calls this contemplative spirituality— from the ring shouting that Priscilla mentioned, to the spirituals, voicing hopes of freedom. Out of the Black church came the civil rights movement with the energy of love, transforming our society. Some of the roots of all this dwell with the Gullah people. I want to understand more."

***

By the time the women gathered again in January for a movie night to watch *Daughters of Dust,* they were rather well-versed in Gullah Culture. Molly served up popcorn and drinks all around, and they settled back to learn about some women leaving the Sea Islands. Priscilla looked forward to their upcoming trip.

Grand Ma Ma Weighs In

I gotta tell you, I'm impressed with these MAMs and how they're helping my great-grandson, Welby. I been lookin' in on him from time to time. I used to haunt him a little to get him to straighten up, thinking if he got touched by an angel, something might change. Sure enough, I thank the good Lord, he's got himself back on the straight and narrow. Makes me downright happy when I see so much bad going on down there with so many of my people these days.

Mm-hm. These MAMs got somethin' goin' on. I can hear gears rattling in Priscilla's blonde little head. Learning the ugly history of my people should be life-changin', you know? Priscilla's feelin' it. Nothing good about how those men done kidnapped my people, stole us away from Africa and brought us over here to make their money off our backs.

Now I hear tell some folk want to take all this history out of the classroom. Not wanting to upset the chilluns, not a-wantin' them to feel bad. But that's the truth of it. They chained people to decks, laying them out in the slave ships, side by side with no room to move. Then they sold them like animals and worked them to death. Honey, I know you don't treat your dog that way. But you gotta tell history or it will repeat itself.

Now here's a good way to spin it. Let's let everyone be enjoyin' life, liberty, and the pursuit of happiness. Stop the discrimination and injustice that started way back then and continues into this day. But instead, these white people don't even want my people to vote no more.

The MAMs got it right, going on this trip and trying to learn the history for themselves. Priscilla and Reagan may need to cry a little, now that they know it's their ancestors we're talking about. But it should make all of you cry. I just hope that this trip makes a difference in their lives. For many Americans these days, the Sea Islands are just another place to go resorting. I think the MAMs know better. Yes, ma'am.

Welby Preaches It

Marcus Welby Jones brushed some lint off his suit, looking out the window. Snow fell gently in the early morning, coating the ground with translucent white. After a year in Yankee land, he still got excited to see snow, a rarity down South where he grew up.

In less than one year's time since they'd sprung him from his five-year sojourn in prison on a drug charge, he felt happy with himself for turning his life around. Well on his way to becoming an electrician, he could now refit houses with solar panels. Just recently, he started taking online classes to complete his college degree. With a little luck, next year this time, he might be living on the campus of a fine seminary and perhaps tie the knot for the first time in his life. At twenty-eight years of age, things were looking up. He gave thanks every day that his Aunt Mabel sent him north to this halfway house of Solar Power.

Today, they'd invited him to preach at Molly Mabra's church, preach and play. What a gig! He packed up his sax to play special music with the Mabra brothers as he reviewed the sermon he would preach later on. It was amazing that they asked him. Pastor Williams heard him speak in town a few weeks ago and invited him to step up. Welby had worked long and hard on what he wanted to say. "Ready or not, here I come," he muttered.

He heard a door slam downstairs, and George shouted, "You ready, Welby?"

"Yeah, man, I'm coming," he yelled back. Grabbing his overcoat, he headed down the stairs, stopping in the kitchen to pour a cup of coffee into a travel mug. Then he shrugged into his coat and followed George outside to his SUV.

"What you plannin' on saying today?" George asked.

"Oh, a little bit of this, a little bit of that. I'll tell my story and then some. I really want them to think about extending that hand of friendship across the great divide. Ain't nothin' goin' change if we can't do that, you know?"

"I'm real proud of you, man. Real proud," George told him, giving him a gentle pat on the arm.

Ever since Welby got down on his knees at the retreat center in

Ireland when the MAMs took them all over there to explore their roots, he felt the call to speak real bad. Sure, he celebrated Martin Luther King, Jr. like the rest of them, but that man died over fifty years ago now. New voices were needed to speak truth to the people. He heard enough fake news to last a lifetime. What the world needs now is truth and love, he believed.

George eased his car slowly along the slippery streets to the nondenominational African American church that he and his family called home, a place that Welby enjoyed also. Getting back on the straight path again felt real good. He just wished his girlfriend, Reagan, would come along, but she preferred a different type of church. He knew they would often go their separate ways, but he hoped that the bridge they found to each other could hold.

Church members greeted them warmly at the door and then they went into the sanctuary to set up their instruments. Welby tracked down the sound man to figure out where to stand and what microphone they wanted him to use. Then he relaxed in a pew to gather his thoughts and pray. He asked for a calm spirit and good words.

The service began, and he waited for a signal from George and Tom to go up for the special music. Today they were doing his old favorite, "When the Saints Come Marching In." George set the cadence on the drums, then Tom belted out some pure, piercing notes on his trumpet. Welby chimed in on his sax as the melody began. As far as Welby could hear, the horns blended into a splendid offering, providing cascading harmonies and bellowing resolve, rising up into the church rafters and reverberating off the walls. In no time at all, the people rose up, clapping and swaying. Then Molly took the mic and ripped out the verses, leading the clapping congregation in a sing-along. Welby didn't know she had it in her. Man, some music. He felt the Spirit dancing through his fingers and all around the sanctuary. How would he ever follow all this?

After their song, Welby returned to his seat, listening as Pastor Williams led the morning prayers and then read the scriptures. Before long, the pastor started talking about Welby, making his ears burn. He couldn't quite believe the nice things the man had to say about him. Really, a convicted felon? The pastor made Welby out as a saint and asked him to come forward. Welby grabbed his folder and high-tailed it up front as planned. Pastor Williams laid a hand on his shoulder, saying, "Let us pray. Dear God, Father Almighty, we just want to give you thanks today for our brother, Marcus Welby Jones. Lord, we do thank you for all you've brought him through. And we do thank you that he's answering your call. We just pray you will anoint Brother Welby with your spirit today. Let your words rise up and lift the roof off our sanctuary. Lord, please cover this conversation with faith, hope and love. We pray now in the name of our holy Savior, the one and only Jesus Christ of Nazareth. We do pray, Amen."

Then the pastor left Welby all alone, standing at the pulpit, and so he began in the only way he knew how, with a prayer. Sure, the pastor already prayed over him, but he needed to say it himself. "Dear God, it's Welby, standing in the need of prayer. Help me speak a good word for these fine people today. Help me to speak truth. Open their ears to hear your Word. Oh Lord, may the words of my mouth and the meditations of my heart be acceptable onto you, my Rock and my Redeemer. Amen."

And the people echoed, "Amen." Welby felt affirmed already. One thing he knew about preaching in a Black church: he would not be alone. The people would be chiming in and commenting and affirming, and he liked that. He missed it over in the white churches. He opened his folder and began, repeating lines from the scripture of the day.

"In the last days it will be, God declares, that I will pour out my Spirit upon all flesh, and your sons and your daughters shall prophesy, and your young men shall see visions, and your old men shall dream dreams. Acts 2:1-21.' The last days are upon us. I'm your young man with a vision." Welby felt goosebumps popping up on his arms as he read the familiar scripture. He remembered the words from his childhood, but didn't expect it to be talking about him.

The Amens started from the back of the church. Others chimed in, "Say it, brother."

"All right, all right."

Welby smiled. It felt so good, almost like home. He replied, "Thank you,"

"You're welcome, son," a lady called out from the front row.

A smile spread across his face. He felt hope springing up from deep inside. He continued. "The Lord poured out his Spirit upon me."

"Okay, okay," a man called out from the middle of the sanctuary.

"Yes, Lord," several women murmured from the choir loft.

"Tell it, Welby!" another man called out. Welby recognized George's voice.

The murmurings continued. Welby's joy expanded. Why did he ever trade this for those drugs? "You all are blessing me," he told them. "I haven't even started, and already, I feel your love. Thank you. Thank you. Thank you." Welby put his hand on his heart and nodded his head. "Thank you, Jesus."

Then he continued, "Today, I want to tell you about my vision. But first, let me tell you a little about Welby and then you'll know that I am just a lowly vessel for God Almighty. Throughout time, God chooses imperfect people to carry the message to the people. I'm no exception, none at all. He called Jacob, who stole his birthright from his brother Esau. He chose David, who stole another man's wife, sending her husband to be killed at the battlefront. He chose Zacchaeus, the cheating and stealing tax collector, as his disciple. And the Lord called me, Marcus Welby Jones, a little Black boy who grew up in North Carolina, to be his servant leader.

"As a young boy, I met the Lord and was baptized in the Atlantic Ocean on a sea island where my aunty and uncle and my Granny Ma Ma watched over me every summer, hands down the best time of my life until recently. Back then, I became their child preacher, sharing my gift of gab in the little church where we would stomp and shout our Sunday mornings away, Sunday nights and Wednesday nights, too, and sometimes other days in between."

"Yes, Lord," someone called out. "All right now."

Welby felt energized by their encouragement. "But then I got involved with the wrong crowd. I carried a chip on my shoulder because I was Black. In North Carolina, that meant I wasn't quite as good as my white brothers and sisters."

"Don't we know it," an old man shouted out from the back.

"Tell it, brother," a woman spoke out.

"No, no. You somethin', don't be lettin' them tell you that," an old lady in the front row told him with a stern look on her face.

Welby smiled. He loved the people in the Black church. "Thank you. That's exactly right, ma'am," he told the lady. "But I didn't think so then. I found other ways of making myself look good. I messed up in school, because those teachers didn't treat me right. I found the girls treated me all okay. I aimed to impress them with my fine clothes. I started driving trucks after high school. That brought in plenty of money to wine and dine the ladies. I started putting drugs into my body to keep me feeling good, instead of depending on the sweet wine of the Spirit. I became one lousy representative of Jesus Christ. Soon, the law caught up with me and you all know when they find drugs on a Black man, that means he's going to do time."

"Yes, sir," a man called out. "They like to lock us up, sure thing."

Welby nodded. "I spent five long years in the penitentiary, which I have to say didn't really change anything inside of me. No rehabilitation at the pen, just a cauldron that brewed up a lot of anger inside me, to be honest.

"But then my auntie shooed me up here to Ohio to the Sun Power House, run by George Mabra and the MAMs, the Magnificent and Marvelous Book Club. I'm ashamed to admit I didn't really want to come. But here in River City, Ohio, these people gave me a second chance. I'm becoming an electrician. I'm learning how to install solar panels. We can help you with that if you want." He paused to smile and turned to George. "George Mabra will sign you up."

George raised his hand and called out, "Just talk to me after worship. Thanks for the plug, Welby."

"Thank you, George Mabra, for working to move our town off fossil fuels." Welby smiled right back. "He's a good man. He'll hook you up." Then he continued, "And then the MAMs took me to Ireland last month. Amazing ladies, they are. On my knees, praying in a closet, I turned my life back over to Jesus on a silent retreat. I even talked to a little leprechaun."

"Okay, okay," a man about halfway called out. "A little green man? You sure about that, son?"

"Ain't that something?" the woman in the front row said. "Be careful with those haunts, boy."

Welby watched saw some raised eyebrows and then one man called out, "You sure you left those drugs behind? Sound like you was trippin'."

Welby laughed. "No, sir, no more drugs for me, no, sir. I know it sounds strange, but the leprechaun spoke for God. You might think I'm just a little crazy. Yes, sir. I'm not ashamed to admit I'm a fool for Christ. I believe the Lord called me to serve as a minister and prophet. I want to bring a message of hope in this very troubled time in which we live."

The murmurings continued. "All right, all right."

"Say it, brother."

"I'm listening, I'm listening."

"Praise God!"

Welby revved up his volume. "The scripture for this morning lays it all out. Jesus says to love God with all your heart and soul and mind and to love your neighbor as yourself. We have our marching orders, yes, but I want to ask, 'Who did Jesus say is our neighbor?' You know, you all know, the Good Samaritan, right? But what gets lost in translation is that the Samaritan was the lowest of the low in Jesus' day. Jesus' buddies didn't like the Samaritans one bit. Here, Jesus tells a story about the foreigners they despised, the foreigner did a good deed when all the other supposed good folks just walked on by.

"Brothers and sisters, Jesus already taught us how to live. He didn't want us putting people down, hating folk we don't like or loving only our family. No, he told us to love our enemies and those people we really don't like.

"We live in difficult times, hard times of division and hate, anger and unrest. I hear some say we're on a path to civil war. I hear political leaders intentionally divide us to get power. I don't know about all that, but I do know we have a call. When they go low, we must go high. We serve the master of love. I know it's not easy when politicians go low. Those attack ads get them elected these days, but that's not our job, no, sir. We Christians are called to love. Racism gets touted as a flag-waving patriotic duty. We know better because we've been taught better.

"So when you hear lies that inflame and divide, know that you are called to a different path. We may be persecuted for our love, but that's okay. We may come in last, but that's okay, because the last will be first. The good book tells us, 'Blessed are you when you are persecuted for righteousness, for Jesus' sake.'" Welby picked up his Bible and held it up high. "Now, I've neglected reading the good book for many years, but I've been turning the pages more these days, and it lays it all out there for us. Jesus turned the world upside down and inside out. Jesus argued with the Pharisees who thought they knew everything and went by the law. But Jesus told them to get off their high horses and start acting out of love.

"So go find that bridge of love. Brothers and sisters, that's our call. Shake hands with your enemy, that person across the aisle. Make friends with those racists. Speak up for common decency. It's not over, no, it's not, and we have a long fight ahead. Like Martin Luther King, Junior once said, 'We must overcome hate with love.'"

Then Welby stopped. They hadn't told him to talk all morning and he figured the pastor might want to say something. Scanning the congregation one more time, he again sensed their affirmation and love. Then he looked, and looked again. Was that a vision or… lo and behold, in the very last row, he caught sight of a very familiar face, peeking out from behind a big man who must have hidden her before. Right back there, holding two thumbs up, a big grin on her face, sat his Reagan. He blinked, confused, just as she rose up and began to applaud. Slowly, he watched the people in front of her follow suit until the whole congregation made a ruckus, clapping and cheering on their feet. Reagan stepped out in the aisle, now in clear view, maintaining eye contact while she kept clapping, letting him know she'd been there all along.

He nodded to the pastor and stepped away from the pulpit. The folks kept the applause going. He felt a little embarrassed, but mostly, he felt real good. He sauntered down the center aisle with his Bible and embraced Reagan, then pulled her down into the last pew beside him. He put his hand in hers, and together, they sat in silence, watching the rest of the service. Welby felt completely dazzled, absorbing the love of both Reagan and the congregation, grateful to God, in love with Reagan and them all.

CHAPTER TWO
THE MAMS HEAD SOUTH

Priscilla Begins the Journey

Priscilla checked over everything in her suitcase carefully before closing it up. She liked dressing well and this trip would be no exception. Whether traveling on a bus, walking on a tour, or attending a service, she aimed to look her best as she explored her roots. "Always dress your best, and you need clean underwear, honey," her mom told her. "Always be prepared, in case you end up at the hospital and have to take off your clothes." Her mother also taught her how to use makeup. "A little makeup goes a long way to show off all your God-given beauty." Long after her mother passed to the other side, Priscilla could still hear her voice. In deference to her mom, she'd visited the beauty shop the day before, hoping her new hairdo would weather the week ahead. The long rides might be a problem.

After closing her suitcase, she lifted the quilt off the rack at the bottom of her bed. This family heirloom came from the South. As a child, she'd admired the stitching and bold colors, now faded with age. Her mother said it held family secrets. When Priscilla asked her mother to explain, all she got was, "Not today, honey. Someday." Someday never came because her mother died during Priscilla's senior year of high school, taking the quilt's story with her to the grave. Priscilla carefully slipped the frayed quilt into a large bag, hoping on their trip, she would finally learn its story.

Then she reviewed the trip itinerary to prepare herself. Today, they would drive all the way to Savannah and then spend the first two days learning history in Georgia. Next, they would visit Charleston, South Carolina, before returning home through North Carolina.

In the living room, she reached up to pull another family heirloom off the shelf. The tattered brown journal held more mystery than the quilt. She believed it also held clues to her past. Her mother gave it to her shortly before she died, for a school assignment to write her family history. She remembered her words, "Maybe this will help, honey." She used the diary in her school paper, but it seemed to raise more questions than it answered.

Priscilla collapsed into the easy chair, gingerly opening the old book and fingering the brittle pages covered with faded ink. Written in longhand with great care, it obviously came from an earlier time when penmanship was taught and expected. She read the first entry.

"July 4, 1864

Dear Diary,

Papa John says he'll come for me soon. Mama tells me not to get my hopes up, that he used to tell her the same thing for many years after I was born. But I love Papa John and I know he loves me. He told me to study hard, become a good writer and always write him, wherever I go.

Mama doesn't want me to go anywhere. She doesn't want to leave the island. It's all she knows. She tells me I'm her baby girl, and that Mama Annie needs her baby girl always by her side. I tell her I'll take her with me when I go, but she says she's too old to go. We fight and I slip away alone to cry. She tells me to quit my dreamin' and do my chores.

We have so much work to do. Even though President Lincoln freed us before he died, the land still belongs to Papa's family. They work us hard. Papa treats me and Mama differently when he's here, but the overseer doesn't like us. He gives me whuppins just like the other kids, if I'm daydreaming. One time, I told him I was going to tell my daddy and he whupped me so hard, I started bleeding. I told Papa, but it didn't matter, because Papa isn't usually here.

Well, they're calling me now. I'll talk to you again later.

Sincerely, Moriya Applebee.

Priscilla fingered the page. Moriya's name came from her mother's family tree, Applebee, until she got married and took the name of Johnson. She knew the Applebees were a respected name in the annuals of Charleston history. The journal seemed clear enough. Moriya was a slave. Why did it confuse her before? Did her mom read this journal? Why did her mother only talk about the high life of her ancestors in South Carolina?

Welby Tripping Again

George called up the stairs, "You ready, Welby?"

"I'm a-comin'," Welby yelled back. He closed his suitcase, stuffed a journal and a book into his backpack and looked at the clock on the wall. Time kept right on marching into the future. He turned his calendar page to February, wondering how January disappeared so fast. Before long, they'd spring him from the comforts of the Sun Power House. Who knew what would happen then, but he hoped and planned to make it good.

"I'm going home," he told George with a grin, pulling his suitcase to the front door.

"Yes, you are," George agreed. "But first, we got some miles to travel and some sightseeing to do. First stop, Savannah. Better get a move on, the ladies are waiting."

Welby smiled, knowing that meant Reagan and the rest of the ladies heading south. "We're going all the way to Georgia today then?" "That's the plan, God willing and the creek don't rise." George nodded.

Welby loved that about George. He knew the phrases Welby grew up on. Could there be a connection between the Mabras and the Joneses way back when? Ever since Ireland, he believed he was connected to everybody, somewhere back there on the common tree of humanity, starting with Adam, or the cave man, or the cradle of civilization: Africa.

However you chose to spin up the creation story, he knew all people are one. Jesus said it and no one could convince him otherwise, although his face fell, thinking about going back South. He knew he had it good in Ohio at the Sun Power House, even though they told him the Ku Klux Klan planned and plotted in the Buckeye state, as well. He shouldn't get starry-eyed, assuming the North was so much better than the South. But since he came up here, things were good. That gave him a brand-new perspective, as he reconnected with God and God's people, which made all the difference. Even if others are stuck in their small thinking, thinking white folk are better than God's other people. What did they know? How would he enlighten them? His calling would be a challenge, for sure.

"Where we stayin' tonight?" he asked George.

"Oh, Reagan didn't tell you? Her people invited us to their manor house, oceanfront, just south of Savannah. Twenty rooms, can you believe it? Her mom and dad are coming down. Oh, man. I hope you'll be okay."

"What?" Welby slapped his forehead. "Oh, man. No, Reagan did not tell me that. Why didn't she tell me?" Nothing like starting the trip off with a bang.

"You know women," George quipped. "Or, I mean, who knows the mind of a woman? Not me. I sure haven't had success in that department."

"Right," Welby agreed. He wanted to get along with Reagan's family, but so far, they didn't see eye to eye. Reagan tried real hard. Abigail and her friend Seamus even led a listening session with her family at the FARM over the holidays. Sometimes Reagan's parents said the right things, but Welby could tell they were none too happy about their little darling matching up with a Black man. Reagan said they'd come around, but he wasn't so sure. Yes, they were somewhat cordial, but Reagan didn't see the looks her father gave Welby when she wasn't looking. Welby believed Mr. Hunter Smith could very well be a card-carrying member of the Ku Klux Klan. Reagan said no, but how would she know?

Now Welby just shook his head. "Man, I don't know. Her parents don't like me."

"Grab your sax and your banjo, Welby," George said. "We might have some time to make some music down there. Maybe that will bring them around."

Welby doubted that, remembering how he played the first night Mr. Hunter Smith showed up at the FARM's fundraiser. All Reagan's father wanted to do that night was to get his baby out of there. Why would this be any different? He frowned, carrying his stuff out of the house, heading for the van.

Antonio and Max, the two other Solar Power guys who'd won the lottery for the trip, followed him out of the house. Welby sure appreciated having some Black guys along. "You got Gullah roots?" he asked them.

"Don't we all?" Max laughed. "Most of the Black people in America came through the Sea Islands, I believe, not that I know any of the details. Henry Louis Gates hasn't invited me on his show yet to find out."

"Right, right." Welby laughed. "We ain't no movie stars. What about you, Antonio?"

"Maybe, maybe. There were slaves in Central and South America, too. I'm Mexican and African. Mutts rarely know where they came from, you know. *Posible, Mama nunca me dice.*" Antonio slipped into Spanish, and Welby remembered enough from high school to understand his mother didn't tell him.

Welby liked both of these guys, the little he'd gotten to know them. Max liked to show out, the kind of guy who liked to iron his jeans. Antonio seemed like a down-to-earth guy, always cracking a joke. Welby would be happy to have them along.

Welby considered the trip ahead. After sightseeing and exploring the Gullah culture, he would revisit the prison that ruined five years of his life. When his parole officer asked him to go back to speak to the inmates, he thought long and hard. After wrestling with it for several days, Welby realized this was exactly his call. He started to prepare; for weeks, he wrote and rewrote, leaving room for the Spirit to speak. As much as he dreaded walking back through those iron bars, he prayed that his words might actually make a difference in the lives of those men sentenced to the misery he knew so well. Being locked up tight with no place to go tended to turn out the light in most men. He longed to offer a glimpse of hope, to light a candle in their hearts. If he could do that, he would be fulfilling his call.

When the MAMs started a Toastmasters Club for the group home residents, he signed up. Honestly, he joined because Reagan wanted to improve her public speaking skills, but he told them it would assist him along his path to becoming the next MLK, Jr. When the leprechaun issued the call back in Ireland, he laughed. He continued to chuckle about it even now, although he truly believed God's call came through that little green man. Go figure.

After making his first ten speeches with Toastmasters, Welby found his groove. His ability to organize and speak effectively improved immensely as he built on his days of preaching back in his youth. The evaluators offered glowing reviews after each of his speeches. Perhaps he wasn't quite ready for prime time, but he thought he was becoming darn good. "Look out, North Carolina, I'm coming home," Welby said aloud. "Here I come now."

CHAPTER THREE
VISITING SAVANNAH

Touring the City with Priscilla

The MAMs did it again, Priscilla thought, as she enjoyed a cushioned swing on the veranda of the Hunter Smith home, overlooking an incredible tranquil view of blue skies and blue sea with gentle rippling waves. She pinched herself to confirm that, yes, that is the Atlantic Ocean out there, and, yes, Reagan's family did welcome them into their oceanfront mansion just south of Savannah, in the little town of Oceanside. The Hunter Smith staff rolled out the red carpet with Southern hospitality, oozing with charm for the MAMs and their crew. Tomorrow, Reagan's parents were flying in. Priscilla nibbled on a fresh croissant and some blueberries. She tried a few bites of grits, a staple of a Southern breakfast, finding it tasteless, until she added some honey and cinnamon at Reagan's suggestion.

"Wow, Reagan, this is really something," Sallie exclaimed. "I didn't know you were this rich." Sallie started her signature belly laugh. Reagan blushed and Priscilla noticed Welby giving Sallie a frown.

Reagan turned to Welby. "It's okay." Priscilla figured she saw that look he gave Sallie, too. "Yes, we've been blessed. My parents have a lot of money."

"How did they get so rich?" Sallie inquired.

Priscilla again felt uncomfortable with Sallie's comments. She told Reagan, "Don't answer that question, dear. It's okay."

"No, no," Reagan said. "It's okay, really. My ancestors had one of the largest plantations in Georgia, back in the day, making their money off the slaves. Nothing to be proud about."

Abigail nodded. "Most of the fortunes made in the early days of America were at the expense of some group of people. In the south, the slaves. In the north, the poor immigrants. Everywhere, stealing the lands of the native peoples."

Katharine chimed in. "Those plantation owners were the richest people in the American colonies. Yes, they thrived with their get-rich-quick scheme in a new land, but without free labor, they would have had nothing."

"So, there you have it. Without the slaves, they'd be dirt poor. I bet you didn't read that in your history book," Molly added.

Priscilla didn't like the discussion, feeling uncomfortable again. "Could we change the subject?"

"Why?" Sallie asked. "We came down here to learn. These are your people, too, Priscilla, on both sides."

"Speaking of which," Molly interjected, "I want to go over our itinerary for today. This morning, we'll walk down to the business district to catch the hop on/hop off tour bus of Savannah. This afternoon, we'll visit a Gullah museum, followed by a nice dinner on Bigbe Island. Tomorrow, we head downtown to the African Methodist Episcopal church for an African American history of Savannah. Then, ladies, we'll have time to shop before heading north to Charleston."

"Oh, bless your heart," Priscilla gushed. "Always looking out for us, aren't you, Molly?" Priscilla had pinched pennies for several months just for this very occasion.

"I aim to please. It wouldn't be a bona fide MAMs adventure without shopping and fun, now, would it?"

After breakfast, Priscilla went back up to her room. She decided to change into her favorite sundress, black with bright pink, green, and yellow flowers. Then she slipped into her favorite pink heels and pulled out a black sweater for a wrap. She freshened her lipstick and combed a few stray hairs back into place. She wanted to look her best for Savannah.

Soon, they strolled down the avenue, heading for Old Town Trolley Tours. "Daddy told me to buy all your tickets. He said, 'Tell them to relax and enjoy.' The tour takes you around the city and explains the town pretty well," Reagan said.

Priscilla raised her eyebrows, always thinking about how much things cost. With the six MAMs, Reagan, Artemis, and Zorastria from the FARM group home, and Welby, Max, and Antonio from the Sun Power house, also Molly's husband, Tom, and his brother George, they were fourteen in all for this trip. She admired the generosity of Reagan's parents. Priscilla boarded the bus, taking a seat by Katharine, ready to explore Savannah.

At the first stop in the Visitors Center, she bought a map. Then she traced their route with her finger as the bus navigated the busy streets. As they traveled through what the map called "Old Savannah", it appeared sparkling new to Priscilla. Nice clean streets with freshly painted buildings and shining windows greeted them around each corner.

The driver called out the landmarks at each trolley stop. "Bull Street Corridor, a marketplace," he told them. Next, he yelled, "Madison Square," then "Forsyth Park." So many beautiful places, Priscilla thought. When he pulled the bus up to the Cathedral of St. John, he recommended the group get out to explore the block, and then catch the next bus. "Here, you can visit the home of the Southern writer, Flannery O'Conner, and the first Girl Scout headquarters," the driver explained.

Priscilla liked how the whole city gleamed, attractive and brand-spanking clean. She regretted they could only stay two days. They passed a City Market and she wanted to get out and shop, but remembered Molly had promised that for tomorrow.

Welby On Tour

Welby started off the Savannah day still upset with Reagan for not telling him they would stay at her parents' house, and he also hated how the tour guide sugarcoateded everything. He talked only about a nice Southern city, saying nothing about the evil that built it all in the first place. After thirty minutes on this hop on/hop off stuff, Welby wanted to hear the truth. He worried about how fake news made all facts subject to reinterpretation and outright lies.

Welby complained to Reagan. "When will they tell about the slaves in these historical tours? Did I miss something?"

Reagan laughed. "They aim to keep the tourists happy, glossing over things. A little bit of history, but not too much. Don't want to upset the tourists on vacation talking about unpleasantries from long ago."

"Well, I'm pissed off, like most of my people," Welby asserted. "I want them to tell it like it is. No use trying to sweep it under the rug. If they want to focus on historical preservation, let them preserve the truth, the real stuff. And why in the hell didn't you tell me we're staying at your parents' place and that they are coming, before I had to hear it from George?" Welby felt bad as soon as that slipped out, but that snub had festered inside him since they'd left Ohio, finally exploding into her face.

Reagan clammed up, but Welby could tell by the look on her face the wheels were still turning upstairs. He tended to push her, often, and she surprised him by never pulling away. A lot of white women didn't even look at a Black man, unless to sneer, especially those with criminal backgrounds. Maybe she wasn't ready to talk about this.

But Reagan opened her mouth. "I'm sorry, Welby. I thought you knew. They passed out an itinerary. I thought you'd say something, so I guessed you were okay with it. I'm so sorry and you're right. I should have told you Mom and Dad were coming, too." She paused for a moment, and then continued. "And I never thought about the tourist thing that way. We do need to hear the story. If we just sweep it under the rug, we can pretend there isn't a problem. You and I know slavery was just the beginning of the problem of race in America."

"How did you get to be so wise?" Welby asked.

"You're a good teacher," Reagan said.

She patted Welby's thigh, letting her fingers linger for a moment, feeling his muscles. Welby jumped, startling Reagan. He gently took her hand and placed it back into her own lap, feeling the energy surging in his groin.

"Please don't touch me like that," he said with a smile. "I care about you, Reagan. I'm trying real hard to take it slow. Don't start something we can't finish."

Reagan's pearly whites flashed in her face; she was clearly enjoying the effect she had on him. She knew the power of a woman and used it well, but then she surprised him with an apology. "Sorry, Welby. I didn't mean to get you going. I'll do better. I care about you, too." Then she patted him on the shoulder. "Is that better?"

"That, I can handle," he replied with a sigh of relief.

The bus pulled into a parking lot as the driver announced, "Anyone who wants to tour the home of Flannery O'Connor or visit the Girl Scout Headquarters, get out here. Another bus will be along to pick you up in fifteen minutes. I suggest you all get out."

"Everybody off," Molly ordered. "Katharine wants to visit this famous author's home and Sallie wants to see the Girl Scout Headquarters."

"Oh, boy," Welby said. "I can hardly wait."

Reagan laughed. "Really, it's a good story, the beginning of the Girl Scouts. You'll see. But first, let's visit the Andrew Low house. The Girl Scout founder, Juliet Low, married this guy and moved in there. She never had children, and they eventually got divorced. After that, she met the founder of the Boy Scouts in Europe and decided to start some groups for girls in Scotland. Later, she returned to the States to start clubs here. All good. Come on, Welby, it won't kill you. We females have our own story of oppression. Girl Scouts teaches the power of girls, you know?"

Welby grinned sheepishly. How could he resist? How could he not go anywhere Reagan wanted to take him, for that matter? He watched her hips sway as he followed her off the bus, remembering her soft hand on his knee just a few moments before. No need for Welby to be a girl scout anymore, he done found his prize and didn't plan to let her go.

He entered the Andrew Low House behind Reagan, trying to imagine white folks living in these houses, letting the slaves toil all day and night.

From there, they continued into the First Girl Scout Headquarters, learning the history of the organization which gave girls experiences and education at a young age, building strong leaders. Yeah, Reagan was right. It was all good.

By the time they headed back to the bus, he'd caught the tourist bug. He wanted to see it all.

Reagan seemed in her element in Savannah and Welby enjoyed that. He sat back, watching the city unfold before his eyes, while Reagan added little pieces of information to what the driver said. When the bus stopped at the Riverfront, Molly ordered them off again and led the entourage for a walk along the river. Welby considered it a perfect day so far, glad that Reagan's parents hadn't shown up yet. With a little luck, perhaps they wouldn't come at all.

CHAPTER FOUR
PIN POINT MUSEUM

Ladies' Day Out: Priscilla Shines at Pin Point

After lunch on the river, the group headed over to the Pin Point Museum. The bright sun streamed through the window, warming Priscilla where she sat beside Katharine, as the day continued to unfold. She felt so happy.

Molly took the lead. "Okay, folks. Next, you'll learn about the resourcefulness of the African Americans after the days of slavery. As property owners, they built houses and etched a living together on the coast. Clarence Thomas, the Supreme Court Justice, was born and raised in this community."

Priscilla beamed. "Oh, how nice. Our Clarence Thomas? The good Republican Supreme Court justice grew up here?"

Priscilla heard Abigail clearing her throat in the seat behind her and then telling Sallie, rather loudly, "Right, he's not on my side of the aisle, either, but certainly on yours, Priscilla. The tide's been turning red on the court, all your way, in recent years."

"I'd say it is," Priscilla agreed. "And now that we've got Brett Kavanaugh? All is well!"

Katharine disagreed. "We do have some differences in this group, don't we? Not all of us consider Kavanaugh a good development, either. Oh, my."

"We're going down," Sallie said. "If I've said it once, I've said it a hundred times. It doesn't look very good for the future of our country."

The MAMs had long disagreed on politics and religion, yet they managed to forge strong bonds through the years because they really liked each other and usually were willing to listen to one another, which Priscilla appreciated. Recently, though, she wondered if she should stay in the group. Most of them were Democrats, except for Jane. Sometimes Priscilla held back what she really thought, because she knew they'd disagree.

"We're here," Molly announced. "Our guided tour starts at two. Until then you can look around. Meet at the front desk for the tour. I think you'll enjoy this one."

As Priscilla followed the others off the bus, she noticed a sign reading Pin Point Museum in front of a small building surrounded by green lawns and water not too far away. She figured they must be close to the coast, but the water looked more like a canal than a river or the sea.

As she walked into the small building, she spotted a gift shop straight ahead. "Oh," she exclaimed. "Shopping, ladies." She headed into the shop with Molly and Reagan close behind. Shelves filled with a selection of tourist items greeted them. Picking up a book about the Gullah people, she told Molly, "Look, you can read more about your people here."

"Well, except my people weren't from Georgia, Priscilla. You know you can't stereotype African Americans. We're not all the same. Maybe those are about your people."

"This is about the Gullah people in general. I thought maybe you'd like to read more." Priscilla shrugged. She didn't mean to offend Molly. She selected a book that told the story of the Pin Point factory to purchase. She found it all fascinating and looked forward to sharing it with her prayer group back home. Next, she eyed the mugs. She drank coffee every day. A mug would be a perfect memento of her travels. After making her purchases, she still had a few minutes to spare, so she headed to the restroom.

Welby at Pin Point

The marshy land beyond the museum opened into the familiar landscape of Welby's childhood. The configuration of the land, the changing sky with clouds and blue rolling over the brown and green grasses, seemed exactly like the place farther north where he'd summered as a child.

"Déjà vu," he told Reagan. "I think I'm home. Let's go for a walk. I wanna check out this place."

"You've been here before?" Reagan asked.

"No, no. I've never been in Georgia, but it feels like home, like the summer place I told you about, where I lived as a child." Welby reached for Reagan's hand, the only public display of affection afforded them. Allowed, but he still looked around to see if anyone noticed.

Sure enough, George's hawk eyes zeroed in on their hands as he yelled, "Don't go far, Welby."

"We're just circling the museum," Welby yelled right back, wishing he could shake off the constant surveillance.

"Okay, man," George replied.

Welby swung Reagan's hand as they walked along the water, feeling happy. As a child, he learned to enjoy simple things. They strolled along, absorbing the beauty of the coastal lands, not saying one word, while he also enjoyed the beauty of Reagan, inside and out.

Then all of a sudden, Grand Ma Ma's voice came rushing back, a rare occurrence these days. Back when he first broke free of the slammer, she checked in almost every day. His inner self perked up, loving the sound of her voice, which always could weave some hope into his heart. So many of his people lost that connection with the ancestors. Perhaps the aura of the marsh brought her memory alive, but for whatever reason, he could hear her clear as day, an echo of one her lectures she gave years ago. "Welby, you gotta know where you are before you can figure out who you're gonna be. You gotta take in the lay of the land before you can make your mark. Look around, figure it out and you'll be a step ahead of the others. You know, boy, most people be in such a hurry to get on with their day that they never stop. Down here in the South, we know goin' slow was never just a way to frustrate the master, but it's a way of livin' that makes a whole lot more sense than that rushing stuff you Yankees do up there in the north. Sure, we slow down in the heat. You ain't goin' be a'running around when the sweat's dripping and the mosquitos biting and the humidity's so thick you can cut it with a knife. No, boy, but even in the winter, like you got here now, you gotta slow down and really give the place the respect it's due. Don't you be a'hurryin', boy. Figure out where you are. Then you'll know what to do. It's a simple thing, really, but it will make all the difference in the world."

"Where are you?" Reagan inquired, jolting him back to the present moment.

"Grand Ma Ma," he said. "I just heard her again."

"She's back? Why can't I hear her? Doesn't she like me anymore, now that you're holding my hand?" Reagan pouted.

Welby laughed. "Come on, Reagan, you know she loves you, too. Why did she come haunt you in Ireland and tell you to be my friend? She's here now, with us both, I swear."

Welby remembered Grand Ma Ma appearing to Reagan like it was yesterday. Ireland seeped with that thin space where the boundaries between heaven and earth blur and the dead speak. Grand Ma Ma wanted to stir something up between them and, as usual, she got her way. Welby would be forever grateful. Reagan even painted a picture of the woman during that spooky, but wonderful, time.

"She just doesn't come around much anymore, maybe because she thinks I'm doing okay. But being here, I remember her. She always taught me to get a feel for a place."

"What do you mean?" Reagan asked.

"It's a little strange, you know. She said, pay attention, really notice things, listen and watch. She told me the landscape would teach me how to be. Black people need to be alert to our environment; maybe we never know what's coming down. I mean, when a Black man can get shot for just being in the wrong place at the wrong time? We gotta pay attention, Reagan."

"Is someone going to shoot you here, Welby? Aren't you exaggerating?"

"Well, probably not. But Armaud Avery got shot right here in Georgia, just out jogging. Reagan, I'm just tryin' to understand this place. Look at the water and think about what happened here. They fished for oysters and crabs. Imagine them and their boats going out in the early morning, greeting the sunrise. Reminds me of fishin' in the backwaters as a boy. Maybe you don't get it."

"Context, yes, I do get that," Reagan agreed. "You start out with the big picture, then dive into the specifics. I do that when I'm looking for things to paint, and when I'm putting the brush to canvas, too. I pay attention, Welby. You'd be surprised." Reagan took out her camera and started snapping pictures. She winked at him as she promised, "I'm going to paint this for you. Tell me, Welby. What about this place feels like home?"

"Well, the geography of the coast, what they call the low land. At sea level, the land becomes flat. Here, the sea water mixes with the small rivers and marshes, creating estuaries that breed new life. Birds flock through, seagulls, herons, kingfishers, always coasting in, landing on the water. Grasses sway in the ocean breeze and above the big sky, always changing. It's the place, Reagan. Beautiful, baby, just like you." Welby squeezed her hand.

"Welby, you're a poet," Reagan suggested with a smile, as she locked her eyes into his, sending a spark he felt all the way down to his toes. She again focused her camera lens on the landscape already etched into Welby's soul.

They hurried back to join the others. Welby didn't expect to learn much beyond what he already knew, but the tour actually surprised him. His ancestors had enjoyed some autonomy on the island, but the overseers kept a firm grip. After the war, a few acquired land, but most still earned a pittance, working for the white man. At Pin Point, however, the Gullah people became landowners of seafront property. Although they weren't rich, the guide Aniya told them, they earned enough to support their families into the 1980s. That sure was something.

While Welby absorbed the story, Reagan read signs and stared at photographs. "What you lookin' for?" he finally asked her. He knew Reagan, knew she searched for a needle in a haystack. "What is it, Reagan? Maybe I can help you."

Reagan shook her head. "Something in that film triggered

something. Did you hear them say Hunter Smith? That's a name in my family. Why would he be here?"

Welby laughed. "Come on, Reagan, really? They gave slaves the masters' names. Why should that surprise you?"

"But these were freed slaves. I get the Brown part, but Hunter? That's a middle name. I can't find the name on any of these pictures, but I swore I heard it."

"What bothers you, really? That you might be related?" Welby asked, trying to understand. "I don't mean to upset you, baby, but you got Gullah in your DNA. You gotta be around here somewhere."

Zorastria bumped into Welby and laughed, telling Reagan, "Yes, we're sisters. We all got Gullah blood. You, me, Priscilla, Welby, Max, Artemis, Antonio. That's why we get to come on this vacation in the first place."

"I know, I know," Reagan agreed. "I just want to know the story. Mom won't tell me. Dad says it's a mistake. There's gotta be an answer somewhere."

"How about you check out the library or historical society?" Welby suggested. "Hey, ask Henry Louis Gates if you can be on his show. You're famous enough with your dad and all. Let him get to the bottom of it for you."

Zorastria laughed again. "Wouldn't that be somethin'? Reagan and her dad star on 'Finding Your Roots.' Go for it, Reagan!"

Reagan frowned. "Daddy wouldn't allow that. He wants to keep it quiet. But, Welby, I like your idea of research. Maybe we could go to the library tomorrow."

Aniya said, "Come on, y'all, circle up. We're going to do 'The Shout.' The Gullah people brought this along from Africa. They sang spirituals in a circle, like a praise dance." She demonstrated with some fancy hand clapping, knee-slapping and foot-stomping. "I'll give you a choice. Do you want to do 'Wade in the Water' or 'Swing Low'?"

"'Swing Low,'" Welby yelled.

"Good choice," she said. "You'd be here all day, singing all the verses to 'Wade'. You're probably used to doing this song real slow and quiet, but get ready for a whole different sound with the Shout."

Aniya led out with a clear alto voice and others began to sing along. She shifted the rhythm, adding claps, knee-slaps, and stomps. Welby worked hard to match her motions as she picked up the pace. She laughed as the MAMs huffed and puffed. First time he ever heard 'Swing Low' sung so fast with fancy syncopation, although it did bring back memories of the summer church with Grand Ma Ma. Welby gave up trying to match all Aniya's motions. Then all of a sudden, she threw up her hands and stopped. "Good job, good job," she told them. "And that's the end of the tour."

Welby followed Reagan into the gift shop. While she browsed souvenirs, he perused the books. He pulled a little book on the history of Pin Point off the shelf and began skimming. Right there, on the second page, he found it. Holding it up for Reagan, he called to her, "Reagan, here they are! James and John Hunter Smith set out on the crabbing boat in the morning. Those your guys? Any family resemblance?"

Reagan grabbed the book from him. "What? Oh my gosh, yes!" She looked a little more closely. "Welby, do you think they're light-skinned?"

"Not particularly," Welby said. "But mixin's like that. Some come out real dark, some real light. Some can pass for white, like you, baby, just like you. Some are black as night, like me. Don't make no sense, but that's how the Good Lord cooks us up. Everybody's different."

"I'll say," Reagan said. "I'm buying this book. We'll see what my parents say to this."

"Now don't get your hopes up, baby. You know they ain't about to tell you nothing if they haven't already."

Reagan disagreed. "You don't know that, Welby. You just never know."

The group gathered outside the bus and Molly announced plans for the rest of the day. "First, we'll tour this area, then it's back to Reagan's for dinner. Then tonight, it's dialogue time."

"Oh, no," Reagan said. "Not again. Do we have to participate?"
Molly nodded.

"Reagan, you gotta try," Welby told her. "Maybe your daddy will come around. Like you said, you just never know. Come on, let's get back on the bus." He followed her up the steps, enjoying the view.

Grand Ma Ma Watches Over

I like this, I do. I'm just goin' along for the ride with the MAMs. Not that they invited me, but that's a perk of living in the hereafter, I can drop back in wherever I darn well please.

What I like about this trip is that white folks with mixed blood are actually trying to find out the truth. Take Reagan, for example. A year ago, she was hooked on opioids and stealing drugs from the hospital. Now she done turned around and is taking up with my boy Welby. Ain't that somethin'? Of course, me hauntin' Reagan on the labyrinth at Emerald Isle may have something to do with it, ya think? We angels still have some work to do from time to time.

My hope here is that these MAMs and their groupies discover we are all connected. Yes, ma'am. It's not about just a little mixin' here and there. No, it's about God mixing up the whole human race. None of us are far removed from the big family tree in the scheme of things. That's what I knows for sure. And if I knows it, you'd think the rest of the world would, too. Instead, they seem hell-bent to continue their ignorant ways, dividin' and fightin'.

Let me tell you this and I hope you hear it loud and clear. If you lift a hand against another human bein', you're lifting a finger on your kin. That's plain truth and I won't add no sugar. Read your Bible, dear. It's all there in black and white.

You see, black skin don't make you stupid or lazy, like some white people say. No, the discriminatin' whites make that happen. Those whites been keepin' the schools separate and unequal for years, which affects the learnin' of our children. And why work hard, if the boss man plans to cheat you out of your fair share anyway?

You gotta see this for what it is. Downright and simple racism. And it's gotten completely out of hand ever since they kidnapped my people in Africa, all downhill from there. Don't get me started. Well, I'm already revved up. I can talk. Now, I'm not trying to put folks down, I'm just tired of all this injustice and wantin' something to change, right now.

I gotta hand it to Priscilla and Reagan for diggin' in their family trees. They want to figure this all out. Bless their souls. But let me tell you, the South holds its secrets tight and don't like lettin' go. Even a native daughter's goin' be put through the wringer, if she tries to find the truth. Just watch.

CHAPTER FIVE
DIFFICULT DIALOG

Welby does Dinner at Reagan's

Just when Welby relaxed, thinking maybe Reagan's parents wouldn't show, here they came, arriving from the airport just before dinner. Reagan's dad gave Welby a perfunctory handshake. Her mother smiled at him, albeit a little nervously. After exchanging quick hugs with their daughter, they climbed the stairs to change, leaving Reagan to entertain their guests. "I hope you brought your appetites," she told the group. "I ordered a good mix of Savannah seafood, along with Southern dishes, for the evening meal." When she gave a rundown on the menu, Welby smacked his lips, making Reagan laugh.

The Hunter Smith ancestral home sat perched high atop a rocky bluff, overlooking the Atlantic. Welby knew Reagan came from money, but this was really something. Large windows in the dining room opened out to a panoramic view of the sea. As they took their places, he watched the brilliant yellow orb slip into the water, leaving shades of orange dancing in the sky and on the water below.

"The best we have to offer," Reagan added, squeezing Welby's hand. "I'm so glad y'all are here."

Welby glowed, happy to share all this with her, although the implausibility of it all still worried him. That her parents would welcome a Black man with an eye on their daughter into their home might mean he was making progress. Yet he also knew better than to count his chickens before they were hatched. Hard telling what these white folks really thought about him.

The kitchen staff delivered platters of fried seafood and assorted sides to the table. "We're serving homestyle tonight," Reagan told them. "Because … we are home!"

Welby hungrily eyed the aromatic spread of hush puppies, candied sweet potatoes, mashed potatoes, greens, and black-eyed peas.

"I love treating my friends," Reagan explained. "You might pass out in a food coma, but you'll have smiles on your faces."

"All this, Reagan? Is the Queen coming, too?" Sallie queried.

"Yes, you're already here. You MAMs are now the visiting queens of Savannah, Sallie. Nothing but the red carpet for the Magnificent and Marvelous Book Club. You're the best."

"Aww." Sallie laughed. "Remember that, guys. You may now stand up and bow to your royal highnesses." She looked around, pointing to the men around the table. "Hear! Hear!"

Welby looked at Antonio and Max and raised his eyebrows before standing and gesturing to them to do the same. Then he led them in circling the table, bowing to all the women in attendance.

When Max reached Zorastria, she turned around in her chair and reached up to pat him on the head. "Well done, faithful servant," she told him.

"I beg your pardon, my lady?" he quipped back. "Your prince, not your servant, has arrived." He held out his hand, which she batted away with a laugh.

Meanwhile, Welby and Antonio finished the trek around the circle, taking a bow to each of the women as laughter filled the room.

"Thank you, thank you, thank you," Sallie gushed. "Fine princes, you may take your seats now. And, Reagan, be sure to thank your parents for us. What a spread!"

"You can thank them yourself." Reagan motioned to the back of the room. They all turned. Reagan's father and mother descended the grand staircase, both decked out in fine evening wear. Welby thought they looked more like they were attending a ball than a meal with ex-convicts. Did her dad have on a tuxedo? And that yellow lacy full length gown of her mother's spoke of privilege and deep pockets.

"Oh, how lovely," Priscilla exclaimed. "Reagan, your mother is absolutely stunning. And your father, so handsome."

Welby whispered into her ear, "The apple doesn't fall far from the tree. You've got the best of both."

Reagan blushed, just as her father took charge. "Welcome to the Hunter Smith Manor. We are so pleased to welcome Reagan's friends into our winter home. I trust the cooks are keeping you happy with the catch of the sea and Reagan's favorite Southern dishes. Now eat! Eat, drink and be merry."

While the Hunter Smiths took their places at the head of the table, an all-male string quartet appeared, bowing and then taking seats in the corner of the room. Soon the hall filled with high-fallutin' classical sounds, somewhat foreign to Welby's musical tastes.

Reagan squeezed Welby's arm. "Will you play your saxophone later?"

Once again, he thought she could read his mind, but then he wondered if that was why they let him in. "Oh, I get it. No free lunch, right? The vaudeville act, live and on stage at the Hunter Smith Manor." He frowned.

"No, no. You don't have to play, but I'd really like to hear you,

Welby. My dad doesn't even know you brought your sax."

With that, Welby cooled down and even smiled. "I'm sorry," he said, feeling bad about the bark in his voice in his retort. "I'll consider it." Then, to change the subject, he raised his drink. "My compliments to the chef for the best food I've eaten in a very long time." He touched his glass to Reagan's and that initiated a ripple of clinking glasses around the table.

Suddenly, the double doors opened and in walked Seamus, Abigail's friend. Welby watched the surprise on many of the faces around the table. The MAMs were well-acquainted with Seamus, their Irish tour guide last October. A romance sparked then between Abigail and Seamus and he knew Seamus had visited Abigail after the holidays,

Abigail didn't look surprised, just happy as she made a beeline for Seamus. They closed the distance between them in seconds, enfolding one another in a tight embrace.

"What's he doing here?" Welby whispered to Reagan.

"I don't know. I didn't know he was coming, either," Reagan admitted. "I bet they want more dialogue. Oh, no. Can we go home now?"

Welby squeezed Reagan's hand under the table. Unlike Reagan, he held hope dialogue could turn Reagan's parents around. If anyone could pull it off, Seamus would, after years of involvement with the Irish Troubles at the Shalem Centre for Peace in Northern Ireland.

Welby got an itch to play his sax. He hit up George for assistance. While the rest of the group welcomed Seamus, George, Tom and Welby scooted up to their rooms for their instruments. When they came back down, they put their instruments in a corner, returning to the table to for second helpings and dessert.

Later, when the string quartet packed up to go home, Welby and the Mabra brothers excused themselves from the table and opened their cases, taking over the corner of the room vacated by the quartet. Soon, Welby led on his sax with the opening notes of "It's a Wonderful World". Tom's clear trumpet joined in on the chorus and George tapped a light rhythm on the edge of his bongo, holding them all together.

A mellow, contented atmosphere filled the room, just as Welby intended. As the others finished up their meal, enjoying shoofly and sweet potato pies with pralines, there were smiles all around. Sallie nodded off a bit. Reagan's parents seemed pleased. Her dad even snapped along with his fingers. Then her mother pulled her dad up out of her chair and darned if they didn't start dancing in the hall adjacent to the dining room. A moment later, Abigail jumped up and pulled Seamus out onto the makeshift dance floor as well. Welby wished he could sway with Reagan, up close and personal, but he had a job to do.

Tom, though, put his trumpet back in his case and made a beeline toward his wife, Molly.

"Another slow one, please," Tom requested, standing with Molly and the others. "How about 'I Will Always Love You'? You got this, right? I need to dance."

Welby nodded and led on the sax, but, after a verse, he stopped playing and started to sing. As his voice resonated through the room, he flashed back to a night in the Dingle pub on the west coast of Ireland. He remembered unlocking his voice for the first time after being sprung from the pen, and felt happy now to be singing again. He watched the couples swaying in love. His eyes connected with Reagan's, hoping she could feel his heart, wishing they could be out there twirling around, too.

After the slow one, George called, "When the Saints Go Marching in!" As the melody poured out from Welby's sax, George kept the beat with the bongo, which brought all the MAMs up and at it on the dance floor. Molly took the lead with a conga line. Holding on to each other at the waist, they snaked around the room, picking up Zorastria, Artemis, and Reagan. Antonio and Max slipped in between the group home women, and Welby wasn't too happy to see Max's hands on Reagan. Even the dressed-out Hunter Smiths joined in the fun. Without drugs, without alcohol, they were all dancing, having a jolly old time. Just what life should be about, Welby thought.

Tom rejoined the band halfway through the song, his trumpet piercing the room with a strong, clear voice. Welby put down his sax and started to sing. "Lord, I want to be in that number," he bellowed, raising a hand to call on God. The conga line continued to snake around the room, and Reagan sashayed along with the rest of them. Just as she got close, he closed out the song, "When the saints go marchin' in." While Tom continued to jazz up the ending and George rumbled his drums, Welby reached out and embraced Reagan in a bear hug, a silly grin on his face.

Abigail addressed the band. "Thanks, guys, for all that fun. And now, on with the show! Listening Circles! What did you see and hear in Savannah today? How does that intersect with your life? Seamus will help us all talk about that together."

"Aw, Abby," Sallie whined. "Do you have to break up our party? We were just getting wound up. Do you know how long it's been since I danced? Don't stop me now."

"Maybe we can dance again tomorrow night?" Abigail suggested.

"Sure thing," George readily agreed, putting away his drums.

Welby pulled the mouthpiece off his sax and dried it off before tucking it all away in the case for safe keeping. Then he took Reagan's hand to go back to table for the last few bites of his sweet potato pie and to grab some pralines. A little sugar could go a long way to get him through the discussion ahead.

Priscilla and the MAMs Listening

Priscilla took off her heels. As much as she loved them, dancing did a number on her aging toes and arches. While Seamus and Abigail arranged a circle of chairs in the nearby room, she massaged her feet, trying to alleviate the pain, and asked for a cup of coffee. She felt sorry for herself. While the other MAMs enjoyed retirement, Priscilla still needed to work, maybe for the rest of her life. She took a deep breath, trying to at least savor her vacation. She did love Reagan's family and this beautiful home, wondering if her own family's plantation had once hosted parties like this. While she looked forward to the rest of this trip and what she might learn about her own family tree, she also felt conflicted, guarded, and unsure she wanted to hear more. Could she unlock the mystery of the family quilt? Tomorrow, she hoped to visit a quilt store to see what they could tell her.

Abigail and Seamus arranged chairs in the big hall. Priscilla carried her cup of coffee into the group, fearing a long night. Abigail started off, thanking the Hunter Smiths for the wonderful dinner and their Southern hospitality. "You make us feel like royalty," she said. "We hope you'll join us for our group activity."

Priscilla detected a slight frown on Mr. Hunter Smith's face, but his wife spoke for them both. "Yes, of course we'll join you. It will be our pleasure." Reagan's mother took her husband by the hand, leading him to open seats among the others.

"The circle is a great way to build community," Abigail explained. "Each of us has a story. Each of us has something important to share. Tonight, we'll start with some fun. Think about the food we ate tonight. What was your favorite dish? Got it?"

Seamus picked it up from there. "Okay, now, stand up and roam the room, saying your favorite food. See if you can find someone else who enjoyed the same cuisine. When you find your person, sit down and share your stories about the food you both liked. Can you remember when you first ate that type of food? Do you have a personal story connected with that particular food? Share what comes to mind with each other."

Abigail cautioned, "Now, if you don't find anybody, that's okay, too. Just find somebody else without a match, sit down and talk food. Okay, go. Ten minutes begin now."

Priscilla didn't want to stand. She could feel the blisters forming under the tight heels she'd forced her feet back into when they'd left the dining room. In a very rare move, she slipped them off again, then stood in front of her chair, "Cornbread. Cornbread." It reminded her of her mother.

The group milled around the ballroom and Priscilla watched the bedlam, reminded of the children's game where everyone made animal noises. Folks seemed to be laughing and enjoying the charade, though. Here came George, and darned if he wasn't chanting, "Cornbread," too.

"Do we have a match?" he inquired.

Priscilla laughed. "I guess so."

George pulled a chair out so they faced each other while Priscilla sat back down, kicking her shoes under her chair and a little nervous to be sitting there with exposed feet, although George didn't seem to notice. "Tell me about cornbread and you," he requested with a smile.

"Oh," Priscilla responded, "my mother made cornbread, called it the food of the gods. She served it up with every meal. Maybe she just didn't want to go to the trouble of making real bread. Don't need to knead cornbread, you know?" She laughed.

George slapped his knee. "No need to knead. You're funny, Priscilla." He smiled as he told her, "My mother liked serving it up, too. Not quite with every meal, but always with beans and company."

"What do you like about it?"

"It brings back memories, for sure. Family gatherings, home, church. Always cornbread, sorta dependable, you know? Smear on some butter and honey, apple butter, jelly, or preserves. It tastes real good. Like you got dessert without waiting 'til the end of the meal."

Priscilla laughed. "I never thought of it that way before. My daddy liked apple butter. I think he had apple butter growing up on the farm. I think of him when I eat apple butter and cornbread."

"Funny how food stays with us that way. We Black folk talk about soul food, and it's a stereotype, but you say the word and everybody knows what you're talking about."

"Where did that come from?" Priscilla asked.

"Good question. Good food touches you deep inside? What do you think?"

"Yes, I think so. Soul food is good home cooking. When my mother died, that's all I wanted to comfort my soul. During slavery, I imagine the people needed comforting food," Priscilla said.

For a moment, Priscilla watched animated conversations underway around the room. Food brings people together. Hadn't her mother told her to serve up some soup when times were hard? Some good grub goes a long way to put hope in your belly and a smile on your face.

Laughing and reminiscing with George about cornbread perked her up. She noticed Welby chatting with Reagan's dad and they were laughing, too. The last time they were together at the FARM, Reagan and her dad fell out. There was much for Mr. Hunter Smith to handle: first Reagan on drugs, now with a Black man.

Abigail rang the brass bowl, calling everyone back into the circle. "So, what did you learn?" she asked them all.

"Talking about food relaxes me," Priscilla said. "Makes me laugh and remember."

Mr. Hunter Smith told them, "Welby and I love fried catfish. As different as we are, we like the same stuff."

"Sweet potatoes bring people together," Reagan chimed in. "Nothing like a good sweet potato pie for Molly and me. Molly learned how to make one as a little girl. We grew up miles apart, but this Southern cuisine unites us."

"Kinda like the menu at Panera and Texas Roadhouse. Ever notice it reads the same in Ohio, Georgia, and California? Comforting and familiar," Jane offered.

"Yes, free enterprise and restaurant franchises are American miracles," Mr. Hunter Smith agreed.

"Isn't America wonderful?" Priscilla felt so proud of her country.

"But what about GMOs, food allergies, production of food laced with high fructose corn syrup, and unhealthy processed foods? Bad stuff is marketed endlessly, everywhere you can imagine. We are overweight, getting cancer, and not living as long as our parents did," Molly lamented.

Abigail said, "Okay, you both make some good points, but let's get back to the topic. Who else found a partner tonight?"

Seamus, Zorastria, Max, and Tom formed a huddle. Seamus stood to speak for them. . "Hush puppies brought us together. These three here have been eating them all their lives, but I just had my first tonight and I'm a believer." Everyone laughed. "Delicious little morsels, aye, they are. I'll try this recipe back in Ireland, I will."

Artemis, Antonio, and Mrs. Hunter Smith bonded over the black-eyed peas. Healthy fare, they agreed.

A large Black woman emerged from the kitchen, pulling off a bright red apron and revealing a shapely figure well-dressed in stylish fashion. Priscilla didn't expect such sophistication from hired help.

"Mama Jack," Reagan called. She raced over to enfold the woman in a hug.

The woman held her for a moment, then pulled away, giving Reagan a once-over. "Well, look at you. You grew up real nice there, honey. Good to see you, Nancy." She planted a kiss on the cheek, then with her arm still around Reagan, she looked at Mrs. Hunter Smith. "Do you still want me to talk to the group?"

Reagan's mom looked at Abigail. "I thought perhaps you would like to hear a little from our chef tonight. She's not only an award-winning Southern chef, but also an authority on Gullah cuisine. Reagan tells me your trip is about exploring the Gullah culture."

Priscilla had thought perhaps a second dessert, but a lecture? Abigail answered quickly. "Oh, yes. That's perfect. Please do."

"Well, then, let me introduce myself," the beautiful lady began. "My name is Sonia Jackson. Some call me a gourmet cook. Nancy calls me Mama Jack, because we go way back. When she was a little girl, she was my assistant in the Hunter Smith kitchen when her family came down here for the winter. I cooked for her family to put myself through college.

"These days, I don't have time for cooking. I teach anthropology for the University of Georgia. I got my Ph.D. in soul food." She laughed. "Not many people can claim that honor. Bet you didn't know that, Nancy, did you?"

Priscilla wondered who she was talking to, but then remembered Reagan's real name, Nancy Reagan, and she did look as surprised as Priscilla. She thought most Blacks in the South didn't even graduate from high school.

Reagan exclaimed, "That's awesome, Mama Jack. I didn't know that and you don't know I started going by my middle name, Reagan, when I turned sixteen. I don't go by Nancy anymore."

"Lordy, lordy," Sonia exclaimed. "Seems we both been about the business of transformation, Reagan dear. Every now and then, the Hunter Smiths talk about serving up a special meal for their guests. Tonight, I fed you bona fide soul food, American cuisine with many influences. Now, here in the South, our people were bought and sold like chattel. It was a despicable era in the American history book, which many of our people would rather forget, but there are some good things that came out of it all.

"You got the strongest men and women in the world in these parts. They maintained their West African cultures in a strange land. Somehow, they managed to keep their humanity, despite being treated like animals. The Gullah Geechee people didn't bring many material possessions along on those slave boats, but they stored up treasures and traditions in their minds. African music, religion, medicine, and food know-how stayed with them for many years to come. They planted their African wisdom in new soil, growing rice, cotton and all kinds of beans. They created all those delicious dishes that now are a regular part of the American diet.

"In the South, you see that mixing races and cultures yields good things, even in the midst of evil. The food created in dark times continues to nourish the soul even now.

"We anthropologists call it resilience. People do endure and even triumph over adversity and oppression. You might be surprised to learn that people didn't actually start calling it soul food until the 1960s when the soul music and Black culture became popular as well.

"And you may be surprised that there are not only strong African influences in soul food, but also Native American contributions. Let me read you something here from a historian, Charles Hudson, who studied the southeastern Native American tribes. 'Hominy, for example, grits, Indian fritters—variously known as hoe cake or Johnny cake—Indian boiled cornbread, corn meal dumplings, and hush puppies are all part of what the Native Americans ate. They also cooked beans and field peas by boiling them, and cured their meats and smoked it over hickory coals.'

"So, you see, the African slaves surely borrowed from the native people, but heated the food the way they did back in Africa and spiced it up, too, with their cayenne and malaguena peppers. From the African savanna and tropical regions, they used pigeon peas, black-eyed peas, and sorghum, as well as domesticated rice. Did you know all that came from Africa?"

"No, I didn't," Jane admitted. "Very interesting."

"There's quite a lot we don't know," Katharine exclaimed.

"That's for sure," Sallie agreed.

Zorastria gave Artemis a high five. "See there, the Gullah people gave us half the food we eat today. Some more of those African American contributions that didn't make it into our American History books."

"You're absolutely right," Sonia concurred. "Rice is a staple of soul food. Think red beans and rice. And then there's sweet potatoes; yams in Africa. They also had something like cornbread which they call fufu, and cooked meat over open pits—barbeque."

"Where did all the fried food originate?" Mr. Hunter Smith asked.

"Now that's a little more complicated," she answered. "People experimented with food preparation for thousands of years, long before the Africans arrived in America. We know the Scots deep fried their chicken back in the Middle Ages, but many believe the Portuguese first gave us fried fish. Certainly, it became popular in the South, way over to Louisiana where the Cajuns gave a particular spicy seasoning for all this."

"Why catfish?" Welby asked.

"Our people back then ate what was readily available. Sea Island slaves, living along inland waterways, could easily catch fish and fry it up for dinner. Catfish, but saltwater fish, too, and shellfish, like the clams and oysters that the Pin Point Factory packaged to make a profit.

"You might wonder why ribs are so popular. That's because ribs were leftovers after all more desirable cuts were served to the whites. You see that time and time again when you study the history of food. The poorer folk take the unpopular items and transform them into fancy cuisine. Ever had fajitas in a Mexican restaurant? Some of the best stuff around, right? But that used to be the part of the animal thrown away. The poor folk figured out how to season and soften it up and now it's what everybody wants. The Pennsylvania Dutch rescue the hog's stomach for cooking. They stuff it with vegetables mixed in with ground hog meat, made from the unpopular cuts, and serve up hog maw, a popular treat for special occasions. The history of food is really something, if you take some time to learn. Ever heard of Paula Deen's cooking school right here in Savannah? You should tour her facility to learn more while you're here."

"Not sure we have time on this trip," Abigail said. "Maybe we can come back."

Priscilla loved all this talk of food and had always dreamed of taking a Paula Deen cooking class in person. "I'd love that," she gushed. "Paula Deen's my favorite in Southern cooking."

Sonia glanced at her watch. "Well, I'm sorry, but I have a class to teach over at the university. The Gen X students like late classes. That's hard for me at my advanced age." She laughed.

"We know what you mean," Sallie said.

"Thank you so much for coming, Sonia," Seamus told her, standing to shake her hand in farewell. "This has been very informative. Thank you for sharing your food expertise with us."

"You're most welcome," Sonia replied as she turned to Reagan's mom. "I'll see you tomorrow, then, Mrs. Hunter Smith."

Reagan's mom nodded, the group clapped, and Sonia made her departure, while Seamus took charge, repeating himself. "Aye, most informative. Now, how about we move into a circle of listening before we call it a night. Let's move our chairs back into a circle. Abigail and I have a few questions for all of ye."

Priscilla watched the group shuffling the chairs, but she herself sat tight, nursing her sore heels, glad she'd never moved in the first place. She just wanted to go upstairs and read in bed, so she hoped they would tie this all up quickly.

Abigail said, "What stood out for you today? Any surprises?"

Welby slapped his knee. "Well, I'm surprised, for sure, to see Mr. Hunter Smith and I share the same favorite food. We both love a good fried catfish."

"Stereotypes," Seamus noted. "We make many judgements, don't we? Here, you find unexpected alliances. What does that tell you?"

Welby thought a moment. "Don't judge a book by its cover?"

Mr. Hunter Smith gave him a look, so Welby corrected himself. "I just mean we're more alike than we think."

"Right," Reagan agreed. "We stereotype, thinking we're separate from others, but really, we all have similarities. Our bodies, for example. In my nursing studies, I learned there's very little variation in our DNA across races around the world. We are all connected internally. If you just focus on the external appearance or socio-economic status, you're being very short-sighted."

"Out of the mouth of babes," Mr. Hunter Smith said. "You wouldn't know she's descended from me, would you? I never knew any of this science stuff very well."

"Is that why the Republicans are down on science?" Molly asked.

Mr. Hunter Smith started laughing. "That's not true of us as a whole, just certain more prominent members."

Priscilla knew he was talking about President Ace Steele. Probably better not to mention his name in this group, but Priscilla also had concerns about science. She had a real problem with scientists who tried to prove the Bible isn't true. Just because they could figure out how things work didn't make them in charge of explaining creation and how people should live. "But sometimes Christians must tell the scientists they're plain wrong. I mean, the Bible is right, you know, about creation."

"So true," Reagan agreed.

"But perhaps the Bible just tells us why God created world. Some of us believe it's okay to believe the scientific version of creation, as well," Katharine interjected.

"Right." Sallie raised her hand. "Me, too."

"Okay, so we have our differences here, but we can still break bread together, right? Seamus asked. "What else did you learn tonight?"

"I enjoyed all that about the history of food and cooking," Jane offered. "I'll be happy from now on when I eat soul food, thinking about how it's a gift of Africans, Native Americans, Cajuns, Scots, and probably a lot more folks."

Reagan's mom started talking. "This reminds me of my mother, who loved to cook. One Christmas, she created a family cookbook for all of us, showing how different foods came from many branches of our family tree. I need to get that out again; Reagan, remind me. I think you'd like it."

"It's about time to call it a night, it is," Seamus announced. "How about a closing song?"

"'What A Wonderful World'?" Tom suggested.

"Yes," Molly agreed with enthusiasm.

Tom got his trumpet, Welby picked up his sax. George made his way over to his drum, and then the three of them took the night home. The music lifted out into the ballroom, circling around the MAMs and the others, enlivening the room with soulful joy.

Mrs. Hunter Smith stood, right before the chorus. "May I join you?"

"You sing?" George asked.

"A little bit." She smiled.

"Be our guest," Tom told her. So then they toned down the horns, while she sang with a raspy alto voice, "I see trees of green, red roses too. I see them bloom for me and you. And I think to myself what a wonderful world."

"Can I join you, Mom?" Reagan asked.

"Sure thing, doll," Mrs. Hunter Smith replied.

Priscilla loved this. She could see the mother's love for her daughter as Mrs. Hunter Smith wrapped her arm around Reagan. They swayed together as Tom played an interlude on the trumpet, with backup from Welby, who winked at Reagan. Maybe they could all be one happy family after all, Priscilla thought. For tonight, at least, harmony ruled the roost. The gentle sounds of the sax and trumpet continued underneath the sweet sounds of Reagan and her mom harmonizing their raspy jazz voices. Priscilla closed her eyes, enjoying the marvel of it all.

On the last verse, Mrs. Hunter Smith dropped out, letting Reagan shine as she as she sang the final line. "And I say to myself, what a wonderful world."

When Priscilla opened her eyes, she saw tears streaming down Reagan's face, and even thought Welby wiped a few away as well. Mr. Hunter Smith joined his wife and daughter, embracing them both. What a beautiful, talented family, Priscilla thought.

As the group broke up, Priscilla headed upstairs with a lot to ponder. She continued to find it hard to get used to the reality of her own Black blood. She wanted to read that journal. She traced the pattern of the quilt she'd brought along with her finger. What mysteries did it hold and could she discover them? Or perhaps not knowing would be better than the truth.

CHAPTER SIX
THE OTHER SIDE OF SAVANNAH

Reagan Connects the Dots

The trip was passing entirely too quickly for Reagan. The music of the night before played in her heart when they gathered for a sunrise photoshoot. She marveled how each day offered a new vista of an everchanging seascape. She hummed to herself, remembering singing with her mom. Yes, what a wonderful world.

After the others returned to the outdoor veranda for breakfast, Reagan led Welby out onto the pier, reminiscing about days gone by. "I love this place," she told him, sweeping her arm around the dock, taking in the view and then the house behind them. But then, as Welby backed up so she could swing her arm freely, he came perilously close to the edge of the dock. "Welby," she called. "Turn around before you fall in!"

Welby's feet shuffled as he looked down, turned, and took a step back, giving Reagan a sheepish look. "Saved me again," he yelled. "Thank you, Reagan."

He laughed. Reagan laughed, too."

Reagan looked out across the water and imagined sailing into the wild blue yonder with Welby. She could see it clearly, the two of them all alone in one of her favorite places on earth. She slipped into her fantasy, mesmerized by the waves.

"Reagan, Reagan. Where are you? What's comin' down, doll?" Welby pulled her close. "Tell me anything," he said. "I can take it."

A tear slipped out of her eye and rolled down her cheek.

"Oh, babe," Welby said as he took a step back, looking into her eyes. "What's wrong? Is it something I did? I'm sorry. I never wanted you to cry." He wiped a tear from her cheek.

Reagan felt a knot in her throat, her words stuck way down there somewhere. She grabbed his hand, then took a deep breath and began to speak. "It's good, Welby. All good. I love this little boat here. See its name down there on the side?"

Welby squinted. "I can't quite make it out."

"Fancy Nancy, from before I started going by Reagan. You know Fancy Nancy?" Reagan asked.

"You're fancy? Now and then?" he responded.

"No," Reagan explained, "Fancy Nancy is a character in a children's book series who liked to dress up. The books were all about building vocabulary."

"Oh, that's where you got all those high falutin' words, Fancy Nancy?" Welby hugged her from the side, saying, "I got you."

"Possibly." Reagan smirked. "Daddy called me his Fancy Nancy and I liked it, along with my Fancy Nancy books and my Fancy Nancy doll. So he gave me that boat for my twelfth birthday, with Fancy Nancy painted right there in bright red letters. When I went all quiet on you, I was dreaming about hopping into this boat and sailing out to the sea to forget about all of them for a while." She swept her arm across her chest, taking in the house and the group gathered out on the porch. She started to hum and before long, she sang the words, "I would give you the world."

Not to be outdone, Welby joined in on the chorus. Once again, his tenor voice joined her soprano. As they harmonized into something beautiful, a crowd started to gather.

Tossing caution to the wind, Reagan pulled Fancy Nancy up to the dock, motioning for Welby to step in. "Come on, let's get out of here." She untied the rope from the dock and joined him. She reached for the key hidden under the dash and inserted it into the ignition. When she gave it a turn, the boat sprung to life, and she laughed out loud. "Hold on, Welby! I'm taking you for a ride." With a wave to those watching from the shore, she headed them out over the waves into the rising sun. For a few minutes at least, she could pretend that she and her dashing prince were the only two people in the whole wide world.

But then a familiar voice shattered her early morning joy. "Reagan, get back here. You know better than leaving your guests like that. Turn that boat around, right now."

Reagan covered her mouth with her hand, stifling a laugh. "Listen to him. He has absolutely no control over me anymore. But keep a straight face, don't let him think I'm shaking in my boots."

Welby acquiesced, putting on a poker face, but with a hint of a smile forming on his lips. "Reagan, turn around. Last night, your dad seemed very civil. Let's not blow it, okay? Remember, we've got breakfast and a tour this morning."

Reagan heard Welby's voice of reason, but also longed to just follow the call to be wild. For years, she'd kept herself under wraps, being just what her daddy wanted. She screwed up big time on opioids after the wreck, but then went right back to her old ways of conforming and pleasing him. That needed to change, so she refused to turn around. Instead she sped out across the shimmering sea. As her friends and family home faded into a speck in the distance, the golden ball of the sun rose on the horizon, signaling new life ahead.

But then Welby called over the din of the engine, "Reagan, turn the boat around. Thank you for this great ride, but we gotta go back, doll. Another time, you can take me out. Oh, yeah. You can take me." Then he put this faraway look on his face, and gently traced his finger along the side of her face.

She punched him for his silliness, which was clearly a sexual overture. "Welby, stop."

"Reagan, stop," he bantered back, raising his eyebrows. "Do I need to put on my pirate persona and tie Fancy Nancy up?"

Reagan looked at him mischievously, but then grunted. "Okay, okay. You men take all the fun out of life. First Daddy, now you. When will I ever get a life?"

She turned the boat toward shore, frowning and slowing the engine, not about to rush back the way she'd sped out. She could send her father a message one way or the other that he could no longer run her life. She doubted he accepted Welby, either. She'd watched him, a true politician, many times work a crowd, keeping his emotions close to the chest. Yes, Reagan knew him all too well.

"You drive," Reagan told Welby. "Let me enjoy the beauty of the morning and our escape for just a few more precious minutes." She moved over, offering him the helm, then pulled her camera out of her pocket, removed its waterproof jacket, and began framing the beauty around her.

First, she shot Welby with a smile on his face, looking ahead to shore, the sun at his back; a portrait of a man who knew right where he wanted to go. He gave her a wink and she captured that, too. Enjoying his handsome face, she experimented with lighting and zoomed in and out, catching the sun shining off his wide smile, getting that soulful look deep in his eyes, then framed those big, beautiful hands on the wheel. She felt her temperature rise, just focusing on him. Her ex-fiancé, Tyler, never had this effect on her. Good thing that didn't work out or she might've ended up a divorced single mother or stuck in a political marriage for the rest of his career.

She switched on the camera's sports mode, snapping pictures of the waves. Droplets hung midair in the wake as Welby opened the throttle, flying Fancy Nancy along toward shore. The sun sparkled on the cascading waves. Then the cool mist generated tiny little rainbows, emerging just above the water. Someday soon, she would make this visual feast come alive on her canvas, commemorating a very special morning in Savannah.

Once again, she turned her back to the shore, arranging the view of the rising sun spreading rays over the water. She zoomed in, shooting the sparkling waves near the boat. She zoomed back out to get it all in, flipping the scene wheel into the panoramic feature for a three-sixty of the moment. She would remember and relish this freedom long after she returned to shore.

The early morning sun illuminated houses along the shore in pastel beauty. She continued snapping picture after picture. One might make a great painting for her parents for Christmas, or maybe her mom's birthday, which was coming up soon. She really loved this place and had missed it for so long. Life had happened, making it difficult to find time to spend here. She tucked her camera away, determined to make the most of this day.

"Welby, here. I'll do it," she said as they approached the dock. He slid over, giving her full berth as she pulled the boat up to the dock, lassoed the rope over the pier post, and reeled them in. "Go ahead, Welby. Step out, one foot at a time." Then she turned off the engine, took the key out of the ignition, and tucked it back away. Welby offered his hand as she climbed out, stepping up easily onto the pier.

"Where did everyone go?" Reagan wondered out loud. "I'm surprised Daddy didn't make them wait or send out the Coast Guard."

"Give your father a break," Welby said. "He just wants you to mind your manners. Don't go all hostile on him. I wish I had a dad to remind me to do the right thing every now and then."

"Do you ever hear from your dad, Welby?"

"Sometimes. He keeps writing, but I'm still mad. Probably I should write back or visit sometime. You know life's not very easy for Black men. His problems weren't all of his own making, but he could've done a better job. He'll be getting out of the pen soon."

"You're right." Reagan changed her tone. "I should be grateful for what I have, but sometimes, I just wish I lived in a different family, you know?"

"Most of us do, Reagan, from time to time. But what the good Lord gave us is what we got. Up to us to find a way to make it work. We can't pass on all the blame. We have choices."

Reagan pondered what Welby said. Yes, she did have choices. She made up her mind to finally find out the truth in her family tree. It was her story. She had a right to know, regardless of how her dad wanted to hide it. And before her daddy kicked the best thing that ever happened to her out of her life because of the color of his skin, she would know exactly how that Black blood got into her veins. And if she'd gotten some, so had her daddy, because she knew for sure it didn't come from her mom.

When they entered the house, breakfast was finishing up. "Grab something quick," Abigail told them. "We leave in fifteen minutes for our eleven o'clock tour."

Reagan poured herself a cup of coffee. "Want one?" she asked Welby.

"Sure thing," he told her.

She poured him a cup, then set the carafe back on its perch and grabbed a croissant, peeled a hard-boiled egg and put them in a bowl. "I'm going to change real quick," she told Welby. She needed her journal, the family history book, and her satchel. She also wanted some dry clothes and shoes.

"Not so fast." George stopped her, and right beside him stood Abigail. He told them, "Reagan, and Welby, too, we need to have a talk." Reagan figured they were in for a lecture. "Now, we gave you two some latitude with your relationship, but we're trusting you to keep it light. I didn't like what I just saw. You can't go off like that, sailing into the sun, especially after Reagan's father called you back. Where's your respect? You just can't do that."

Abigail chimed in. "Yes, we know you care about each other, but keep in mind you are still under supervision. You need to be with one of us at all times. You know our rules."

Reagan nodded. She felt guilty, especially for Welby, because he'd wanted her to turn back. "I'm sorry," she told George and Abigail. "It won't happen again."

"Welby?" George asked.

"We'll be good. Sorry, man," Welby agreed, but didn't place the blame on Reagan.

A few minutes later, they all gathered in the front hall. "The gang's all here," Abigail announced. They filed out of the house into a large van waiting in the circular drive. Welby scooted behind Reagan in line. They entered the vehicle together and shared a seat for the short ride into town, but didn't talk much. Reagan was happy to escape her father's reprimand, or so she thought, but then her phone chimed. There, a message from him scolded: Start behaving like a lady, Reagan. You're no longer a child. She fumed and turned off her phone.

As they pulled away, Seamus' resonant Irish brogue filled the van. Reagan closed her eyes, and, for a moment, imagined she was back on the Emerald Isle where they'd first met the jolly tour guide. She'd watched love unfold right before her eyes, between Abigail and Seamus, between her and Welby. She loved Ireland, and Savannah didn't measure up. A dark pall hung over the city, probably because of its sordid past. The Black blood in her veins called her to understand and uncover the truth about her own family and the darkness that simmered just below the surface of this town.

"Today, we be off to the Second African Baptist Church, we are, for a Black history of Savannah," Seamus announced. "Then we'll stop for some more delicious Southern cuisine, before we pack up and head north. Tonight, destination Surfside Beach, South Carolina. Now just sit back and relax and we'll have ye there in no time, no time at all."

Reagan used the time to peruse her family history, "The Hunter Smiths of Savannah," wondering if there lurked any clues about the Gullah Hunter Smiths of Pin Point. On the family tree page, she noticed a gap. Martin Hunter Smith, the patriarch born in 1801, owned a large plantation, and also a bank. She remembered her dad pointing out his picture in the museum, telling her to be proud of the man, who had been a prominent founder of Savannah. But how many slaves had he owned, and how did he treat them? Her father never said a word about that.

The book noted that Martin married twice, and had a total of five children. The first wife and two of the children were listed on the family tree, but no branches extended from them. And there, she saw her great-grandfather, Charles, one of the other sons. The branches led downward to her dad and eventually to her. Who were those other children? What happened to the first wife, Sarah? Did they die or perhaps they went to Pin Point? She checked her phone for the photo of the Hunter Smith names she'd found in the book at Pin Point. Sure enough, she found a match.

"What's up, Reagan?" Welby asked.

"Oh, nothing," she lied. "I'm trying to figure my family out." God knew there had been enough lies already when it came to her family, but she didn't want to say anything until she could be sure. She flipped to the index in the back, searching for Sarah and the two boys' names. Nothing. Everybody else in this history book was listed in the back. Why were they left out?

Before she could tell Welby the truth, they arrived in downtown Savannah. While Seamus parked the van, Abigail led them to the city square across from the church to meet the tour guide. An attractive middle-aged Black woman with dreadlocks introduced herself to the group. "Welcome to Savannah," she told them. "We will be waiting a few minutes for a few others who signed up for this tour. Just have a seat, or enjoy the square, and we'll start soon."

Welby took Reagan's hand, leading her to a park bench. The tree-lined square provided a beautiful place that Reagan enjoyed. "The original developers of Savannah planned these city parks that provide nice shady spots all over downtown. But today, I'm glad to be sitting in the February sun," she explained to Welby. "It's weird, as many times as I've toured Savannah, I never heard about this one. I wonder how they found it."

"Abigail spotted it on Groupon. The lady cut us a special deal because we're a group. When she explained about the re-entry grant, she reduced the price even more."

"How do you know all this?" Reagan inquired.

"I listen, Reagan. You daydream. You were there when she told us that."

Reagan laughed. "You're right, you know me so well, Welby. That's what I like about you."

"I watch you, Reagan. While you daydream. I'm dreaming about you, about us." He traced circles in her palm, sighing as he said, "Baby, baby."

Reagan took a deep breath. This man oozed sexuality. His way of experiencing the world touched and changed her. Over the months they'd been together, she'd felt herself becoming more like him.

"I'm so glad you're trying to learn about your people, Reagan, especially your Black ones," Welby told her, continuing to trace his finger around her palm, soothing and exciting her with such a simple touch. "Maybe what you discover will change your dad. Maybe he'll come around about me."

"Don't you think he already knows? I always thought he left something out. This goes way back, and it's deep." Reagan frowned. Welby liked to be optimistic with all his born-again faith, but some people never change and her dad was one of them.

Breakfast in Bed with Priscilla

Morning came early on the coast. They served breakfast at the crack of dawn with a sunrise photo shoot. But while others "ooh"-ed and "ahh"-ed over the new day, Priscilla slept in. For a working woman, nothing beat the luxury of a morning in bed. At nine, she considered getting up, but then snuggled down under the downy coverlet just a little bit longer, appreciating the comfortable mattress and the picturesque view of the Atlantic out her bedroom window.

A knock sounded on the door. "Can I bring you some breakfast?" a voice inquired.

Priscilla slipped into her robe to answer the door. She didn't recognize the voice. Hired help perhaps?

"Good morning," a young woman greeted her. "I'm Kayletta, on a mission to wake you up. They told me to tell you the van leaves at ten thirty. Would you like breakfast in bed?"

"Oh, wow," Priscilla responded, pinching herself to confirm what she'd just heard. "That would be simply marvelous. Coffee, fruit, a scrambled egg, and a piece of toast? Is that really possible?"

"Yes, dear. Your wish is my command. Back in ten," Kayletta promised with a smile.

Priscilla shut the door, and then her eyes. The last time anybody waited on her like this was when she was a little girl. Her mom had done her best to make up for what they lacked. Sometimes she did serve breakfast in bed. She looked back with fondness on those days, so very long ago, remembering the day her mom brought in a plastic crown, placing it on her head and crowning her "Princess of the Manor."

Now, she tried to imagine her ancestors, living life on a plantation. Where had they lived and what had they done? She hoped this trip would take her there.

Her uncles still flew the Confederate flag. She knew many people got upset about that flag these days. She read about the changes coming down: folks tearing down the statues of the South, renaming schools, stealing their favorite icons of yesteryear. Her uncles complained loud and long at family gatherings.

She understood. Maybe the Yankees won the war, but why did that mean the Confederates needed to give up the past? Her mom always taught her there are always two sides to every story. That's why President Steele got elected. White people were tired of immigrants and minorities getting all the jobs. Weren't the white people running the country, anyway? Just because they worked hard and succeeded, should they give it all up to these others? And what about all those people living off the government?

God knows, she didn't get a break. As a single working woman, she scrimped and saved. She never could even afford a vacation, until Jane and the MAMs started bankrolling these trips for her. As an administrative assistant, she could barely pay the bills and struggled to keep a cushion in a rainy-day fund. Unlike those welfare cheats, she worked hard every day.

When Kayletta knocked again, Priscilla jumped up and opened the door. Then, leaving her pity party behind, she reveled in the luxury of the morning, becoming a princess once more. She thanked Kayletta for the food, closed the door, and carried the tray right back to bed. For a few minutes, she would enjoy the luxury of this brilliant new day.

In a little while, Abigail knocked. "The van's leaving."

"Go ahead without me," Priscilla told her. "I want to take the morning off, okay?"

"Are you sure? You'll miss the tour."

"Yes, go ahead. I need to rest a little." Then she dressed slowly and decided to go down to the veranda on the ocean. She grabbed the mysterious journal and headed down the grand staircase.

Passing the study, she heard loud voices. Never one to eavesdrop, she couldn't help but recognize Mr. Hunter Smith's distinctive voice through the open door, announcing loud and clear, "She'll tire of this infatuation soon enough. If I lay low and pretend I'm okay with it, she'll be on to a more appropriate partner soon. If I protest, she'll dig her feet in."

"People are already talking. They saw your daughter holding hands with that Black boy on the street. This will ruin your career. Let me help. I'll just pick him up for questioning, include him in a line-up. That will shake her up a little and it won't come from you."

Priscilla heard footsteps on the stairs. The door to the study swung shut and she looked up to Mrs. Hunter Smith coming down. She waved briefly and then escaped out the door to the deck. Her hand shook as opened her journal She couldn't read now. What were they plotting and what were they going to do to Welby?

The Tour, Continued

As they waited for the Black History Tour of Savanna, Reagan fretted over her ancestry. Life used to be so simple, but now everything she thought she knew about her heritage seemed to be turned upside down and inside out. Yet, when Abigail called her and Welby back to the group, Reagan smiled, somehow knowing she was born for this moment, for whatever would transpire on this tour. "Let's do this," she told Welby as they headed to the church to begin.

The attractive tour guide circled them up near the church doors and launched right into her narrative. "It's hard to tell the history of Savannah without the story of the Blacks who once resided here," she explained. "The African slaves who were kidnapped from their homes and brought here against their will built this city. When you enjoy the beautiful houses and mansions along the river, tour the large buildings, consider the plazas and the wealth displayed in so many ways, you need to be thinking about the slaves who built this place.

"James Oglethorpe originally founded Savannah back in 1733 as a debtors' colony. At that time, they brought in white slaves to work off their debt. But when Eli Whitney invented the cotton gin in 1790, capitalists clamored for profit in cotton production. In order to make money, they required cheap labor. That is why they needed the slave trade. In the 1800s, the Confederate entrepreneurs bought and sold kidnapped Africans like chattel. Unlike many forms of slavery throughout world history, the cruel American version disrespected family connections."

She pointed across the plaza. "Right there, in that small building, they conducted slave auctions. They paraded the men and women in chains to be bought and sold. If they acted up, the ruthless sellers would break their legs and teeth to serve as a message to the others. In 1862 alone, the slave trade profit totaled two million dollars. They didn't mind sacrificing a good sale now and then to keep the rest of the slaves docile."

Reagan looked at Welby. "How could they do that … to other human beings?"

"I know, I know. It's so bad. So hard to comprehend," Welby agreed. "All about money, greed, evil."

"We're going into the church," the guide said. "The African Americans built this church in 1802 and trained more pastors here than any other church at the time. The members built and installed these benches in 1810." She demonstrated how the backs of the benches flipped back and forth. "If they were having church, the benches would all face forward. For political meetings, they flipped the benches to face the back. The politicians didn't speak from the pulpit."

"Very cool," Welby commented quietly to Reagan.

George seemed impressed, too, moving one of the bench backs to try it himself. "Did they get a patent on this?" he inquired.

The guide laughed. "I don't think so. They probably wouldn't give a patent to the Black folks back then, but it served them well." She continued, "Now, we do know that after the war, General Sherman met with twenty Black clergy here in 1865 to ask about the needs of the emancipated slaves. When they asked for land, he arranged to give them forty-acre parcels of land on Skidway Island. After slavery, the plantation owners abandoned many of the Sea Islands and didn't want the land."

Soon, she led them out of the church and down the street, stopping in front of the slave auction building. "I want to tell you a story about Weston Hunter Smith, who shopped for slaves here. Born into two leading families of early Savannah, the Hunters and the Browns, Weston would eventually become the black sheep. When his parents, Annabelle Hunter and Malachi Brown, married, they combined their names to reflect their high station in Savannah society. Weston, though cruel and ruthless, has a very interesting story."

Reagan cringed as she heard her family name, not surprised when Molly asked, "Is this your relative? Hunter Smith?"

"I honestly don't know," Reagan replied. "I've never heard about him, but that's our name and it's Savannah. Probably so, don't you think? A slave owner." She shuddered.

"It's not your fault," Welby told her, putting his arm around her and giving her arm a squeeze. "Let's hear the rest of the story."

"Well, okay," the guide responded. "Let me warn you, first, it's not pretty. Weston chose a very beautiful, light-skinned, former slave named Sophie for his mistress. He decided to marry her, but Georgian law prohibited mixed marriages. First, he captured her partner and sold him away, then moved Sophie into his house. Together, they created seven children, with varying skin hues. Weston didn't like his dark-skinned children.

"Not only could they not get married, but they also had to live with other freed slaves. Mr. Hunter Smith wanted to live in a better neighborhood, so he needed a legitimate marriage, He therefore petitioned the Georgia legislature to pass a statute declaring Sophie to be a free white woman. The legislature complied with his request, even though common knowledge said otherwise. Subsequently, they married, moved to the white side of town and all was well, until Weston took a fancy to a young Irish maiden, divorcing Sophie and marrying his new love, Mary O'Reilly. He cut off support to Sophie and her children.

"But Sophie showed her mettle, suing Weston Hunter Smith in court, and she won. The judge cited the Georgia statute that declared her a free white woman and granted her alimony and a portion of Hunter's holdings."

Reagan's head spun with the details of this revelation. This man must be a part of her family tree. Could he possibly be the connection between her Savannah's society roots and also the Pin Point entrepreneurs? His darker children perhaps obtained land near Pin Point?

"Wow," Welby said. "What a lady! You should be proud, Reagan."

Reagan nodded. Yes, this strong woman had stood up for herself and her children. Reagan wanted the truth now. Her father must come clean. She resolved to make him fess up.

For the next hour, they followed the guide through the streets of Savannah, learning more about the slave markets and evil of the slave entrepreneurs. As they neared the oceanfront, she stopped by a building labeled Warehouse. The sign further explained products were stored in this windowless building after being unloaded from ships in the harbor. Inside, the tour guide pointed out a French drain running around the circumference of the large single room. "What that sign doesn't tell is that this was actually a holding cell for the slaves. They were locked in here, awaiting slave auction. Their excrement was swept into the drains."

Reagan shivered in the dark building, suddenly yearning to get back outside into the light of day. She'd actually like to slam the door and never look back, but she also knew she couldn't do that and still live with herself. No, this was her story now and she needed to know it all.

Soon, they stood in front of a statue of an African American family, dressed in their Sunday best, but with chains around their feet. "This statue was the subject of some controversy. For one, they wanted to put this by the church we visited, to keep it out of the limelight of the harbor promenade. Then, they dressed the family in Sunday clothes with shoes. Slaves weren't allowed to wear shoes. Maya Angelou was invited to write a script for the statue, which read, We lay back to belly in the holds of the slave ships in each other's excrement and urine together, sometimes died together, and our lifeless bodies thrown overboard together. The Savannah City Council would not approve this statement, so Maya added another line, reading, Today, we are standing up together, with faith and even some joy.

"But they left the rest of the quote in there?" Welby inquired.

"Yes, they did," the guide explained, "but also added the sentence to end on a positive note."

"Glad to see there's some truth-tellin' here," Welby commented as they walked along the waterfront promenade. "You see how these white folks want to revise the history, pretending it's all so pretty? Dressing slaves up in Sunday go-to-meeting clothes? Really? They don't want the truth, because it sucks, plain and simple."

Reagan understood, but it did also bother her that the Black history of Savannah included so much suffering, which didn't bode well for tourism. As she began to learn the truth about Savannah and her own family, she felt sad, disturbed, and uneasy. Why did she never learn any of this growing up? Why did her family cover the facts? How could good Christian people do all this in the first place, and continue to discriminate in the years since?

After the tour, they returned home for lunch on the veranda. The beauty of the afternoon, the closeness of Welby, the fun of having the MAMs close by made Reagan happy. For the time being, she put aside the growing revelations of her family history, and decided to enjoy the luncheon. All seemed right with the world as the sea breezes blew in across the sunny deck, and they partook of a delicious meal of fried fish and chips.

Everything seemed almost perfect, until the Oceanside police showed up, looking for one Marcus Welby Jones to take him down to the station for questioning.

"What?" Welby said. "What's this about?"

George stood by Welby and approached the police officer. "Sir, could you please tell us what this is about? We've only been in here for two days and Welby has been under our supervision the entire time."

The officer seemed undaunted by George's protest. "Sir, Marcus Welby Jones is a person of interest in a rape of a white woman that occurred late last night, around one a.m., just a few blocks from here. We'd like to take him down to the police station for questioning."

Reagan's mouth hung open in surprise and dismay. Welby would never do such a thing. He was sound asleep at one a.m. She remembered wishing him a goodnight, but then she wondered if he could have slipped out.

Welby spoke up for himself. "That's crazy, sir. I was sound asleep at one a.m. George here can testify to that."

"Yes," George agreed. "Welby and I slept in the same room last night. I'm a light sleeper. I would've heard him leave. How did you even know he was here?"

The policeman seemed nonplussed by their protests. "We get notifications of felons entering our state through an inter-cooperative law enforcement with other states. Ohio files when probationers go out of state. When the rape was reported, we searched for criminals with records in the area and Marcus Welby Jones' record residing at this address surfaced front and center. You need to come with me, son," he said. And then he started to read Welby his rights.

George stopped the man. "Something's fishy here. We've got several other men on parole here, and some women, too. In fact, we have two other Black male parolees along with us. Why you singling out Welby?"

"Do you want me to take the others as well?" the officer asked.

That dumbfounded George. "I don't want you to take any of them."

"Sir, I'm sorry, I need to proceed with reading Welby his rights."

Reagan wondered the exact same thing that George asked. She knew something was very wrong with the whole situation, but wondered if it surprised Welby. She remembered he'd told her earlier, "Things are never safe for Black men in Georgia." She hadn't believed him at the time. She began to cry.

As the officer finished up, George asked if he could come along. The MAMs started consulting about arranging an attorney and, suddenly, the blissful afternoon became a nightmare in the first degree. When they led Welby away, Reagan disappeared up to her room. She couldn't believe that Welby would do such a thing, but more than that, she found it even harder to believe they would find him here. Something was very wrong about this situation.

CHAPTER SEVEN
WELBY AND THE POLICE

The MAMs Luncheon Stopped Short

Priscilla came downstairs to enjoy a luncheon with the MAMs after spending the morning to herself. There was a lovely spread on the veranda, and a beautiful ocean breeze with a matching incredible view across the water beyond the well-manicured lawn. She must be a little late, because Reagan and Welby and the other group home members were nowhere in sight. Fortunately, the buffet table seemed well-stocked. She fixed herself a plate and joined Jane, Molly, and Abigail at a table.

She sensed tension in the air. "What happened?" she asked. "Is something wrong?"

"They just took Welby down to the police station for questioning," Molly said. "Hard to believe. We're here two days and they're framing a Black man on vacation."

Priscilla's stomach sank. Suddenly, she didn't want to eat. She knew what she'd heard in the study. Her conscience nudged her to speak up right away, but she couldn't quite form the words. Instead, she asked, "Why? For what?"

Jane said, "A woman was raped a few blocks from here last night. They say they had Welby in their system. We're guessing because all of our residents had to report this trip to their parole officers, it must've gone into a national tracking system. We're not sure. They're questioning him as a person of interest."

"Welcome to the South," Molly said. "For African Americans in Georgia, four hundred years after slavery, the injustice continues. Don't you think it's strange that they only picked up Welby? Why not the other men? Something's rotten in the State of Denmark."

Sallie and Abigail came over to join the discussion and Sallie contributed, "Good point. We need to talk with that attorney brother-in-law of yours. This certainly puts a damper on our vacation. This is awful. What can we do to support Welby?"

"George went down to the station with him," Molly said. "Tom already contacted his brother, Leo, the attorney back in Ohio, to get legal representation. Leo will fly down, if necessary. We can't just assume that Welby will be okay. Law enforcement has a long history of framing

Black men for crimes they didn't commit. We will stand by him through this. We will probably not be able to leave for Charleston tomorrow."

"Ladies, we need a plan," Abigail said. "The other tours are off for this afternoon. Tom jumped at the chance to take the group home members out sailing, something he's been itching to do since he saw that Hunter Smith sailboat sitting there by the dock. Why don't you go freshen up in your rooms and meet me down in the main hall at two-thirty for a meeting?" And then she dismissed her friend. "Seamus, you can go with Tom."

Priscilla's thoughts reeled as her whole body shook. She needed speak up. "Wait a minute," she said. Her heart seemed to be beating twice as fast as usual. "Stop. I need to say something. Sit down."

The MAMs took their seats obediently, and Tom and Seamus sat as well. All eyes turned toward Priscilla. "What is it?" Abigail asked for them all.

"When I came down for breakfast, I heard voices in Mr. Hunter Smith's study. I didn't mean to eavesdrop, but the door was open. They were talking rather loudly."

"Who was talking? What did you hear?" Molly asked.

"Some man told Mr. Hunter Smith that he needed to stop Reagan's relationship with Welby because it could hurt his political career. Mr. Hunter Smith said he didn't want to say anything to tell Reagan to stop, because it might cause her to dig in her heels. Then the other guy said that people were already talking after seeing Reagan and Welby holding hands. Then whoever it was offered to pick up Welby for questioning and put him in a lineup to scare off Reagan."

"What?" Molly yelled.

"Calm down, dear," Tom told her. "Let's think about this." His calm voice made Priscilla feel better. "Priscilla, do you know who he was talking with?"

"No. Right after he said that, someone closed the door. I didn't see the other man, but I recognized Reagan's dad's voice. It was clear the guy had the authority to pick up Welby. He must've been a policeman," she said.

"No policeman worth his salt would ever make such an offer," Tom said. "I retired from the River City Police Department after thirty years and never in my career did I hear of such a thing. Not only is that unethical, but it's also illegal. If that was a police offer, he should be fired immediately."

"We need to talk to Reagan," Abigail suggested. "Ladies, go take that break to freshen up. Take ten, and then come back down and we'll figure out what to do. Tom and Seamus, before you leave, what do you think?"

Priscilla left the table, her plate still full. Her stomach turned as she hurried up the stairs to her room, afraid that she might actually vomit. Once away from the others, she calmed quickly and decided to read her Bible for a few minutes and pray. At home, the pastor was leading a Bible study on the Psalms. She opened her Bible to Psalm 63 and read the passage.

The soothing scripture and beautiful view of the ocean helped her to feel much better. She bowed her head to praise God and ask for guidance. It seemed fairly clear that Reagan's dad and the visitor were framing Welby. After her prayer, she freshened up her make-up and headed down to join the MAMs for the pow-wow. She felt much calmer, knowing she just needed to tell the truth and that the MAMs would take it from there.

Welby at the Station

Welby tried to keep his cool at the police station, but déjà vu placed him on high alert. He flashed back six years when that highway patrolman searched his glove compartment, found illegal drugs, then handcuffed him and transported him down to the county jail. Okay, he broke the law, but he didn't hurt anybody and that didn't justify five long years in the penitentiary. This time, he'd done absolutely nothing to warrant an inquisition, other than making the mistake of being born Black and coming back to the South.

George reassured him. "Leo's going to help us, man. He'll fly down if needed."

Well, that was something. Last time he faced the music, he was entirely on his own. This time, he had friends and support.

"We're just going to put you in a line-up," the officer said. "If you are innocent as you insist, then this goes no further."

Another officer appeared with a camera and asked Welby to stand by the wall. They gave him a number to hold up and snapped his picture. A mug shot. Hadn't been back in the South three days, and already they were trying to frame him for a crime he never committed.

Sweat rolled down under his shirt. As innocent as was, he knew they could send him back to the pen with very little effort. He'd talked to guys there who insisted they were innocent. Maybe some of them were guilty, and probably some were telling the truth. He almost had it made: the love of a beautiful woman, technical skills to support himself, and a vision for a future. But this could stop everything.

"Now we just want to ask you a few questions, Marcus," the officer said.

"He goes by Welby," George said. "And hold your questions until our attorney arrives."

The officer looked at Welby. "Do you want to wait for an attorney, Welby?"

"I didn't do anything. What do you want me to tell you? I slept hard last night. There's nothing more to say," Welby said, dismissing the officer.

"Then you will have no problem with us taking a saliva sample to prove that your DNA was not present in the victim," the officer replied.

George put his hand on Welby's shoulder. "Don't let them do this, Welby. They have no reason to even suspect you of this crime, much less collect evidence. Wait until we get your attorney."

"But I didn't do anything. Why do I need an attorney to tell them I'm innocent?" Welby argued. "There's no way in hell they'll find my DNA in any woman that was attacked last night. I've never laid a finger on a woman in my life. Just because I'm Black and went to prison for having some recreational drugs in my glove compartment does not make me a rapist. I want to put an end to this fabrication now."

"I understand, Welby." George tried to placate him. "But we also want to make sure that your legal rights are respected here. Already, I think they are overreaching to pull you in on this."

The officer admitted, "Well, you certainly have a right to an attorney. We'll give you twenty-four hours. You are not to leave the area until you come back with your attorney and we finish the questioning. Understand?"

Welby's manners kicked in. "Yes, sir," he responded, then went silent.

"We'll be back, with legal representation," George promised.

The officer replied, "Then you are free to go."

Welby made a beeline for the door, with George following close behind. When they climbed into the van, Welby let out his breath. George patted him on the back. "It will be okay, Welby. Don't worry. We've got your back here."

"Thank you, George. I appreciate you, man. You don't know how much. That whole scene in there took me way back. It felt like it was all coming down again."

"I'm sorry, Welby," George apologized. "I don't believe they have the right to even pick you up without evidence. I just don't want anything bad to happen to you. It's a lot safer to have an attorney there to keep them honest. The last thing we want is for you to take the rap for a crime that the local authorities can't solve. It wouldn't be the first time, though, unfortunately."

"Do they really track people like me when they leave the state? That seems crazy," Welby complained.

"Didn't you report your trip to your parole officer?" George asked.

"Oh, yeah." Welby remembered and slumped in the seat. If he'd worried about Reagan's parents before, now any flicker of hope they could come around was completely blown out. He hated even returning to the Hunter Smith house. It looked bad, even if he was completely innocent. How do you prove you're asleep?

The MAMs Put Their Heads Together

Half an hour later, the MAMs gathered in the main hall around a large dining table. Priscilla wanted to trust the MAMs to figure this out.

"Let's talk," Abigail started. "What should we do now?"

"Support Welby, for sure," Molly said. "George just texted me from the police station. They took Welby's mug shot, wanted a saliva test and to ask him some questions. George put a halt on all that until we can get an attorney in there to represent Welby."

"But do you think he might have actually done it?" Jane asked.

Molly frowned. "Come on, Jane. Do you really think he's guilty? Don't you know this is the way things go down for Black men in the South? Remember when we read *Just Mercy*? Remember that guy who was throwing a party at his own house when a murder occurred? They still pinned it on him, even with all the witnesses who attended the party saying there was no way. That man served years for a crime he didn't commit. We don't want that to happen to Welby. Did you hear what Priscilla said?"

"But you don't really believe they lock up people who are innocent, do you? Don't you think that's just a rare occurrence, few and far between?" Jane responded.

Abigail chided, "Jane, come on. You heard what Priscilla said. I have a friend who is a death penalty attorney. He helped get people free, off death row, who were completely innocent. It happens more than anyone likes to admit."

Tom chimed in. "You're right. Unfortunately, African Americans have been framed for crimes they didn't commit for years. Fortunately, Priscilla heard their plan to do it to Welby. We need to stop this little charade right now."

"How do we do that?" Molly asked. "Reagan's father will deny it." Molly looked around the group and then stopped. "Hey, where's Reagan?"

"I knocked on her door and she didn't answer," Sallie reported.

Abigail jumped in. "I'll call her. We need her before we do anything." The group listened as Abigail called Reagan to join the group downstairs. "She'll be right down."

A few minutes later, when Reagan slowly descended the stairs, Priscilla could tell she'd been crying. That fresh coat of makeup couldn't begin to hide the evidence.

"It's okay, Reagan," Abigail told her. "This isn't your fault."

"No, not your fault," Sallie said, "but maybe your father's."

"What?" Reagan asked. "What did Daddy do?"

"Priscilla, you tell her," Tom said. "Priscilla overheard your dad in his study."

"Oh, Reagan, honey, I'm so sorry," Priscilla offered. "I skipped the tour this morning to get some beauty rest. When I came down to breakfast, I heard voices in your dad's study. I recognized his voice, but I didn't see the other man."

Reagan frowned and then asked rather impatiently, "And what did they say?"

"A man told your father people are talking about you being with a Black man, that it could end his political career. Your father said he didn't want to interfere, afraid that would push you to like Welby more. But then the other man offered to pick up Welby for questioning and put him in a line-up. He thought it stop you from liking Welby."

"No, no. How can that be?" Reagan cried. "Did Daddy agree?"

"The door closed after that," Priscilla said. "I didn't hear the rest."

"But it's obvious, don't you think?" Molly interjected. "A little later, they pick up Welby? Geez, I knew the South was bad, but this is so hard to believe. Tom, we need to do something."

Tom nodded. "Yes, but let's talk to Leo before we rush into anything. We may want our first step to be confronting Reagan's dad, but Leo may think otherwise."

Just then, Reagan's mother entered the front door. She waved to the group and turned to go up the stairs.

"Mom," Reagan stopped her. "Come here. You need to hear this."

Mrs. Hunter Smith came over to the table and sat in an empty chair next to Reagan. "What is it, dear?"

Reagan burst into tears. "The police came and picked up Welby for questioning. Priscilla overheard Daddy talking with someone in the study. They want to scare me out of liking Welby by picking him up for a line-up. Mom, Dad framed Welby."

Reagan's mother's mouth dropped open and she gasped, but then she closed her mouth and put her arm around Reagan, drawing her close, trying to offer comfort. She told Reagan, "Now, honey, that doesn't sound like your father. I think you're mistaken." Reagan scanned her mother's face. She'd just gasped, but now her face looked stoic. Priscilla thought she detected some nervousness, as she continued to hold Reagan, stroking her arm.

"Priscilla, you tell her," Reagan requested.

Priscilla repeated the words she'd overheard. Mrs. Hunter Smith became very agitated. She pulled her cellphone out of her purse and placed a call.

Tom stood and announced, "I'm calling Leo again," then walked out of the room.

Reagan's mom connected with her husband, telling him, "Ronald, you need to come home right now." After a pause, she continued. "I don't care what you have on your schedule. Come home now." Her face turned beet red.

"Is Daddy coming?" Reagan asked.

"He says he'll be home for dinner," her mother whispered, then continued the call. "Ron, did you frame Welby?" She pushed the speaker button and Mr. Hunter Smith's voice flooded into the room.

"What the hell? Why would I frame Welby? Martha, what are you talking about? Who is talking to you?"

"One of the MAMs, Priscilla, overheard you talking with someone in your study this morning. She said the other man offered to frame Welby, bring him in for questioning. That just happened. Welby's down at the police station right now."

"Martha, you know I wouldn't do that," Reagan's dad yelled. "Who is this Priscilla woman and what's she got against me? Is she a Democrat or something?"

"Honey, you're on speaker phone," his wife cautioned.

"Well, why didn't you tell me?" Ronald's voice barked through the crowded room.

"Sorry, dear," Martha replied. "I'll take it off." She pushed the button. "There," she said. "They can't hear you now."

Martha held the phone to ear for a few more minutes, then she put it down. "He can't get away right now. He'll be home at six, like planned. We can talk with him then."

"No way," Reagan yelled. She took out her own cellphone. "Dad, you come home right now. I don't care who is on your fucking schedule. You need to answer to us." Then she frowned. "He told me he didn't do anything, too. He won't come home until later." She put her phone down with a sneer.

Tom walked back into the room. "Leo's catching the next flight down. I'm picking him up at the airport. If we can't get the police to come clean the nice way, we'll take it to the press. It won't be pretty."

Martha cleared her throat. "But Ron said he didn't do anything. Priscilla, dear, are you sure what you heard? My husband is a good Christian man. He wouldn't lie about something like this. You can't go to the press if you don't know what happened."

"Mom," Reagan chided. "Look at the facts. It's clear. Daddy is lying. He is so not telling the truth. Look at what happened. A few hours later, they pick up Welby for a rape that happened last night? Welby's never done anything like that in his whole life. He was in prison for drug possession. He was sound asleep all night. George shared the room with him and said so. I wonder if there was even a rape. I bet they made that up, too."

Priscilla's stomach started turning again. She knew what she'd heard, but Mrs. Hunter Smith questioned her report. What if the police didn't believe her, either?

Tom spoke up. "Let's wait for Leo. We'll let our attorney handle this. For Welby's sake, I think we better wait and do things by the book."

The front door opened and George and Welby walked in. Reagan ran to Welby and embraced him, sobbing in his arms. "I know you didn't do anything. We need to get out of this place, now."

"I can't leave," Welby said. "I have to stay in town while they investigate."

Reagan took Welby by the hand and led him over to the group seated at the table. "Tell him, Priscilla. Tell him what you heard," she demanded.

Priscilla looked at Reagan's mother and then at Welby. Welby needed to hear the truth, but she felt nervous with Mrs. Hunter Smith sitting right there. She remembered her prayer time earlier and took a deep breath. Her mama always taught her to tell the truth and that's exactly what she aimed to do.

But then George interrupted. "Tom called us and told us what Priscilla heard. We'll deal with this when Leo arrives. Until then, Welby's right, he can't leave the Savannah area. We will stay until his name is cleared. Then we will high tail it to Charleston."

CHAPTER EIGHT
SOUTHERN JUSTICE

Grand Ma Ma Buckles Down

Now, this trip's gettin' downright ugly fast. I don't like it one bit. It's all good for Reagan and Priscilla to find out about their roots, but I didn't expect the demons of the South to show up for a bunch of tourists. But this ain't nothin' new. No, this here's as old as slavery. Or take it all the way back to Adam and Eve, if you want. I watched it time and time again in my lifetime. Down here, the white men hold the power and they lie. They do whatever is needed to keep my people down. After the Emancipation Proclamation, they kept their feet on our throats. First, kept us from owning our own land. We ended up serving the same masters as sharecroppers, not much better off than being slaves. The Jim Crow laws let them throw our men in jail for looking at somebody wrong.

But I sure hope they don't get away with this one. Welby's got good people on his side, along with his innocence. No relative of mine would ever rape a woman. Mr. Hunter Smith is one very sorry man. I hate to say it, but he deserves whatever happens next. I don't blame Reagan one bit if she never speaks to the man again, nor her mother as well. It's not right. But here you see it, plain and simple, what the white folk do. Anything to keep a daughter from mixing with one of mine.

Funny thing is those Hunter Smiths are all part of us, too. Reagan's hot on the trail of her ancestors. Don't let that truth get buried in all of this craziness. Her dad might just be one more dirty scoundrel, descended from that no-good Weston Hunter Smith back years ago.

I'm countin' on my Welby to rise above this mess, and Reagan, too. I see her shining and branching off her sorry family tree in a whole new direction. You just watch these young'uns. I'll place my cards on them. You watch now.

Welby's Backup for the Showdown

Welby hated watching a woman cry. He worried about what could come down, but put his concerns aside for Reagan's sake, telling her, "It'll be okay, Reagan. You'll see. Things will work out. I didn't do anything. They can't charge me for a crime I didn't commit." He said it so many times, he began to believe it himself, although it sure hadn't felt that way down at the police station earlier. The bad feelings that resurfaced from his first arrest haunted him still.

"I'm so sorry, Welby," Reagan told him. "I worried about Dad accepting you, but I never dreamed he would go this far. We should not have come here. I should've known better."

"It's not your fault," Welby responded. "I worried, too. Not only am I a Black man, but a Black man with a record. That's a tough match for your dad's little princess."

"Don't try to excuse him, Welby," Reagan protested. "Nothing gives him the right to frame you. This is all about his political career, it's not about you. I hope it comes out in the press. Serves him right."

Although Welby agreed, he wasn't about to tell her that. He tried to temper his own anger for the man, remembering it was her father. He knew exactly what it felt like to be embarrassed by a father. How many times did he wish his own dad was someone else? So he reassured her, rather than expressing his own thoughts and fears. "We'll get through this together, Reagan. I know we will."

When the MAMs planned dinner out at a local restaurant, Welby and Reagan decided to stay home and wait for Leo's arrival. With George and Tom, they ordered in pizza and sat out on the back deck, taking the sunset into early evening. Things seemed too quiet in the Hunter Smith mansion, with Reagan's parents strangely absent.

Just the day before, Welby skipped along on top of the world. Now, despair clouded out those happy feelings. Twilight brought shadows on water below, echoing into his life. He appreciated the support of Reagan, Tom, and George, but worried about the future. When darkness fell, they moved indoors to the living room.

"We got your back, man," George told Welby, sliding in next to him on the couch and slapping his shoulder, as if he could read his mind. "We won't let them get you. Don't let this get you down. You've come too far to let this blip send you off course. It's just another day in the life of a Black man. But we're stronger than them. You can't let them win."

Welby nodded, not quite sharing George's confidence. He'd seen too much. Life wasn't fair. He didn't do anything wrong, but they framed perfectly innocent good folks every day.

"I'm going to go get my dad," Reagan announced. "He needs to call off his thugs right now."

George put his hand on her arm. "Wait, Reagan. Leo will be here soon. We want to get this right. We need to protect Welby before anybody tries any more crazy stuff. Right now, we can't trust the police or your father to do the right thing. We don't want to give him a head start. I know it's hard, but just take a few deep breaths and wait."

Reagan frowned, clearly not happy with George's request.

Suddenly, Welby noticed her face light up. "Wait a minute," she said. "I've got an idea." She walked across the room to a big rolltop desk and pushed up the cover. She pulled out a small laptop. "My dad is hyper security conscious. The house is vacant most of the time, so he hires a security service to keep tabs on everything. If I remember correctly, these cameras record on a seven-day cycle. A few years ago, someone broke in. We were able to track not only how they got in, but exactly what they did in the house. My dad's so proud of this system. There's a website where we can view all the videos."

"Does that mean that we can prove I never left the house the night of the rape?"

"Yes, sir," Reagan told him. "And I think the cameras probably picked up the conversation in the study as well. I doubt my dad turned them off just because we were all here for a few days."

"So, the question is, how do we get this evidence before your father erases it?" Tom asked.

"Good question," Reagan said. "Maybe I can contact the security company and ask for copies of the videos? I'm going to put this away so I don't remind him of anything." She slipped it back into the desk, pulled the cover down, and returned to sit with the group.

"Can you get the copies without alerting your father?" George asked.

Just then, they heard footsteps on the stairs. Looking up, they saw Mr. and Mrs. Hunter Smith descending slowly together. Reagan's mother held on to her husband's arm. Their unsmiling faces were hard to read. Welby wanted to get out of there as quickly as possible, but realized he needed to stay. The security system gave him hope, but Reagan's father was a smart man. Welby doubted he would keep any information that could smear his face with mud.

Reagan remained silent. Welby supposed, because she'd already confronted her father on the phone and heard his denial, as well as hearing her mother supporting him, she didn't have anything more to say. Surprisingly, the Hunter Smiths didn't even try to talk to the group about the elephant in the room. Instead, Reagan's mother said, "We're going out. We'll be back late. Don't wait up for us." They walked with pomp and circumstance like they owned the place. Guess they do, Welby thought.

The front door closed, and Welby let out his breath. "Okay. Wasn't that something?"

George and Tom looked at Reagan, who smiled. "Perfect!" she announced. "This gives us just the time we need. I'll call the security service to come over right now."

George's cellphone buzzed. "George here," he answered, then

paused a moment before speaking again. "Leo! So glad you're almost here. We need you, man. I'll meet you at the door. Park out front, there's plenty of room in that large circular drive." George hung up, then told the group, "Our man has arrived. Two minutes away," He looked at the large front doors. "Do you think your parents have left yet?"

"Oh, yes, no problem," Reagan assured him. "My dad keeps his Mercedes on the circle. When he makes up his mind to go somewhere, he's gone."

George opened the door and peered out. "Coast is clear and here comes our man driving up right now."

A moment later, George hugged Leo at the front door and welcomed him in. Tom walked over to give him a hug as well. Leo approached Reagan and Welby, placing a hand on each of their shoulders, telling them, "I'm here to help."

"Thanks for coming," Welby said. "It means a lot."

"Sure thing," Leo replied. "We know what Southern justice looks like and we don't want to let them mess with you, bro."

Welby smiled for the first time all evening. "Thanks, man. I'm going to owe you big time."

"You can pay me back by paying it forward. You've got a bright future ahead of you, Welby. Don't let this mess trip you up. We've got your back," Leo fired back.

The support amazed Welby. It'd been a long time since anyone pulled for him. Years ago, his great-grandmother and mother went to bat for him, but then they died, leaving him to fend for himself. It felt good to have this group surrounding him with love and assistance once again.

Tom walked over to the desk, rolling the cover back up. "I think Reagan already solved our problem. Look at this. Security cameras record everything that goes on in this house. We should be able to hear Reagan's father, ID the policeman he talked with about framing Welby, and clear Welby with the tapes of the house entrances the night in question."

Leo rubbed his hands together. "Looks like the Good Lord is pulling for you, Welby. If we can get those videos, this whole situation might evaporate right before your eyes. So how do we access them before the big man has them erased, if he hasn't already?"

"Reagan was about to call the security company and ask for the data. Her father doesn't need to know," Tom explained.

Leo smiled. "That's a whole lot simpler than getting a court order to release the information. But are you sure your father hasn't already thought of this?'

Reagan shook her head. "I mean, it's possible, but he's so arrogant.

He just took my mom out for the night, acting like there is no problem. Before that, he stayed away, working all day."

"It's worth a try," Leo said. "If we go the formal route, he could easily erase the videos before they're turned over."

Reagan went back to the desk. Fortunately, her dad had taught her long ago what to do in the case of any suspicious activity. During her college years, Reagan and her friends sometimes came down for spring break. If she called the security company, they'd send a man out right away.

"Here goes!" Reagan placed the call, then looked at the clock on the wall. She smiled and announced, "They'll have someone here in thirty minutes."

"Now," Leo suggested, "let's make a list of what we need."

"They're trying to pin a rape on Welby that allegedly occurred the night before last at one a.m. So, I think we need to have the entrance scans from ten p.m., which is when I tucked Welby in. I mean, we were in the same room until morning," George suggested. "That will prove no one went in or out of this house that night."

"Right," Leo agreed. "And maybe the hall outside the bedroom door, too? To show that the door stay closed all night?"

"Yes," Reagan said. "Perfect." She gave Welby a side hug. "You're going to be just fine."

"It's not over yet, Reagan," Welby warned. "Wait until it's a wrap. We haven't even seen the videos yet, if they even still exist." Welby had no reason to believe that Mr. Hunter Smith hadn't already erased the evidence.

"And video of the study," Reagan told Leo. "We need yesterday morning's video of the study and the front door from eight a.m. to noon. Then we can see this policeman who visited, get his license plate, and also determine what time he came and left. With a little luck, it should pick up the conversation in the study. I know there's a camera in there, to protect my dad's private papers. If we can get that conversation, he's definitely sunk." Reagan smacked her hands together. "We've got this one in the bag, guys. My dad's going to be so sorry, and I don't feel for him one bit. He deserves everything he gets."

"Then what, Leo?" George asked. "Say we get all these videos and review them. Then what? How do we prove the videos are legit? What do we have to do to get the police to view them and exonerate Welby?"

"The videos should have date and time stamps on them, along with address and location imprints. Security companies are in the business of preparing evidence. Although they may usually be erased after a week, we can ask them to leave selected videos on the portal. But let's also ask them to download copies onto Reagan's laptop or external hard drive. Then we will need to get the police to look at what we have. If the videos implicate the police chief, we may have some obstacles in our way."

"My daddy knows all the bigwigs around here," Reagan said. "It very well could've been the police chief."

"One more thing, before any more time passes," Leo said. "We need a record of the police report for this alleged rape."

"Would they give you that?" George asked.

"Most police departments prepare a daily blotter with a list of crimes committed. The newspaper requests that information daily. I often prepared that for the River City Times when I worked the evening shift at the station," Tom said.

"Would it be in the newspaper?" Reagan asked.

"Probably, yes. There may be a day or two delay, though," Tom said.

"Could we just call the newspaper and get it?" Reagan suggested.

"I've got a better idea," Leo said. He pulled out his cell phone and, in a minute, started to smile. "Right here on the Oceanside News Facebook page is a link to their police blotter. Two nights ago, you say?"

"Right," George confirmed. "Can you find it?"

Leo scanned the information. "I'm not seeing any rape reported that night."

"I knew it! I knew it!" Reagan said. "They made it all up. Oh ,my God. How could he do this to Welby? To me?"

Priscilla and the MAMs at Dinner

Priscilla, the MAMs, and the other group home members piled into the van for an evening meal at a seafood restaurant on the water. Reagan had selected one of her favorites, but now would miss out. Priscilla regretted that Reagan couldn't come along and she also felt sorry for Welby. The more she thought about the whole situation, the angrier she became. Although she'd respected Reagan's dad in the past and followed his political career ever since Reagan moved into the FARM, now she found herself with second thoughts. How could he throw Welby under the bus like that? It's one thing to be upset about his daughter dating a Black man, but charging him with a rape he didn't commit?

Even without Welby, Reagan, George, Leo, and Tom, they still had a big crowd with the six MAMs, Seamus, Artemis, Zorastria, Max, and Antonio. Abigail forgot to call ahead, and now the group needed to wait forty-five minutes for a table. The veteran tour guide, Seamus, knew better than to let people stand around while they could be having some fun.

"We're near the historic district," Seamus said. "Let's go for a walk and check out some of the old houses before dinner."

"Do we have to?" Zorastria complained.

"Well, we could split into two groups," Seamus suggested. "Who wants to stand here for forty-five minutes?"

"Probably we could sit down," Artemis corrected. "See all those benches over there?"

Seamus chuckled. "Okay, yes, you're right, Artemis. Who would like to go for a walk?"

He always has such a good disposition, Priscilla thought. She tried to decide. She should go for a walk, but also felt exhausted by the day's events. In the end, she stayed on the bench with Zorastria and Artemis. "I'll give them my cell phone number, so they can text me and then I'll text you when we get our tables," she told Abigail as the rest of the group walked off.

Zorastria asked to go the bathroom, so Priscilla suggested, "Good idea, let's find it together." She didn't want Zorastria wandering off on her watch. They entered the restaurant and soon crowded into the small two-stall restroom. Priscilla touched up her makeup while waiting for the others.

Soon, Zorastria joined Priscilla at the mirror, asking, "Do you think Welby's guilty? I thought he turned over a new leaf. He doesn't strike me as the type to attack women. He's always been very respectful of me."

"No, honey," Priscilla answered. "Welby didn't do anything. Unfortunately, I think Reagan's dad doesn't approve of her relationship."

"Doesn't surprise me," Zorastria said. "But just think about it. If Reagan's got African blood, her father probably has some, too, especially if they're related to that Weston Hunter Smith we heard about on the tour today. Why are these pretend white people so ugly, Priscilla? You strike me as a nice white woman. Where do the white people get off on putting my people down?"

"I don't know," Priscilla replied nervously. "It's not right. I wasn't on the tour today. What did you learn about the Hunter Smiths?"

"Oh, they told us about a Weston Hunter Smith, some business guy back in the days of slavery, who made a lot of money the wrong way, and he liked this mixed lady. So, he got the Georgia legislature to declare her white. Then after he had a bunch of children with her, he tried to cut her off because he shacked up with another woman. The judge told him he'd married the first lady fair and square and there was state law to back it up. He ordered him to pay alimony and give her part of his fortune."

"Oh, my," Priscilla said. "That's Reagan's ancestor?"

"Sure sounds like it," Zorastria answered and then looked closely at Priscilla. "You got some of our blood, too, don't you?"

"Yes, I do. I didn't know about until we got our DNA tested," Priscilla replied.

Artemis came out of the stall and asked, "Can we go look at the river now?"

Priscilla checked with the hostess. "We've still got thirty minutes to wait. Yes, let's go check out the river, ladies."

The earlier conversation didn't sit well with her. The more she learned, the more disturbed she became. Knowing from the journal that one of her ancestors chose a slave girl as his lover bothered her as well. Was that rape? She was pretty sure she was descended from their child. That made her family about as good as the Hunter Smiths. She turned to the Savannah River, hoping that perhaps for a few minutes she could forget about it all.

She draped her arms around Artemis and Zorastria as they strolled along the river. Priscilla realized she still had a lot to learn about her heritage, about racism, and about each of the people on the trip.

When the restaurant texted to let them know their table was ready, Priscilla texted Abigail, then herded Artemis and Zorastria back to the dining room. The others arrived just as they took their seats. Soon, they ordered as lively conversation ensued. Priscilla puzzled over the good spirits of the group. All the laughing and joking seemed odd, when she personally couldn't relax or feel happy. The conversation between Reagan's dad and the policeman kept playing in her mind. They might have the power to seriously frame Welby.

When she found a lull in the conversation, she jumped in. "I think we should move out of the Hunter Smith mansion tonight."

"What?" Jane responded, sounding disturbed. "We've got great accommodations, and the Hunter Smiths aren't charging us a dime. Why move out? We're leaving tomorrow, anyway."

"We can't leave until Welby gets released to leave. Actually, we may be here for a while," Abigail explained.

"It's just not right," Priscilla insisted. "Mr. Hunter Smith framed Welby. We should leave, now."

Abigail looked at Seamus before speaking. Priscilla didn't think Seamus would know what to do. Couldn't Abigail see for herself? Then Abigail spoke. "I know how it looks, but Welby was ordered to stay here. And, frankly, we don't have the money to move into a hotel. We've made reservations for the rest of the trip, but adding more nights in a hotel could be very costly. We don't know how long and how this situation will play out. Remember, Mr. Hunter Smith denied the conversation you think you overheard. Really, they might ask us to leave. I don't think they're very happy with you right now."

Priscilla shivered. Did Abigail believe Mr. Hunter Smith more than her own friend? "I know what I heard," Priscilla insisted. "Don't you believe me?" Obviously, Abigail didn't.

"That's why we called Leo," Abigail said, avoiding her question. "We are going to fight this the right way. For now, we need to stay put until Welby is cleared."

Seamus nodded. Even Molly agreed. "I know what you're saying, Priscilla, but we can't afford to just leave our free lodging. Especially because we don't know how long this might continue."

"Okay, but what if they do ask us to leave?" Sallie asked. "I agree, they aren't very happy with Priscilla's accusations. If we don't have the money for a hotel, what then?"

The MAMs all looked at Jane. Jane looked at the ceiling.

Sallie tried praise tactics. "Jane, you've been so good to us in the past. Surely you could just help us out in a bind?"

Jane snickered. "You just think I'm made of money, don't you? I've worked hard for every dime I've got. You just want me to cough it up?"

"No, no," Sallie said. "I know you've worked hard. You've been very generous. It's just if we're in a bind, could you help us out?"

Jane smiled. "I'll think about it. But hopefully, that won't be necessary."

Priscilla tuned out the conversation and silently fumed. They came down here to learn about the Gullah people. Instead, they were getting a lesson in how racism worked. In the past, she'd complained Black people cried wolf all the time, trying to get themselves off the hook even though they were usually guilty. She always posted "Blue Lives Matter" on Facebook to support her local law enforcement heroes. Not that she regretted that, but suddenly, she began to get the other side. Black lives matter, but only to some, it appeared. Couldn't Reagan's dad see how Welby had changed? Couldn't he see Welby as a nice Christian man? He certainly forgave Reagan for stealing from the hospital. Welby was only arrested for possession of drugs, and then served five years. Didn't he deserve forgiveness as well? Could he only view Welby as a dreaded Black face?

CHAPTER NINE
SAKING THINGS UP

The Police Station Revisited

Welby's head reeled from the events of the day. George and Reagan flanked him, with Leo and Tom close behind, as they entered the police station. He held Reagan's hand tightly, squeezing it from time to time to let her know he appreciated her presence. Armed now with new evidence—the links to the home surveillance videos and a police blotter quiet on an incident of rape—he really began to believe this might be over soon. He prayed silently, for the umpteenth time today, that all would go well. After watching the videos, Reagan was able to I.D. the guy talking with her father. Fortunately, he was the assistant chief, who reported to the chief.

Leo knew how to work the system. It surprised Welby that the police chief would actually come down to the station at eight p.m. to meet with them. But according to Leo, the chief asked Leo to set the time and place. Perhaps he wanted an excuse to fire the assistant chief. Or maybe this would be the norm in a small Southern town. With the furor of Black Lives Matter protests in recent months, this could start a riot. Hell, he felt like swinging a few bats himself. Maybe he could ask George to take him to a boxing gym to let him punch his anger away.

The police chief greeted them from behind the counter, then walked out and shook all their hands, before inviting them into a small room behind the desk. "Now," he started, "thank you for coming down tonight. I want to deal with this situation quickly and put it behind us. I don't like the sound of it at all. Show me what you've got."

Leo first explained that he was an attorney from Ohio, representing Welby. Welby felt his heart warm, listening to Leo. "Sir," he told the chief, "our group came down here on tour to explore their roots. Welby, and five other young men and women, have turned over a new leaf at group homes managed by my sister's group, the MAMs, The Magnificent and Marvelous Book Club."

The chief's lips twitched. "Okay," he said. "Let me understand this. The MAMs brought Welby down here to explore his roots, out of a group home? Excuse me for questioning you, but really? This sounds rather strange."

Leo laughed. "You don't know my sister and her friends, sir. They read about things and then take action. They took some of their group home folks to Ireland last year. They got a re-entry grant to do this."

"Oh, I see," the chief said. "This is where our federal money is going these days."

Welby cringed. He was beginning to have second thoughts. What made him think that this police chief would be any different than the rest of them?

George spoke up. "Sir, I'm a recovering alcoholic myself. I've been clean ten years. And you well know that we have a serious drug and alcohol problem in our country. I'm on the board of the MAMs' group homes and, believe me, their programs are changing lives. Welby has been an exemplary citizen since he joined our Sun Power House last year. He's an electrical apprentice and also starting college. He plans to attend seminary.'

Then Tom Mabra piped in. "Sir, I just retired from the River City Police in River City, Ohio, after twenty-five years of service. As a police officer, I lived through the war on drugs and it's clear to me that, although we thought we were doing the right thing at the time, we've not solved our drug crisis by throwing people in jail. If anything, we've made it worse."

Now Welby let out his breath, which he didn't realize he was holding. It felt so good to hear his bros speaking up for him. He smiled and squeezed Reagan's hand again.

Leo said, "Could we get to the matter at hand? I believe that my client, Marcus Welby Jones, was framed by your assistant chief, Tad Matheo. We are prepared to go the press if you don't want to work with us on this."

"Now, now," the police chief said. "I invited you down here, didn't I? But you know and I know there are always two sides to a story."

Yes, always the truth and lies, Welby thought.

"Tell me what you got," he repeated. "I already told you that I don't like the sound of this."

Leo took over. "Sir, this is Reagan Hunter Smith, daughter of Ronald Hunter Smith, a well-known politician who has roots in Savannah and waterfront property here in Oceanside. You've probably heard of him?"

The police chief nodded, but maintained a poker face. Welby watched enough police shows to know he was trained to do that.

"Reagan and Welby are good friends," Leo said, then smiled. "Actually, they've developed rather strong feelings for each other, during the trip to Ireland. But they are finishing up their year in the group homes and are only permitted to have a platonic relationship. They are complying."

Welby smiled himself at that, knowing he deserved a gold medal for his behavior; keeping his hands off Reagan had not been easy. Loving Reagan tested him every day, but so far, he kept to the straight and narrow. Leo got that right.

"It appears," Leo continued, "that Reagan's dad doesn't want her to be involved with a Black man. Although he was friendly enough, welcoming this group into his home, behind the scenes, we find another story. One of the other MAMs, Priscilla, overheard Mr. Hunter Smith talking in his study with a man who offered to frame Welby to deter Reagan. She might have misheard the conversation, but I want you to watch this. Reagan, could you show him the video?"

Reagan opened her laptop. "Sir, our house has twenty-four-hour security cameras in most rooms and on the entrances and grounds of the house. My family lives in Ohio, so we don't spend much time down here. I was down on spring break with friends a few years back and someone broke in. We were able to give the police enough evidence to make an arrest, so I know how this system works. We talked to the security company earlier. Here's a video of my father's study yesterday morning, at the time Priscilla heard the conversation."

Welby realized Reagan was handing her dad over on a silver platter to the police chief and she didn't blink an eye. In fact, she had a hard edge to her voice, like anger seethed just below the surface. Welby appreciated the way she stood up for him very much.

She pushed the play button. Together, they watched her dad in conversation with the man they now knew to be the Oceanside assistant police chief.

"The people are watching," Tad Matheo told Reagan's dad. "They've seen your daughter with a Black man. It's just a matter of time before this gets out. It could ruin your career."

To his credit, Reagan's dad said he didn't want to interfere. He didn't want to cause Reagan to dig in her feet. If left alone, he believed she would tire of Welby soon. Smart man, Welby thought, he worried about that himself. But then the assistant chief made an offer.

"We can pick Welby up for questioning. You don't have to do a thing, Ron. That should make your daughter think twice about this Black man."

Welby thought maybe Mr. Hunter Smith would object, but instead, he nodded and asked, "You can do that?"

"Easy as pie," the man replied. "Consider it done."

"Okay, thank you, then," Reagan's dad replied. "Thank you very much."

Reagan stopped the video. "Seen enough?" she asked.

Leo said, "We can also show you video of Matheo getting out of his car, entering the house, and leaving again, with the license plate and time, if you want. Any questions?"

The police chief shook his head. "Any other evidence?"

Leo continued, "Later that day, your officers came and took Welby down here for questioning. They took a mug shot to put him in a line-up. They said he was a suspect in a rape that occurred the night before. Said they had Welby in their database of convicted felons in the area. However, sir, Welby's never been convicted of a sex crime. He served five long years for drug possession, obtained on an illegal search of his glove compartment, I might add. Furthermore, according to your police blotter, there were no rapes that night. George here was sleeping in the same room with Welby that night and said he didn't stir. Home surveillance videos also indicate no one left that room during the hours of the alleged rape, nor were any exterior doors opened during the night. What we have, sir, is clear evidence that your assistant chief framed Marcus Welby Jones. We are asking that you exonerate him immediately and expunge that record, or we're going to the press."

The police chief ran his hand through his hair and sighed. "Let me check our police record for that night. Sometimes things aren't reported when the crime is under investigation." He went over to a desk and signed on to the computer.

"He doesn't believe you," Welby whispered to Leo.

Leo placed his forefinger up to his lips, signaling Welby to be silent. They watched the police chief scan the computer for the information. Welby hoped nothing would be found.

The police chief finished his research and rejoined the group. Welby could feel his heart beating and held on to Reagan for support. "And?" Leo asked what they all wanted to know.

"You're correct. There's no report of a rape that night. I personally will make sure that Welby's record here is wiped clean. We will also be conducting an internal investigation. Reagan, would it be possible for me to get copies of that video you showed me?"

"Of course," she said. "Do you want to get it directly from the security company, or do you just want me to share the file with you?"

"Just share the file with me, for now. Later, I might need to request the official copy from your company. Please, if you could provide me with your contact information. You're all free to go. And on behalf of our department and the City of Savannah, I sincerely apologize, especially to you, Welby." He reached out to shake Welby's hand. "Congratulations on staying clean and sober. I'm glad to hear you're on a good path. Best wishes with your romance." He laughed, smiling at Reagan.

But Leo wasn't done. "I'd like something in writing before we leave here tonight," he told the police chief. "A note that Welby was mistakenly picked up for questioning for a crime that did not occur. And an apology, on your letterhead."

"I understand, not a problem," the chief responded. He went back to the computer, typed up a letter, printed it out, and signed it on the spot. "Will this do?" he asked, handing it to Leo.

Leo scanned the letter and nodded. "Thank you, sir. We appreciate you coming down tonight to resolve this situation." He reached out to shake the chief's hand and added, "Good night."

When they walked out of the police station, Welby let out a long whoop and Reagan cheered. George gave Welby a hug, while Leo and Tom patted them both on their backs.

"You did it, bro," George told Leo. "Great job, man. There's a reason why I'm glad I'm related to you."

"Yes, way to go!" Tom also offered his kudos. "That assistant chief is an abomination to our profession. Men like him give us all a bad name. I hope they fire his ass out of there."

"Notice the chief didn't make any promises," Leo cautioned. "We all know about internal investigations: a little hand-slapping, a written complaint, and a release right back out into a new game."

Welby certainly hoped Matheo would be punished, but he celebrated the fact that the truth had set him free. He lagged back to help Reagan into the van, planting a kiss on her cheek. She surprised him, turning back so their lips could connect. He enfolded her in his arms and slipped his tongue into her mouth. His hands moved down her back, settling in on her warm and smooth butt. The guys in the van didn't say a word. Welby soaked in Reagan's warmth, knowing that temptation would be knocking at his door loud and clear that night.

Reagan Confronts Her Father

That night, Reagan waited up for her parents to come home. Long after everyone else went to bed, she paced in the grand hall. She dismissed Welby to bed, telling him she needed to do this by herself. Never had she felt so betrayed. Sure, they had spats from time to time, but usually there was a lesson involved. This time, there was absolutely no excuse for his behavior.

People had warned her to expect some flack for dating Welby. The Black women didn't like white women stealing their men. White men didn't like seeing white women chasing Black guys, either. Families were often entrenched in the racism of the past. Many Black parents held too much anger to welcome white people into their family. Likewise, many white parents held on to racist attitudes. They didn't like to be accused of being racist, but let their daughter or son bring home a Black lover and they showed their true colors. She had really believed her dad was above that. What did it mean to be a Christian if you were going to reject somebody by the color of their skin? Jesus made it very clear. The Good Samaritan, a foreigner, is your neighbor. Love your enemies, he told them. The greatest commandments are to love God and your neighbor as yourself. Of course, this meant also loving and forgiving her dad. Right now, she just wanted him to suffer.

The outside porch light flashed on. Here they come, she thought, as she braced herself for the confrontation. She didn't plan to forgive him anytime soon.

Her mother entered the house, alone. "Hi, honey," she said when she noticed Reagan sitting on the couch. "You're up late."

Reagan snickered. "I didn't think you were a night owl yourself. Did that liar make you go out tonight because he didn't want to face me and Welby?"

Reagan knew what would come next. "Nancy Reagan Hunter Smith, how dare you? After everything your father has done for you? He's defended you right and left through all your drug problems. You're calling him a liar?"

"He lied, Mom. Pure and simple. He lied to you and he lied to me. I hope that police friend of his gets canned."

Then in came the Mr. Ronald Hunter Smith, no longer Reagan's favorite politician. She felt embarrassed and ashamed. "How could you, Dad?" she blurted and burst into tears.

"Well, good evening to you, too, Reagan. What burr have you got up your butt tonight? Do you still believe that conniving Priscilla woman over your own father?"

Reagan wiped her tears with her hands. Anger replaced sadness. "How dare you? Did you forget you've got cameras posed on every single room of this house? Did you forget to cover your tracks? You're slipping up, old man." Reagan never talked so disrespectfully to her father. "Did you forget you taught me all about that system years ago? You know perfectly well there was no rape, don't you, Dad? Your friend, Tad Mathieu, concocted that whole story to try to break up Welby and me. Don't try to deny it. And don't you, Mom, try to defend him, either. Do you want to watch the video? Do you want to hear the whole conversation, Mom? Priscilla told the truth. She heard exactly what Dad said. Dad agreed to the plan for the police to pick up Welby for questioning, thinking that would turn me off. When we showed the police chief the video tonight, he expunged Welby's record on the spot and apologized. I think your friend, the assistant police chief of Oceanside, is in a heap of trouble. How could you, Dad? How could you do that to Welby and me? I have news for you. I love Welby and I intend to marry him and nothing you can do or say will change my mind. We are leaving in the morning, and I won't be back. You lied. You also lied about my heritage. I heard the real story as we toured Savannah. Our ancestor, Weston Hunter Smith, was a despicable, racist man. He loved our ancestor, a mixed-race woman, until he didn't. First, he petitioned the Georgia legislature to get her declared free and white. Then when he wanted to take up with another woman, he asked the judge to annul his marriage, because it was illegal to marry a Black woman. Guess what, Dad? The judge sided with her. Some of her dark-skinned sons worked at an oyster factory at Pin Point with freed slaves. Why didn't you ever tell me about this? Why didn't you tell me that I am African American, Dad? And why in the hell would you throw Welby under the bus when he's just like us?"

An uneasy silence filled the hall. For once in her life, her dad didn't have a response. How could he? Instead, the color drained from his face. He grasped his chest and fought for breath, collapsing right in front of her eyes. His right leg buckled as he fell onto his side, landing on the rug with a soft thud. His eyes remained open with a vacant stare.

Reagan's mother screamed. "Reagan! Look at what you did to your father!"

Reagan's nursing training kicked in. Pushing her anger aside, she jumped into action. "Mom, call 911. Keep them on the line. Tell them we need an ambulance, now." She checked for a pulse. Feeling none, she rolled him onto his back, undid his tie, and opened the buttons on his shirt, wasting no time to begin CPR. Finding a steady rhythm, she pushed firmly on his chest and then blew into his mouth. As her father's life teetered on the brink, she hoped against hope that her efforts would bring him back. Praying silently, she pleaded with God. "Please, please don't let my father die," even as she realized he already had.

Meanwhile, her mother made the call, and Reagan listened in as she reported to 911. "My daughter's doing CPR. Yes, she knows what she's doing. She's a nurse. Please, we need an ambulance now! When will you get here? Hurry, hurry. My husband is Mr. Ronald Hunter Smith." She repeated the address several times. All color drained from her mother's face and Reagan began to fear for her mom, too.

As she pressed on her dad's chest, she tried to calm her mom. "Sit down, Mom. Take a few deep breaths." She stopped talking to again blow air into her dad's mouth, pushing the recent events out of her mind. Her dad's life depended on her now. Would she be enough? She continued to pray. As angry as she was, she didn't want her father to die. No, she wanted him to live and answer for what he did. If he died on her now, it would look like it was all her fault.

"Reagan, you're hurting him," her mother said.

"No, Mom, I'm trying to save his life. He stopped breathing. I'm trying to get his heart going again." Reagan stopped to check again for a pulse on his neck. Just then, her father's mouth opened and he exhaled. "He's back," she reported. "He has a pulse!"

The sirens became louder, the porch light flashed on outside the window, and they could hear a vehicle pulling into the front drive.

Her mother rushed over and opened the door. "He's here, on the floor. My daughter just did CPR. He's breathing again."

Two uniformed men entered the house, carrying a stretcher and a big black bag. One pulled an oxygen tank. Jane, Molly and Priscilla came stumbling down the stairs.

"What's going on?" Priscilla asked.

Reagan's mom put her fingers on her lips to silence her. Reagan gave report to the paramedics, which answered Priscilla's question quite well. "He fell from a standing position, fainting, about fifteen minutes ago." She looked at the clock. "His right leg buckled under him when he fell. It could be broken. I'm a nurse, so I checked for a pulse. Feeling none, I began CPR. A minute ago, he let out a breath and I believe his heart is beating again."

"Good work," one of them said. "Looks like you saved a life today."

While the paramedic attached a blood pressure cuff and checked her father's pulse, the second one took a needle attached to a vial out of the bag, rolled up her father's sleeve and jabbed it in his shoulder.

"Beta blocker?" Reagan asked. He nodded.

"One eighty over one twenty," the paramedic reported. The other placed oxygen tubing in her father's nose, hooking it up to the cannister they brought with them, then took supplies out of a bag to start an IV.

"We'll be transporting him to the nearest hospital, Savannah Regional. Is that okay, ma'am?" he asked.

"Of course," her mother answered, still sounding rather hysterical.

"Mom, are Dad's ID and medical card in his wallet?"

"I assume so, Reagan. They usually are."

"They'll need them at the hospital," Reagan explained. "I think his wallet is in his back pocket," she told the paramedic.

As they rolled him onto the stretcher, one of the guys felt his pockets on both sides. Clearly, there was a lump on one side. "Should I get it?" he asked Reagan.

Reagan nodded and so he pulled it out and handed it to her. A moment later, the paramedics were ready to roll.

"Can you meet us at the hospital, ma'am?" he asked Reagan's mother.

"I'll bring her," Reagan said, not trusting her mother's ability to drive, but she really didn't want to do this alone.

As the men carried her father out to the ambulance, Reagan turned to Molly, Jane, and Priscilla. "Would one of you go to the hospital with us?"

Priscilla raised her hand. "I'll go, honey. I will never get back to sleep after this."

Jane nodded. "Sounds good to me. Priscilla, you sure? I can drive you all."

"That would be awesome," Reagan responded.

"We got you," Jane said. "Let me tell Abigail and change out of my pjs. I'm surprised nobody else woke up."

"Me, too," Priscilla said. "I'll change quickly." She followed Jane up the stairs.

Reagan told her mom, "It's going to take them a while with Dad. They won't let us see him right away. We'll be there in good time."

Looking ahead, Reagan began calling her brother, Dean. No way in hell did she plan to wait this one out alone with her mother.

Last Day in Savannah

When Welby woke the next morning, he sensed something was wrong. He'd slept like a baby, with his fears relieved, but a new uneasiness set him on edge. He hopped in the shower, shrugged into some sweats, and then headed downstairs for breakfast. He hoped Reagan worked things out with her dad last night. God only knew how that conversation turned out.

He poured himself some coffee and joined Tom, George, and Leo out on the veranda. Abigail hurried over as soon as Welby sat down. Just then Zorastria, Artemis, Antonio, Max, and Seamus joined the breakfast group.

"Listen up, everybody," Abigail said. "We had an incident last night."

"An incident?" Welby asked, remembering the odd feeling he had when he woke up. "Is Reagan okay? What happened?"

"Reagan's father had a heart attack last night. His heart stopped, Reagan did CPR and got it going again, then the EMTs took him to the hospital. Reagan, her mother, and Priscilla are at the hospital now."

"Is he okay?" Welby asked. "Is he going to pull through?"

"Priscilla called a few minutes ago. They're prepping him for surgery now. He needs a triple bypass. It's up to the doctors now," Abigail explained.

"Oh, man," Welby said, rubbing his head with his hands. "Can I go? I want to be with Reagan. Could someone give me a ride to the hospital?"

"Reagan and Priscilla are on their way back here. They should be here any time," Abigail said.

"What?" Welby asked. "You mean she's not staying there with her mother? That doesn't make sense."

"She can explain it all when she gets back. I believe her brother arrived at the hospital a little while ago. You know, Reagan and Priscilla haven't slept all night," Abigail noted.

Just then, the door to the house burst open. Reagan hurried out onto the veranda, making a beeline for Welby. He stood and embraced her. She began to cry. "It's okay, baby. It's okay. I've gotcha," Welby reassured her. "Do you want to talk? Do you need something to eat? What can I do for you, Reagan?"

"Just hold me, Welby. Just hold me."

As Welby continued to provide solace to Reagan, he listened to Priscilla's report. "Last night, Reagan waited up for her parents. When they finally came home, she confronted them with the videos, and the family history of Weston Hunter Smith, from the Black history tour of Savannah. Her father collapsed. When Reagan checked him, she didn't get a pulse, so she began CPR and saved his life. She got his heart beating again and the paramedics took it from there. Reagan's mother is blaming her for the heart attack. But the surgeon told us this morning that she saved his life in more ways than one. He was a time bomb waiting to explode, because he didn't know he had a heart problem. The blockage was so severe, he was living on borrowed time. With surgery, his prognosis is very good."

Priscilla patted Reagan's arm. "Don't feel bad, Reagan. God is taking care of your daddy. All things work together for the good for those who love God and are called according to His purpose. Why don't we all pray for Reagan's father and the surgeon right here and now."

"Sounds like a good idea," Tom said. "Let's circle up and hold hands."

Welby let go of Reagan. He used his handkerchief to dry her tears, then grabbed her hand and Tom's. "Yes," he said, "let's pray."

"Heavenly father," Leo said, "we beseech you this morning to guide the hands of the surgeon as they operate on Reagan's father. We pray that you will hold him in your care and that he will emerge a whole person, sound in mind and body."

Welby admired Leo's example. He decided to add a few words of his own. "Lord God, we give thanks for the life of Ronald Hunter Smith. We especially thank you for the gift of his daughter, Reagan. We pray for a good outcome today with his surgery. And we pray for restored relationships also." He squeezed Reagan's hand and opened his eyes. Her face seemed contorted. He imagined she had a whole range of emotions running through her mind and body right now.

"Amen," shouted Tom. "Amen! Now you ladies sit down and have some breakfast before you go back in and get some shuteye."

"What can I get you, Reagan? Have a seat. I'll go get it for you," Welby told her.

"I'm not very hungry," Reagan answered. "Just some eggs, a piece of toast, and some juice. I don't want any coffee. I need to sleep."

While Welby gathered the items from the breakfast buffet, Abigail outlined the schedule changes. "We've been thrown off course on our trip, but plan to get moving fairly soon. This morning, we've scheduled a boat ride at the Savannah harbor while Priscilla and Reagan catch up on their sleep. You all get something to eat now, so we can get on the road. We need to leave in thirty minutes. We'll return for lunch, pack up, and head north. Reagan, you can stay here for a few days, as your father recovers from surgery."

"No way," Reagan announced. "I am not staying here to look after my father after what he did to Welby. I saved his life, but that doesn't mean I've forgiven him. My brother is coming to help Mom. I want to leave with you."

"Are you sure, baby?" Welby asked. "I'll stay if they let me. Don't you want to be here?"

"No, I don't. My brother is all my parents need. I feel sorry for my father, but that's all."

Welby understood. He knew how angry she was, but also knew she might regret this later. He heard the determination in her voice, so he kept his mouth shut.

"Are you sure, honey?" Priscilla asked. "Your parents need you right now."

Welby doubted Reagan would agree and, sure enough, she wasted no time letting them know exactly how she felt. "No, Pricilla, I am not staying here. My mother is blaming me. I've had enough. He framed Welby. He has lied to me my whole life. Why didn't he ever tell me I'm Black? He had a heart attack because of his sick heart. That's not my fault. The doctor told them I saved his life. He could have croaked at any time. No, I need to stay away. If I'm so upsetting to him, let my brother and my mom take care of him. He'll be okay."

Abigail looked puzzled. "Reagan, I think you might regret this. How about we get you a cellphone to keep in touch with them, in case he takes a turn for the worse?"

Reagan smiled. "Okay, that would work. I wouldn't mind a cellphone, but I'm not staying here."

"Hey," Zorastria said. "My sister's about ready to have a baby. I need a cellphone, too."

"Yes, and my mama's got cancer." Artemis looked at Abigail. "Why's Reagan so special? Maybe we all should get cellphones?"

Max nodded. "I'd like a cellphone, too," he said. "I need to keep up with my family back home."

Welby thought Abigail looked flustered. She told them, "We'll discuss this more when we get home. Reagan's father is very sick, so this is an exception, and she will give it back when he's out of the woods. But I want to know more about your families and make sure you're able to communicate with them when they are in crisis. We will work this out. Thanks for speaking up."

Welby thought Abigail handled that smoothly, but Reagan looked embarrassed. Personally, he didn't think she needed the phone; she needed to stay put. But when Reagan dug in her heels, nobody could turn her around. He admired her spirit, although he also worried. Would she eventually blame him for all of this? None of this would have happened if she wasn't dating a Black man.

Welby wished it could be easier for them, but racism complicates life and sometimes turns everything downright ugly. He aimed for a path of love and forgiveness. Being Black, he knew too well that hate could consume you. He learned long ago he needed to let it go and ask the Good Lord to help him forget the ugliness he experienced. Holding the pain only hurts more.

CHAPTER TEN
HEADING TO HILTON HEAD

The MAMs Head to the Beach

Priscilla tried to nap when she got back to her room in the morning. The events of the last few days, coupled with the excitement of moving on to the place of her ancestors soon, caused turmoil as she tossed and turned until her alarm went off at 11:30 a.m. After a quick shower, she read the journal one more time. The mother of the writer of the journal settled in Mitchelville on Hilton Head Island after the war. The daughter moved to Ohio, where her father, a legislator, arranged for her education, at least through high school. The daughter obviously missed her mother and hoped to visit. The journal ended before that happened. The Hilton Head branch of her family was a mystery to Priscilla. She read now,

Dear Diary,

I miss my mother so much. I want to visit her. Papa tells me to wait until I'm older. I don't think he cares for her anymore. He has a new family now. He travels back and forth from South Carolina to Washington, DC, where he serves in the new Congress. I ask Papa to take me to see Mama, but he won't take me to visit her or to meet his other children. He tells me to study hard and that he'll find me a job when I get done. People in Oberlin accept me, even though I'm colored. My skin is light. I want to attend the university here, but Papa says he'll find me work with a good family when I finish high school. I can be a nanny, he tells me.

I want to go to Mitchelville, a freed slave colony on Hilton Head Island in South Carolina. I want to go see my mama there and maybe I can get a job. But Papa says no, he has other plans for me now.

Abigail knocked on the door. "Ready?" she asked.

Priscilla closed the journal and slipped it into her suitcase. "Yes, I'm coming." She pulled her suitcase down the stairs and out the front door, where the bus awaited. She handed her suitcase to George who reached out to help her up into the van. Priscilla glanced back at the Hunter Smith mansion one more time, remembering her initial excitement at the beauty of the place and admiration for Reagan's family. Now, the dwelling seemed tainted by the recent events. Money didn't solve everything, often creating problems of its own. She felt very sorry for Reagan.

Priscilla took a seat alone, hoping for some time to think. Unfortunately, Abigail started right in. "Today, we head back north. We hope to arrive by three at our Airbnb on Hilton Head and, with a little luck, we'll go out and enjoy the beach before dinner. Tonight, a Gullah historian will provide a history of their people in Mitchelville, where they started a freed slave community after the war. We'll visit a healer, Molly's distant cousin, to learn about root doctors. Tomorrow, we plan to take a Gullah Tour of Hilton Head, go for a bike ride, and to the beach. In the evening, we've booked a sunset cruise. The next morning, Charleston."

Wow, Priscilla thought. Tonight she would learn about Mitchelville. Were some of her ancestors still living there? Could the historian explain her quilt? She knew the plantation owner's name was Johnson, but would that be enough to find her family? Eventually, the girl married, and her surname disappeared. Such a coincidence, that her mother married a Johnson. Priscilla could barely keep her eyes open as she wrote questions for the historian. Eventually, she gave up and let the sandman reign.

A couple hours later, she startled awake, hearing Abigail announce, "We've arrived! Carry your bags in and change for the beach. Meet by the front door in fifteen if you want to go. It's too cold to swim, but we can look for shells."

Priscilla rubbed her eyes, combed her hair, and reapplied her lipstick, waiting to disembark. Feeling almost human again after the nap, she absorbed the bright sun, smiling at the beach out the window. How awesome to stay by the water again. God love the MAMs. Where would she be without them? Most likely, just back in River City, working away. Leave it to the MAMs to bring good things into her life.

As she stepped off the van, a flock of gulls swooped down, almost like a welcome. Nearby waves lapped the sand. She longed to go for a walk along the shore, but first, she needed to take her suitcase in and find a room.

After moving in, she joined the group by the front door. While George, Tom, and the group home crew started a game of beach volleyball, Priscilla and the MAMs decided to walk along the beach. Seamus tagged along with Abigail. They chatted and picked up shells. The exercise invigorated Priscilla and, for once, she happily walked in her new Nikes, rather than her heels.

The saltwater spray cleansed her from the inside out. She began again to form questions for the Gullah historian as they returned to the house. Her eagerness and curiosity pushed out any lingering shame about her Black genes. She wanted to understand and embrace this new aspect of her identity. She wanted to live her truth—if she could find it.

A day after her father's heart attack, and a few hours down the road, Reagan began to have second thoughts. Should she have left so abruptly? But her anger drove her away, as she continued to puzzle over how her father could do that to Welby. Could she ever trust him again?

She took out her frustration on the volleyball, making a few good spikes, but then the lack of sleep, the stress of the past day, coupled with the afternoon sun wiped her out. She ducked out of the ruckus of the game and asked for permission to take a nap. Back inside, she collapsed on her bed.

Three hours later, Priscilla woke her for dinner. By the time she got downstairs, most of the group were done eating and the Gullah historian already arrived.

Reagan served herself a plate of the leftovers, then sat cross-legged on the floor in front of Welby, who sat on the couch with George and Tom. A picture window framed the ocean in the large room.

An old African American man with a grey beard stood in front of the window, addressing the group. He gave Reagan a nod, then continued his discourse. "So, you see, Mitchelville was created for the freed slaves right after the Civil War by the Union Army stationed here. The Union Army used some of these sea islands for their bases against the Confederacy. When they won the war and freed the slaves, many former slaves flocked here. They developed Mitchelville like a regular town. They built roads, offered one-quarter-acre lots, and established a church. A process of election and governance led to various laws addressing such issues as community behavior and sanitation, collection of taxes, and a compulsory education law for children ages six to fifteen. Many freed slaves initially worked for the army. They built little houses and arranged for teachers for the children from a missionary society. When the army jobs disappeared, the fifteen hundred residents worked as subsistence farmers, often experiencing food shortages.

"Today, over a hundred and fifty years after the Civil War began, our local Gullah people, direct descendants of Mitchelville, carry on the traditions of their history-making ancestors. We work with a diverse group of islanders to preserve and promote Mitchelville and its story of freedom."

Priscilla raised her hand. "Do you have the names of the freed slaves that lived here? Is there a place I could look up those records?"

"Well, ma'am, we're talking 1862 when they obtained their freedom. Remember, the slaves weren't allowed to read and write. They didn't keep a whole lot of records at the beginning, but there are some, yes, a few. You might want to visit our little museum and talk to the people over here. Eventually, the Gullah people showed up on the South Carolina census. Some of us are descendants of those early freedmen." "I'm wondering if you have any Johnsons who live here?"

The man scratched his head. "Well, now, Johnson, you say? My wife came from a long line of Johnsons. She's a Sheldon now, my name. She's got many a story to tell. Do you know Johnsons back up north?"

Reagan knew Priscilla wanted to find her family, just like Reagan, and it looked like she'd hit paydirt.

"Oh, my," Priscilla exclaimed. "Oh, my! I'm trying to find my lost ancestors. Johnson is my family name. Could it be the same? Is that possible after all these years? I have a young girl's journal who writes her mother lived in Mitchelville, after slavery. But the girl moved to Ohio. You see, her father was the son of the plantation family. He arranged for her to get educated up north. She wanted to visit her mother, but I don't think she ever got to come back down here."

"Excuse me, ma'am. Forgive me for asking, but you think you are a relative of my wife? You sure don't look nothin' like her. She's as black as you are white. Are you sure about this?"

"I know, I know," Priscilla replied, blushing. "It sure doesn't look like I've got African blood. But, yes, I do, according to my DNA test, and I've got the journal of this Johnson slave girl. If your wife is a Johnson, then maybe I'm related. Could I meet her?"

"How long you goin' be here? And you know that's a very common name," the man cautioned.

"Yes, I know. We'll be here one more night, leaving the following morning," Priscilla answered.

"Maybe I could ask her to come over for breakfast tomorrow. Can you get up early? She's an early riser, but starts work at eight-thirty. Would seven do?"

Priscilla nodded. "Yes, sir, that would be wonderful. And there's one more thing I want to ask. I brought a quilt from home. I believe it came from my Southern family." Priscilla unfolded a large quilt, asking Sallie to help her hold it up. "Have you ever seen anything like this around here?"

"Well, I'll be," the historian exclaimed. "What you got yourself there is an Underground Railroad slave quilt. Our oral historians tell us they hung those on clotheslines as messages for escaping slaves. See that log cabin on your quilt? That meant slaves could seek shelter there, announcing a safe house. You find some quilts with a bear paw, telling them to follow the animal tracks through the mountain to find water and food. Now, truth is, we're not really sure. Some researchers say that's just fancy false folklore. But you've got your quilt passed down through the generations, and there are many more. Who's to say? Seems like quite an inventive way to communicate, don't you think?"

"Yes, sir," Priscilla responded. "So, wow! You think this was actually a slave quilt?"

"Sure looks like it to me. Show that to my wife. She knows a lot more than me about the quilts. She's even made a few herself. You'll see some old ones, and also replicas displayed in our little museum."

Reagan's phone buzzed in her pocket. She glanced at it and almost turned it off, but her brother's name flashed across the screen. "Excuse me," she told the group. "I need to take this. It's my brother."

Zorastria frowned. "Explain to me again why Reagan's allowed to have a cell phone."

Abigail quickly responded, "Because her father's very ill, we agreed to this, but just until he gets better. Go ahead, Reagan."

Reagan nodded and walked out the front door and sat on a nice wooden swing as she took the call. "Dean?" she asked. "Is that you?"

Her brother wasted no words. "Get back here right now, Reagan. Dad needs you. What were you thinking, running off like that? Think about someone else for a change!"

Reagan bristled. How dare he talk to her like that? "First of all, I'm in a court-ordered group home. I need to stay with my group," Reagan replied. Her anger continued to surge. "Furthermore, that's not fair, Dean. If Dad needs me so much, why did he lie and frame my boyfriend? He got Welby picked up for a rape that didn't happen. Welby's never hurt a fly in his life. If our father wants to be a racist bastard, that's his choice, but don't expect me to come running back to nurse his sorry ass. Let Mom do the job. No, I'm not coming, Dean."

"Reagan, listen," Dean insisted. "Dad's in the ICU. He's fading in and out, murmuring your name. And he adds 'I'm sorry,' almost with every breath. The docs aren't sure he'll pull through. They think he needs you."

Reagan fumed. "Now he's sorry? Right. How could he do that to Welby, to me?"

"I know, Reagan. He shouldn't have done that, but he figured that out. He had a heart attack, for God's sake."

"Yes, I'm sure he's worried about how all this affects his political career. He's lucky I walked, instead of going to the paper. He's got Welby to thank for that." Reagan could hear her sarcasm and anger, but she couldn't help it. Damn her dad.

"Reagan, come back. You'll live to regret this," her brother pleaded.

She balked. "I'm not coming, Dean. I can't and I won't." But then she remembered her feeling earlier that she should have stayed, and she relented. "I'll talk to him on the phone, but I'm not coming back. I need to finish my trip and my year of recovery. I'm not free to just leave the group like you want."

"Okay," Dean agreed. "Better than nothing. Can you do Facetime?"

"Of course," she responded.

"I'll call you back," Dean said. "Mom's in there now. I'll go in when she comes out. We can only be in there for five minutes every half hour. Thanks, Reagan. Maybe this is better. They aren't sure he's going to make it through the night."

Dean hung up and Reagan stared at the phone with a hundred thoughts racing through her mind. Tears started to come. She looked out to the sea, watching waves lap the shore in the dark. A lone seagull picked at the sand at the water's edge. Her brother's words echoed in her heart. Her dad might not make it through the night.

The door creaked, then opened and out walked Welby. "You cryin'?" He closed the distance between them in a flash, joining her on the swing. He wrapped an arm around her and took her hand. "What's wrong, honey?" He took a handkerchief out of his pocket and dabbed at her cheeks, but she couldn't stop her sobs.

"Dad might not make it through the night. My brother says Dad keeps saying my name and that he's sorry. The doctor wants me to talk with him." Reagan put her head down, covered her face with both hands.

Welby massaged her shoulders, handed her the handkerchief, staying with her in the pain. "I'm here for you," he assured her, but he didn't tell her everything would be okay. Only God knew what might come out of this freaking mess. She realized that, in spite of everything, she still loved her father. The thought that he might die terrified her.

"Should I go back? Would they let me?" she asked Welby. "What do you think?"

Welby hesitated. "You only get one father, Reagan. That's it. If you don't go and he dies, you could spend the rest of your life regretting that. I know I regret the times I stayed mad at my mom. She didn't live long enough for me to make it up to her. By the time I could think like an adult and apologize, she was long gone and six feet under. Didn't Abigail tell you that you can be with him? It's your call."

"I told my brother I'd talk to him on Facetime. He's calling back soon. That might be better, don't you think? I mean, if he's going to die tonight, I might not make it there in time. If he needs to hear my voice, see my face, the phone is more immediate." Reagan stopped talking, wiping her face off with Welby's handkerchief. She knew talking to her dad was the right thing to do.

The front door creaked open again. The MAMs and the others filed out. "We're going to visit the healer now," Abigail said. "Everyone in the van. We won't be long, one hour tops. We'll be back before ten, so you can get a good night's sleep."

Welby removed his arm from around Reagan. "We better go."

"I can't go like this," she told Welby. "I'm a mess."

"It's okay, dear. You're beautiful with or without makeup. You're fine, but when is your brother calling back?" Welby asked.

"I … I … I don't know," she replied.

"Bring your phone and don't turn it off. Tell Abigail you'll need to take the call. She'll understand," Welby instructed.

Reagan couldn't think straight, so she thanked God for Welby's advice. As they left the porch, Reagan took Abigail aside to tell her. "My brother just called. My dad might not make it through the night. He's going to call back soon on Facetime so I can talk to Dad. If I step out, that's why."

"I'm so sorry, Reagan," Abigail replied, giving her a hug. "Certainly, take the call, that's fine. Perhaps we can ask the healer to help your father."

Reagan nodded. Definitely, she needed the healer tonight, to bring her father back, and also to provide solace to her own broken heart. Just when she thought her life was coming together, everything seemed to be falling all apart. The thought crossed her mind that a few pills would help her feel better. Welby took her hand. She followed numbly, unsure of herself, or anything, for that matter.

Welby led her to the back of the bus and kept holding her hand. "Let me pray for you, Reagan," he said. They closed their eyes. "Dear Lord, we ask for your love to surround Reagan and her family tonight. We pray for healing for her father and his heart. We pray for healing for Reagan's heart, also. God, we know you don't like brokenness because you're the God of wholeness, goodness and love. Bring your love down and help us all. In the name of Jesus, I pray. Amen."

Reagan took a deep breath. "That was beautiful, Welby." Light and warmth surged into her heart. "Thank you. God is with us. You're right. Love is the most important thing. You're the one that should be mad and there you are, praying for my father who set you up. You're my teacher, Welby. I want to grow up to be like you."

"Don't put yourself down. We all need God. Just when you think there ain't no way, God shows up, and that's when we need Him most. God's love is better than all the drugs in the world."

Could Welby read her mind? Did he know she craved her pills? What she needed was Welby. She grasped his hand tightly. He wrapped his arm around her shoulder and pulled her close.

"I'm with you, Reagan," he whispered. "We'll make it through this together."

Reagan hoped Welby was right. She could only hope.

A Visit with Madame Biddy

Priscilla gazed out the window as their bus passed by the seafront promenade, then wound its way through a little village. They stopped in front of a small house, barely visible through the trees. The group disembarked and walked a narrow path, through a jungle of trees and plants, approaching the weathered brown house that was dwarfed by the humongous trees in the yard. Fenced gardens filled every inch of the lot with verdant plants.

A small dark, plump woman waited on the porch beneath a sign that read simply MADAME BIDDY. "Welcome, welcome," she greeted them as they stepped onto her porch "Come on in. Tea's on. I've been waiting for you." This offer of hospitality from a total stranger touched Priscilla's heart.

"Hello, ma'am," Priscilla responded, extending her hand. "Thank you for having us over."

"Oh, yes, I'm happy to have you," Madame Biddy replied, firmly shaking Priscilla's hand. "Any friend of Molly Mabra is a friend of mine."

Molly came in right behind Priscilla, beaming at the lady's comment. Madame and Molly embraced one another.

"So good to see you again, Mrs. Biddy," Molly said. "It's been such a long time."

"Yes, chil', don't you know it?" Madame Biddy replied. "Why, you were just a little wee one last time you came with your mama and papa, and now look at you!"

Molly laughed. "Yes, I'm old and gray, but look at you! You haven't aged a day. How do you do it?"

"Ah, that's what you come to find out. The fountain of youth and the mysteries of the root. Come in now, all of you, and let me pour you some tea." Madame Biddy opened her arms to her guests, gesturing them into her house.

Priscilla took a seat on a folding chair in a circle. A single white candle flickered in the center, creating a spooky atmosphere. Did Mrs. Biddy practice voodoo? Priscilla worried at the candle shadows dancing on the walls. As she sipped her a cup of tea, she shivered, hoping the devil wouldn't join them.

Madame Biddy served tea to all who asked before taking a seat herself. "Now, ladies and gentlemen, thank you for coming. I'm honored that you visit me. As you know, Molly and I go way back. I met her when she was a wee little thing. Her mother and I are cousins of some sort. Most of us around here are related in some way." She smiled.

"Now, I understand you're wanting to learn about the Gullah Geechee culture. I'm fixin' to tell you about the root doctors and the medicine of the early Africans, brought here to work the plantations, against their wills."

Priscilla shivered, wishing she'd brought along a sweater or jacket.

"Now, let's get down to business. It's late and I don't aim to keep you here more than an hour. First off, I'm a medicine woman for the Gullah people here. I practice healing techniques passed down to me from my mama, who learned from her mama, and so on through the past. The Africans brought their knowledge of healing with them across the ocean.

"Maybe you don't know, but at one time, Africa and North America were all one continent. When the land masses split eons ago, they shared similarities, even though the Atlantic Sea began to span the distance between them. Those early slaves found healing plants they used back home. The Native Americans taught them to use more. Upwards of four hundred plants were in their medicine bag back then. 'Course, they learned through trial and error, too.

"On the Sea Islands, they had no doctors and no hospitals. When the slaves got sick or injured from overwork, they made do with what the Good Lord provided. Healing herbs came right out of the good earth. You know God already done told you that in the Bible. 'The leaves of the trees are for the healing of the nation.'"

Priscilla blurted out, "Yes, ma'am, Revelation 22:2." Then she felt embarrassed. The woman didn't ask for that information.

Instead of getting upset, the healer burst out in laughter. "Now ain't that somethin'. I see you got the Spirit, too."

Priscilla didn't know what to make of this lady.

"It's okay, honey," Madame Biddy assured her. "You and me, we're one. That's another thing in the Good Book, Jesus prayed that, didn't he now?"

"Yes, ma'am. John 17:21," Priscilla offered without thinking. Scripture verses committed to memory in her childhood were always on the tip of her tongue.

"There you go," the healer responded. "That's what I'm talkin' 'bout. Sure enough."

The shadows continued to flicker on the walls, but now Priscilla focused on the flame in the center of the room. Was God present, or was it the devil? What she read with the MAMs about the root doctors scared her. She didn't like it. But now Madame Biddy was quoting scripture? Something didn't compute.

"Now, don't you go scared on me," Madame Biddy said, looking straight at Priscilla. "I know you probably done heard all about voodoo and the root doctors casting spells and taking people away. Yes, that's part of our story. The Gullah people did all that, but my mama only taught me the good ways of healing. She taught me to focus on the goodness of God with my doctoring. All the medicine you need for your whole life, you'll find right outside my door in my gardens and in that little jungle you walked through a minute ago. The ways of the human heart aren't too different, whether you're as white as a ghost or black as the darkest night. Inside, God made us all the same. Figure that out, then you know the truth. The truth will set you free."

"John 8:32," Priscilla whispered.

"You got it, girl," Madame Biddy responded. "You and me gonna be friends, I can see that now. What's your name, honey?"

"Priscilla Johnson," Priscilla offered guardedly to the woman.

"Now, you a Johnson, are you? We got lots of you Johnsons in these parts from the old Johnson plantation, on the other side of this island. They gave everybody the big man's name. You're okay then, Priscilla Johnson. You're one of us."

Could that be a good thing? When Mrs. Biddy smiled at her, Priscilla felt the warmth of her heart and felt right at home.

"Now, the people come to me for doctorin' of their hearts and spirits. The Good Lord gave me an extra sense, and I uses it to serve Him. Like I said, my mama had the gift, and her mama before her. They say it's passed all the way down the line, coming over on the boat from the old country. P'haps not what you heard about root doctors, but that's my story and you know we got somethin' going on. Now, who of you want me to help you out?"

Reagan held up her hand, bursting into tears. Welby patted her on the back. "She's been through a lot recently," he told the lady.

"Landsakes, girl," Madame Biddy responded, picking up her teapot and refreshing Reagan's cup. "This tea will comfort your soul. It's my special recipe. Why don't you just take a deep breath, dry those tears, and tell Mrs. Biddy what's got you in a tizzy."

"Thank you, ma'am," Reagan managed to spit out, after taking a sip of the warmed tea. "I love Welby here." She put her arm around him and patted him on the back. "My dad just framed Welby for a crime he didn't commit. Dad doesn't want me dating a Black man. When I confronted him, he had a heart attack. He's in the ICU now and they're not sure he'll live through the night."

"Now, now, honey," Madame Biddy told her. "You let me take care of this situation here. Let's put it in the Good Lord's hands."

Mrs. Biddy closed her eyes and stretched out her arms. Priscilla thought she was going to pray, but she didn't say anything. Silence filled the room. The shadow of the candle kept dancing on the wall.

Priscilla felt nervous, worrying about the devil. Madame Biddy said she only did good doctoring, but Priscilla couldn't be sure. After what Reagan's dad did, perhaps Mrs. Biddy would just decide to do him in.

After what seemed like the longest time, Madame Biddy opened her eyes and looked directly at Reagan. "No need to worry, dear. I see your daddy's upset about what he did. He wants you to forgive him, sugar. That's not an easy thing to do, but I believe you'll get there. Your daddy needs to hear your voice. He's going to pull through. He'll be okay. He's a-knowin' he done you wrong. Yes, he's going to come through this just fine, but watch out for him to flip back on you when he gets to feelin' better."

As if on cue, Reagan's cellphone buzzed. "I gotta take this," she said, hurrying out of the circle, heading toward the front door.

Mrs. Biddy didn't skip a beat. "Anybody else got a problem here you want me to hear?"

"Can you tell me about my family?" Priscilla asked. Somehow, she believed that Madame Biddy might be able to tell her what she longed to know. Maybe tonight she would learn the truth.

"Now, what you be a-wantin' to know about them, dear child?" Mrs. Biddy asked.

"Well," Priscilla started slowly, "I found out a few months back that I have African DNA. I have a journal written by a slave girl who lived on a Sea Island. Her daddy was the son of a plantation owner. He entered politics and deserted her mama after the war. He arranged for her to move to Ohio to be educated. That girl's my great-great-grandmother. She was light-skinned back then and now several generations later, you can't even tell I'm descended from a Black woman. I didn't know it, either. This girl's mama lived down here, though, and I don't think she ever got to see her daughter again. That's what I'm trying to figure out."

Madame Biddy closed her eyes and again stretched out her arms. The candle's flame danced and Priscilla's heart raced as she waited for a response. She hoped the woman would come through. Maybe she had connections all the way up to heaven. Priscilla looked at her friends. Sallie seemed about to laugh. Jane's eyebrows were ready to lift on her forehead. Even Molly's eyes were open wide.

After what seemed like the longest time, the healer opened her eyes. "You done already figured this all out. What more do you need from me, Priscilla?"

Priscilla didn't know. What did she want to learn? Something more about her Black relatives here? "I want to know who my relatives are down here."

Madame Biddy smiled, looking at Priscilla with warm eyes that seemed to peer all the way into her heart. "Honey, you got relatives down here like the grains of sand on a beach, girl. You know those Johnsons be all over the place. You got a big family, girl. You ready to add all these Black folk to your life now? Or maybe you want to know about the head of the Johnson Plantation, responsible for this clan?"

Without hesitation, Priscilla said, "Yes. I want to know it all." Maybe she wasn't quite prepared to meet all these Black people who shared her DNA, but she sure wanted to know about them.

"Half the people in these parts be related to you in some way, girl," the healer said. "Matter of fact, I got some of that Johnson blood myself. Now, you come over here and give me a hug and we'll call it family, okay?" Mrs. Biddy held out her arms to Priscilla.

Priscilla walked straight into her embrace. Madame Biddy enfolded her tightly in her bosom, rocking back and forth, whispering, "You gonna be all right now, baby. You done found your Black family and you've got a brand new home here with us."

Priscilla absorbed the love the woman freely offered, realizing and accepting they were one, just like Jesus prayed. Right then and there, Priscilla saw no reason to think Madame Biddy was of the devil.

"We be fulfilling Jesus' dream, we are," the woman said, reading Priscilla's mind. "This here is that John 17:21 you just quoted to me awhile back. Mm hm, mm hm. We be one, just like Jesus wanted."

It felt good to be held, but also so very strange. Priscilla's whole world was upended. She couldn't tell black from white anymore, and maybe that was the whole point. A light flickered on deep inside her soul. Madame Biddy stepped back, telling her, "Now, you go sit down, honey. Let's see who else needs some help tonight."

Priscilla backed up to her chair and sat. Now the candle's shadow seemed to be making a happy dance. Darkness still lurked in the corners, but the light seemed to be overcoming it somehow. Around the circle, the light reflected on the faces of her friends. It made shiny the Black faces of Molly, George, Tom, Welby, Zorastria, and Antonio, and also dazzled the white faces of Jane, Sallie, Katharine, Abigail, Seamus, and the others. One light, one God, all together, just one, Priscilla thought. They'd come to the root doctor and got a Bible lesson— certainly the last thing she'd expected for this visit.

"Well, it's gettin' close to my bedtime," Madame Biddy told the group. "You got any more questions before we call it a night?" Silence filled the room. "Just remember, don't you believe everything you hear about root doctors. My people are believers for the most part. Back then and right now, we gotta believe to get past the darkness of the white man. We pray and we hope. We use the good plants God created. We do what we can to heal our people."

Molly raised her hand. "May I ask a question?"

"Sure thing, baby. What you want to know?"

"Why did my family leave?" Molly asked. "Why didn't they stay? You have a strong, good community here."

Madame Biddy got a faraway look in her eyes. "Didn't your mama tell you that, honey?" She paused and rubbed her forehead. "Life sure wasn't simple back then."

Molly shook her head. "I don't know the story. I found out I have Irish DNA recently. Does that have anything to do with it?"

Madame laid her hands on her knees with palms open and closed her eyes. She took some deep breaths. Priscilla wondered what was going on.

After a short while, she opened her eyes and looked directly at Molly. "Your great-great-grandmother tell me it's time for you to know your story." She leaned back and folded her hands in front of her ample belly. "Back in those days after slavery, the lines blurred between the slaves and the freed. The plantation owners didn't want to give up their slaves. They still owned most of the land, so they forced the freed slaves to keep doing the work for a pittance. Now, here on Hilton Head, the Union Army gave land to the freedmen and founded Mitchelville. 'Course they stole the land from a plantation owner.

"Things weren't right. The plantation owner had his way with your double-great-grandma from the beginning. She wasn't but a baby herself, but she birthed three babies by him before the end of the war. Things weren't easy, but she met another freed slave, your great-great-grandfather Henry Miller, who took her and the children in. Together, they came out here and joined the freedmen's colony, getting a piece of the free land.

"But, you see, the land was owned by the freed slaves together, and that community ownership passed down from one generation to the next. When the developers started coming in to make vacation houses for the rich, property values skyrocketed. The folk here could barely afford to pay the taxes. And, you know, there never were any good jobs here for the Blacks. This created a lot of pressure to sell. When they sold, it hurt the whole community, but sell they did. Sometimes they didn't have much choice. Your grandfather had an itching to go north. Like all of us, he wanted to get out from under the white inhospitality. He sold his land for pennies, but enough to take his family north.

"Upset our people here, it did, but he hightailed it out and didn't have to deal with them. Eventually, much of our land was sold or stolen by developers. Understand?"

Molly nodded. "That's a hard story. Mom probably didn't want to upset me. I guess I know now why I got white Irish blood."

Madame Biddy nodded. "Yes, honey, just like most of us. Those plantation owners did whatever they wanted with our people back then. But don't think that white blood gave us any privilege. Nope, that's just for purebreds or those who passed." She laughed then and Molly joined her, but Priscilla didn't see the humor.

Welby raised his hand. "I'd like to ask you a question. Do you contact the living and dead in your work?"

"Yes, at times," Madame Biddy replied. "Sometimes I get blocked, but often I can get through."

"This is crazy, but then I want to know about my mother and father. Do they have anything to tell me?" Welby asked.

Madame Biddy got back into position with her open hands on her knees. After a little while, she opened her eyes and this time, looked at Welby. "Your mama's long gone, I see that. Passed to the other side when you were a young'un."

Welby nodded. "Yes, ma'am."

"She tells me she wants you to know she's a-watchin' over you. she be real proud of the changes you're a-makin' in your life. Don't worry about not being a doctor. No, son, she just wanted you to be somebody and you sure enough are."

Welby smiled. "My mama named me Marcus Welby after that white TV doctor. Crazy. She always said she wanted me to be a doctor. I never saw that happening, so I'm glad she's finally letting that go. It's about time. I'm getting my life back in order after doing five years in prison. Thank you. Sometimes I can feel her love. Knowin' she's watching and proud? That's priceless."

Madame Biddy nodded again. "These powers I'm using are open to all of us, but most people just don't listen. Now, about your daddy. Looks like he's doing some serious time?"

Welby nodded, but didn't speak.

"It's time to give him a second chance. He's a brand-new man and wants to tell you all about it. He wants to apologize."

"Right," Welby said. "I've heard that before. Sounds like he's lying to you now, too."

"You're wrong, son. How long you been avoidin' him?"

Priscilla looked at Welby, noticing a sheepish grin on his face like he didn't want to admit that Madame Biddy spoke the truth.

Mrs. Biddy continued. "Just give him a chance, hon. You'll be surprised. Your dad's about to get out and he's got some inheritance to share with you."

"Sounds like another one of his scams," Welby said. "Lure them in, then sell their souls to the devil. Ain't no money in my family. That's bullshit."

"You don't know everything, Welby. Give your father a chance." Madame Biddy blew out the candles and flipped the light back on. "Now I really want to call it a night," she said. "It's time for you to get on out of here. Molly, I want to give you a little present, a medicine kit for you to take home."

Madame Biddy opened her closet and pulled out a little black suitcase. Embroidered bright green cursive letters announced "Madame Biddy's Medicine Bag." Surrounding the letters were flowers of every color of the rainbow.

"People pay a lot of money for my medicine bags, but for you, Molly, it's all free. It's a present from the land of your people. This land gives us everything we need to be healthy individuals. My people never could afford those high-falutin' doctors, but most of the time, we do just fine with these herbs."

She unzipped the bag and flipped the cover up where a diagram showed the names and pictures of the herbs. She pulled out a small book entitled *Madame Biddy's Guide to Good Health*. "Read this book and you'll learn how to use your new medical kit, along with some advice from me on the side. It's your heritage, Molly. This doctorin' advice goes way back to the old country." She returned the book to the suitcase and zipped it up. "Now get on out of here and have a good night." She pulled the little suitcase over to Molly and gave her a hug.

"Thank you so much," Molly said. "Thank you, Mrs. Biddy."

The group heaped thanks and good-byes on Madame Biddy as they left the little house and walked back through the now-darkened path to their van. Priscilla waited until most of them were out the door so she could give the lady a hug of her own. "Thank you, Mrs. Biddy. Thank you for giving me all this."

Madame Biddy enfolded her in her arms one more time, and Priscilla felt a deep kind of love she remembered from her mama. As the others straggled out, Mrs. Biddy took Priscilla aside. "Honey, there's something else I want to share with you. When I was a-listenin' for you, I heard another name. Is there a Sun man in your past?"

Priscilla felt like a deer caught in the headlights. "Sun? Moses Sun? Really?" How could Madame Biddy know about him? Her thoughts raced back through the years, back to her early dates with Moses Sun, the man she once thought would be her husband, and then to the MAMs Archaeological Expedition in Search of Thecla when Moses followed them and shot Katharine and Emily, Abigail's granddaughter. She remembered the mediation on Patmos where the MAMs forgave him and he turned over a new leaf. Then she thought about the traveling they did together to visit churches with the message of the scrolls the MAMs dug up in Kusadasi, Turkey. All that was water under the bridge now, because she fell out with him a couple years ago, when he went back to that right-wing think tank in Colorado. She found him just a little too much for her tastes and sensibility. Although they shared Jesus and many political views, she parted ways with him on his conspiracy theories. Also, he had too many guns. She could never forget what he did in Turkey. Sometimes she wondered if he would do it all again, given the chance. He gave her the willies.

Madame Biddy waited for her response. She heard her name being called to get on the van, but she wanted to know more. "What about Moses? What did you hear?"

"Be careful, dear," Madame Biddy said. "He's coming around again. He may say he's changed, but an acorn doesn't fall too far from its tree. Okay? I don't want anything bad happenin' to my relation. You got it?"

Priscilla nodded and shivered. She sometimes thought the devil resided in people like Moses Sun. "Thank you, I'll be careful."

"Priscilla!" She heard Abigail calling her name again from the sidewalk. She gave Madame Biddy a quick hug and kissed her cheek, then hurried down the dark walk, worrying about when Moses might show up again.

CHAPTER ELEVEN
FINDING FAMILY

Reagan and Her Dad

Reagan walked onto Madame Biddy's porch to take the call from her brother. A million thoughts raced through her head. Her anger still simmered, but she also held a lifetime of love for her father. Most of the time, they were tight, like two peas in a pod. He gave her the world, taught her right from wrong, paid for her education, never gave up on her when she got hooked on drugs, and always believed in her, his princess, his baby, his queen. And yet, with Welby, he messed up royally.

Reagan now understood that when racism gripped the psyche, good men could do terrible things. Before Welby, she never gave it much thought. She accepted the justifications for why Black people stayed down. They were lazy, stupid, criminal, or just plain inferior. After a few months of getting to know Welby, everything changed. How did she ever believe such things before? And how could anybody who followed Jesus treat human beings as less than human? But her father, whom she used to call a model Christian man, did exactly that. She used to call him next to perfect. Now, she called him racist.

"Reagan," her brother said, "I'm with Dad. He's asking for you again. I told him I'd call you."

"Is Mom there, too?" Reagan asked. She still harbored some anger for her mother, but also knew she must be going through hell.

"No, you know the rules. Only one person in the ICU at a time. She's in the waiting room."

"Tell Mom I'm praying for them both, okay? Give her a hug from me," Reagan said. She knew she upset her mother when she left with the MAMs with her father in critical condition.

"Okay," her brother responded. "Thanks, I'll do that. I'm sure she'll appreciate that. Now, are you ready? I'm switching to Facetime."

Reagan took a deep breath. Hell, no, she would never be ready, but this was her only father. "I'll try," she told her brother as his face appeared on the screen. He gave her a thumbs up. Then she heard him tell her father to open his eyes. She tried to make sense of the tubes and wires hooked up to her father. His face looked white, and his hair, mussed. She could barely recognize him in that hospital bed. She knew well the monitoring devices in the ICU from her nursing days, but usually the people were total strangers, not her daddy.

"Well, if you aren't a sight for sore eyes," her father said. His words sounded normal enough, but the rasp in his voice told a different story. "Nancy, dear, I've missed you." When he paused to get his breath, she worried about his labored breathing and wondered if he should even be talking yet, but he continued. "Thank you for talking with an old man who's got a few failing body parts."

"Oh, Daddy," Reagan said. "I'm sorry you had a heart attack. I'm so glad you're pulling through." Reagan felt like an observer watching herself saying the right thing, but harboring anger for the man. Seeing her dad in an ICU bed did something awful to her insides. All she could do was be kind. She knew positive words were important. She couldn't even correct him for calling her Nancy.

"Nancy, baby, the Good Lord just gave me a second chance." He struggled to get the words out. "I want to do it right." His once booming voice barely came out in a whisper. He began to cough as the monitor started to beep.

"It's okay, Daddy," Reagan said. "You need rest. It's going to be okay."

Her father cleared his throat, clearly not finished. "God sent me back to tell you I'm sorry." He paused again, struggling for air. "I don't know how long I've got, but …" He coughed and the beeping continued, but he pushed the words out. "I want to make it up to you and Welby." Then he fell back on the pillow and closed his eyes.

A nurse rushed in, checked the monitor, adjusted his oxygen, and took the phone from his hand, handing it to her brother. She heard the nurse scold him. "What were you thinking, having him on a phone call? He's not strong enough for this yet."

Dean then disagreed with the nurse. "It's what the doctor ordered, actually. He's been restless and wanting to talk with my sister. The doctor thinks he needed to apologize and ask for forgiveness."

The nurse bristled. "Well, it's not in his chart and those doctors don't know everything. We're the ones with the patients and we know how they're doing."

"But," Reagan heard Dean say quietly to the nurse, "he's been asking and asking to talk to her. The doctor thought it would bring him comfort and rest to get it off his chest."

Then she heard the nurse respond, "Well, keep it short then. You know he's still very weak."

Reagan worried about her father and wondered if Dean would hang up. She told her brother without stopping to think, "Tell him I forgive him, Dean." If they didn't know if he would make it through the night, she wanted him to know she forgave him. It was the least she could do for him now. She knew that it might just be the meds talking, maybe not true repentance, though. She knew full well what medication can do to the mind.

Her brother held the phone up so she could see her dad again, then leaned over and touched his face. "Dad, Reagan wants you to know she forgives you, okay? Now you get some sleep. You can talk to her again when you wake up."

Dean left the phone focused on her father's face. She saw his lips turn up in a brief smile, and then back down, as his breathing evened out and he began to snore. For once, that sound was music to her ears.

"Reagan, thanks," Dean said. "You did good. I think he'll come around now. Love you, sis. I'll call later with an update."

Dean signed off, leaving Reagan alone, staring into the jungle of Madame Biddy's front yard. She felt so full of emotions she couldn't begin to unpack. The wild growth of the South Carolina foliage brimmed with life. Perhaps Mrs. Biddy was right. Perhaps her father really had come around, but it seemed too good to be true. Could he do a one-eighty like that? If and when he recovered, would he even remember his apology? Would he really do the right thing by Welby? Or, once all the medication wore off, would all his racist attitudes return front and center? Wasn't that Madame Biddy's warning?

She prayed hard for her father, that he would indeed make it through the night and live to make it up to Welby. She prayed that her own life might flourish like the Southern jungle crowding all around Madame Biddy's yard. She shuddered, thinking how many times in the last few days she'd longed for the ease of an opioid fix. Even now, she could imagine just how soothing that would be, although she had no clue where to get a pain pill in this place.

The door opened and the group began to file out of Madame Biddy's house. When Welby arrived, he plopped right down beside her on the porch love seat. "You okay?" he asked. She nodded. He wrapped an arm around her. She leaned into his shoulder and began to cry.

"Let it all out, baby," he told her. "It's okay to cry. You've been through a lot."

Reagan appreciated that Welby didn't pump her for information, but just comforted her. She wanted to tell him all about it, but right now, her heart felt raw. She realized she actually wanted to be at her father's side. Her brother said the conversation did him good, but she needed to see that for herself. If she were there, she could reassure him. What if he died tonight? Was she wrong to leave in the first place? Did her forgiveness make a difference? She hoped her dad really changed, and that he would be okay. "Do you think I should go?" she asked Welby.

"Baby, if you want to be there, yes. Go." Welby responded. "You may only get one chance and you certainly only get one father. Madame Biddy told me the same, after you left."

"What?" Reagan asked.

"You know my father's in the pen, right?"

Reagan nodded. Welby continued, "He's been writing me letter after letter, most of which I don't open. He's been trying to convince me he's a new man, but I just don't trust him. I worry he just wants to use me all over again. Madame Biddy said he's accepted the Lord and he's telling the truth, and even something about an inheritance he wants to share with me."

"Wow, Welby. You and me, our fathers. It's the same thing. I want to believe my father, but it's hard, after what he just did to you. My dad just told me he's sorry and he wants to make it up to you," Reagan said. "Can you believe this? Both of our fathers did us wrong, but want to make it up to us now?"

"Welby! Reagan!" George called. "We're leaving. Come on, you two. Get in the van so we can go get some shut-eye. You're holding us up!"

Welby took Reagan's hand, pulled her up, gave her a quick hug and a kiss on her cheek. Then he scooted her behind a bush, where George couldn't see, and gave her a sound kiss on the lips before tugging her hand in the direction of the street. "If I ever wondered if we were meant to be, there's no question in my mind right now. I love, love, love you." He spoke quietly enough that only she could hear. Reagan wiped the tears off her face and felt the warmth of Welby spreading through her fingers all the way up her arm and into her heart. How did she ever get so lucky after all she did wrong? No way in hell would she take another pill if she could help it.

Priscilla and the Johnsons

Priscilla startled awake when her alarm blared into her slumbers at six a.m. She pushed the snooze button, wanting to return to her dream. What just happened? Did Moses Sun really propose on one knee? She opened her eyes, remembering exactly why the alarm went off. Time to get up and prepare to meet the historian's wife for breakfast. Perhaps today, she would find out more about her people.

Why in God's name was she dreaming about Moses Sun after all this time? Madame Biddy told her he would be showing up soon and to watch out. Her dream seemed entirely different. Beware of the wolf in sheep's clothing, a voice sounded in her head. No, she would not be fooled again by that man.

When she finally descended the stairs, a tall woman in an African dress stood in the living room, chatting with Molly. Priscilla admired her beautiful face and graceful neck.

"Priscilla," Molly called. "Meet Rita Mae Sheldon, the historian's wife."

Priscilla eagerly walked over to the pair and reached out to shake the fine lady's hand. "Pleased to meet you, ma'am."

"No, no," Rita Mae insisted with a smile. "Let me have a hug. We're sistas, I hear."

Once again, Priscilla felt the love of these strangers, part of her family tree. The hospitality dazzled her. How could she possibly be related to this dark, beautiful woman? Yet all the facts seem to lean in that direction.

"Thank you," Priscilla whispered into the lady's ear as they embraced one another. "Yes, I do believe we are."

"Now, let me look at you," Mrs. Sheldon said as she pulled away, taking both of Priscilla's hands in hers. "You sure don't favor me, but there are some Johnsons in these parts that definitely share your looks. Most are a little darker, though." She smiled.

Priscilla nodded. "I know it's hard to believe I'm part Black, isn't it?"

"Now, no, not for me. We Blacks come in all shapes and sizes and colors of the rainbow. Some of us are more white, some yellow, some brown. We're a mixed bunch. Of course, that's a whole discussion, about light and dark. I'm not saying it doesn't make a difference, because you know how people can be. Tell me your story, Priscilla. What do you know about your family tree?"

"Well, I don't know much. I hoped you could tell me. I have a journal my mom gave me about a young slave girl who grew up on a sea island in South Carolina."

"Coulda been right here, then," Mrs. Sheldon said.

Priscilla nodded. "She and her mama worked the plantation, but her daddy was the son of the plantation owner. Before the Civil War ended, her dad moved her to Ohio, where she attended high school and became a nanny before marrying. Later, her father served as a congressman in Washington, DC, marrying someone other than her mother. Her mother settled in Mitchelville after the war. I don't think mother and daughter were ever reunited. That's about all I know."

"Well, I'll be," Mrs. Sheldon responded. "I have some stories for you, sure enough."

"I also have this quilt, a family heirloom, that my mother gave me. Your husband told me it's an Underground Railroad quilt and you could tell me all about it." Priscilla pulled it out of her bag and unfolded it, draping it over her knees.

"My, my," Mrs. Sheldon said. "Sure enough, hon, sure enough." Then Mrs. Sheldon opened her eyes wide and placed a hand over her mouth, quietly looking at the quilt.

"What is it?" Priscilla asked. "You look like you saw a ghost."

Mrs. Sheldon remained silent, simply shaking her head. Finally, after what seemed like the longest time, she started to cry. Priscilla couldn't figure out what could be so emotional for a total stranger.

"Honey child," Mrs. Sheldon finally spoke. "Cat got my tongue for a minute there. You see, this quilt look just like the one my mother put in my hope chest years ago. In fact, I swear that piece of indigo fabric stamped with white dots is exactly the same material in a quilt my mother passed on to me. You see that?"

Priscilla nodded. That meant that Mrs. Sheldon was not just some distant relation, but part of her very own family tree. Perhaps they both descended from the mother of the girl who wrote the journal. A million thoughts raced through her head, along with so many questions she wanted to ask. The immensity of the moment filled her with awe and also tied her in knots.

"Land's sake, girl." Mrs. Sheldon smiled. "Welcome to the family, dear. Now, let me tell you a little "bout this quilt and the family story passed down to me. Our female slave ancestors dyed uniforms for Union soldiers in the Civil War. They used the indigo plants to dye the deep blue material. Now, 'course, the plantation owners made them sew britches for the Confederate troops, but we like to tell this story. Our people smuggled britches out for the Union soldiers, and got paid too, honey. Once the Union ships got close enough, they'd paddle out and do the exchange. What's got me dumbfounded about your quilt is that not only does that indigo match,   but some of the other materials do, too.

"These quilts helped the escaping slaves on their trip north. The infamous seamstress Matilde Johnson, our matriarch and common ancestor, kept the master's family in the finest clothes, but also managed to do a subversive assortment of quilts on the side. Our storytellers say her quilts were smuggled north, along with other goods."

Priscilla asked. "How did these quilts help the slaves escape?"

"Oh, well, you see, we believe they hung them on the clotheslines at the safe houses and the symbols gave them directions. You see that basket there? If you saw the basket on the quilt, that meant you could get supplies and spend the night there. That's a symbol for the safe house. Now those bear paws? They would point in the direction of a path through the woods to go to safety and also where you could find food and water, following the animal's trail, although you also have to watch out for the bears!"

"Really?" Priscilla asked. "All that from a blanket hanging on a clothesline?"

"Yes, that's the story passed down to me. I do believe it's true."

Priscilla smoothed the quilt with her hands, looking at it with new eyes. "Matilde Johnson? Tell me about her."

"Matilde Johnson's a legend in these parts. The plantation owner's son took up with her, not that she had a choice. Back in the day, she thought the sun rose and set on that lad who came over to sow his wild oats. Left her high and dry, once he became a politician and went north to the capital, stealing their child up there to Ohio to be raised with the white folks. Never did see the girl again, although, just as your journal tells it, she got more than a few letters over the years."

"Oh, my gosh," Priscilla responded. "That's my Matilde, from my family tree? I'm getting goosebumps. Give me a moment." She took a few deep breaths and closed her eyes. Could this really be happening, she wondered. She wanted to know more. "Tell me, how did Matilde become a legend?"

"Well, after she figured out how that boy did her, she vowed to never depend on a man again, although she did find a good one in Mitchelville after the war. She took up with Harvey Johnson, another survivor of the Johnson Plantation. She pushed a total of ten more babies out after that. Five survived to adulthood, and those five multiplied down through the years. You got a whole bunch of Johnsons around these parts, although many left for the north and west."

"Do you know where Matilde and the other Johnsons are buried? Do you have anything written down about their family tree?" Priscilla's thoughts raced quicker than her words. She wanted to know it all.

Mrs. Sheldon paused. "Well, now, there's some burying grounds on the island, but back then, they didn't have much money for fancy burials, so we can't pinpoint one grave over another. And there really aren't written records, either, but the stories stayed alive, passed along from one generation to the next.

"Now, Matilde made a living with her sewing skills. Rumor had it she could stitch up almost anything. She supplied shops in Savannah and Charleston, along with local stores, too. She lived to the ripe age of a hundred and sewed right up to the very end."

"Wow," Priscilla said. "That's really something. My mama taught me how to sew, too. Do you sew? Is it in our genes?"

Mrs. Sheldon started laughing. "No, can't say that I do. I've taken the medical route myself. I studied to be a nurse in my younger days, then I became a nurse practitioner. I'm semi-retired, but I still help the local doctors in the clinic here a couple days a week. In fact, I need to be getting over there real soon. It was a pleasure to meet you, Priscilla."

"Same here," Priscilla replied. "I hoped maybe I'd find out something about my quilt. I never dreamed I'd find my family!"

"Now, you keep in touch, honey, okay? Here's my card. You can email me. If you have more questions, just let me know."

"Thank you, ma'am," Priscilla said. Mrs. Sheldon hugged her again before collecting her things and leaving. Afterward, Priscilla sat still, fingering the basket on the quilt, trying to imagine the life of Matilde, her ancestors, and all that transpired.

Gullah Tour Hilton Head

Welby followed Reagan off the bus into the parking lot of the Coastal Discovery Museum. Reagan made a beeline for a table with some baskets. Leave it to a woman to start shopping, first opportunity. Welby recognized those baskets from his childhood. In fact, his grandmother taught him how to make one of those back in the day.

"Sweetgrass baskets," Reagan told him. "Aren't they cool?" She picked up the largest one on the table. "Out of my price range, though. Two hundred and fifty dollars!"

The woman behind the table picked up a smaller basket and said, "Here's one for fifty."

Welby held his tongue, knowing the sales were bread and butter for these women. Prices had sure escalated from what he remembered. He shared, "I made these as a boy."

"Oh." The sister smiled. "You from Hilton Head?"

"No, Wilmington and Raleigh," he answered. "They sent me out to the island for the summer with my grandma."

"Ah, yes. Up north of here then?"

"Right," Welby said.

"The Gullah Geechee Corridor begins around Wilmington and extends all the way down to Florida. You're one of us, then, of the northern ones. You know our people lived on the sea islands while enslaved and we kept much of the African culture we brought along over here."

"So I hear," Welby said. "I hope I'll learn more on the tour."

"Yes, it's a great tour. If you're on the ten o'clock, you have about fifteen minutes. Go check out the Coastal Discovery Museum inside."

Welby took Reagan's hand, pulling her away from what she couldn't afford and leading her toward the modern building nearby. "Now you can learn all about me," he told Reagan.

"Aren't you going to buy me a basket?" Reagan asked. "Oh, what am I thinking? That's too expensive for both of us!"

"If you want a sweetgrass basket, I'll get one from my auntie when we go to Wilmington. It might be worth two hundred, but for us, it's free," Welby told her.

"Cool," Reagan replied.

Welby's head reeled with memories of sweetgrass baskets, fishing expeditions, and those simple younger days as he wandered through the little museum with Reagan. Panels interpreted the geography and natural history, along with the plantation history in this place called Honey Horn. He skimmed the information and enjoyed holding Reagan's hand, feeling the soft, gentle pressure of her palm on his, and smelling the fresh, clean smell of lemon in her hair.

"Read between the lines, Reagan. This exhibit tells it all. Hurricanes, beach erosion, extinction. Planet Earth is going down," Welby warned.

"But no," Reagan disagreed. "Look what they're doing. They replenish the beach with sand, a sixteen million dollar project. Look at these endangered species: the ivory-billed woodpecker, the American alligator, the bald eagle, and piping plover. They're all coming back. They haven't had a hurricane here since 1989. Hugo was thirty years ago! Look at the bright side, Welby. Your glass is half full, don't call it half empty."

"Well, aren't you little miss sunshine today?" Welby countered. Growing up with a silver spoon gave Reagan a positive spin on things. He lived the downside of life, far from her glory. "I still hope, Reagan, but the planet is heating up. Hurricanes are getting bigger because of the warm ocean water. It's just a matter of time before they blow all of this development on Hilton Head away. Hell, this whole island will be under water once the polar caps melt."

"You don't know that, Welby," Reagan argued. "Come on, let's hurry. It's almost time for the tour."

They quickly perused the rest of the small museum that also summarized the history of slavery on the island leading into modern times of development.

Then George showed up. "Reagan, Welby, the bus is about to leave. Come on now."

A few minutes later, Reagan and Welby sat in the front of the bus. A nice Black man, dressed in a blue shirt, with a mask on his face, led the tour. He introduced himself as Maurice Campbell.

"Do we have to wear masks?" Reagan asked.

"Up to you," the man said. "It's the safe option, so we all wear them, but it's optional for you."

Welby leaned back, enjoying the warmth of Reagan's body beside him as the guide began his spiel. He didn't feel like wearing a mask.

"The Gullah Tours Company is owned by the Campbell family. I'm from the fifth generation of the Gullah people on Hilton Head and our driver is sixth generation. This is a family business," he explained.

"Blue. What does the color of blue mean to the Gullah?"

"Tranquility," Sallie shouted.

"Somewhat," the guide responded. "Blue is the color of peace in the Gullah tradition, and also is said to ward off evil spirits, which is why our uniform shirt is blue. Hilton Head was named after William Hilton, who claimed the island in 1600. Before the Civil War, there were twenty-five plantations on Hilton Head," Mr. Campbell said. "The island was very isolated until 1960 when a bridge was built. The bridge led to development. Now the island swells to forty thousand residents in the summer, but only ten thousand the rest of the year. Back in 1960, before the development, there were twenty-seven hundred Gullah people. Today, there are still twenty-seven hundred Gullah people living here."

Welby half listened to the guide and half carried on a conversation inside his head about the sea island, this one in particular and the one he knew so well. Before the bridge, the Gullah people could roam the island as they wished. After the bridge, the mainland came to the island. He remembered enjoying island life as a child. It sure beat the hell out of his life in Raleigh. He liked the isolation from the modern world. His people always talked about the bridge as a mixed blessing. Yes, it connected them to supplies and the city, but it also brought the white man into their world which caused them more problems. Sounded like the bridge down here at Hilton Head did the same thing as their bridge up north.

"Before the bridge, the people farmed and fished to survive here. Everybody had a horse or two. There are ten Gullah neighborhoods. All the Gullah communities had three things in common: a school, a church and a cemetery. The people were very independent, but they depended on each other."

He continued, "Today, seventy percent of the island is gated. That leaves thirty percent for the rest of us. First, we will visit the Squire Pope community, the largest neighborhood. Many of these people were commercial fishermen. You'll see a variety of houses here, mobile homes, affordable housing, and family estates." A Squire Pope Neighborhood sign announced the community.

The bus continued on its trek and Welby spotted a Stoney Neighborhood sign as the guide announced, "Next up, the Stoney Neighborhood. See those blue bottles over there? The Gullah people make blue bottle trees to ward off evil spirits. Speaking of blue, my mother painted the kitchen and dining room blue to keep love and peace while we're eating and no evil talk about her food." He chuckled, then continued. 'Now, this neighborhood was one of two downtown neighborhoods. There used to be a market here and a school. The schools were funded by the neighborhoods until 1954. What happened in 1954?"

"School desegregation," Welby said. When the Koch brothers tried to get the North Carolina schools resegregated a few years back, he'd done a little research and it stuck in his mind, like a lot of other things he'd rather forget. For some reason, his father appeared in his mind's eye. Had he really turned over a new leaf like Madame Biddy said?

"We're coming up to Jonesville now," Mr. Campbell pointed out as Welby spotted yet another neighborhood sign.

"I love the trees here," Reagan commented. "So green, so nice." Her eyes took on a dreamy look. Welby wished she was talking about him rather than the trees.

The tour guide told them, "Caesar Jones bought land here. They named this neighborhood after him, an auto mechanic. There weren't many cars on the island, so he fixed them to work for only a couple weeks, so they would come back soon. He needed to keep making money, you know."

Welby laughed. Reagan shook her head and said, "Glad he's not my mechanic."

"Back in the day, the blacksmith also lived here. Now we're approaching the best neighborhood, Spanish Wells. Why is it the best? Because I live here." He laughed and pointed across the road. "That's my family estate."

Welby liked the wooded area he called the estate. With such very nice houses surrounded by trees, he imagined these Campbells enjoyed wealth, too. Someday, he hoped to make enough money to buy Reagan a nice house. Could he do that if he went to seminary? Would Reagan want to have children? Would she be okay, having children together? Hell, would she ever really agree to marry him? Sure, she hung tight with him now, but once the FARM sprung her out, would she still cling to him when she could have anyone?

Lost in his thoughts, Welby missed some of the tour. The bus abruptly stopped to visit Bradley Beach, Mr. Campbell said. "In the time of segregation, this was the only beach where the Gullah people could play. My family always came for the Fourth of July, Labor Day, and Memorial Day, and then sometimes in between."

Welby held Reagan's hand as they walked off the bus and onto a boardwalk leading out to the sea. Memories rushed back as the salt-infused air tickled his nostrils. He always loved the sun and sand, welcoming him to the edge of the world.

"Hey, are we going to get to swim?" he asked.

George, who walked right behind them, keeping tabs on Welby as usual, replied, "It's in the plan for this afternoon, if all goes well. We're going to ride bikes to the beach, actually."

Several hours later, Welby found himself back at their accommodations, preparing for a bike ride and a swim in the Atlantic. Could life get any better than this?

A Bike Ride

Abigail came up with the brilliant idea of renting bikes to give everyone some exercise and a different way of exploring the island. Although not in the trip budget, Jane agreed to pay, and now Reagan found herself pedaling along a Hilton Head bike path lined with trees. The stories of early Africans, some her ancestors, kept resurfacing in her thoughts. They rode by little houses, some built right after the Civil War when the Union Army built this town for the newly freed slaves.

"Nice bike trails," Welby observed, pedaling beside her. "I read that Hilton Head got an award for being a bike-friendly place. Not only do they have all these trails, but also extra lanes on the roads for bikes and signs to share the road.'

"Yes, it's a great place to ride," Reagan agreed, even if she felt slightly nervous.

"Woowee," Welby yelled. "What a life!"

Reagan laughed. "If you're happy, I'm happy. After all we've been through, we need this."

"Yes, ma'am," Welby agreed. He stayed close to Reagan, pedaling alongside her when possible, and following her when they switched to single file. It had been a very long time since Reagan rode a bike, but they said you never forget. Her leg muscles felt out of practice, and her butt began to ache after about a half hour. Her cellphone buzzed in her pocket. She pulled it out, trying to maneuver the bike with one hand as she read her brother's name on the screen.

"Be careful, Reagan," Welby called.

She braked and then everything went wrong. She felt herself flying through the air, over the handlebars, somersaulting onto the pavement below. Later, she remembered putting her arm out to try to stop her fall, but then her helmet made contact with the ground and she blacked out.

When Reagan woke up a few hours later, she opened her eyes to a hospital room and Welby. He wasted no time getting up from his chair and standing by her side. He touched her face as he said, "Reagan. You're back! I've been so worried about you, dear."

"What happened?" Reagan asked. "Wait, I fell, didn't I? We were riding bikes. My brother texted, and I was checking my phone."

Welby nodded. "Don't text and ride!"

Reagan managed a little laugh. "My phone. Where's my phone?"

Welby pulled it out of his pocket. "It went flying when you fell. I rescued it for you."

"Thank you," Reagan told him. As Welby handed it to her, she reached out with her left arm. "What?" She looked down at her arm and the heavy cast circling her lower arm. "What did I do?"

"You broke your arm, Reagan," Welby explained.

"Great," Reagan complained sarcastically, but continued on her mission to check for messages. "I need to check on my dad." She fingered her phone with her right hand and awkwardly held it with her left.

"Really, Reagan?" Welby scolded her. "Let it go. Think about yourself for a change. Don't you want to know what happened to you? You just goin' read your brother's text? Are you in pain?"

"Welby, my dad might be dying, might be dead. This is more important than me right now," Reagan asserted. She read the text and smiled. "He's getting better. He made it around the corner. They think he's going to pull through. Mom told Dean to tell me thanks. They think my call did it. Ah, that's so sweet. Welby, I'm so relieved."

Welby squeezed her hand. "That's great news. And I'm glad you woke up. How are you feeling, Reagan? I need to give Dean another report on you. I called him a while ago."

"Thanks, Welby, but don't worry Dad," she said.

"Your brother's got a good head on his shoulders, Reagan. He doesn't plan to tell your dad about your fall, but he and your mom send their prayers," Welby replied.

Now that she knew her dad was okay, Reagan took stock of her situation. She fingered a bandage on her forehead. She kept looking at the cast below the elbow. Funny, she felt fine. What kind of meds did they have her on that she couldn't feel any pain? Just yesterday, she wanted some of those drugs, but now, she just worried about getting hooked again. After all the mess addiction caused in her life, she did not plan to open that door again.

"Welby, what did they give me? I can't feel the pain. Oh, my God, you don't think it's opioids, do you? Let me talk to the nurse," she told him. "No, it's not possible. The MAMs wouldn't let them, would they? Where's the nurse?" She became frantic, trying to get out of the bed. Fortunately, the sides were up. Only with help could she get free.

"Calm down, Reagan," Welby said. "They got your back on this. I'll get the nurse, but you stay put. Don't create any more problems than you've already got. A concussion and a broken arm are enough for now."

Reagan tried to remain calm like Welby said. She took a few deep breaths, but only felt fear growing inside. After all this time, she still loved that liquid gold in her veins, spreading euphoria throughout her body. It was a good feeling that had made her seek more time and time again. She checked out the IV pole, wondering if it was programmed to give her another fix in an hour or two.

Welby returned with a nurse and Jane after what seemed like hours. "We're so glad you woke up," the nurse told her. "You gave us all a scare there, honey."

Jane put both thumbs up. "Welcome back, Reagan. Sorry our little bike excursion tripped you up. We've been worried about you. You brought all the MAMs to their knees. Priscilla's back at the house, leading a prayer vigil for you, even as we speak."

"Tell her thank you, Jane. Thank you all so much. God answered your prayers. I'm doing fine and I can't feel a thing." Reagan frowned and then turned to the nurse. "Are you giving me opioids? It sure feels like it. I'm a recovering opioid addict."

The nurse seemed startled. She grabbed Reagan's chart from the wall. "Did anyone tell us that when you came in?" she asked.

Jane put her hands on her head. Welby grimaced. Reagan started in on them. "What were you guys thinking? When you bring an opioid addict to the emergency room, that should be the first thing on your minds!"

"No, Reagan, we were worried about you, not drugs. Your arm cocked out at a strange angle when you landed on the ground. You completely blacked out. Although the EMT got a pulse, you didn't respond. I didn't want to lose you, baby. Saving you was the only thing on my mind, and I think for the rest of our group, too," Welby said, obviously trying to get back in her good graces.

Reagan turned to the nurse. "Well?"

"No," the nurse reported. "No opioids. Our ER's policy prohibits opioids. There are way too many addicts in the community these days. We don't want to take a chance of throwing people in recovery off balance, or getting new addicts started. Don't worry, dear. You've just got some strong Ibuprofen in your system. At home, you take two hundred mg. Today, you've got our hospital version of six hundred mg. You're fine."

"But I feel like I'm floating," Reagan said. "Are you sure?"

The nurse checked the chart again. "You're on another drug to relax you, but don't worry, it's not opioid-based. And you've received your last dose of that."

Jane put her thumbs up. "Awesome. You're right, Reagan. We should have thought about that when they brought you in. You gave us a major scare."

"Boy, I'm really messing up our little trip, aren't I? First my dad, and now this." Reagan didn't like all the attention on herself. "How does this affect our plans?"

"You let us figure that out," Jane said. "Concentrate on resting and getting better. They'll spring you out of here soon. Enjoy the pampering while you can."

"You're good, Reagan. You're going to be just fine, you've got this. You've got me and God in your pocket, too. You've got everything you need. I'll be happy to walk slowly with you for a couple of days," Welby told her.

Reagan gave Welby a half-hearted smile. The last thing she wanted was a setback. The whole situation felt too much like the car accident that led to her addiction in the first place. But Welby was right, she had him and God in her corner. She would need to summon determination to push through the next six weeks as her arm healed. "Thanks, Welby," she said. "I'm going to need you and God both."

Regrouping at the Airbnb

Priscilla joined the MAMs in the living room for a pow wow. After the aborted bike ride, they'd cancelled plans for a swim at the beach. Instead, they hightailed it back to the bike rental place to drop off the bikes and came home. While George and Tom chaperoned the group home folks in a beach volleyball game out front, the MAMs put their heads together to come up with a plan. Jane and Welby had accompanied Reagan to the hospital.

"Get out your Madame Biddy Medicine Kit, Molly," Sallie suggested. "We can use those herbs on Reagan. God knows she's going to need it."

"Yes," Priscilla agreed. "We'll learn about the Gullah healing techniques and help out Reagan at the same time."

"Let me go get my iPad," Katharine said. "I've got that *Blue Roots* book on Kindle. You know, I read that when we read about the Gullah people."

Katharine and Molly left to get their things, leaving Sallie and Abigail to shoot the breeze with Priscilla for a few minutes. Priscilla continued to stew over Madame Biddy's prediction. "She told me Moses Sun is going to show up soon. Do you think that's possible?"

Sallie said, "I thought you told him to get lost a long time ago."

"We did go our separate ways, yes," Priscilla said. "He started to scare me. I used to think he was a man of God and we'd get married someday. But he started building up his gun collection again, then returned to work with that Colorado think tank organization.

Remember the one he worked with when he shot Katharine and Emily?"

"Oh, no," Sallie said. "You're better off without him," She gave her famous belly laugh. "You can be like me, enjoying the single life. It's not all bad."

Abigail got a starry look in her eyes. "I wish both of you could find a Seamus. What about that Gullah Tour guide, Priscilla? He was so very handsome and intelligent. He didn't have a ring on his finger."

"Abigail, why are you looking?" Sallie chuckled. "I'm going to tell Seamus."

"You stop." Abigail laughed back. "You know women notice things."

"I didn't notice, did you, Priscilla?" Sallie teased.

Priscilla nervously giggled. "I may have some Gullah blood, but I'm not ready for a Black man yet. I'm still processing everything. Can you believe that I have relatives here on Hilton Head? I don't really know them, though, and I can't really say we have anything in common, other than an antique slave quilt. What does it mean to have African blood?"

"That's deep," Sallie said. "Journal about that and give it some more thought. Will it change your political views? You know those Republicans don't want anybody talking about race anymore. Heck, they want to pretend slavery never happened, nor racism, for that matter."

Priscilla didn't know what to say. Republicans aren't racist, she thought. The Democrats want to give Blacks special privileges. All her familiar political views looked somewhat askew. Would Black blood change her politics? Fortunately, Molly and Katharine came down the stairs and she could forget about that for a while.

"Okay, ladies," Molly said. "Let's check out Madame Biddy's Medicine Kit." She placed the suitcase on the floor in the center of their chairs and unzipped the bag, while Katharine perused her iPad.

"What I'm wondering," Katharine said, "is how much the root doctors were about herbal medicine and how much about voodoo. The tour guide said the enslaved people didn't have doctors, so herbs and roots were all they had."

"Madame Biddy said the same thing," Abigail reminded them. "But they brought voodoo from Africa, too. Remember that novel, *Mama Day*? All those fixes and spells were downright scary, really."

Priscilla shivered. "That stuff seems like evil to me. I don't like it at all."

"Me either," Molly agreed. "But let's focus on the positive, the healing aspect of herbs. Let's listen to Madame Biddy." She opened the book tucked inside her new medicine kit. "Here's a table of contents with a list of common ailments. I'll find something good for Reagan."

Katharine began to read from *Blue Roots* on her iPad. "Traditional African medicine taught that sickness had its origin in spiritual evil and drugs alone would not guarantee physical health."

"We know that, right?" Sallie said. "We are a unity of mind, body, and spirit. Everything is interconnected. We often need more than drugs to heal illness. Sometimes people vilify what they don't understand."

"But casting spells and putting fixes on people to hurt and punish them? That's what I don't like," Abigail argued.

"Here on page eighty-three in *Blue Roots*, it says that Alligator root is a sedative," Katharine told them. "Do you have any of that in your kit, Molly? That might help calm Reagan."

"Alligators don't have roots," Sallie complained.

Priscilla Googled it. "No, Sallie, Google says that Alligator weed is a wetland plant that can be found in waste places in ponds, streams, and along some rivers."

"That makes sense," Katharine said. "They definitely had wetlands on the sea islands."

"Yes, but it says alligator weed is from South America. It creates problems. It's very invasive," Priscilla cautioned.

"We're a bunch of quacks." Sallie guffawed with her signature belly laugh. "Let's be careful about giving Reagan alligator weed. That's a sedative. Let the doctor prescribe what she needs. But I do believe that the Gullah people used herbs for healing. I mean, think about it. What else did they have? The book I read said they learned some of the things in Africa, some from the indigenous people here, and also by trial and error. Okay, Molly. What more do you got in that bag of yours for Reagan?"

"Basil. Good for relieving anxiety and stress," Molly offered.

"Oh, my goodness," Katharine said. "Basil? I didn't know that."

"Mullein," Molly continued. "Anti-inflammatory. Great for a broken arm. It can also help joint pain. You can make it into a tea or poultice. By the way, it's also good for lung ailments and asthma. Amazing stuff."

Abigail's cellphone buzzed. "It's Jane," she told the group.

"Put her on speaker phone," Sallie demanded. "We want to hear, too."

Abigail pushed a button, bringing Jane's voice booming into the room. "You can all relax. Reagan's going to live. The broken arm is a simple fracture. They've put a cast on it. They do think she might have a concussion, so she's gotta lay low for a few days. She's awake and doing well."

"Praise Jesus," Priscilla said. "I'm so glad to know that our girl

Reagan will be all right."

"Yes, thank God," Sallie exclaimed.

"They decided to watch her overnight, then spring her in the morning if all is well. Then we can move on to Charleston as we planned. They'll release her at eight, so we'll be back to pack up. I'm letting you know now I'll be sleeping on the bus tomorrow. No noise, ladies, please."

"Thanks for the update, Jane," Abigail said. "Glad she's doing well. Is she in much pain?"

"We've got some herbs for her," Sallie yelled.

"What?" Jane asked. "I didn't hear that."

"We're reading about Gullah healing techniques, looking to find some herbs in Molly's new medicine kit for her," Abigail explained.

"Okay," Jane said. "But we best stick with the doctors here. As soon as Reagan woke up, she wanted to know if they gave her opioids. She was worried about getting hooked again. I can't believe none of us thought about that! Good thing they've got a policy against opioids in the ER. Too many people in recovery these days, they said."

"Oh, my," Abigail said. "She's right, though. We should have thought about that."

"I gotta get goin'," Jane said. "Welby wants to spend the night. I plan to stay to keep him company. I'll see you all in the morning."

As Abigail clicked off the call, the volleyball players strolled in from the beach. Seamus reminded them all, "We should get down to the dock by five thirty for our sunset cruise."

"Oh, I forgot all about that," Abigail said. "Right. Everybody get cleaned up. We'll put out fixings for sandwiches with chips and veggies for dinner. We don't have much time, so hurry. The cruise will be a lot of fun. We might even see some dolphins."

An hour later, Priscilla and the MAMs, minus Jane, with George and Tom, Seamus, Artemis, Zorastria, Max, and Antonio, arrived at the Mermaid of Hilton Head for an evening cruise. The setting sun still shone brightly in the sky, creating dazzling lights on the boats bobbing in the water near the pier. They checked in at the office, then made their way down to a small open building to wait for the boat.

A cool breeze blew across the water. Priscilla snuggled into her jacket, glad she brought it along. Molly snapped photo after photo with her new camera. The group home folks huddled together to keep warm. George hung close by to them, probably to make sure the guys kept their hands off the women. She remembered that problem in Ireland with Welby and Reagan.

Some families joined them in the small shelter. A young woman arrived and introduced herself as their tour guide. She led them to the end of the dock, then offered a hand to steady each person as they stepped into the boat. Fortunately, the open seacraft provided ample comfortable seating for the thirty-some passengers. Priscilla chose a front seat and began snapping photos with her cellphone. The wind whipped the water, creating whitecaps. A churning sea set against a changing sky filled with puffy white clouds created great beauty.

She pinched herself as they pulled away from the dock, once again grateful for traveling with the MAMs. The young tour guide stood near Priscilla, explaining the types of fish found in these waters, and she also mentioned dolphins.

"Will we see dolphins?" Priscilla asked. "I've never seen one before."

"We certainly did on our cruise this afternoon." She lifted up a cardboard poster displaying dolphin fins. "Every type of dolphin is unique. Here are dolphins that we've spotted in these waters. We also give each dolphin a name." She handed the poster to Priscilla.

Priscilla perused the fins of a variety of dolphins in different sizes and colors. She laughed at the names. "Gator, Smitty, Nick, Carlos, Mango. Who comes up with these names?"

"Our employees," the woman answered.

Priscilla passed the poster on to Molly and Tom, seated behind her. The guide said, 'Look, there's a dolphin over there now." She pointed to the right side of the boat. "Keep looking."

Sure enough, Priscilla saw a fin in the distance, but it disappeared so quickly, she couldn't get a picture. The children rushed up to the front of the boat. Their parents followed with their cellphones, busy capturing the magical moment. Over the next hour, the dolphins surfaced time and time again.

"Dolphins swim near the surface to breathe," the guide explained. "They can stay under water for up to ten minutes when they dive. So, that's why we have to keep looking!"

As the golden ball of the sun fell beneath the clouds, then sank into the ocean, Priscilla found herself mesmerized by the beauty, capturing pictures of the changing skies and sparkling water on the horizon. She absorbed the wonder of it all while the sky turned pink and orange, creating a dazzling scene. She realized her ancestors had lived in this very place and wondered if they'd treasured the sunsets. Had the beauty momentarily eased the suffering for her enslaved ancestors? She could only hope.

When the sun finished its journey into the water and the colors faded into night, the captain turned the boat back toward the dock. Priscilla never wanted this cruise to end.

Grand Ma Ma Weighs In

Okay, now. All these chillun's are makin' me laugh. Do you see those MAMs trying to make themselves into Gullah root doctors? I don't think that's happening in this lifetime, but I hope they're having some good plain fun. God knows they need it right now. What a trip. Those men framin' my baby Welby, a heart attack, and now a broken arm. This whole adventure's not for sissies, but neither is being Black in America. Yes, ma'am, they're learning what it's all about.

I can tell you I'm real proud of Reagan, standing up to her daddy that way. I'm sorry it knocked him down, but he was like a tree ready to fall anyway, and according to the angels up here, that heart attack saved his life. He's got another opportunity to get it right. I'm all for second chances—for Reagan's dad, and Welby's, too. It's never too late to begin again. If there's one thing I know for sure, you gotta forgive and forget and keep loving your folk even when they mess up time after time. If you don't, your anger's going to eat you all up inside.

Now, I'm not sayin' you make up with people when they're hangin' with the evil ones, like those Proud Boys, gangstas, and terrorists. No, you gotta stay clear of their mess. Like right now, Ms. Priscilla gotta watch out for that Moses Sun from her past. He showed his colors in Turkey, I heard. The MAMs forgave and forgot, giving him a pass into respectability. But he's done taken advantage of their good hearts and is starting to mess up all over again. I wouldn't trust him one bit. You watch now and you'll see.

People call our root doctors evil. True, some of them put fixes on people, which Jesus don't like. But I also see the evil fixes in the racism of those Proud Boys, and the ones who want to rewrite history, cancelling out the truth of racism. Faulting critical race theory, my foot. That's just code for keeping the truth in the closet.

We Gullah people lived some good years on our islands, keeping our culture and ways to ourselves. Not an easy life, but at least we could fend for ourselves, keepin' the white man off our backs. Bridges and development turned all that upside down. Nobody's really got that island life anymore. America done came to the islands, trying to build paradise. Between you and me, they got it all wrong. Paradise was here before the developers came in. Now, you just got fancy houses and miles of fences. Some say fences make good neighbors, but I say they're just trying to keep my people out.

Welby at the Hospital

Welby stood up and stretched. Feeling disoriented, he tried to shake the sleep out of his eyes. A glance at the hospital bed across the room woke him into reality real quick. His beautiful Reagan lay there, all banged up with a cast on her arm. He wished he could turn back the hands of time and beg off that bike ride. In the corner, Jane stretched out on the only recliner. At least she got a good night's sleep.

Reagan seemed peaceful enough in her slumber, so Welby sat back down to ponder his own plight. Before he'd left town, his parole officer had suggested he go to that prison that sucked up five years of his life, to give the current inmates a pep talk. Yes, Mr. Peabody thought hearing how Welby turned over a new leaf might inspire them to change likewise. Welby took the request seriously, because ever since Ireland, he did believe God wanted him to tell it. Now that that speaking gig loomed on the horizon, his feet turned cold. Sure, he'd constructed and rehearsed what he planned to tell them at the Toastmasters Club back in River City. But actually delivering the message to guys in the pen would be a whole different ballgame. Hell, when he left, he promised himself he'd never go back again.

Yet he knew deep inside he had to do it. He remembered his own sentence and bleak darkness closing in. Yes, he knew all about living without hope behind prison bars. His life stopped within the North Carolina Department of Corrections, where they warehouse Black men. Sometimes the men deserved what they got, and also, you could find a complete travesty of justice, a function of the color of your skin. He owed it to his people and to God to speak hope. He wished he could fling open the prison and set those guys free. He still wore some of those chains inside, but being on the outside felt so incredibly sweet. The MAMs gave him a second chance. Now he wanted to give back. Instead of backing out, Welby reviewed what he wanted to say, praying that his story might truly make a difference for a least one man that day.

He thanked God for his memory as the speech he'd rehearsed remained fresh in his mind. He'd brought the paper copy along, too, but packed it away in his suitcase. Yes, he could do this, and make the MAMs and God real proud. But then he thought about visiting his dad, something he'd vowed he would never do. The words of Madame Biddy really sunk home. Welby knew he needed God's forgiveness as much as his dad. Sure, his father screwed up, yes, but so did Welby many a time.

Jesus sets the bar high. You gotta forgive how many times? Seventy times seven? Welby didn't even come close. He wanted to believe that his dad had turned over a new leaf. Could it really be true? His past experience only told him his dad was lying, but perhaps he really did change. He knew prison could do that to a guy. Welby himself didn't make a change until he got out, but he watched other guys transform in the cells. They call it foxhole religion in war, but the same sort of thing happened in the pen.

He imagined, for a moment, his father as a new man in Christ. Could he be genuinely sorry and regret what he did to Welby? Holidays and celebrations might be something to look forward to if his dad was really all new. If he could actually be proud of his dad, what a difference that would make in Welby's life. Was it too much to hope? Or did he need to let go of his own jacked pessimism and take his dad at his word? Maybe Welby was the one stuck in the past.

Welby stopped considering his dad when Reagan opened her eyes. She looked confused and disoriented, the way he'd felt when he woke up in this same room a few minutes earlier. "Hey, babe." He smiled her way, getting up to close the distance between them. "Good morning, beautiful. How are you feeling?"

Reagan grunted. "Maybe like death warmed over," she said, but then she started laughing, which sounded like heaven to Welby's ears. "Like I've got a millstone on my arm? Oh. My. God." Reagan's voice got louder as she spoke. "What am I going to do?"

Her voice woke Jane. Jane rubbed her eyes, pushed the recliner up and sleepily said, "Good morning, Reagan, glad you made it through the night. How are you?"

"I've been better," Reagan said, "but not too bad."

"You're looking good," Jane responded. "Can you excuse me a moment? I need to find the restroom."

As soon as Jane disappeared, Welby took the opportunity to lean over and give Reagan a kiss on the cheek. "You're going to be just fine." He wanted to reassure her, even though he imagined this might slow her down. "Just think, you can paint with your good arm and use it as an excuse to take it easy for a while. Six weeks max, you'll be good as new. This sorry episode will be all over before you know it."

"That's easy for you to say," Reagan retorted. "We're in the middle of vacation and I've got a concussion and a broken arm. How will I play tourist anymore? Think about the next few days, never mind six weeks."

"You'll be fine, Reagan. You'll be okay. Speaking of which, they're springing you out of here after you eat a little breakfast. Abigail's packing your things. Jane and I need to go back to pack, too. Will you be okay alone for a little while?"

"Welby, I told you that you didn't need to spend the night. Yes, I'll be just fine. Thanks for being here, though." She reached out and grabbed his hand. Tears leaked out from her eyes. "You're so kind to me. I'm so glad God brought us together."

Welby nodded. "God and Grand Ma Ma, right? Crazy still after all these days between, thinking about Grand Ma Ma spooking you on that labyrinth in Ireland, telling you to be my friend, and then you painting a spitting image of her. Reagan, we are meant to be."

"A great story to tell our children someday," Reagan responded.

"What?" Welby said as her comment registered. Did Reagan just fast-forward into the future, envisioning a reality of them as husband and wife? Before Welby could take that thought any further, Jane appeared at the door.

"We gotta go," she told Welby. "The nurse will help you get dressed, Reagan. We'll be back in an hour to pick you up."

Welby kissed Reagan good-bye with a warm smile. "Let's pick up this conversation later. See you soon." Then he followed Jane out to the van, trying to imagine that future that Reagan could already see. Children? A white picket fence? Would she really marry a Black man and take him in, baggage and all?

CHAPTER THIRTEEN
CHARLESTON

Sunday with Priscilla

Priscilla looked forward to visiting Charleston, but the things that excited her in the past seemed less enthralling now. The beautiful houses along the oceanfront and the large mansions of antebellum times which she loved reading about and perusing in *Southern Living* magazines at the library didn't hold their former allure. She now realized that they were symbols of a plantation culture that used humans like animals to build fortunes. She descended from those plantation owners, but also from Matilde Johnson, a slave. The two parts of herself did battle within. Although she learned many months ago about her African blood, this trip put a face on her actual relations. Discovering a common story changed everything. She wanted to learn about the Black history of Charleston. What was it like for the freed slaves in those days after the Civil War?

Priscilla made the mistake of drinking some coffee to fully enjoy the sunset cruise, and that caused her to toss and turn all night. She finally gave up at four in the morning, pulling out her iPad to look for something to read. Could she find some history of Charleston on Hoopla, the library app? Hoopla always came through for her binges on romance novels. Although the MAMs long ago left romance reading behind, Priscilla still enjoyed the genre, hoping to find true love herself one of these days.

Her search turned up *Sojourns in Charleston, South Carolina, 1865-1947, From the Ruins of War to the Rise of Tourism.* This collection of essays focused on the wealthier part of Charleston rebuilding after the war. But then she found "Inside Southern Cabins", by Eliza Houston Barr. This woman wrote about the life of the freed Blacks, comparing the ones who lived well in nice houses and others who lived in slums. She made the observation that those living in the nice houses acted the same as the whites in nice houses. A lot of the criticisms against the poor Blacks, she said, would be true of anyone assigned to live in poverty. She wondered why life was so unfair. Priscilla read until finally she couldn't keep her eyes open.

Next thing she knew, Abigail knocked on her door, calling her to get up and pack. "Priscilla! Reagan's home from the hospital. We're leaving this morning. Get your suitcase packed. Bring it down so we can load the van, then get some breakfast. It will be a while before lunch."

Priscilla looked at the clock. How did she sleep past nine? She hurried through her morning routine with a quick shower, applying make-up, brushing her hair, and dressing for travel. She carefully folded the quilt, fingered the journal before slipping it into her large purse, and then packed everything else into the suitcase. She made it down to breakfast in record time, but they were putting the food away already. She poured herself a cup of coffee, fixed a bowl of granola, grabbed an orange, and figured that would have to do. She gulped down the cereal in very unladylike fashion and tucked the orange in her purse, then found a lid for the paper coffee cup. She headed out to the van, then waited while Welby helped Reagan up into the vehicle.

Her cellphone buzzed just as she took a seat by Sallie near the back. By the time she found her phone in the bottom of her purse, the buzzing stopped. Who could be calling now? She checked for a number, then gasped. Moses Sun? Goosebumps popped up her arms, Madame Biddy was right.

She dialed her voicemail to listen to his message with dread, then pushed the speaker phone button on her phone so she could hear his familiar voice. "Hey, Priscilla! I see you're coming to Charleston. That's great. Come help me preserve the Confederate monument down here. There's a rally today. Some people want to knock down these important historical statues. Call me back, doll. I miss you." Priscilla shuddered and silenced her phone.

Sallie overheard and asked, "Who was that? That sounded like Moses Sun. I thought you told him good-bye. Saving confederate monuments, really?"

"I know," Priscilla responded, glad Sallie overheard. "He scares me, Sallie. What should I do? How does he even know I'm down here? I haven't talked to him for two years."

"You know Abigail. She lives on Facebook. It probably wasn't too hard for him to figure out with a little cyber stalking. I imagine you're in some of her photos," Sallie said.

"Oh, gosh," Priscilla said. "You're absolutely right. He spends hours on Facebook."

"Just ignore him," Sallie recommended. "Charleston's a big place. He can't find you. Even if he does, we've got your back. You don't owe him a thing. Let it go."

Priscilla looked at her phone. Good manners taught her to respond, but she didn't want to speak to the man again. Why would Madame Biddy tell her to be careful if he couldn't really find her? Certainly, he knew where she lived. If not on the trip, then back home, he could find her easily.

"I'm going to ask Abigail to quit posting," Priscilla thought aloud.

"Better tell Molly, too," Sallie said. "Molly's been blogging the trip. Ask her to delay her next post until after we leave Charleston. Keep him guessing."

Priscilla nodded. Life used to be so simple. Now everything seemed confusing.

She glanced up front and noticed Abigail and Seamus beside Reagan, a flashback to their travels in Ireland with Seamus as tour guide. Abigail took the microphone. "We'll start our tour of Charleston at the Angel Oak on Johns Island," she announced. "The tree is somewhere between three and four hundred years old. Then we'll head into town for a Gullah Tour. After that, we'll find a park to eat the box lunches we brought along. The rest of the afternoon we will spend on a hop on/hop off tour. Tonight, we stay at an Airbnb up in Monck's Corner, northwest of the city."

The MAMs packed so much into this trip. Priscilla would like more breaks, but she did find the history interesting. Her sleepless night caught up with her and she yawned. Her eyes fluttered, then closed completely. She slipped into a much-needed nap.

Reagan Adjusting

The ride to Charleston gave Reagan time to think. Her broken arm would be a hindrance in the weeks ahead. She'd planned to start working out to get in shape for returning to work when her year at the FARM ends. Yet slowing down might not be all bad. In her younger days, she rarely stopped, racing through days, focusing on goals to create a good life. Even after the accident, she pushed herself, eventually stealing drugs to keep moving forward at all costs.

Her arrest and rehab stopped her dead. But soon, she focused on getting out, clean, and back to her old life. The MAMs and the FARM taught her that her old ways wouldn't cut it anymore. Moving ahead must look very different. Also, Welby was a game changer. She realized taking it slow seemed right. Perhaps the cast could be the silver lining in the cloud of her life.

She thanked God that the ER in Hilton Head didn't give out opioids. What a great trend across the country, helping addicts and everyone, really. Reagan made it through the pain without narcotics. By the time she woke up, her arm was set and the pain subsided. Now she only had to hope that itchy feeling under her cast wouldn't drive her crazy.

She dozed off, worn out from the trauma. When she woke, she noticed a sign announcing they'd arrived at the Angel Oak Tree of St. Johns Island. Reagan googled the tree on her phone. *Some say it's the oldest tree east of the Mississippi River.*

Before long, Welby offered an arm to help her out of the van, saying, "At your service, ma'am." He gave her a wink. "Should we walk under the branches, or stay out here on the pavement?"

"Let's stay out here first," Reagan suggested as she perused her phone. "That ground doesn't look real even. Do you know why it's called an angel?" she asked Welby.

"Can't say I do," Welby replied.

"Google says if a branch touches the ground and then starts to grow back up, that makes it an angel tree," Reagan told him. "What's that all about?"

"Beats me," Welby said. "Ain't never seen an angel, except maybe Grand Ma Ma."

"Exactly," Reagan said. "That's what I'm talking about." The massive tree, with its wing-like branches, covered a huge area. Quite a few indeed touched the ground, then grew back up, like giant elbows leaning on Earth. "Google says this tree may be three to four hundred years old, maybe even five hundred. Some think it was a burial ground for Native Americans."

"It was certainly here during slavery, then," Welby noted.

Reagan enjoyed sharing privacy with Welby, staying back from the rest of the group who were busy exploring under the branches. Another silver lining in the cloud of her broken arm, which she appreciated very much. "Hey, here's a YouTube video about the real legacy of the Angel Oak." She pushed the button to listen, holding the phone up so Welby could hear, too.

An African American lady talked about the beauty of the old tree, but then told a tale supposedly by a freed slave at a nearby plantation who said that they hung slaves here.

"Oh. My. God," Reagan said. "I don't like it. Lynchings, Welby. Killed right here."

Welby put his arm around Reagan's shoulder and squeezed her tight. After a while, he agreed. "Mmhm. Too much suffering in the history of our people. But I'm with this sister on YouTube, the story needs to be told. It's plumb hard. That grief, that terror, that ugliness, still camps out in the psyche of our lives and bodies. Maybe not in yours, but certainly in mine."

"I've never heard that story," Reagan admitted.

"No, they don't want you to know. Don't want to mess up your pretty little vacation. That's white folks, sugarcoateding the past," Welby said.

"But who's white, Welby? I'm white, you're white? I'm Black, you're Black. Who's doing the sugarcoating, you or me?"

"Neither of us, babe. I'm just sayin'," Welby said. "They want to keep it quiet. Not you, not me, but them."

Reagan looked at the old tree, wishing it could whisper secrets about everything that happened under its branches over the years. As she watched the others snapping photos and posing with the ancient giant, she felt sad, wondering what kind of evil would make a person kill someone just because of the color of their skin. She hated the thought of her ancestors treating her other ancestors like animals.

"A penny for your thoughts?" Welby offered. "What's going on in that big, beautiful head of yours?"

"It's a lot, Welby. I'm trying to wrap my head around my white ancestors hanging my Black ancestors. Trying to understand evil. How could my dad even do that to you?"

"You're right, Reagan," Welby said. "It is a lot. Being Black in America, I've lived with that reality every day of my life. You keep thinking something will change. But then some crazy white supremacist goes and shoots up a bunch of Black people. You realize nothing's changing. If anything, it's getting worse." Welby hung his head, but then his eyes lit up. "Hey, maybe you could paint something to make a statement. Maybe you could paint this tree."

Reagan thought about it. "Yes, maybe I can say it without words, show the sorrow of the tree. I need to take some pictures." She reached for her cellphone with her broken arm, forgetting about her problem. She switched to her good arm, then placed the phone in her left hand, thankful she could still use her fingers. "Let's go under the branches, so I can get some pictures close up, too."

They ducked under the low branches. Reagan held her phone at different angles to provide many perspectives on the old tree.

"Hey, Reagan," Abigail called. "We want a group shot with the tree." She rounded up the group, as they straggled into the center. George and Tom, Molly and Sallie came first. Pretty soon, the others arrived.

"Isn't this tree amazing?" Artemis asked Reagan. "I love how it just hangs over us, creating a canopy of love, an umbrella for life."

"But," Reagan countered, "did you know they used to hang slaves from this tree?"

"Oh, no! Why don't the signs say that?" Artemis asked. "Are you sure?"

Welby responded. "You know these white people don't want to air their dirty laundry. Hell, yes, it happened. Are you kidding? We found a YouTube video where a sista laid it all out."

"Oh, my God," Artemis exclaimed. "Let's get out of here. This place is haunted."

Abigail frowned. "Let's get our picture. Thanks for sharing, Reagan and Welby. We need to know the truth. That's why we're here. We want to expose the truth, not hide the places of evil. But it's not the tree's fault. Once again, it's the humans that caused the problem."

"I'm out," Artemis announced. "I don't want my picture by this tree. I'm sorry. I don't think it's a place to smile or celebrate."

"But it's important to tell the story," Reagan argued. "I want the picture so I can remember to tell people about this tree and what happened here."

"Not me," Artemis replied. "You all just go ahead. I'm sitting this one out."

So the group assembled beneath the branches, without Artemis. Reagan stumbled and Welby seized the opportunity to put his arms around her, supposedly to steady her, she imagined, not that she minded. As he held her close, she felt her body awaken. Tingles from all the places their bodies connected surged through her body, coming together at her womb-center. She longed to unite with Welby. In a few more months, they would be free to do as they pleased. She could hardly wait.

George tagged another tourist to do the honors, and Reagan handed them her cellphone to capture the moment. They waited patiently while the tourist obligingly snapped pictures with all the MAMs' phones and cameras. Reagan didn't mind more time close to Welby. She smiled, safe in the arms where she hoped to spend the rest of her life.

A few minutes later, they climbed back into the van, heading to Charleston. Reagan studied her photos of the Angel Oak. She imagined creating a mystical scene, depicting both angels and devils hanging around the old tree. She wanted to expose the evil and make a statement with the art. She pondered the thought as they sped along the highway, getting closer to downtown.

Gullah Tour Charleston

For the second time in one week, Priscilla boarded a bus for a Gullah tour, this time in Charleston. The friendly man first greeted them by the side of the bus outside the Charleston Visitor Center. Now he stood, talking through a little headset mic as he prepared to take them on a two-hour romp around the city. He mentioned a guide he'd written, *Gullah Guide to Charleston,* and she found it on her iPad so she could follow along with his narration.

"Do you know where the Gullah language originated?" he asked. When no one responded, he continued. "Lorenzo Turner of Howard University researched this. When visiting South Carolina, he heard the Low Country dialect. Later, he traveled to Sierra Leone in Africa, finding a similar language there. It's a Creole language, which means mixed. In this case, Gullah is a mix of African languages with English. I bet you didn't know many Africans spoke English before they were kidnapped."

This sounded familiar to Priscilla. Between reading with the MAMs before the trip, the Gullah Tour on Hilton Head, and now this, it was sinking in. Her cellphone buzzed in her pocket. She almost ignored it, but decided to fish it out and glanced down discreetly. The tour guide had asked them to turn off their cellphones. She didn't want to appear disrespectful. She held it low, behind the seat, so he couldn't see it, as she looked. "Moses Sun," she whispered out loud. "He's calling me again."

Jane, sitting beside her, must've overheard because she said, "Let that loser rot."

Priscilla tucked the phone in her purse where she wouldn't feel the buzz if he called back. She did not want to talk to the man. He gave her the willies. She wanted to focus on the tour, but she couldn't help being distracted. She tried to push Moses Sun out of her thoughts and just listen to Alphonso Brown.

"Phillip Simmons," Alphonso said, "was a talented African American ironworker who lived to the age of ninety-seven." He stopped the van near a green space and announced, "This ironwork is Simmons' Gateway to the City, commissioned by the City of Charleston." An ornate black iron gate with decorative swirls at the top graced the small park. Priscilla tried to imagine how he made the gate.

The tour continued as they wound through the streets of Charleston. He paused at various houses to note significant African Americans who once lived here. He pointed out the iron gates created by Simmons. Brown also told them, "Phillip Simmon's ironwork is displayed at the Smithsonian Museum in Washington, D.C. He once was commissioned to create a gate during the National Folklife Festival on the National Mall."

As they neared the end of the tour, the van stopped at the former house of Philip Simmons. Here, Priscilla learned how the gates were made. They met Simmons' nephew who kept the craft alive. The modest house included a workspace in the back, where the nephew worked, hammering black iron, holding it over a flame to make it soft enough to bend. On the workbench, Priscilla saw a sketch of a design. The man held the design close to his work, then continued hammering, oblivious to their group.

"Philip Simmons lived a simple life. He preferred to keep this house and never spent much money. He went to church and focused on what was important, not material things," Alphonso told them.

They next visited a cemetery next door to a church. "The Blacks and whites were buried together in this place, which was very unusual in those times. We are all related," he commented. "I could be a member of the Daughters of the Confederacy, if I were a woman." Priscilla wished he would say more about that, but she wrote it down in her notebook. He must have mixed blood like her.

The commentary, which highlighted the African American history, also often included digs at the white oppressors. "You can become very rich with free labor," he noted. "The slave plantation crops of indigo, rice, and cotton made Charleston rich."

He talked about John C. Calhoun drafting the articles of succession. The Gullah pronounced his name 'Killhoun.' Some said it was Gullah dialect, but Alphonso said they knew exactly what they were saying. "Our politicians participated in the evil of slavery. Strom Thurman had a daughter with a Black woman. She was killed when she was twenty years old. George Washington took all the teeth from a slave to make a set of dentures for himself. The father of the country did that. It was common when the men were traveling to offer a slave to sleep with the man for the night."

Priscilla didn't like hearing this history. She felt embarrassed and ashamed, even as she realized these things were being done to her people, the Black side of her family tree. Her head hurt just trying to comprehend the reality of it all. Dark clouds cast shadows over the city, mirroring her feelings. She understood why some tours hid this ugly side of Charleston life and the Confederacy.

As she held her purse close for comfort, she felt her phone buzzing again. She dreaded the thought that Moses Sun was trying again and left it buried in her purse this time. The MAMs were right. He couldn't find her. Abigail and Molly had agreed to slow down their social media posts, so hopefully, he wouldn't have a trail to follow.

CHAPTER FOURTEEN
SOUTHERN PLANTATIONS PART I

Boone Hall – Charleston

Welby again helped Reagan onto the van when they left the Charleston Visitor Center, enjoying a chance to touch her after the Gullah Tour. She took a seat for herself, putting her legs up and leaning against the window, with her broken arm up over the edge of the seat. "Sit there," she told him, pointing to the seat behind.

They chatted as Seamus drove them to the Boone Hall Plantation, and soon, Seamus began to talk. "The Boone Hall Plantation provides a good overview of what life was like back in the days of slavery. They have a very popular live performance which interprets the history of the Gullah people. We will also attend a presentation on the slave houses and the life of the slaves on the plantation. Boone Hall is unique in that it is still a working farm. We will go on a tractor tour of what they grow today. If we have time, you can walk through their gardens and the butterfly house, a new addition."

"They're still making money off us, aren't they?" Welby complained to Reagan.

"All these plantations turned into money-making tourist destinations. Go figure."

"Yes, but it's our history, Welby. It's so important to tell the story," Reagan replied.

"Well, let's see how much they sugarcoat the truth," Welby said. "You heard Seamus. They planted gardens. People gawk over beautiful flowers and impressive mansions. Give 'em what they want."

"But we're going to hear about the slaves, Welby. I think they want to tell the truth at Boone Hall," Reagan responded.

Welby continued to stew as they arrived at the plantation, but Reagan distracted him from his anger. They walked down the paved main drive to a little outdoor theater. Stately oak trees lined the road, creating a place of beauty, even though the whole place remained tainted, in his eyes, with evil.

A buxom Black woman greeted them at the outdoor theater. They sat in the front row. The woman nodded at him, offering a warm smile, then began to rap about the Gullah people. "Now, I'm going to tell a story, and your part is 'Spread the Word,'" she instructed. "Have you heard?" She pointed to them, and they said, "Spread the word." Then she began telling the story of the Gullah people, which sounded familiar after hearing it on Hilton Head and again in Charleston. But Welby liked the way the sista here made it all come alive in an art form he appreciated, in the music he loved. She ended the rap, saying, "Medicine for the spirit and medicine for the soul."

Reagan was right, Welby realized. They told the story here to keep history alive and remind people of the evil of slavery. Only with telling our history can we make sure not to repeat the mistakes of the past.

Afterwards, he went up front to tell the woman she did a great job. She smiled, accepting his praise. "You from around here?" she asked.

"Wilmington and Raleigh," Welby told her.

"Oh, you Gullah?" she asked.

"I think so," Welby responded. "I loved your rap. You remind me of my childhood."

"Help us keep our story alive," she told him.

Welby nodded and promised, "Will do."

They walked on to the next event, passing little brick houses identified as slave quarters, and stopping at benches between two of the houses, where Seamus said a presentation on the slave life would begin soon. Welby tried to imagine life in these houses. It was such a beautiful place, but such wicked treatment. How did they manage to keep the faith and stay alive? The shadow of slavery had haunted him since he learned about it in school.

Here, they learned all about slave life at the plantation, and they didn't seem to sugarcoat it at all. In fact, the picture they painted was downright horrible. Later, on the farm tour, they rode through the fields, learning about cash crops the current farmers planted. Although they sold some crops, they said they made more money on special events, such as a pumpkin patch and Halloween maze.

"So, Welby, after visiting Boone Hall, do you still think they're just sugarcoating and making money here?" Reagan asked. "What do you want them to do differently?"

"I know I said that before," Welby replied. "But they do a good job of telling the story here. Sure, it's a beautiful place to visit, but they speak the truth along with the beauty. I think this place got it right."

Welby and Reagan visited the butterfly house so Reagan could take some pictures and talk about her plans for a painting of the plantation. She wanted to make a mystical scene of slaves flying away, like monarchs. Welby wondered if America would ever transcend the evil of racism. Forgiving and loving didn't come easy.

Cypress Gardens

Reagan leaned against Welby's arm as the van left Boone Hall, heading for the last tourist destination of the day. Her head hurt a little, but all in all, she felt a gradual return to normalcy. Welby wrapped his arm around her. She rested her head on his chest. Their self-appointed chaperone, George, didn't seem to notice, or perhaps he just wanted to give them some space after the trauma of the trip. Reagan mouthed a silent prayer of thanks for Welby. What would she do without him?

Abigail and Seamus perched in the front of the van, tag-teaming as tour guides. Abigail held the microphone and announced, "Our final plantation for the day will be Cypress Gardens. Originally, Dean Hall established this plantation in 1750 to grow rice, using the fresh water from the Cooper River. Benjamin Kittredge acquired the property in 1909, digging out an area for a swamp at the end of the Cooper River and turning it into a place for duck hunters. During the Depression, two hundred men built four and a half miles of walking trails. They opened to the public in 1931. In 1963, Benjamin's son gave the land to the City of Charleston who later turned it over to Berkeley County. The County continues to manage the property, now known as Cypress Gardens Nature Preserve."

"This doesn't sound like a real plantation," Reagan commented.

"No, my lass, not anymore," Seamus agreed. "It's a garden now, a nice place to walk. Many a movie and TV series have been filmed there."

Abigail read from a book. "'The Patriot, North and South, Cold Mountain, The Notebook, The Swamp Thing, were all filmed there.'"

"This reminds me of that tour in Ireland when Seamus told us about all the movies made in the Wicklow mountains," Welby commented to Reagan.

Seamus overhead. "Ah, yes, you be right, my lad. The filmmakers like our Emerald Isle, too, they do. And the Americans like to watch movies made in Ireland."

Seamus took the book from Abigail and continued. "Hurricane Hugo in 1989 caused much damage to the park, causing it to close for a year. Then massive flooding in South Carolina in 2015 caused millions of dollars of damage to the botanical gardens. The County announced they would apply for FEMA funds. Four years later, they re-opened."

"Climate change," Abigail said. "Areas close to the coast in the United States are starting to feel the effects of rising sea levels, an increase in the number and severity of hurricanes, as well as increased rainfall and flooding. The sea islands that once preserved Gullah culture were opened to development, displacing many Gullah people. Now the changing climate destroys newly developed beach getaways. Daufuskie Island is a case in point. We thought about taking you there, because it was originally a Gullah community. Now only a handful of Gullah people live there. A major golf resort and private residences fill the island. Some of them were destroyed by a hurricane. You don't hear much about that because the tourist industry doesn't want to dissuade people from visiting."

"They'll probably let the Gullah people move back to the Sea Islands eventually," Welby said. "Once they're flooded and gutted, the rich white folk won't want them anymore."

"But I doubt they'll be livable, once the sea level rises. The ice caps are melting. It's just a matter of time," Abigail said.

Priscilla exclaimed, "Jesus is coming back soon. We'll be okay."

"I don't think we can put all our eggs in that basket," Abigail cautioned. "The early Christians thought Jesus would return in their lifetime. It's been two thousand years now. The Bible says we can't know when he'll come back. We need to be good stewards of what God has given us."

Reagan hoped Jesus would come soon, but she also thought Abigail had a point. "It's a lot to think about," she told Abigail.

"How are you feeling, Reagan? Do you still have a headache?" Abigail asked.

"No, I'm feeling okay," Reagan answered. "I think I'm going to survive."

"We're going on a boat ride next, so that should be easy on you. After that, you'll be free to walk around the gardens, or rest if you prefer, before driving on to our lodging for the night."

After arriving at Cypress Gardens, they walked together along a path near the water. Spanish moss hung from the trees, creating a magical feeling. Early spring flowers bloomed near the water. Welby held her hand, following her pace. Daffodils seemed to be shining almost everywhere in the afternoon sun, reflecting onto the water. She took pictures with her cell phone, hoping to paint them later. Some of the trees were budding, including delicate pink blossoms on the red maple and redbud trees. A sign read Yellow Jessamine: State Flower of South Carolina. These bright five-petaled yellow flowers sparkled along the path. Frogs croaked in the waters. Reagan loved spring up north. It was cool to experience it early in the South, and then, when they returned home, it would happen all again.

The MAMs paid for their boat rides, and soon they stepped into the little boats. Reagan shared a boat with Welby and George, Artemis and Priscilla. George and Welby did all the paddling. They floated among the trees, enjoying the early colors of spring. Reagan felt like a queen, floating along, breathing in the crisp, cool air.

"This is nice," Priscilla said. "The flowers are so pretty. I'm glad they turned this place into gardens."

"Much better than a slave plantation," Welby agreed. "But the shadow of the past hangs over the place nevertheless. The sign says people get married here. This is the last place I would choose for my wedding."

"Where do you want to get married?" Reagan asked.

Welby turned red. After a moment, he said, "That's a good question. I'm not sure. What about you, Reagan?"

Reagan had to give that some thought. She'd known the answer when she planned to marry Tyler. But now, if she married Welby, that would be a whole different ball game. Fortunately, Reagan didn't have to answer the question, because a boat pulled up to theirs.

A man called, "Priscilla!"

The Return of Moses Sun

Priscilla had thought life couldn't get any better, floating in the beautiful swamp. But then it took another U-turn. Here came Moses Sun, paddling his own swamp boat, not even six feet away. With a big smile on his face, she knew he was up to no good and it freaked her out.

She quietly whispered to George, "Could we please get out of here? That's Moses Sun." George knew the story, and immediately turned the boat around, heading back for the dock. Priscilla watched the other boats heading deeper into the swamp, and out of sight. Meanwhile, George told Welby to pump it back toward the dock.

Moses Sun was not the sort of man who could be easily dissuaded. "Priscilla, there you are! I found you. What a sight for my poor eyes! I missed you! Come here, baby."

Priscilla avoided making eye contact. Welby and George stroked quickly, making good time, but Moses Sun kept pace entirely too well. He must still be on his weight training, she thought. She didn't want to ruin the trip for the group and she didn't want to deal with the man. Madame Biddy had said to watch out. She didn't trust him, especially in the South. She knew exactly what he thought about Black people. She didn't want him to be mean to her friends. She knew he would take up the Confederate cause.

George and Welby wasted no time in returning to the dock, but Moses Sun was right behind. Even if Priscilla wanted to hightail it out of Cypress Gardens, she'd have to wait for the others. She figured the only sensible thing would be to deal with him. Bid the man good riddance once and for all.

"You okay?" George asked, touching her arm.

"I think so," Priscilla said, trying to convince herself. "Thanks for trying to make a getaway, but it looks like I'm going to have to talk to him. I'll tell him to get lost." She said it loud enough, hoping Sun would hear, but he was too busy docking his boat. She braced herself for the confrontation.

George stayed back while the others headed for the path. "I'll be here for you if you need me."

"Thank you, George," Priscilla whispered. "I appreciate that. I don't think this will get ugly, but with Moses Sun, you just never know. He's not a very stable man."

Priscilla took a moment to appreciate the beautiful lake, shining in the late afternoon sun with splashes of spring color everywhere, perfect for staging spring weddings that often occurred here. So much for a picture-perfect afternoon, she thought. She wondered how she'd ever once hoped to tie the knot with Moses Sun. Even after he shot Katharine and Emily, she forgave him. Along with the rest of the MAMs, she gave him a second chance. But she imagined some people like Moses are just too broken inside. As much as she tried, eventually, he slipped into his old ways. His fascination with guns bothered her. She didn't want her Second Amendment protections taken away either, but she also believed some people couldn't be trusted with guns. She feared Moses Sun was one of the dangerous ones. She pushed him away before. Now that Madame Biddy confirmed what she knew in her gut, she didn't want to give him the time of day. If he shot two white women friends, what might he do to her Black friends?

Moses Sun greeted her and motioned to a bench. "Let's talk, Priscilla," he said. With George hanging close by, Priscilla felt safe. But as soon as she sat down, Moses Sun claimed her, wrapping an arm around her, leaning close, turning her head toward his, then wasted no time in plastering his lips on hers. He held her tight with his strong arms. She couldn't wriggle out of his grasp. When he stuck his tongue in her mouth, she bit it. Two could play this game.

Startled, he pulled back and she took the opportunity to slap him across the face. Now she would give him a piece of her mind. "Moses Sun, I told you we were over two years ago. I'm not opening this door again. What don't you understand? Why did you follow me? Are you crazy? Do I need to call the police?"

George pulled out his cellphone and held it up, hovering his finger over the screen. He raised his eyebrows to ask her. She wasn't sure she wanted to go that far. Did Moses Sun have a gun on him? She checked him over, looking for any bulges. It was perfectly legal to be out in public with a concealed weapon, and she knew if anyone would have one, it would be him.

"Priscilla, stop," Moses Sun countered. He turned to George. "You do not need to call the police. I love her." Then he told Priscilla, "I missed you, babe. I thought you felt the same. Don't you remember how good it was between us? God brought us together. You can't fight God, Priscilla, dear."

"Well, guess what? God told me to stay away from you," Priscilla told him. "I'm sorry, Moses, it's over. I thought I made that very clear a long time ago. I'm not giving you any more chances to get it right. You are so not a man of God. I don't want to have anything to do with you."

Moses' eyes bulged out of their sockets and Priscilla started shaking. She knew he could get very angry at times. Then he began to point at her and said with an accusing tone in his voice, "Priscilla Johnson! I can't believe I'm hearing these words come out of your mouth. We love the Lord. We both have sinned and fallen short. Nobody is perfect. Are you saying you're perfect and I'm flawed? Did you forget to read your Bible today? Our country needs the Christians to make it better again. I thought we were on the same page, dear."

How could he turn this all on her? Talking about loving the Lord with that anger in his voice and trying to excuse his own behavior. Priscilla shook her head. "I'm done. Leave me alone, or I will call the police."

Moses Sun looked stunned. He got up off the bench and reached for her again.

She pushed him away. "What don't you understand?"

George stepped in between Priscilla and Moses. "You heard the lady. Now, do I need to get security or are you going to back off?"

Moses Sun patted his pocket. "Who are you and what do you think you're doing? Nobody comes between me and my woman."

Maybe he did have a gun. "Let's go," Priscilla told George. She took his arm. "Let's get out of here."

"What's goin' on, Priscilla? You got a Black boyfriend now? You're better than that," Sun told her. "Let go of him."

"George is my friend and he's a better Christian man than you. You can't tell me what I can and cannot do, Moses. Behave yourself. I said we're done."

To his credit, George didn't allow Moses to ruffle him, but she knew Moses would not be easily ditched. Sure enough, he followed them as they walked toward the park exit. She turned around and got in his face. "Didn't you hear me? What don't you understand? I'm through with you. Leave me alone."

Moses grabbed her arm and George went into action. "Don't mess with her." He grabbed Sun's arm and twisted him around, away from Priscilla. George towered over Sun by almost a foot.

Priscilla ran into the small store just inside the gate and heard George tell Sun, "Now leave. Get out of here, or I'm calling the police. Goodbye. You're finished here."

Priscilla slipped into the store and closed the door and started shaking.

The cashier asked, "Are you okay, honey?"

"There's a man out there who won't leave me alone," Priscilla explained.

"You need help?" a large man behind the counter asked.

"I think so," Priscilla said. "Could you make him leave?"

The man picked up a phone. A moment later, a security guard came in. "Tell me what happened, ma'am," he said.

Priscilla took a deep breath and began to explain what happened. "I think he has a gun," she told him. "He won't leave me alone. He forcibly kissed me. He's a dangerous man."

"What is he wearing?" the security guard asked.

"He's got a red baseball cap and matching red jacket. He's short, wearing blue jeans."

"Stay here," the guard told her. "I'll take care of this."

George entered the store and told Priscilla. "He headed toward the parking lot when I told him to get lost."

"I'll make sure he leaves," the guard said.

George stayed with Priscilla while the others finished their rides and walks. Artemis, Welby, and Reagan had ventured out on a hike around the lake after their short boat ride and they weren't back yet. Priscilla felt scared and threatened. She knew he had a gun. None of them were safe. He was gone for now, but he wouldn't go far. All she could do was pray.

CHAPTER FIFTEEN
SOUTHERN PLANTATIONS PART II

Brookgreen Gardens and Huntington Beach State Park

Priscilla couldn't sleep. They arrived at their rental that night with no further interference from Moses Sun, but she doubted he was really gone. How could she enjoy the rest of the trip with him lurking nearby? Between her ancestral revelations and Moses Sun, she felt agitated inside. How could she reconcile both slave master and slave on her family tree? As a lifelong Republican, she believed she always stood on high moral ground. Now things didn't add up. Moses Sun was a case in point. She read her devotions and prayed, then twisted and turned all night.

In the morning, she rose before the sun, fixing an early breakfast with coffee, hoping it would see her through. She longed for home, the safety and comfort of her own bed. Going back to work would be a relief. Three more days of vacation loomed on the horizon.

Today, the MAMs planned to play. That was the last thing that Priscilla wanted to do, but she had no choice but to go along to Brookgreen Gardens and Huntington Beach State Park. She packed the journal in her bag. She hoped to read through the pages one more time on the beach in the afternoon. She wanted to fully absorb the backstory of her family in the South.

Abigail seemed in good spirits when they assembled for the day. Laughter echoed through the small bus. "We're going to the garden, ladies," she told them. "I'm glad you got the memo to wear your flowering MAMs t-shirts." Priscilla smiled at her friends, decked out in the brightly colored shirts Jane gave them last Christmas.

The MAMs also agreed to wear hats today, expressing their unique personalities. Sallie's hat was red, trimmed in purple, something she bought for Red Hat Society meetings. Jane pulled on a bright orange ball cap. She liked sporting events more than concerts. Priscilla chose a floppy yellow hat with pink flowers to match her shirt. Katharine expressed her more conservative nature with a navy hat, trimmed with brown straw. Environmentally-minded Abigail loved a green hat. Molly explained that her multi-colored, flat-rimmed hat with Guatemalan stripes came from Central America.

"We must get a picture," Molly suggested.

"Right," Abigail said. "When we arrive at the gardens, we'll stop at the entrance. A day to remember, ladies. Remind me if I forget." She chuckled. Priscilla knew forgetting seemed much more common among all of the MAMs these days.

Surprisingly, Molly took the microphone from Abigail. "Now, ladies, I want to tell you about Brookgreen Gardens and Huntington Beach State Park. I love these places. Tom and I often come to Myrtle Beach for winter vacations. I try to spend at least one day at them each year. Have any of you been here?" Only Reagan held up her hand.

"Oh, my," Molly told them. "Then you are in for a surprise. You'll like these places. The garden has a labyrinth! Once again, plantations were transformed into something good.

"During the Civil War, Union troops freed slaves. Plantations struggled without free labor. By 1910, they quit growing rice in this area. When these plantations fell into disrepair, a sports club purchased the four plantations of the Oaks, Springfield, Longhill, and Brookgreen. The Brookgreen Gun Club used the old plantations as a hunting preserve for many years."

"What did they hunt?" Jane asked. "Can we try?"

"Alligators," Sallie yelled, immediately following up with her signature belly laugh. "Jane wants to go on an alligator hunt. I gotta see this!"

"I'd love that," Jane replied.

George piped up from the back, "Me, too!"

Molly frowned. "Let me finish. It's not a hunting preserve anymore, guys. In the 1930s, Archer Huntington and his wife, Anna Hyatt Huntington of New York, purchased the four plantations. Archer had inherited a railroad fortune and patronized the arts where he met Anna, a prominent sculptress at the time. They married later in life in 1923. She was forty-seven and he, fifty-three. They never had children. When Anna contracted tuberculosis, a doctor recommended she spend time in the South on the beach. Thus they built a beach house and outdoor sculpture garden."

"This is so cool," Reagan said. "Archer helped create an artist's dream. Her sculptures are in the gardens. In their house are Anna's art studios. She kept big animals for her projects. I love Brookgreen Gardens and their house, Atalaya."

Molly nodded. "I'm no artist, but I'm impressed, too. This was a very poor region back then, not much work to go around. Anna and Archer respected the local people, hired them, and maintained good relationships. Gullah people helped with the landscaping in the gardens and built the house on the beach, Atalaya, modeled after a Scottish castle. After we tour their house, we'll visit the beach at

Huntington Beach State Park. Long after Archer and Anna died, the Brookgreen Gardens Foundation continues to employ local people and tell the story of the Gullah people, as well as provide a place of beauty and nature for tourists and locals alike. Their creative director wrote a book about the Gullah people. He often lectures and provides Gullah activities at Brookgreen."

"Will flowers be blooming in February?" Abigail asked.

"Remember, it's the South," Molly said. "Tom and I often come down in February for Presidents Weekend. Yes, it's amazing how much blooms here in February. Like March in Ohio, you'll see many blossoms: daffodils, dogwoods, and more."

Priscilla appreciated the background information. Now she looked forward to their tour, as long as Moses Sun didn't show up again. As they neared Brookgreen Gardens, she donned her yellow hat. She happily joined the MAMs for group shots in front of the long drive leading to the gardens. Majestic oak trees lined the road.

"These are three to four hundred years old," Molly told them. "They were planted for the original plantation here." They smiled and posed with the ancient oaks, making great pictures with their colorful shirts and hats.

Reagan Does Brookgreen

While the MAMs posed by the Brookgreen Gardens sign, Reagan told Welby everything she could remember about the place. "It's cool, Welby. You'll love it. It's spring, so everything will be blooming, plus there are sculptures everywhere. Mother Nature meets art and they kiss with joy."

"Okay." Welby chuckled, obviously amused with her perspective. "What exactly does that art smooching nature look like?"

Reagan laughed. Welby liked to tease her. "Not like that, but you'll see. I mean, already, aren't these huge oaks spectacular? They're from the original plantation, planted over three hundred years ago. Beautiful."

"But, Reagan, like that Angel Oak we saw in Charleston, they're haunted with the evil of the plantation. Nobody knows the troubles they've seen!"

"Hey, that's a song," Reagan said.

Welby opened his resonant tenor voice and began to sing it. Reagan looked at him with admiration. "You've gotta do more with that voice of yours, Welby. You're real good."

Welby smiled and Reagan continued the topic at hand. "You gotta hand it to Archer and Anna. They turned this place into something beautiful. Like the Bible talks about turning swords into plowshares?

They hired descendants of the slaves. Part of what they do here is tell the story of the evil. They lift up the Gullah people, too. Their creative director used to be on that Gullah show on Nickelodeon. We can't go back and erase slavery, but how we treat people today is important. We have to change. This is one of the good places, Welby. They don't sugarcoated the past here."

"Okay, okay," Welby said. "Bring it on. Brookgreen Gardens, here we come."

After the MAMs photo shoot, they wanted a picture of the whole group. Abigail asked them to gather in front of a huge statue of fighting horses which Reagan remembered admiring on a previous visit. The large horses stood on their hind legs, wrestling with front legs, seemingly suspended in midair.

Abigail orchestrated them. She directed the MAMs to the center with herself on the left with Seamus and Molly on the right, with Tom and then George. Then she placed the group home members on either side, women on the left, men on the right. Seamus snagged someone to capture the group shot. Reagan passed them her cellphone to get a copy for her dad.

"Say cheese!" Sallie laughed. Once she started, laughter rippled through the group, creating a jolly picture for posterity. Reagan enjoyed the levity. She looked forward to a relaxing day with the flowers, art, and the beach.

Morning dew sparkled on the plants as they walked into the gardens. Flowers opened to the morning sun. Pink azalea bushes, bright yellow daffodils, pastel snapdragons, and brilliant gold marigolds lined the paths. Reagan snapped picture after picture, capturing flowers with sculptures nearby. She zoomed in on dogwood blossoms, capturing four-petaled, delicate pink and white blossoms, then zoomed out to get the whole tree which was bathed in pink early light. She focused on micro and macro in the daffodils, as well. Zooming in, she photographed the bright yellow daffodil trumpet. She zoomed out to a whole bed of daffodils lining the path. Welby just walked along quietly, as she oohed and ahhed. She remembered the sculptures from her last visit: the nymph, the flutist, and the archer Diana with the bow and arrow in the center of the fountain.

Welby posed with a silly grin, imitating Diana the archer, shooting an imaginary bow at Reagan. "Call me Cupid," he told them.

Reagan giggled. "Do that again! I want to get your picture with Diana."

"Did you get the arrow? I aimed straight for your heart."

"Yes, I got it." Reagan tapped her heart. "I feel it right here."

Welby took the opportunity then to enfold her in his arms and plant a big kiss on her lips. Unfortunately, George was only a few steps behind. "Okay, Welby, let's move on. Enough with the public displays of affection."

Reagan's broken arm ached from holding her phone steady to get the pictures. She gave up on the photo shoot and let Welby take her hand. Then, together, they walked quietly through the gardens. She warmed, at one with the beauty of nature and the exquisite love she enjoyed with Welby.

Atalaya and Huntington Beach State Park

Despite her earlier reservations, Priscilla enjoyed Brookgreen Garden and the plain fun of vacationing with the MAMs as they all delighted in the fragrant blossoms of spring surrounded by sculptural art. Once home, the lion of winter would continue to roar for another six weeks. She looked forward to a second spring up north. Her worries subsided as the ladies laughed together, posing for pictures with sculptures, flowering trees and bushes, and fountains.

At a sculpture of a young woman playing a flute on a mushroom, Abigail and Sallie struck poses on either side, pretending to play flutes of their own. Priscilla laughed at their frivolous play, jealous of their long-term friendship since college, which Priscilla never got to attend. By the statue of Anna and Archer, labeled Visionaries, Abigail asked all the women to line up in front. "We MAMs are visionaries, too," she announced.

"How so?" Priscilla asked.

"We've traveled the world, casting light on the book of Revelation with our archaeological dig. We're leading the way with our recovery and re-entry homes. We work for the Earth with our organic farm and solar training house. And look at our revelations in the roots in Ireland. I say there's groundbreaking stuff going on whenever we MAMs are around," Abigail explained.

"They should make a sculpture of us," Sallie quipped.

"Right," Jane said. "And I suppose you want me to pay for it?"

"Great idea!" Sallie agreed. "You're our personal money bag. You always help us out."

Jane laughed. "Find me a sculptor and I'll negotiate, but don't get upset if it's true to all your various forms."

Sallie raised her eyes. Abigail laughed. Molly nodded and put both thumbs up. Priscilla didn't think they were serious, but who knew?

The nudes made Priscilla very nervous. She didn't think they were appropriate, even if they were works of art. She turned the other way when they passed a nude woman squatting with her hand behind her head, as if to pose. Her exposed breasts seemed like downright pornography. Another statue depicted a sitting woman, leaning forward, holding onto a stick behind her back Her breasts were full and hanging down in plain view. Priscilla wondered why an artist needed to expose women's bodies to get a point across. There weren't as many statues of nude men. She worried the MAMs would think she was a prude, so she didn't complain, but still, it just didn't seem right.

Midmorning, they attended a presentation about the Gullah people in the theater. Most of the information sounded very familiar to Priscilla now. The staff person told the story through a quiz game and the MAMs won because they knew almost all the answers, which surprised the speaker. In the gift shop, Priscilla purchased a photo card by a Gullah artist, depicting a woman in a brightly colored hat and dress. She planned to send her co-workers a note with it later.

Afterwards, Abigail led them to the labyrinth by the river. "We've gotta walk the Brookgreen labyrinth," she said. "We can get some prayer time in before lunch." They followed Abigail's lead, soon arriving at a path leading out to a flat, grassy area by the river.

"Hey! This is really cool," Molly said as they approached the labyrinth, made of gravel, asphalt and brick. "Feels like home!"

"But it's quite different from the Living Vine Labyrinth," Sallie noted. "It's okay, but a new experience." She laughed. "Let's try it out, ladies."

Abigail reminded them, "Pray and set an intention before you go in."

Priscilla certainly needed a time of prayer after viewing all the nude statues. More than that, she needed to spend time with God after all she'd discovered on this trip and her fears about Moses Sun. She personally didn't prefer a labyrinth as a place of prayer, but she had to admit it was growing on her a bit. She loved how this labyrinth was by the river and all the trees. It was really quite a beautiful place to pray.

"The last time I was here, the labyrinth was closed because it flooded," Molly told them. "I think they've reinforced it to protect it for the future. All these bricks are new, along with the asphalt."

Priscilla didn't mind the well-defined path. She appreciated there was more room to walk than on the cloth labyrinth that Jane made which they often walked in the barn at the FARM.

"Okay." Abigail said. "Get to it. You have thirty minutes. After this, we're going to the garden café for lunch."

Priscilla sat down on a bench to pray. She asked for peace. So many thoughts raced through her head as she tried to hold her diverse ancestry in her thoughts. She also needed to stay clear of Moses Sun. She invited Jesus in to clean out her frustrations and worries. He said to cast your cares upon him, so that's exactly what Priscilla aimed to do.

She would practice letting it all go, giving it over to Jesus, as she walked the labyrinth. Like Carrie Underwood, she asked Jesus to take the wheel.

By the time she finished praying, the MAMs were already on the path. She left her backpack on the bench and approached the labyrinth, following Katharine, several steps ahead. She walked slowly, trying hard to let go. She breathed in God's love, then breathed out thoughts crowding her brain. She enjoyed the view of the river in the distance and green trees swaying in the breeze. The path wound around and around, providing ample time for her to let go. She imagined her slave ancestors, perhaps enjoying this riverbank, years ago.

When she reached the center, she joined Katharine and Molly who already stood in the inner circle. Tears begin to flow. She felt the Lord's presence with her. Whenever she faced troubles, she always found God right there for her. Lately, she realized she'd been carrying the burden all alone. Placing it all at the feet of Jesus provided needed relief.

"You okay?" Molly asked.

Priscilla dried her tears with her fingers. Katharine handed her a tissue. Priscilla responded, "Yeah, I'm okay. Just feeling God's love. So good, you know?"

"I agree," Molly said. "I feel it too. This is powerful stuff."

"Thin space," Katharine suggested. "Like the holy wells in Ireland, the labyrinth connects us to the other side, to God, to the spiritual realm."

"For me, it connects me to Jesus, my Lord," Priscilla squeaked out through sobs. "He's always there, whenever we turn to him. What a friend."

Molly nodded. She gave Priscilla a hug, then turned to walk back out. Katharine followed her. Priscilla stood in the center, all alone. Goosebumps formed on her arms. She felt so close to God and, all of a sudden, she realized everything would be okay. She could embrace her ancestors and love them in the Lord, knowing that all people make mistakes. God forgives. She bowed her head to give thanks, praising Jesus, and then raised her hands high, shouting, "Praise Jesus! Praise the Lord!"

Abigail and Sallie were already done with their walk, sitting on a bench near the labyrinth. Sallie laughed and Abigail gave Priscilla a very strange look. Katherine turned around on the path and raised her eyebrows. Did it bother them that she was praising the Lord? Well, it bothered her that they didn't want her to express her joy in the Lord. She decided to just ignore them and enjoy the moment. She smiled and almost danced, she was feeling so happy, as she left the center to journey out of the labyrinth for the rest of the day. She walked confidently, somewhat quickly, and full of hope. She could do this. Yes, she could.

After morning in the gardens, they ate at the Garden Café. She enjoyed delicious clam chowder and a grilled cheese sandwich. Chatting with her friends, she almost forgot about Moses Sun. She hoped he would heed her words and get lost.

In the afternoon, they drove to Huntington Beach State Park, touring the home of Anna and Archer Huntington. Priscilla wondered what the place looked like when they first built it. The rather primitive-looking structure, obviously weathered by the years, looked like quite a strange house. Only the stone walls and ceiling remained, fashioned after a Scottish castle. She liked that boats sailing on the intercoastal waterway could sometimes see a fire burning on the front hearth, signaling that the Huntingtons were home and open for visitors. She found Anna's studios impressive. Large animals could pose there for her sculptures. Although the animals wouldn't stand still, with Anna's artistic hand and photographic memory, she could capture the nuances and essence of the creatures.

After the house tour, they explored boardwalks covering a marsh by the sea. She imagined slaves once built canals for the rice plantations in this area. A sign admonished them: Do not feed the alligators.

"Are there really alligators?" she asked Molly.

"Oh, yes," Molly said. "They're here, all right. They may be sleeping, but I imagine we will see some."

Sure enough, they spotted a group of gators lying on nearby rocks. Priscilla gasped at their long bodies, covered with greenish scaly skin. She couldn't tell if their eyes were open or closed. Two were over ten feet long, two others, she would guess around six, and one only three feet. Maybe it was a family. "Won't they eat us?" Priscilla asked.

"Yes, of course," Jane told her. "You better run, Priscilla."

"No running! Sudden movements are not good," Sallie chided. "She's just messing with you, Priscilla."

"But they could attack, couldn't they?" Priscilla asked.

Seamus had done his research. "These alligators have other sources of food. They don't come after humans very often, unless someone tries to bother them. There have been no attacks at this park in recent years. You'll be fine, Priscilla."

But Priscilla felt relieved when they left the marsh and boardwalk behind. They walked onto the beach and put out blankets to lie in the afternoon sun. The temperature climbed to sixty degrees by midafternoon. The sun made it feel much warmer. She enjoyed the calm ocean which gently sent waves rippling into the shore. After applying sunscreen to her face and arms, she stretched out on her blanket and closed her eyes. The trauma of Moses Sun far behind, she slipped into a sound slumber.

She startled awake awhile later, at the sounds of the guys yelling while tossing a football back and forth on the beach. She sat up and pulled the journal out of her backpack and began to read it all over again. Right here by the water, she could almost imagine the life of the young woman, her foremother, the slave whose father liberated her to life in the North. How hard it must have been for her to leave her mother and never return. She reread the early entries, then turned to the last pages of the diary.

Dear Diary,

I wish I could go visit Mama, but there is no money for travel. After working as a nanny, I now have a family of my own. Ben Johnson took a liking to me and didn't seem to mind my light brown skin. He's as white as an Easter lily. He works hard on the railroad, which doesn't pay much. We have three children, two boys and a girl. I take care of them, making meals, and keeping house. They're growing up so fast.

Things are nice up here in Ohio. We have running water in our house and even electricity, but I still miss the sea island where I was born. I miss the ocean. I miss my Mama most of all. Sometimes, though, the past doesn't seem real to me anymore. I haven't heard from Papa for several years. He was pleased when I got married, sending a telegram with money to buy a house. That was the last time I heard from him.

I tell my children about the ocean and what I remember. That helps me keep the Sea Island alive in my heart. I pray for Mama and hope she's doing well. She probably misses me as much as I miss her.

Priscilla shut the book and looked out over the water. She felt sad for the young mother. After all these years, she'd finally closed the loop. She traveled where the young woman could not. She didn't visit the girl's mother, but certainly her descendants, the Johnsons of Hilton Head.

As the waves lapped the shore, Priscilla focused on the span of blue water in the distance. She tried to imagine her ancestors on a slave ship, forced against their will to come to this strange land. She then imagined her ancestor, the plantation owner, treating her other people like cattle. She fathomed the young man taking advantage of a slave woman on the Sea Island. This was her story now. It didn't seem congruent with the beauty of the big blue sky and tranquil ocean. This new reality forged sadness in her heart and made her head ache. She lay back and closed her eyes again, hoping she could fall back asleep to ease the pain.

Then she sat up, remembering she'd turned this all over to the Lord. She chastised herself, remembering her time on the labyrinth. Her ancestors are forgiven, but was that enough? What did Jesus want her to do? She needed to pray some more. She lay back down and closed her eyes. The peace of the labyrinth returned. She slipped into a second afternoon nap.

***

"Priscilla! Time to go!" A voice awakened Priscilla. She opened her eyes, feeling disoriented and confused. She sat up, feeling the soft sand beneath her blanket. She looked again out to the waves lapping the shore.

Molly approached her. "You went to sleep?"

Priscilla rubbed her eyes and nodded. "I guess so. I feel refreshed. It's so beautiful here, do we really need to go?"

Molly nodded. "Yep, it's time to head to dinner. Hard to believe our trip is coming to an end, isn't it? One more stop in Wilmington, and then in two more days, we'll be home."

"What a trip," Priscilla said. "For me, but also for you, right?"

"Yes, we learned about our ancestors, didn't we? And maybe that we have some ancestors in common," Molly added.

"You think so?" Priscilla said.

"There's a good chance," Molly said. "As white as you are, you got some African blood, just like me. I think we both came through the Johnson plantation."

"That's a good thing," Priscilla said. "We're blood sisters, then."

"Whoda thought?" Molly responded. "Here I am, thinking I'm in a book club with a bunch of white ladies, but no! You and me are sistas. Yes, ma'am!"

Priscilla laughed, feeling warmed not only by the sun, but by Molly's friendship. She folded up her blanket and gathered her things. Then she locked arms with Molly. "Shall we go, sister?" Together, they walked toward the rest of the group to head out of the park.

As they neared the parking lot, Priscilla did a double take. A man stood at the edge of the lot, looking too much like Moses Sun. As she looked again, he pulled a ball cap over his head and headed for the beach. He didn't seem to notice the MAMs. But had he really been stalking her all this time? She shivered and prayed and hurried into the van. Perhaps it wasn't him, or perhaps he would never let her go.

CHAPTER SIXTEEN
WILMINGTON, NORTH CAROLINA

Welby Comes Home

The trip seemed to be flying by for Welby once they left behind the drama in Oceanside and Hilton Head. He could get used to playing tourist and taking care of Reagan, He liked learning more about the South and places he never visited in his youth. But now it was about time to go home. The van pulled out of Huntington Beach State Park and headed north. They picked up some fast food to eat on the road, and headed toward Wilmington where they would spend the night in yet another Airbnb.

Welby mulled over the good and the bad, the crazy times of days gone by. For the most part, his memories of Wilmington and the summers by the water were good. It was after he went up to Raleigh with his dad that things got hard.

"What ya thinkin'?" Reagan asked.

"It's a lot," Welby replied. "I'm looking at my life, thinking back to my childhood, Wilmington and summers in Navassa, Grand Ma Ma, my mom. This trip puts it into perspective, learning about the Gullah Geechee culture, and thinking about who I really am inside and the people who shaped me."

"Yeah, that's a lot," Reagan agreed. "Will we go to your house where you grew up?"

"I grew up in the projects, Reagan. I couldn't even tell you where that would be today. My family's long gone. There's nobody here for me now. Now, if we could go to Navassa, I might be able to find Grand Ma Ma's house, but that might be torn down by now, too."

"Navassa? Where's that? I thought you lived in Wilmington."

"Well, my mom lived in Wilmington, but she grew up in Navassa. Around Wilmington, most of the plantations were on or near Eagle Island, inland from the Atlantic Ocean along the Cape Fear River. After the Civil War, many of the former slaves settled in Navassa, on the west bank of the river where it meets the Brunswick River."

"Why did they call it Cape Fear? Was it a scary place?"

"Back in the 1500s, a ship ran into some rough waters in the river. They started calling it Cape Fear. There are ghost stories associated with Wilmington and the river," Welby explained.

"Ooh," Reagan responded. "That's weird. Did you have any scary things happen?"

"No, not really. The river could get rough when a storm came up, but we tried to do our fishing at other times."

"Did you eat the fish you caught?" Reagan inquired.

"Oh, yes, we learned how to clean the fish, the whole deal. That was part of the fun. Those were good times back then, fishing and eating our catch."

Abigail took the microphone up front. "In about a half hour now, we'll reach our destination for the night. Tomorrow, plan to get up bright and early. After breakfast, we'll take a Black history walking tour of Wilmington, then hop on the Eagle Island boat ride. In the afternoon, most of us will go to the beach, while Welby, George, and Tom will be heading over to the prison where Welby's addressing the inmates. We're real proud of you, Welby."

Welby looked at Reagan. "Do you think I'm ready?"

"You got this." Reagan nodded. "I heard you preach it at Molly and Tom's church. You're a natural-born speaker. You speak from your heart. You're going to reach those guys where it counts. If anybody can, you will."

Welby felt embarrassed, but he knew he wasn't a bad orator. He thought out loud, "You know, I do love to talk to a group of people, but it's scary going back in the pen and talking to those guys. They aren't your everyday sort of men. They can be very rough. But they are a lot like me, thrown in there and losing out on their lives for some minor infraction that never would have got them time if they had any money to defend themselves or a different color of skin."

"I never knew how unfair things were until I met you, Welby," Reagan said. "I had no idea. I think about what I did, and what you did, and it doesn't make sense. I was stealing drugs from the hospital. I went to rehab. You had recreational drugs in your glove compartment, and you went to prison for five years?"

"You got that right. Life's not fair for the Black man, especially in the South. They take so many Black men away from their families. It's no mystery that so many Black families are broken."

Molly overheard and added her two cents worth. "First there was Jim Crow, and then the new Jim Crow."

"What was Jim Crow?" Reagan asked.

"After the Civil War, they freed the slaves. Some of the freed slaves even got property and began to make a life for themselves. But the white folks in the South didn't like that. They passed the Jim Crow laws, designed to keep the Black people as second-class citizens."

"Why did they call them Jim Crow?" Priscilla asked. "Who was he?"

Katharine stepped in to help out with her vast academic knowledge.

"Have you heard of the minstrel shows? In these Southern variety shows, often a white man would put on black face and sing and dance and make fun of the Black people. Back in the 1830s, a white actor, Thomas Dartmouth 'Daddy' Rice, developed the character of Jim Crow, a buffoon, reinforcing racial stereotypes. He donned the black face makeup and danced around like a fool, belittling African Americans with his antics. Later, the name became associated with the laws to keep the former slaves from full citizenship in the emancipated society."

"What were Jim Crow laws?" Reagan wanted to know.

"Basically, they didn't let the Blacks and whites mix in marriage, in schools, hospitals, or places of business. Blacks could get in trouble for things they didn't even do. White people lynched Black people while law enforcement looked the other way," Molly said. "Eventually, with the civil rights movement, these practices became illegal. Then came what some call the new Jim Crow. As part of the war on drugs, they took away rights related to search and seizure. A professor at Ohio State wrote a book that our MAMs Book Club read a while back. The war on drugs was actually a plan to put Black men in prison. The Black people didn't realize at the time what was happening, none of us did. We don't believe in crime, so we thought it was reasonable to lock people up for criminal behavior. But now, we realize there was nothing fair and just about what they did. Black people were thrown in prison for years for having a little bit of marijuana. While they slapped rich white boys on the wrist for such antics, it could mean a lifetime in prison for a Black man."

"I need to read that book," Reagan said.

"I'd like to read it, too," Welby agreed. "Do you have a copy, Molly?"

"Yes, remind me when we get back to Ohio. I also can email you a list of the main points in each chapter. It's a dense book, so the summaries might be easier to digest."

"The story of Wilmington goes deep," Welby commented. "These are my people. Before the late 1800s, they were doing pretty good down here. Grand Ma Ma bragged about her folk all the time. She never let it go."

"What happened?" Reagan asked.

"Wait 'til tomorrow. You'll hear it all soon enough," Welby told her. "Let's enjoy the moment." He circled Reagan with his arm. She leaned into him and no more words were exchanged. Welby enjoyed the feeling of Reagan's body close to his, relaxing into the evening. After all the water under the bridge they shared and the new Jim Crow, could they find a happy life together? Although mixed marriages were now legal, that doesn't mean accepted. While he held Reagan, he was all too aware of how her father framed him, of how white people still mistreated Blacks, and the way Black sisters dissed their brothers who went white on them. But then, his life had never been easy. He was well-prepared to do hard. He could handle tongues wagging and evil looks, but he never wanted to handle prison life again. Speaking of which, he decided to rehearse his prison talk one more time.

Reagan's eyes closed. He felt her gentle breathing so close. He closed his own eyes, for a moment, imagining them being much, much closer and he longed for the future to arrive soon. Then he started rehearsing his talk for tomorrow, silently within his thoughts. He aimed to inspire and knew he had it in him.

Grand Ma Ma's Lament

These chillun getting' ready to tour my stomping grounds. The old people talked about those days after slavery. Our men died, fighting with the Yankees. The colored troops helped the North win the war. They fought for us all. But freedom comes with a price, don't you know it? Those plantations lined the pockets of those owners, making them the wealthiest businessmen in the history of 'Merica, all because of my people. But the only way they could get rich was through cheap, almost free labor. They barely kept our ancestors alive, treating them worse than animals, and buying new ones when the old ones failed. Those Southern white folk were downright angry when the North took their slaves away. They weren't about to take that sittin' down. No, sir.

For a while, though, things looked up for our people. The Feds gave us land. We started farming for ourselves. Those whites didn't like that at all. Givin' plantation land to the former slaves? So before too long, to keep the white Southern folk happy, the Feds took it all back. Yes, ma'am, the states returned that land right back to plantation owners. Sure enough, once again, my people were servin' the white man as sharecroppers, living not much better than slaves. They passed those Jim Crow laws to legalize treating us bad and keeping us separate from the white folks. Although they all went to church on Sundays, they somehow lived with the idea that we were less than human and so they could treat us however they wanted to keep on making money. That's not in my Bible, but then why you suppose they never let the slaves read? Now you know and I know the Good Lord made us all and that there's not much difference in our DNA related to the color of our skin. That there's a difference was somethin' those who want to justify mistreating dark people made up, a greedy hypothesis that has absolutely no basis in fact.

In Wilmington, you got Blacks starting to make a life for themselves, get an education, and be professional. These chillun's goin' tour the

Black history of Wilmington and you'll see it firsthand, the houses they built. They had their own newspaper. Once they got the right to vote, they started electing their kin. Of course, the white people didn't like that one bit.

One day, the Black newspaper owner wrote a column against lynching, callin' it out for what it was, a despicable act of evil men. I mean, who could approve of what they did? They would pick up an innocent Black man, torture him, and hang him in a tree just because they hated having the Black people living free. How those white devils could sleep at night after doing something like that is beyond me. And that's not all. Those whites got so doggone angry back in 1898 that they burned the Black newspaper down. Before I was even born, the whites declared war on my people. What were they so afraid of? It wasn't like we was takin' over the South. No, my people wanted to work hard and make a decent life like the rest of them.

But let me stop chatterin' so you can get on with the story. I'm just sayin' the history of my people ain't right and it ain't good and it's about time that someone put an end to treatin' people like they're not all children of the Good Lord. It ain't biblical. It ain't Christian. And it ain't nothin' nobody got no business doing, especially all those folk clamorin' to keep God in the public schools. Why do they want God there and not God's ways? It's beyond me. Who they really want, God or the Devil? The way people be these days in the USA concerns me quite a bit as I'm lookin' down from heaven on what's going on.

I also be a-wonderin' if I made a big mistake encouragin' that girl Reagan to befriend my boy Welby. I saw the chemistry heatin' up back on the Emerald Isle and thought they could do each other some good, religiously speaking. But I fear for them, I do, to tell you the truth. I wasn't a-countin' on Reagan's dad to be such a mean old racist codger. I'm beginnin' to wonder if he'll ever come around. If not, that won't be any good for neither of them. And then also Reagan to see that the Black women don't like their Black men going after white women and those white men don't like it neither. Just because you got a lot more mixed marriages and mixed blood these days, don't mean it's easy. If you're looking' at my family, well, we've been mixed since the slave master took up with my great-great-grandmother way back then. My people don't like it, but it's our blood and you got to make peace with who you are, or it tears you up inside. I'm a-prayin' for them and wishin' Welby and Reagan the best, but they got a hard row to hoe.

Priscilla and the MAMs Take a Walk

Priscilla rubbed her eyes, stretching and enjoying vacation, <u>once again</u> staying in bed a little longer. Tomorrow, she planned to get up bright and early, to get her body back on schedule for work next week.

When she visited interesting places, going back to the humdrum of daily existence always dogged her. After sailing the Mediterranean, playing archaeologist in Turkey, and having fun with the MAMs in Greece, her secretarial job seemed boring. She flashed back to their trip circling the Emerald Isle, where she'd enjoyed Irish music and dance and retreating with the nuns. She hated going back to work. But this time might be harder than usual because the trip turned her world upside down. Seeing the South from a whole new perspective, looking at it with the eyes of her newfound Black ancestors, affected her in ways she never imagined.

Molly knocked on her door. "Priscilla, you up? We leave in fifteen. Better get a move on. Get something to eat."

"Okay, I'm up," she lied. Well, she was awake at least. "Be there directly," she told Molly as she eased out of bed. She dressed, brushed her hair and added a little spray, fixed her face with foundation, some blush, eyeliner, mascara, and a little lip gloss. Then she hurried out to the kitchen where she grabbed a banana and a packaged cup of vanilla low-fat yogurt, and quickly buttered a piece of toast, adding some strawberry jelly. She liked to take time with her appearance and makeup and hated rushing breakfast. She hoped she didn't look too disheveled, not that the MAMs would notice. Sallie and Abigail didn't believe in wearing makeup and Jane and Katharine used very little. Funny how she was the most respectable one in the group and she never even went to college.

When she made it out to the van, the rest of the gang was already situated. Abigail jabbered away, "For exercise this morning, we're going on a walking tour. Here's a tour booklet for each of you. Read about the points of interest now. We'll drive some of the tour and walk some to make it down to the riverfront for our Eagle Island Cruise by ten thirty."

Priscilla glanced at her watch. It was already nine. She wished she had worn her sneakers. Her heels might be a problem. Oh, well, she imagined the good people of Wilmington folk would appreciate her appearance, touring with class. Her mother told her to always look her best and she tried.

"Now I'll shut up and give you some time to look over your booklets about the Black historical sites of Wilmington." Abigail turned off the microphone.

Priscilla opened the little booklet, "A Guide to Wilmington's African-American Heritage". She scanned the pages, checking out the names of the buildings they would soon see. Why did they even have to walk all over God's creation to see these things? The guide laid it all out, complete with pictures and descriptions. Maybe she could stay in the van and read?

On the first page, she learned that President Lincoln issued an emancipation proclamation in 1861, freeing the slaves to serve in the Union Army. She never knew that. Dr. John Haley, the author of the book she was reading, had also added 'The African Americans who served in the Union armed forces were not merely combatants. They also served as liberators, helping to free their sisters and brothers from the bondage of servitude. Ratified in December, 1865, the Thirteenth Amendment to the Constitution of the United States abolished slavery nationwide.'

Why do they celebrate Juneteenth if the slaves were freed in December, she wondered. She Googled it. 'Ratified by the required 27 of 36 stateson December 6, proclaimed on December 18, 1865' Hmm, she thought. She googled Juneteenth. In Texas, slaves were declared free on June 19, 1865, according to the 1862 Emancipation Proclamation. Weird, she thought.

She read on. '1898 Monument and Memorial Park.' She couldn't figure out what the picture showed. Maybe a modern sculpture. Were those people? Maybe she would have to get out of the van.

Right then, Seamus stopped the van. She looked out the window and spotted that very weird collection of statues portrayed in the booklet.

"We're here," he announced. "Now ya can see for yourself. First stop, number one in your booklet, the 1898 Monument and Memorial Park."

Priscilla picked up her purse off the floor, opened her cosmetic bag to check her makeup. She freshened her blush and added some lip gloss.

"Come on, beauty queen," Sallie teased. "Time to go. We've been waiting for you all morning."

Priscilla laughed nervously. Didn't Sallie believe in looking good? She never seemed to worry about makeup or fancy clothes. "I'm trying to look my best, honey," she told her.

Sallie let out one of her signature belly laughs. "You look great, Priscilla, absolutely wonderful. Now get out of the van."

How did Sallie do it? She could yell at you and make you laugh at the same time. Priscilla chuckled as she stepped out of the van on her high heels. She would do her ancestors proud, glad to know she looked absolutely wonderful.

Looking at the strange statues close up, she discovered they were actually canoe paddles. Before she could ask why, Welby started talking.

"I'm glad you're learning the history of my town today. I've got to warn you, it's not very pretty," he said.

"What is this?" Sallie asked. "What happened in 1898 and why are these canoe panels all sticking up in this park? It doesn't make sense."

"Okay, it may be a little strange at first," Welby replied. "But what you don't know is that Africans believe that when you pass from this world, you take to the water for the voyage home. It's a memorial to the African Americans that lost their lives in the violence of 1898, as we imagine them paddling on into the afterlife.

"At that time, the African Americans made a good life for themselves in Wilmington. They could vote. They opened their own newspaper and built houses. Before the war, the slaves built all the houses in Wilmington, so they had all the skills. Finally, they got to build them for themselves. You'll see some of their houses on this tour. The whites didn't like the colored, as they called us, getting a piece of the good life. The African Americans started electing their folk to the City Council. The Black newspaper editor wrote an article, calling out lynching."

"Lynching?" Priscilla asked. "Was that common back then?"

Katharine put her hand over her mouth. Sallie's eyes popped out. Even Jane looked bewildered. Priscilla wondered what was wrong with her question.

"Maybe you haven't heard much about lynching, Priscilla," Welby said with respect and no expression such as the faces the MAMs were making. "The white people used lynching to take my people out after the emancipation. Often, the person didn't do anything wrong, or maybe they looked at someone the wrong way. It really picked up in the late 1800s. Didn't really matter what a person did, if a white didn't like it, they would get a group together and go take you out."

Katharine added some information. "Priscilla, the white people killed the Blacks in a brutal way. They would capture and torture them and then kill them. Sometimes they hung them in trees, sometimes they displayed their mutilated bodies in the town square. Have you heard of Emmet Till? They made a movie out of his story recently."

Priscilla shook her head. She remembered a little from a high school history class, but she hadn't thought it happened very often. She didn't want to hear this stuff. Welby said it wasn't pretty, but she had no idea.

"I'm so sorry they did this to your people, Welby." Priscilla stopped, realizing they weren't just Welby's people, they were her people, too. "Our people. They're my people, too."

Molly, standing nearby, held up a hand to Priscilla. Priscilla just stared at her.

Then Sallie whispered, "She wants to high-five you, dear."

"Oh," Priscilla responded. She held up her hand and pushed it into Molly's.

"Yes, ma'am, blood sisters." Molly embraced Priscilla with a side hug. Priscilla smiled, even as her stomach turned as she thought abut a lynching.

"So, what more did the whites in Wilmington do back in 1898?" Sallie asked.

"They rioted," Welby said. "They burned down houses and businesses of the African- Americans. They burned the newspaper to the ground. They killed people. They kicked our Black people out of office."

"How could they do that?" Sallie said. "That's not right."

"Simple," Welby said. "White people got the power. They do want they want, right or wrong."

Priscilla looked at the paddles and imagined her African ancestors leaving for home in the water, the same way they came in the first place, except finally they were free. Paddling home didn't make sense, but then she didn't know really what happened after death. She wondered for the first time if people really go to heaven or hell. Would God really send people who never met Jesus to hell?

They milled around the paddles and the monument until Seamus called them back to the van. "We're off to stop number two, the Bellamy Mansion Slave Quarters," he told them as they drove on.

"I thought this was a walking tour," Jane complained.

"Well, yes," Seamus said. "But the first few stops are a great distance. I promise ya will get your morning exercise in, Jane."

Priscilla didn't agree with Jane. Personally, she enjoyed driving around. Maybe walking would be minimal after all. Back in the van, she pulled out the booklet and read about the Bellamy Mansion. Sure enough, built between 1859 and 1861, probably by the slaves, according to Welby. The mansion is 'an exuberant example of Classical Revival antebellum architecture,' built for plantation owner John D. Bellamy, M.D., who lived from 1817 until 1896. Actually, it had been constructed largely by both free and enslaved African American artisans. Behind the Bellamy Mansion was the Negro House, or slave quarters, which served as the home to enslaved house servants for the Bellamy family. She read on, learning that it was actually one of the most intact urban slave quarters in the country.

Maybe some slaves weren't quite as bad off as others. The ones on the Sea Islands were left to themselves, although they had mean overseers. Here in the city, the domestic workers had a little more freedom and could read and write. Some had even learned trades, such as blacksmithing and midwifery.

"This is a museum," she said. "Are we going in?"

"Not today," Abigail responded. "And we're here! Get out. Check out the house and slave quarters. Don't miss the carriage house in the back, then hurry back to the van."

Priscilla smiled that she wouldn't have to walk much on high heels. She could get used to this. She joined the others as they circled the mansion and other buildings. She enjoyed visiting historic buildings. The Bellamy Mansion was beautiful. Even the two-story brick building labeled slave quarters looked fairly nice. Yet the whole place seemed tainted with slave owners living there. She wondered how much say the slave had in anything. Her journal seemed to suggest that her ancestor loved the owner's son, but why didn't he marry the woman? Did he love her or just use her? Why did he move his daughter to Ohio, leave her mother on the island, and then start a whole new family? Maybe he couldn't marry her. The laws didn't allow that in the South. Why didn't he move north? Why didn't he move the whole family? Priscilla didn't get it, or maybe she understood perfectly, and didn't like it. Whatever could she do about the all the skeletons on her family tree?

They continued the tour, stopping at a few more places before Seamus deposited them on Red Cross Street to start the walking tour in the Brooklyn Neighborhood. In the 1890s, a mix of people, immigrants and African Americans lived here, according to the booklet.

As they walked, Priscilla read about the places in the booklet. She got confused, because the numbers weren't in order with the actual locations on the street.

First, they viewed #34, the C.D. O'Neal House and the Alpha Kappa Alpha House at 417-419 Red Cross Street, the first African American sorority in the nation built in 1932. Next up was #19, St. Stephen's African Methodist Church at 501 Red Cross. The former slaves left the other Methodist Church in 1865 and built their own. Good for them, Priscilla thought. Later, they added an annex with a library, a swimming pool, a physician's office, and services for the elderly. Priscilla was impressed.

Her heels began aching as they walked down Red Cross Street. At 510 Red Cross Street, her booklet explained a tiny house used to be the North Carolina Mutual Life Insurance Company, founded in Durham in 1899. Eventually, it became the largest African American insurance company in the nation with over seven hundred agents. Priscilla wondered if they started a life insurance company because of the threat of lynching. How would a family support themselves if their head of the household got lynched? Sudden death could certainly be rough on a family

They passed by Shaw Funeral Home at 518-520 Red Cross. Priscilla grimaced. Why did everything seem so depressing today? Lynching, life insurance, funerals. Was there any joy in the South for African

Americans? Her feet hurt. At Campbell Square, they viewed a graveyard for the African Americans, but also a school, a library, and a church.

At Campbell Square, Seamus told them that they were short on time. "Now, on special request by Welby, we'll visit the African American newspaper site. After that, it's off to the riverfront for our boat ride."

Priscilla didn't mind one bit getting back in the van. She took off her shoes and rubbed her aching feet, making a note to buy some flats sometime soon.

Welby Does Wilmington

Welby enjoyed retracing familiar steps with landmarks of Black history in his hometown. He remembered visiting these places as a teenager and being inspired by the legacy of his people, the attorney, the doctor, the writer, and the business folk, included on the tour. He always felt proud of what the newly freed slaves accomplished.

"They were something, weren't they?" he commented to Reagan back in the van. "I wrote a paper about them in high school. Think about it. They started their lives as slaves and then, once freed, they really made a new life for themselves. Some went to college, others built houses. They inspired me a lot back then. I used to preach about it at my church."

"What'd you preach, Welby?" Reagan asked.

Welby smiled. "Look at our ancestors and see your future. They didn't let slavery stop them, no. They were being beaten down and treated like animals, but they stepped out of all of that and spread their wings. Those caged birds learned to fly. The scripture tells us, 'Those who wait for the Lord shall renew their strength, they shall mount up with wings like eagles, they shall run and not be weary, they shall walk and not faint.' And they sure did."

"Isaiah 40:31." Reagan commented.

"You know that scripture, too?" Welby asked.

"Of course. I love the image of flying like an eagle. Do you know the song?" She started singing in her beautiful soprano voice, "And I will raise you up on eagle wings."

Welby joined with his resonant tenor, "Hold you on the breath of dawn." Then he broke into a laugh. "That's what I'm talking about. You got it, girl." He put both his arms around Reagan, as much as he could sitting beside her on the seat. For a moment, he absorbed the warmth of her body, wishing he could get her alone to do what he hadn't done for over five years now. But before George noticed him, he decided to kiss her on the top of her head and let her go.

Good thing, because only a second later, Seamus announced.

"We've arrived. And now I'm going to turn this over to our hometown tour guide to take us through this next stop. Come on up and tell it like it is, Mr. Welby Jones."

Welby eased out of the seat as all eyes turned on him. He took the mic from Seamus. "It's great to be home," he said. "I love this place and this tour. These are my people. They inspired me when I was young, and they're speaking to me again today. If they could do all that, then so can I and so can you! That's what they teach me. I asked Seamus to bring us here, to the Black newspaper place that I told you about. Gather 'round. I'll tell it quick."

They stood in front of a little building that looked like two-story house with a storefront for a porch. White letters painted above the store windows announced The Wilmington Journal. "And this," Welby said with a bow, "is the home of the *Wilmington Journal*. In the 1890s, the African Americans had their first newspaper across the street." He pointed to the place. "*The Wilmington Daily Record* building was right there. The whites did not like this one bit, not the competition or the fact that the Blacks were beginning to speak their mind about what was going down back then. In 1898, After the *Daily Record* published an editorial protesting lynching, a white mob burned the Black newspaper building and press to the ground.

"But do you think the African Americans quit publishing in Wilmington because of the fire?" Welby paused. When no one answered, he did himself. "Hell, no! It took a while, but three years later, a noted Black man, R.S. Jervay, founded the Jervay Printing Company, and in 1927, published the *Cape Fear Journal*. His son, Thomas Jervay, Senior, renamed it the *Wilmington Journal* in 1940 and won honors with the paper. That paper continues today as a family-owned newspaper.

"That's what I'm talkin' about," Welby told them. "Our people were beaten, burned up and thrown in jail, and yet they rose up. They didn't let the white man keep them down. They triumphed in spite of it all. That's what gave me hope as a young boy and inspires me today. Sure, I've created some of the problems in my life, but also some were thrown my way without my consent. But ... because I've got strong genes, because my people are strong, because I serve a risen Savior, I am strong, too. That's what this tour means to me. It's about winning against the odds. It's about good people who did good things. It's about how I will follow in their footsteps."

"You already are," Reagan said. "You already are, Welby."

"Say it, brother," George called.

"Amen!" Molly agreed.

"Well said, me lad Welby," Seamus agreed. "Thank you for that. And it's time to go down to the river for our boat ride. Is that all,

Welby?"

"Yeah, well, I'd like you to complete the tour. Since we don't have time, read the booklet and let's call it a day," Welby replied.

As the group filed back into the van, Welby lingered just for a moment, soaking in the view of the *Wilmington Record*, still thinking about his people writing through all the discrimination and problems over the years in Wilmington.

Back in the van, Reagan used her good arm to rub Welby's back. "Thanks for sharing that, Welby. I'm glad you showed us the newspaper and what it means to you. That's cool."

"I'm glad I got to show you. Some days, that history is what keeps me going. You grew up with your family, a big house, security and stability. I had none of that. This is the rock I stand on, in addition to Jesus, if you know what I mean."

"I think I do, Welby." Reagan nodded. "You draw strength from all this. I'm so glad I got to see your hometown."

"We're not done yet." Welby smiled. "The boat ride will be closer to my stomping grounds and the good times."

The van eased onto a highway and exited near the docks. They parked in a public lot and used the boardwalk to approach a flat white boat labeled Wilmington Water Tours. The open-air vessel provided tables and chairs under a roof, complete with a snack bar and restrooms.

Jane sprung for sodas and snacks. They scattered out around the small tables while the boat pulled out of the harbor. A tour guide provided a running narration. Welby had never taken this ride before, because they didn't have extra money for things like this while growing up. He found it interesting how the guide spun the history of Wilmington. He sat back, sipped his Coke, and took it all in.

"The Cape Fear River is the largest river in North Carolina," the man explained. "From Wilmington, it winds twenty-six miles to the Atlantic Ocean, the only river in the state that connects to the sea. At one time, Wilmington was the largest city in North Carolina, partially because this river made it a port.

"During the antebellum period, there were fifty-eight plantations scattered about Eagle Island and the banks of the Cape Fear River. They all grew Carolina Gold, a brand of rice. Today, you only see what's left of them. Look closely, and you'll the canals the slaves built to irrigate the rice paddies. They brought their agricultural expertise all the way from Africa."

Welby took in the skyline of Wilmington to the right and Eagle Island to the left. The tour guide talked about the railroad bringing trade to Wilmington. After the war, their main trade items were turpentine, pitch, and lumber. Welby kept trying to figure out why everything here looked so different than it had the summers of his youth.

Somebody once said you can't ever go home. He felt that way about the island. After all these years, it seemed more like visiting a strange land than going home. This wasn't the place he remembered, and, furthermore, his people weren't here anymore anyhow.

Reagan picked up on his sadness. She asked, "What's wrong, Welby?"

"It's not the same. This isn't my home. It's not what I remember."

Again, Reagan comforted him, putting her good arm around him and rubbing his shoulders. "Things change. It's hard. Everything looks different when you're young. Maybe you lived near here, but not right here?"

The tour guide explained efforts were underway to preserve Eagle Island as a wildlife sanctuary.

"Do people live on Eagle Island?" Welby asked.

"Not many," the guide answered. "After the Civil War, the freed slaves settled in Navassa on the west bank of the river."

"Will we go by there?" Welby followed up.

"No, not today," the guide said. "We're just going down the river a short distance and circling back."

Welby sat back, dejected, while the others chatted and seemed to be having a good time. The MAMs wore their red hats for the ride. His fellow group home folks were busy taking pictures, laughing, and milling around the boat. The universe could continue spinning without him. Why did he feel like a fish out of water even here, in his hometown? On his old stomping grounds of the Cape Fear River, he felt like a stranger. This didn't make any sense.

But, hey, he chided himself. Why live in the past? His future beckoned. Today, he would talk to the men at his old prison. Perhaps he could focus on making a difference. Let those Wilmington old-timers, the lawyers, the doctors, the artists, the architects, light his path and inspire him to do good. He rehearsed his speech in his mind once more, as the boat hung a U-turn, heading back to the Wilmington dock.

CHAPTER SEVENTEEN
THE RETURN OF MOSES SUN

Luncheon at Elijah's

Priscilla really enjoyed the boat ride and offered a quick prayer of thanks as they approached the Wilmington dock. Before long, they were deboarding and walking back onto the riverwalk boardwalk. A blue sky, fluffy white clouds, and the midday sun created a nice ambience, even on the slightly chilly February day. Priscilla buttoned up her raincoat. As much as things seemed good, she felt bothered about something she couldn't quite place. She knew lunch was next on the agenda. "Where is the restaurant?" she asked Seamus.

"Oh, it's coming up soon. We're only a moment away," he replied with a smile and a chuckle.

Seamus' Irish accent and jolly laugh made Priscilla smile, even while her stomach turned somersaults for some unknown reason.

Abigail called the group together. "Ladies and gentlemen, you have thirty minutes to explore the waterfront." She pointed to a restaurant down the way. "See Elijah's down there? We'll meet up there at one o'clock sharp. Sun Power guys, go with George. FARM ladies, stay close to me. The rest of you are on your own."

"Can't I hang with Welby?" Reagan asked with a pout.

"You can join George's group, Reagan," Abigail directed.

Reagan gave a thumbs up while the other FARM ladies frowned. Priscilla didn't blame them. Reagan got special privileges all the time. It would bother her, too.

Jane nudged Priscilla. "Let's go look at the architecture. Wilmington still has much of its antebellum architecture. They didn't get much damage during the Civil War, like some of the Southern cities. It's all still here. We visited some of the African American highlights, but there's a whole lot more belonging to the white folks."

"Great idea," Katherine said. "How do you know all this, Jane?"

"I've been reading my tour book," Jane replied. "I like to keep tabs on the place when I travel. The historic district is right here, by the water, of course. Let's go. We don't have much time." She led Katharine and Priscilla away from the river, providing a running commentary as they walked briskly. Once again, Priscilla wished she hadn't worn her heels. Why didn't she learn or why couldn't she let go of her appearance for comfort?

Fortunately, the tour distracted Priscilla. She almost forgot about her uneasy feeling, which she decided must be about Moses Sun, as they strolled through the old business district and ogled elegant houses. She imagined there must be a lot of old money in the town because everything seemed so well-maintained, unlike her town in Ohio. Too soon, they turned back to the riverfront for their luncheon reservation at Elijah's. When they rejoined the group in front of the restaurant, sure enough, there stood Moses Sun with a big grin on his face. No wonder she was worried. How on earth did he find out where they were eating?

"What are you doing here?" she asked him. "Didn't you hear me tell you to get lost?"

Moses turned toward the entrance of the restaurant. As if on cue, the door opened and out walked Mr. and Mrs. Hunter Smith.

Priscilla's jaw dropped. Reagan's face turned white. While Priscilla stood frozen, Reagan approached her parents. "Daddy?" she asked. "Mom?" She embraced her mother, and then her father with a perfunctory kiss. "Daddy, you shouldn't be traveling yet. What on earth are you doing in Wilmington?"

"My doctor released me to fly. On our private jet, with a special duty nurse, I'm good to go. Isn't it amazing what modern medicine can do for you these days?" he responded.

Reagan's mother frowned. "I didn't think we should come, but you know your father."

Reagan's father chuckled. "You women, always trying to control us. We don't like that, do we, Moses?" Her father gave Moses's arm a forceful slap.

"How do you know Moses?" Priscilla blurted.

"Moses and I go way back," Mr. Hunter-Smith explained. "We attended high school together. Recently, we discovered our shared connection to the MAMs. When Moses called me yesterday, we decided to get together again. I called Abigail to see if we could meet up with you to make amends. I feel awful sorry, Reagan. Now let's get in there and sit down. Like you know, I am recovering from heart surgery. I don't want to overdo it, but a man's gotta eat, now, doesn't he?"

With that, Reagan's dad held the door open for the group to enter Elijah's. Moses shooed him inside and took over door duty. "Go sit down and relax, Ron," he said. "Keep your women happy." Reagan's dad seemed eager to comply.

Moses greeted Priscilla with a big smile. "I've missed you." He gave her a kiss on the cheek before she could turn away. She hurried into the restaurant and didn't look back.

Reagan sat at the long table, in between her mom and dad. Across from her dad was the infamous Moses Sun. Directly across from her, Priscilla. The somewhat small restaurant seemed to be catering to their party exclusively for lunch in their dining room, although through the window she could see others seated outdoors. She enjoyed the ambiance of the place with dark wood floors, wooden beams stretching up the walls and across the ceiling, and a fire burning in a small fireplace. Paintings of various ships and smaller boats on the walls matched their seafood fare. Reagan missed Welby ever since he left to speak at the prison. She looked out the window to the river where they'd cruised in the morning. So much had transpired on this short trip.

Then she returned to the situation at hand, perusing her father's face and body, still alarmed that he would venture out so soon after a major heart attack. His color seemed fairly good, but then he always had a ruddy complexion and never stayed down for long. Was he pushing himself, or did the doctor really tell him he could make the trip? She had no idea. She added 911 on speed dial on her cellphone and planned to stay alert for any sign of difficulties with him.

As much as she longed to relax and believe her dad could hold his own, she remembered he almost died a few days earlier. She didn't want to fight. She promised herself she would not allow him to push her buttons again. That was what started his heart attack in the first place. Although his actions were dead wrong, she also felt guilty for expressing her anger. The fact that she also saved his life, both with CPR and by triggering the attack that led to needed surgery in the nick of time didn't ease her remorse. How did life get so complicated? Why in God's name did her father have to be here now?

"Where's Welby?" her dad asked. "Did he leave you already? I told you not to trust that man."

Reagan fumed. After all the deathbed apologies, now this? She couldn't risk upsetting him again. She must play nice. "Dad, you apologized. Now here you go again. Welby has a speaking engagement this afternoon at the prison. He's a motivational speaker. He's been asked to give the inmates a pep talk."

"Well, isn't that special?" her dad quipped.

Reagan clamped her mouth shut. She silently prayed to God to heal her dad of his ignorance, while she tried to let his retort go. Unfortunately, anger simmered beneath her calm demeanor.

"We are very proud of Welby," Abigail announced. "He's quite the orator. Today, he hopes to plant seeds of hope in the hearts of the prisoners. Welby is a very special man, Mr. Hunter-Smith. He knows exactly how those men feel. They'll listen to him."

"Yes, Welby's a good guy," Sallie chimed in. "He got a bad rap. He wasn't dealing drugs. He wasn't even using when he got pulled over by the highway patrol. Reagan was stealing them from the hospital. Welby, on the other hand, used recreational drugs from time to time. He went to prison for five years. That's Southern justice for you. I'm glad Reagan didn't do time, but think about it. You need to get to know him."

"As a society, we need to give people a chance to reform. Do you have any idea how many Black men they've locked up in the South? It hurts the whole community when they take the fathers out of the families. It's well-established that the War on Drugs was a plan to put Blacks in prison," Molly pontificated.

"Amen," Artemis shouted from the other end of the table.

Then Antonio piped up. "You think you're better than Blacks because you're not locked up, but it's politicians like you who made the rules to start throwing all of us in jail. This country is jacked."

While Zorastria gave a thumbs up and Max pounded Antonio on the back, the rest of the table went silent. Reagan knew Abigail and Molly were right, although she doubted her father believed anything they said. A year ago, she hadn't believed it either. Her mother cleared her throat and whispered in her dad's ear. Reagan couldn't quite make out what she said, but assumed she told him not to respond.

Moses Sun tried to fill the uneasy void by changing the subject. "The Daughters of the Confederacy now have custody of the Wilmington Confederate monument, after Black Lives Matter protests in 2020. North Carolina has a law protecting historical statues, but the City of Wilmington got around that on a technicality. They established that the original monument belonged to the Daughters of the Confederacy, making it privately owned and excluded from the statute."

"Removing tributes to our soldiers doesn't sit well with me," Reagan's dad interjected. "We need to honor those who served. Just because they lost the war doesn't mean their sacrifice should be forgotten."

Reagan's mom nodded in agreement. Reagan would have agreed with them in the past. As she learned about her own mixed heritage, she could no longer condone the Confederacy. A war raged within as she listened to her parents and Moses Sun. She avoided expressing her thoughts by asking, "Priscilla, what do you think?"

Priscilla laughed nervously. Did Priscilla share Reagan's internal conflict? "I don't know what I think," Priscilla said. "The plantation system was evil. I have ancestors who were enslaved. The Confederates fought to protect their right to hold slaves and continue making money with the plantation system. I think you have slave ancestors, too, Mr.

Hunter-Smith. Doesn't it bother you?"

Reagan's dad's face turned red as a beet, but he didn't answer.

"Don't upset him, please," Reagan's mother requested. She put her hand on his shoulder and said, "It's okay, honey."

Mr. Hunter-Smith's face relaxed and he regained his composure. "My ancestors helped build the South. They were wise entrepreneurs. Don't try to rewrite history."

Reagan opened her mouth wide at her father's denial and Priscilla's courage. Priscilla said exactly what she should have said, and she would have said it if Welby was by her side. She worried too much about her father's reaction. How could he ignore the truth? "Let's change the subject," she proposed. "This is not the time for this conversation. I can tell Daddy's not going to let this go." She turned to Abigail across the table. "Tell him about our garden tours, Abigail."

"You mean the plantations?" Abigail asked.

"Oh, no." Reagan's heart dropped into her stomach. How could she be so focused on the flower, forgetting the fact that the places were former places of torture for the slaves? And she also wondered what they could discuss that wouldn't bring up more rants by her father or protests from herself.

"It's okay, Reagan," Abigail said. "Remember our listening circles in Ireland? Maybe we need to just take some time to listen to each other, rather than trying to all agree on everything? In fact, I have the listening stick in my purse. Let's pass it around and let each person have a chance to share what the trip has meant to them. Then we'll also let your parents and Moses Sun to tell us something they've been thinking about recently. How does that sound?"

Reagan's dad put his thumbs up. "Reagan, why don't you go first?"

Abigail stepped in. "How does this sound to the rest of you?" Those at the end of the table didn't hear the initial proposal, so she repeated the idea. Soon, everyone agreed to go along, with some good-natured grumbling.

Abigail removed the listening stick from her bag and held it herself, rather than passing it to Reagan, which caused Reagan great relief. "For me, this trip has been a learning experience. I gained new respect for the Gullah people, how they brought their culture to a new land and kept it going, within the limited framework permitted. That their culture survived through three hundred years of slavery into the present day is amazing as well. I have some new recipes I want to try out and some books I want to read, that the MAMs can read." She passed the stick to Jane, sitting beside her.

Jane took the stick, but didn't say anything. She seemed to be thinking. Usually, Jane had a quick comment ready for almost anything, but now, she stalled. "We're divided. It's the truth. I'm not sure anymore what the solution might be." She passed the stick to Molly.

"Well, it's hard to tour the South without racism rearing its ugly head. You all saw what happened to Welby. That's just the tip of the iceberg and it's been going on here for generations. As a Black woman, I'm angry. I'm ready for this to stop. Black Lives Matter? Hell, yes. But now you got all those white folks wanting to pretend we don't have a problem. They're all concerned about worrying the children about it. They want to keep history out of the schools and that's very dangerous, because history will repeat itself if you don't educate yourself to learn from your mistakes. That's what scares me."

Mr. Hunter Smith started to mutter something under his breath.

"Do you want the stick?" Abigail asked him. "We'd like to hear what you said."

Reagan's mother shook her head rather emphatically. Reagan held her breath as her dad leaned forward toward Molly with an extended hand. Abigail grabbed the stick from Molly and passed it into Mr. Hunter-Smith's open hand.

"What they want to do is teach our children to hate. That's what's wrong. Put that critical race theory in our schools and get the kids all riled up and thinking they've done something wrong. That's what we're against. You just don't teach children that way."

Reagan thought her father seemed surprisingly calm. Maybe he could have this conversation without blowing up and jeopardizing his heart. Maybe she shouldn't worry so much.

He passed the stick to Seamus. "I be a-learning about the Troubles here in the States on this trip. Ya know we have the Troubles in Ireland, too, with our divisions between the North and South, the British Loyalists and the Irish Nationalists. Back home, it's not about the color of your skin. I know how divided a people can get. But you must build a bridge, just like Abby and me are constructing a road across the ocean between our hearts. You must try. It can be done, but it takes hard work."

Molly started humming a song. Seamus passed the stick across the table to her "Remember this song?" Then she began to sing, "'Love can build a bridge between your heart and mine.'"

"Don't you think it's time?" Sallie chimed in with her off-key voice. "Don't you think it's time."

With that, the group erupted into laughter, bringing some levity to the otherwise difficult conversation. When the group quieted, Katharine began to speak. "Touring the South, yes, you see the evil of slavery and the ways some white people continue to treat African Americans as second class citizens, but you also see the triumph of a people who couldn't be kept down. You see the Gullah culture bringing lively music, art, and food into the present day. You see the community of color and the Black churches which birthed the civil rights movement. And more than that, you see love, the love that binds people together that refused to respond to hate with hate, that continues to teach and preach the love of Jesus. Like Michele Obama once said, 'When they go low, we go high.' I stand on the side of love."

"Amen to that!" Reagan's dad lifted his glass and touched it to the side of Moses Sun's glass. Moses Sun held his glass up and said, "Cheers to all." Then he stood and walked the short distance to where Priscilla sat. Reagan wondered what he was up to now, not sure she wanted to know.

"Could I have that stick?" he asked.

Molly tossed it over to him. "Priscilla, would you stand up for a moment?" he requested. Priscilla seemed reluctant, but he pulled out her chair and she complied.

"Now what?" she asked.

Moses Sun dropped to one knee, pulled a little box out of his pocket, and placed the stick on the floor beside him. "My dear Priscilla, I've followed you around the world. We've had hard times, but more good times. Remember the happy times? Like when we toured the churches, taking the story of the scrolls you ladies found in Turkey. I've made mistakes. We all sin and fall short of the glory of God. But Priscilla, I want to make it all up to you. Will you do me the great honor of becoming my wife?"

Reagan watched the color drain from Prisicilla's face as she wobbled and grabbed the table for support. The nurse in Reagan kicked in. "Let her sit down," she told Moses. "She's as white as a ghost."

"My pretty white lady, you are so beautiful to me," Moses said, oblivious to the problem.

Reagan gave him a piece of her mind. "She's not all white, Moses, but that's beside the point. I'm a nurse. She looks ready to faint. Please, pull that chair back out and let her sit down before she falls."

Only then did Moses grasp the situation. He pulled the chair out. Priscilla sat back down. "Are you okay, dear?" he asked.

Priscilla closed her eyes and dropped her head.

"Priscilla!" Reagan said in a firm voice and rushed to her side. She picked up a glass of water and touched Priscilla's head. "Here, drink some water. It will help." As Priscilla took a drink, Moses Sun returned to his seat.

"Well, that went over real well," he complained to Mr. Hunter-Smith.

"Women!" Reagan's dad exclaimed. "Can't live with them, can't live without them. Give her some space. She'll come around. Did you tell her about your inheritance?"

"I haven't had the chance," Moses answered. "She kicked me to the curb back in Ohio and when I showed up at Cypress Gardens, she called the police. I know she's running scared because her father left her mother years ago. She never got over it."

"Like I said," Mr. Hunter-Smith insisted, "give her time."

Priscilla drank the water, but kept her head down and didn't look at Moses Sun.

"Isn't this when you're supposed to give me an answer? Priscilla?" Moses Sun said, speaking loudly. "I asked you a question, dear." He picked the stick up and handed it toward her. Molly passed it over to Priscilla. Priscilla took the stick with a shaking hand, still looking rather pale.

"I-I-I-I don't know," she responded. "This isn't the time or place for a proposal. You know that. I have nothing more to say."

"Don't push it," Reagan's dad whispered. "You'll lose ground the more you push."

Whew, Reagan thought. She noticed her dad didn't seem nonplussed by the whole scene. Probably he enjoyed the opportunity to tell someone what to do. He always relished calling the shots.

"Do the rest of us get the stick?" Sallie asked. "I want my turn."

Seamus winked. "We need to slow down here a wee bit. Let's just relax and enjoy our food. Save this conversation for another day."

Abigail nodded. Reagan felt relieved. She felt a whole lot better about letting it all go. The rest of the luncheon seemed anticlimactic after all the drama, but Reagan was perfectly okay with that. She could make small talk as well as the next person and that certainly was all she wanted to do with her parents at this point. Someday, she hoped they would revisit the problems, but not right now.

CHAPTER EIGHTEEN
AN AFTERNOON IN NORTH CAROLINA

Welby Visits the Pen

While the MAMs and the rest of the entourage headed for a fancy lunch and an afternoon at the beach, Welby took the back seat in a car George rented for the day, heading back to Pender, which he knew as the pen. With only thirty minutes to go, so many thoughts raced through his mind. First and foremost, he realized how much had changed for him since he left that place less than a year ago.

While the Mabra brothers shot the breeze in the front, Welby reviewed his notes and reflected on his life in the back. Today marked a new beginning. His calling to be a Martin Luther King, Jr. for the 21st century started now. Although it had really started in Ireland and he did speak a while back at the church in River City, speaking to the prisoners in North Carolina seemed a much bigger deal. Not for the first time, he doubted his ability to pull it off. Did a leprechaun really visit him? Did God really call him to do this?

"I'm real proud of you, Welby," George said, interrupting his self-doubt.

"Yes," Tom agreed. "We're both proud of you. You can talk to these guys like nobody else because you've been there. You know what it feels like to be stripped of your dignity and locked up. They'll listen to you. If I tried to get up there and talk to them as a retired cop, they would boo me off the stage."

"Thanks, guys, that helps," Welby responded, encouraged by their kind words. "I have to admit I'm beginning to doubt myself. Did God really call me to this, or did I make it up, wanting to be famous?"

George laughed. "You don't get famous being an ex-con, Welby. You're not trying to be a movie star. I see you wanting to speak up, speak out and make a difference. You want to address the problem of a racist system in this country. That's not going to make you popular. Remember, they killed Reverend Doctor Martin Luther King. If you hear this call, it's God. They killed Jesus, too."

"Will they kill me?" Welby asked, suddenly a little scared.

"You're certainly safe today," Tom said. "You know how tight security will be at Pender. I agree with George. You are trying to make a good difference. That's what God asks all of us to do. And we know working for the good is an uphill battle."

Welby fingered his notes, letting their affirmations sink in, calming his stage fright. "Could we say a prayer before we go in there?" he asked. "I know what I want to say. I know I have something to tell them, but part of me doesn't want to go back to the pen. It's going to freak me out. I may clam up when I get in there. What if they boo me off?"

"Sure, we'll have a prayer for you, but you're good," George said. "Let's do it now, before we get out of the car. Let's talk to God and ask that the Holy Spirit to go with you. You'll be fine. I promise. Trust the Lord."

Tom nodded. "After all you've been through, this is the easy part. Share what you learned. Give these guys a lifeline. You understand them. They'll sense that. You've got this, Welby."

"You are going to make their day, Marcus Welby Jones. Trust me," George encouraged. "Hey, we lined up a visit for you with your dad, if you want to go."

A thousand thoughts raced through his head while Welby felt his heart starting to race. "You did *what*?" he yelled at George. Why on earth would they do such a thing? They knew full well that Welby didn't talk to the man. For years, Welby ignored all his overtures and he had no intention of changing now.

"Difficult conversations are part of healing, Welby. The twelve steps are all about asking for forgiveness. You need to forgive him, Welby. You've sat through enough AA and NA meetings to know that full well. Your dad's no different than you, than all of us. He deserves a second chance, don't you think? I think it might do you some good." George nudged Tom. "But it's up to you. What d'ya think, Tom?"

"Always good to give people a second chance," Tom agreed. "Your dad's had more than enough time to think about everything he did wrong. He wrote to us, telling us he wants you to hear him out. You're right to be cautious. It could be all talk, but perhaps you'll be mighty pleased."

Then the psychic's words came back to Welby. Madame Diddy and her little house in Hilton Head materialized in his mind's eye. She told him that his father was a new man and to give him a second chance. She said he was getting out soon and wanted to share an inheritance with Welby. Welby didn't believe it, but what if it were true?

All of a sudden, he realized his dad might be in the chapel this afternoon. He always pictured speaking to some former fellow inmates and other unknown inmates, but the thought never crossed his mind that he could also be speaking to his own father. He didn't associate the pen with his dad who did serious time elsewhere. But recently, he got moved, and Welby knew that. Why did he never put the two together?

Not sure whether to be happy or sad, he gazed at the farmland rolling by. In a matter of minutes, they would arrive. He closed his eyes, folded his hands, and bowed his head. Only God could help him now.

An Afternoon at the Beach

Priscilla enjoyed the view out the window as their van cruised slowly along the bridge leading to Wrightsville Beach and an afternoon in the sun. The ocean rippled and sparkled in the distance, with waves crashing into the coast below. Abigail introduced the beach as their next destination, where they could watch surfers, walk on a famous fishing pier, and catch some rays on the sand. "Let's have some fun before we go home," she told them.

Separated from the mainland by this bridge, she said this little town served as a popular vacation mecca. Priscilla thought it looked more like a city than a beach. Large buildings lined both sides of the divided road leading out to the ocean. She imagined they held condos and places for people to stay, but, still, it didn't seem like a beach to her.

Abigail took the microphone. "Wrightsville Beach was named after Tylerua Wright, of Wilmington, who had a real estate company. If you're like me, you might have wondered if it was named after our Ohio Wright Brothers, because they did come down to North Carolina to fly their plane. But, no, Kitty Hawk, where they flew, is actually four hours north of here.

"In 1724, the Lord Proprietor of England gave Charles Harrison this land as a land grant. In 1881, the town of Wrightsville was established. In 1883, the Carolina Yacht Club formed on the island. In 1889, the Shell Road and bridge provided a better access from the mainland.

"This area is a high-risk hurricane zone and has weathered many storms. In 1899, two major hurricanes hit the island, devastating the community. Since then, scores of hurricanes have damaged this beach."

Priscilla half-listened to Abigail, while rehashing events of the day. Did Moses Sun actually propose? That was the very last thing she expected, and so hard to comprehend. It left her reeling. Ten years ago, she wanted a ring from him so badly.

Old feelings for the man stirred in her heart. Did fear stand in the way of her happiness or did fear warn her of danger lurking in the shadows? She honestly didn't know.

At the end of the causeway, they crossed another body of water. Priscilla enjoyed the boats lined up in the dock and admired the large mansions, each with their own walkway out to the sea. A long fishing pier extended out into the ocean, which must be what Abigail mentioned. They followed signs for beach parking, soon stopping a short distance from the water.

As Seamus turned off the van, Moses Sun pulled in right beside them in the next parking spot. Priscilla's heart dropped.

"You have a couple hours to explore," Abigail said. "FARM women, you're with Jane and Molly today. Solar House men, you will explore with Seamus and me. Priscilla, Katharine, and Sallie, you can join one of our groups or explore on your own. Be back at the van at four thirty p.m. Tonight, when Welby, George, and Tom return, we have a sunset dinner cruise booked, but first, we'll be checking into our accommodations for the night. It's hard to believe we head home tomorrow!"

Sallie spoke up. "Abigail, I'd like to hang out with you and Seamus and the guys."

"Sure, no problem," Abigail responded.

"I think I'll go with the women," Katharine announced.

Priscilla hesitated. "Moses Sun just pulled up." She pointed to his car.

Seamus stepped in. "Priscilla, do you want me to tell him to leave? You do not have to talk to the man."

Priscilla thought about it. "No, I think I need to tell him how I really feel. He obviously hasn't heard me, or doesn't want to accept reality, but it's time. How about we trail along with you guys? Keep an eye on us. Check in from time to time." Okay, maybe I'm sure of myself after all, Priscilla thought, as she heard herself speak.

"Sure, no problem," Abigail agreed. "Seamus and I will stay at the back of the group. You can trail us. We're all here for you, Priscilla. Sound good?"

"Thanks," Priscilla agreed, then lingered in the van, feeling hesitant. She remembered tucking her sneakers in her backpack and decided to put them on. Certainly no one would fault her for wearing them in the sand. How could she possibly manage on heels in the sand, anyway? She didn't like what it would do to her overall appearance, but sometimes sacrifices were necessary. Surely her mother would understand. When she finally stepped down after making the change, Moses Sun stood in front of the door, offering her a hand.

"Welcome to Wrightsville Beach, my lady," he said. He firmly wrapped her hand around the inside of his arm. "Shall we explore?"

"Thanks for the help down, but I'm good. You can let go." Priscilla removed her hand off his arm. "I came to enjoy the beach. I'm tagging along with Abigail and Seamus and the men on our trip. What are you doing here, Moses? I didn't invite you."

"Priscilla, I just asked you to marry me. I want a proper answer. I'm not about to leave you alone."

"I don't want to marry you, Moses."

He looked uncomfortable. Rather than acknowledging her assertion, he asked, "Can I join you for a walk on the beach then?"

"Why? This is my vacation. I didn't invite you here." Priscilla realized she really disliked the man.

"Humor me, Priscilla. Let's just relax and have a good time."

Priscilla didn't want to cause a scene. "Okay, but only if you behave."

They fell in behind the group. Priscilla appreciated her sneakers, glad she'd thought to change out of her heels.

Moses Sun began to talk. "When I was younger, I spent some summers near here with my cousins. It's been a while, but I still know my way around. Nothing beats walking along the beach and watching the tide flow in. Hey, let's go out on that fishing pier, then find a place to sit and have some iced tea and catch up."

Priscilla let out a breath she didn't realize she held. At least Moses didn't badger her about her response to his proposal. A walk in the ocean air would help clear her mind.

"I'll check with the others," she told him. She took a conscious deep breath in, inhaling the saltwater air and cool breeze coming off the water. It cleared her sinuses, if nothing else. As she let the breath out, she tried to let go of her fears and concerns. She wanted to enjoy their afternoon and see where it led.

Priscilla caught up with Abigail and Seamus. "Moses suggested walking out on the fishing pier, along the beach, and then find a place for some drinks."

"Aye, that sounds like a nice afternoon," Seamus replied. "If the guys want to do something else, we could make it a foursome." He put his arm around Abigail. "A little double date for us all?"

Priscilla frowned. She didn't think of this as a date. "Yes, check with them. Maybe we can all just stay together," she suggested.

Seamus and Abigail caught up with Sallie and the group home guys, while Moses used the opportunity to talk. "You got a little hot under the collar at lunch, Priscilla. That's not like you. What's happening to the sweet, politically correct Priscilla? Why did you come down on Mr. Hunter-Smith so hard?"

Moses' question brought a realization to Priscilla that he had no idea. How could she explain to him what she only was beginning to understand herself? Her inner turmoil seemed to increase rather than subside. She didn't want to get into all of it with Moses right now.

"Cat got your tongue?" Moses asked. "Did they tell you that you have African DNA, honey? Could that be a lie? Don't you think Democrats want to confuse us like that? They started the pandemic to make the president look bad."

Priscilla wanted to explain the trip to Moses, but he couldn't understand. Conspiracy theorists are crazy. "Moses, come on. Think for yourself. Don't believe everything you hear. Why would someone start a pandemic that has taken millions of lives? It's clear it originated in China, probably a freak of nature," Priscilla countered.

"Have the MAMs pulled you over to the other side, Priscilla? What happened to you?" he questioned.

"I'd rather not argue, Moses," Priscilla said, proud of herself for cutting him off in a nice way. Today, she wanted to enjoy the beach. She'd be back at work in a few days and didn't want her last memory of the trip to be a fight with Moses Sun. Clearly, she would not be saying yes to him anytime soon.

Seamus and Abigail returned. "The guys want to stay together. First stop, the fishing pier! We're almost there."

"Great," Priscilla responded. "Thank you." Then she turned to Moses. "You ever go fishing down here, Moses?"

"Oh, yeah," Moses shared. "First thing every morning, we headed out to the pier before it got too hot. I've spent hours fishing on this pier."

"What do you like about fishing? Isn't it gross, catching them? They don't smell very good," Priscilla said, letting out her feelings for the great American pastime.

"Ah, but we're doing something worthwhile, catching food for the family. There's nothing quite like a tug on your line, then reeling in a whopper."

Priscilla tried to imagine the younger version of Moses, waiting for a fish to bite. It took her mind off the elephant between them.

Moses changed the subject. "I just got elected precinct captain for the Republicans in River County."

"Oh, that's nice," Priscilla said. "You decided to serve the country?"

"We must maintain control," Moses asserted. "That last election was stolen. We can't let that happen again. We need to make sure these elections turn out right."

Priscilla cringed. Why were they trying to pretend they won the last election when all the numbers added up otherwise? She didn't agree with their plan to take control and make sure the results came out right, regardless of how the people voted. They aimed to steal the election one way or another and Moses Sun wanted to help.

"Mr. Hunter Smith and I are working on getting more of our people in place, so we don't have an election stolen from us again," he said.

"That's not democracy," Priscilla countered.

"Oh, baby, let's get real," Moses argued back. "You know we can't let those immoral Democrats take over, with those criminal Mexicans and the illegals and gays. That's not what God wants for the United

States of America."

Priscilla looked out over the water, wondering how to respond. In the past, she believed that the Republicans were the moral ones, for sure, and that God wanted them in power. But she thought they needed to win that leadership fair and square. Keeping people from voting, trying to control the election was not the way she thought they should go about things.

"I don't get it," she finally told Moses. "It's not right to me. On the one hand, you say the last election was stolen when all the evidence shows that just didn't happen. Now you want to rig it so you can steal the election next time. It's sick thinking, Moses. It's not honest. That's not what God wants."

"Priscilla, what happened to you?" Moses' voice grew louder. "Are they brainwashing you on this trip? God is on our side. You know that!"

Thankfully, Abigail materialized at her side. "You okay?" she asked Priscilla.

Priscilla sighed and shrugged. "Moses and I don't see eye to eye anymore, Moses doesn't like it." She turned back to him. "You don't need to raise your voice to get your point across, Moses."

"God gave us vocal cords to use for emphasis." Moses laughed. "She'll come around, Abigail." He started humming the "Love can build a bridge" tune. "She just needs some time."

"We're arguing about politics," Priscilla said.

"Oh," Abigail said. "Hard to find agreement on that these days."

Seamus chimed in. "How 'bout we catch some photos of us all at the end of the pier? Let's remember we're tourists here."

The photo shoot occupied them all for the next several minutes as groupings were captured by the water at the end of the pier. Seamus tried out a new camera, calling directions and snapping shot after shot. Then the group found a small café for cold drinks and shakes, and they settled in on Adirondack chairs to watch the waves and soak in some rays. Priscilla sat beside Abigail and Seamus, which kept Moses from revisiting the previous conversation, or any of a more personal nature as well, which made her very happy.

Priscilla began to sort out her feelings and clarity returned. Madame Biddy was right. Moses Sun was not the man she once thought would be her husband. She wanted to steer clear of any future romantic involvement. He wasn't the kind of Republican that she could support. She made a decision to bid him goodbye for good and refuse further communication.

Priscilla knew from experience that when one door closes, another opens. She wanted to learn more about the Gullah people on the African side of her family tree. She couldn't begin to figure out how this might change her life and perspective. Perhaps down the line, a man would come along. For now, sorting all this out would be more than enough to keep her occupied.

You Have a Dream

George's big hand covered Welby's scalp and his other massaged the back of his shoulder. Tom grasped Welby's hands in his. They stood in a small huddle, bowing their heads in the prison parking lot. George led. "Now, Jesus, we know you walk with the sinners and you came to set them free, and you are right here with us in this moment. Thank you, thank you, Jesus. Thank you for your son, Welby, who answered your call to rise up, serve, speak and inspire. Thank you, Jesus, for Welby. Thank you that he heard your voice and wants to speak your Word to these men today. Cover him with your Spirit. Give him words they can hear. May he feel your love as he shares your love with these men, so thirsty for the living water you give."

"Yes, Lord," Tom chimed in. "Thank you, thank you, thank you for Welby. Thank you for his journey that brought him to this place. As he returns to this prison which held him down for five long years, may he soar with your love as he inspires these men to believe they can dream again. We know, Lord, that you care about each and every one of them and you want them to live an abundant life. Use your man Welby to speak to them today. We pray in the name of Jesus who teaches us to always forgive, who never gives up on us, who shows us the way of love. Amen and Amen."

"Whew, boy," George said as he gave Welby a hug and lifted his hands. "If you didn't feel the Spirit there, you gotta be completely unplugged. God is showing up for you, Welby."

Welby laughed. "You got that right. Thanks, man. I do feel the Spirit. Thanks for your prayers. You guys are the best." Then a thought came to mind. "Hey, you know you can't take anything into the prison with you. No wallets, no cellphones. Better lock them up in the van before we go."

"Oh, okay," George replied. "I didn't realize that." He pulled his wallet and cell phone out of his pocket and opened the glove compartment, placing them within and stood back to give Tom and Welby room to put their belongings in as well.

"What about keys?" Tom asked.

"Best to leave them here," Welby instructed. "But, of course, George needs a key, so I'm not sure if they'll keep that or not, until we come out. Hey, we need our IDs, though."

"Good call," George agreed. He reopened the glove compartment, handing out wallets. They pulled out their IDs and then stuffed the wallets back in the compartment. And with that task completed, they headed over to the prison.

Welby felt remarkably calm, poised and ready. Yes, he could do this. He could walk right back in that place he hoped never to see again. He felt a spring in his step, even surrounded by barbed wire fences, a drab compound, and concrete buildings, sprawled out over several acres. Welby knew this place like the back of his hand. Nevertheless, he took a deep breath as they approached the gate.

The prison guard greeted them stiffly, requesting they remove everything from their pockets. He placed a bowl on a conveyor belt to go through the screening machine. Then they each walked into a metal detector door frame, facing a plastic wall with their hands over their head, until the guard motioned them out where they were frisked physically by another guard. Welby remembered the routine all too well. Last time, he came in here in handcuffs, the beginning of a very long incarceration. Fortunately, this time, he would be out in a matter of hours.

After they passed through physical screening, they encountered another guard behind a desk for further examination. "What brings you here for today?" he asked.

"Speaking at the chapel," George answered for them all.

"All three of you?" the guard asked.

"No, Welby here is speaking. Tom and I are just along for support," George answered. "We filled out your screening form online and have been approved for this visit." He pulled out his driver's license, along with the most recent email about their visit.

The guard asked for Tom and Welby's IDs as well, then turned to his computer. He typed a few things and then stared at the screen. He turned to Welby. "You've been an inmate here, Marcus?" he asked.

"Yes, sir," Welby replied.

"Don't try anything. We usually don't permit former inmates back in for five years. The chaplain requested a special accommodation this time, seeing as you are going to speak in the chapel. We are assigning a guard to be with you at all times. We know you're still on parole and any missteps could land you right back in this pen. Understand?"

"Yes, sir, I aim to do right. I'm only here to speak today. Believe me, I wouldn't want to come back here," Welby said, somewhat nervously. He didn't know they were going to put him under such scrutiny, making him feel like a criminal all over again. He hated this place, that much, he knew for certain. He wondered what would they consider stepping out of line. He certainly didn't want to cross it. He would mind his Ps and Qs and keep a low profile.

"Okay, then," the guard said. "Go to the building straight ahead to check in, and they'll direct you to the chapel."

It felt so strange to enter the pen as a free man, hoping to serve, knowing that in an hour or two, he'd be back out in the free world. He watched families waiting, remembering that whole process all too well. But before he could go down that hole, a guard called their names and led them to the chapel.

As he walked, memories flooded into Welby's consciousness, such as the familiar cadence of footfalls on these paths, often single file, under watchful eyes and absolute control. Now, the guard made small talk about the weather, which seemed to be shaping up to another nice day.

At the sight of the brick chapel, more memories surfaced. Back then, it provided an escape, one more way to get out of the cell block for a few. He enjoyed brief encounters there with people from the outside world, not that he paid them much mind. No, in fact, he was so mad at God, he didn't hear much of anything.

Welby really hoped he would break through to the guys, but imagined some of them would be as shut down as he used to be. When you're stuck in prison, you don't see much light, let alone hope and dreams. It had taken everything he had to make it through each day. He focused on what was right in front of his face, and none of it was good.

Sun streamed in through the chapel windows. Today, he could actually sense the presence of God again, something he never felt in this place back in the day. The place looked the same. The same building, the same wooden pews, the same room, but what changed? Suddenly, Welby got it. He himself changed and that made everything new.

In the front of the chapel, the guard introduced them to the prison chaplain, Rev. Brown, a large man with a kind face and a clerical collar. The pastor smiled, nodded at George and Tom, and then extended his hand to Welby. "Welcome, Welby," he said, with a firm handshake. "I don't believe we've met."

"You new?" Welby asked.

"Yes, just started last month," the reverend replied. "Thank you so much for coming. It's a very special day in the chapel when one of our own comes back to preach. You probably know that this doesn't happen very often. Actually, they don't allow much, and never before five years out. I got them to bend the rules for you. The men will be hanging on your every word."

"Wow," Welby replied. "You're right. I don't remember hearing a former inmate speak when I did my time." He paused. The gravity of the situation sunk in. "I'll do my best, Rev. I have a lot to be thankful for. I hope some of them will have the opportunity to begin again like me. I owe a lot to these guys, Tom and George Mabra. Their Sun Power House up in Ohio has made all the difference for me."

George disagreed. "Welby, you made the difference. You listened to God. You've answered the call. We provided the opportunity, but this is on you. Maybe you can recruit some of them to join us."

Welby felt a light come on deep inside. Some of these guys could come to Ohio? He grinned. "Yes, that would be way cool."

The chaplain looked at his watch. "The men will be coming in anytime now. Let's get your lavalier mic set up and do a sound check."

Welby pulled his notes out of his pocket and placed them on the lectern. "Will I speak here?" he asked.

"Yes," Rev. Brown responded. "But feel free to move around, it's a remote mic." He turned on the microphone box and tucked the little apparatus into Welby's shirt pocket, fastening the small microphone on his collar. "Try it out. Say something."

Welby led out, "Testing one-two-three. Welby here, reporting for duty." He laughed.

"Sounds good," the chaplain responded, giving him a thumbs up. "I'm turning off the mic, so feel free to talk. Why don't you guys sit here in the first row, and I'll call you up when it's time."

Part of Welby wanted to watch the inmates filing in, but then he decided to use the time to review his notes and say a few more prayers. In the back of his mind, he also realized he might be seeing his father for the first time in over twenty years, and he didn't quite know how he felt about that. Would he even recognize the man? Some men aged quickly in the pen. He asked God for help. He heard what George and Tom said loud and clear about giving his dad a second chance, and he knew Madame Biddy had some truth in her words, too. He just had to try a little harder to find some forgiveness in his heart. Everybody deserved forgiveness, that was God's grace. Deep down, he knew he couldn't withhold the grace he so freely received himself.

Welby felt goosebumps from the clear answer that flooded into his heart with the morning sun sparkling on the cross. He would meet with his dad, because that's what love requires. God gave that second chance to everyone. Behind him, he heard the door open and footsteps clumping up the aisle. He turned his head to see the seats beginning to fill. He looked for a familiar face, for his father. The men looked haggard and worn. He didn't see his dad, but recognized a few faces, greeting them with nods.

He turned back to read over his notes one more time and then just slipped into silence, asking God for the words to move the mountains of resistance within the men's hearts.

The next few minutes were a blur as the chapel filled. He turned around again, just as his father entered the chapel. Definitely an older version of the man, with grey hair, and wrinkles around his eyes. His prison suit hung on his frame like he'd lost some weight, but even from a distance, he could recognize that face anywhere.

Their eyes connected and something surged through Welby's whole body, scaring him as much as he suspected it was the love he needed to share, that perhaps his father was sharing with him. When his dad sat in the very last row, Welby turned back around as the pastor opened with prayer. The piano player led out with an old spiritual, "It's a me, it's a me, it's a me oh Lord, standin' in the need of prayer." Welby sang loud and clear, no cat holding his tongue this time. The old Welby sat many days in this very place, clammed up like a shell, refusing to sing, but not anymore.

The pastor introduced Welby, and although he wanted to crawl under the pew at the kind words, he figured the warm intro might make his dad proud. Still, Welby felt embarrassed.

George patted him on the back. "Be proud, Welby." Could the man read his mind? "You came a long way. You chose to follow Jesus. You've only just begun. Now go do us proud."

Welby grabbed his notes, took a deep breath, and closed the short distance between the front row and the lectern. He shook the reverend's hand. "Let's pray," the good pastor said and laid his hand on Welby's shoulder, still holding his other hand. "Lord, we give thanks for your servant, Marcus Welby Jones, who follows you. Thank you, Jesus, for his new life. Thank you that he came to speak your Word to these good men today. Open his mouth to tell us your truth. Open his heart and set it on fire. We pray in the name of Jesus. Amen."

Now it was his turn. Welby placed his notes on the lectern and looked out over the crowded sanctuary at the upturned faces. Black faces, brown faces and a few white here and there, all focused on him. He saw himself in those faces, and as he scanned the large room, again his eyes met his father in the back row. He looked at the weathered face, remembering the pain the man brought to his life. Could the old codger really change? God knows he waited and stalled long enough. Another hour or two wouldn't matter at this point, but it did tug at his heart, knowing that his dad would be listening to his every word.

Welby wasted no time, but spoke out boldly. "Good morning, good sirs. Good morning. Thank you for coming to listen to me today. Not too long ago, I was sitting right out there with you. I know it's not much fun. You're probably glad you got out of the cell block this afternoon. That's the way I used to look at this place. Never paid much attention to whatever horse and buggy show they dragged in here. I'd heard it all before. Not much use in telling me again. Back then, I didn't even listen. Nope, I tuned out, spending chapel time looking out those windows and considering freedom and what I was going to do when I got out. I know you may not pay me any mind, but I'm here because God gave me some words for you, and because you got possibilities. Your life ain't over just because you're locked up. I'm here to tell you that you've got a better day coming. The sun is shining, right here at Penwell Correctional Institution. That same sun that will be shining when you get out. Your new day doesn't have to wait until you're out. It can start right now, right here, in this place, in this time.

"Let me tell you my story. They call me Welby, not Marcus Welby Jones, unless my mom was yelling at me. You know how that goes?" Welby laughed. Guffaws rippled through the sea of faces out there. Maybe they were going to listen. "Yep, I'm Welby. I grew up playing in the waves and enjoying summers with my Grand Ma Ma, not too far from here. My mother wanted me to be a doctor with that crazy name she gave me. I didn't intend to be no doctor, TV or otherwise. Now, don't get me wrong, I used to be a good boy back then. They put me up in front of the sanctuary and told me to preach it and I did. Before I even hit my teenage years. I was a child preacher, a prodigy, they thought." Welby slipped into his old child preaching routine. "Say amen, brother." Then he clapped and put his head down. "Let me hear you all out there, say amen!"

Just like in the good ole days, the responses came right back, "Amen!" The cacophony of loud voices sounded real good and was what he needed to keep him going on.

"Yes, sir, you got it. I hear you. I hear you, stay with me now." Then Welby let it all out. He told the men how he got sent up to Raleigh to take care of his father's children and how his world fell apart and how, before long, he fell right down with it. "Now, I don't think they treated me right, and I imagine some of you out there got the raw end of the stick, too. And sometimes when everybody's against you, you start to turn on all of them. I was one angry dude." He stopped a minute to check on his dad, whose face bore a grimace and he didn't meet Welby's eye. "Eventually, my dad got thrown in prison, and I got to live with my aunt and uncle who cared about me, they really did. I straightened out to some extent. After high school, I started driving a truck and I enjoyed the women, wine, and songs, you got the picture? I had a nice little lady, and we used some recreational drugs now and then. I wouldn't say I was an addict, but I always had some weed and coke on hand for special occasions, kept it right in the glove compartment, in fact. And when that highway patrolman pulled me over one day, there it was, right in plain view when my sorry ass opened the glove compartment for him to see.

"You know, we Black men don't always know our rights. I sure had no idea about searches and seizures and what they were allowed and not allowed to do. I've learned a lot since back then, and maybe you have, too. I spent hours reading here. *The New Jim Crow*? Any of you read that?" A few hands went up, but not too many. "Yes, well, I suggest you all get your hands on a copy or ask somebody to tell you about it. You need to know that the War on Drugs was nothin' more than a very tactical plan to throw Black men into prison. Lock us all up. They executed their scheme mighty well, didn't they? Illegal searches and seizures became legal. The feds armed the local police, decking them out with riot gear and everything needed to take us into custody.

"Now, I'm not sayin' we're saints. I'm not. I know most of you aren't either. But we also know the color of our skin says a whole heck of a lot about whether or not we end up in this place.

"When I got picked up, I was just minding my own business, driving down the highway, not even speeding, and I got pulled over for driving while Black. The man found drugs in the glove compartment and here I come, locked up in the pen for five long years.

"Was that fair? No, absolutely not! Nothing fair about the situation and I knew it. Like I said before, I was one angry dude for a very long time. Maybe you feel the same way. How many of you don't think you should be locked up?"

The majority of the men raised their hands, and several called out, "Say it, brother," "Don't you know it," "Amen and amen!" He scanned the back row, noticing his dad hung his head and his hands remained in his lap. Maybe the guy did repent, Welby thought.

When the affirmations died down, Welby smiled. He loved the way the Black church had always welcomed him as a young preacher. These grown men, locked up here, still knew how to treat a preacher. He could make an educated guess that most of them started out their lives sitting in pews, just like Welby. Now, all he needed to do was to bring them back home.

"Oh, man, you got it," he told the men. "Yes, you got it goin' on. You're here with me, ain't you? You hear me. You know it. You know I'm tellin' the truth, because you've lived it just like me. But I'm here today to tell you it doesn't need to be that way. I'm here to call you to wake up and do something new. Yes, sir, I hope today will be the day you change your life."

Welby looked out and knew the men were with him. He heard a few answering him back. "All right, then." "Okay, then." "Tell it, brother."

"Well, yes, I was drivin' down the highway with some drugs in my glove compartment, but what I didn't tell you was that I also carried explosives back in the trunk that they never found, because they didn't need them to send me away. But I fully intended that day to blow up the headquarters of the fossil fuel folks who been messing with our schools in North Carolina, heating up our Earth and trying to pull the wool over our eyes. Don't get me started. But I know full and well that if I followed through with my plans, I might've killed myself and, if not, I know I wouldn't be standing here today.

"Actually, I got off easy. Five years and then I got my freedom back. When I got out, they offered me a place at a group home in Ohio called the Sun Power House. They told me I could learn a trade, how to install solar panels, and get my head screwed back on right. The Lord done saved me again, and I give him all the glory."

Sweat poured off Welby's head. That always seemed to happen when he got worked up. He paused. He took his handkerchief out of his pocket and wiped off his face, trying not to waste too much time. He didn't want to lose the guys.

"You with me?" he asked. He saw the heads nodding and hands going up.

"We hear you," one man said. "Yes, sir!" another yelled. "Tell it, brother," a third cried.

Encouraged by their words, Welby continued. "Yes, I got saved from something a whole lot worse that day. And when my auntie found Sun Power House for me, I really hit the jackpot. George and Tom Mabra, could you stand please?"

George and Tom stood and waved to the men.

"These are my rocks, George and Tom Mabra. They've got my back. We've been to Ireland together. They invited me to their church. And on our trip to Ireland on a silent retreat in this little place run by Catholic nuns, God spoke to me through a leprechaun. And you may think I'm crazy, but now I'm goin' back to school and to seminary someday and I'm goin' to be a bona fide preacher and I have my hero, the Reverend Doctor Martin Luther King, Junior, who is showing me the way. You know what he said? I think you all know. 'I have a dream.' And I do, and I want you to have a dream, too.

"If you're anything like me, you quit dreamin' long ago. I know I did. But today is your day to dream again. I want you to shake out those old dreams and pull them out of your sleeves and bring them into the light of day. I want you to say with me, out loud, now, all of you. 'I have a dream.' Please stand and say it now. Let's say it together. I want to hear you." Then he paused and led out, putting his hands up like he was a choir director. "I have a dream."

Murmurs bubbled through the sanctuary as the men began to stand. He checked on his dad in the back row, who sure enough was rising along with the others. He even punched his right arm up in the air, his lips moved in sync with the crowd. Soon, the inmates throughout the sanctuary were giving themselves a standing ovation, expressing hope.

Welby heard them all loud and clear. Their volume rose, almost lifting off the roof, as the men chanted, "I have a dream! I have a dream! I have a dream!" They stomped and they yelled. Welby cheered along, leading all in the affirmation that meant they each had a future. Welby felt real good because he knew he'd broke through into their hearts by getting them all up and speaking out their truth. At times like this, you could feel hope rising and he wished it for them all.

And then the door to the chapel opened and in walked ten more guards. Now, in addition to Welby's personal guard, and the ten guards already stationed along the aisles, the watchmen lined the back wall, with two in front of the door. One of them yelled, "Keep it down or you're going back to your cells."

Welby considered his options. One moment, he flew high on their excitement and willingness to dream again; the next moment, all seemed squashed flat, like a fly beneath a swatter. The reality of the situation and their confinement sank in. He decided to act quickly, with respect. "Thank you, kind sirs. You may be seated. Thank you for doing that chant with me. Yes, I thank you for taking a moment out of your sorry time here to stand up and raise your voices to the possibilities of your life.

"Now I want you to consider this day to be the first day of the rest of your life. Go back to your cell and write that down somewhere, I have a dream. Etch it in your mind, if you don't have any paper. I want you to carve it into your soul. But don't stop there, no, don't just stop there. I want you to actually begin dreaming again about who you want to be and what you want your life to become.

"Now, we all know that there are a lot of people in this country who want to say we're no good. If you're Black, then go back. Once you get out, you know and I know we're branded as ex-offenders. It's like you've got a tattoo on your forehead, saying you're scum of the earth. But today, I am here to tell you that is absolutely not true. First of all, God made each and every one of you and God doesn't make junk, no, sir." Welby looked directly at his dad and paused to let the words sink in. If he said it out loud, perhaps he would start to believe it when it came to his dad. And, if not for him, Welby never would have seen the light of day. "Each and every one of you is special. Each of you have gifts and each of you have the potential to make a difference in this world.

"Now, I know you may not be following Jesus and the Golden Rule, but God will forgive you. You can start over right now and intend to do right. I believe in you. I know that you can turn over a new leaf right here today. This can be your beginning of a brand-new day.

"Now, don't be shy. I'm not going to ask you to come down front, but I am asking you all to close your eyes now for a prayer. If you want to ask God to forgive you, if you want to turn over a new leaf to discover the dream God has for your life, I ask you to raise your hand."

Heads bowed throughout the sanctuary, and hands began to go up. At first, there were just a few here and there, but Welby couldn't quite believe his eyes as the place filled with raised hands. Certainly not every single man, but a large majority sat with eyes closed and a hand up, including his dad in the back row. Did that mean his dad still needed to turn over a new leaf, or that he was looking for a new dream? Was it possible for him to become a good father this late in the game? Welby paused that thought and concentrated on his task at hand.

"I see you," Welby told them. "God sees you. Praise God. You can put your hands down now." Then Welby began to pray. "Now, dear Lord, we thank you this afternoon for each of these men who want to dream again. We ask you to forgive their sins. May they feel washed clean by your love. Now, if they need to make amends to some people, I pray that they will start writing letters and reaching out to those they've hurt to say they're sorry. Lay it on their hearts to make things right and to start to live by a rule of love, rather than hate.

"God, we know you want goodness and justice to roll down like a river. I pray that you would help these men feel the goodness of your love inside of their hearts. Help them to believe that they can be good again. Help them know they can do the right thing and rise up above the injustices that brought them here. Help them become the men you created them to be.

"Dear Lord, I pray over the next few days and months and during the rest of their sentences that they will figure out the dream you have for them. I pray that they take advantage of opportunities here to prepare them for getting out. I pray they will share their love with their families and friends on the outside. I pray they will be good to each other right here, inside these walls, too.

"God, I praise you and thank you for these men and their decisions to follow you this afternoon. May you walk with them and guide them and hold them in your love. I pray in the name of Jesus, Amen."

CHAPTER NINETEEN
FATHERS

Accolades for Welby

When Welby finished his speech at the chapel, you could hear a pin drop. Even the guards in the back seemed calm and in no hurry. He remembered praying earlier that he could deliver a good message, but the reception he received blew him away.

The chaplain filled the silence with an altar call. "Come all of you who are weary, come to Jesus. Confess your sins and be forgiven. Today, you can start a new life."

Welby blinked his eyes in amazement as whole pews of the inmates filed up to kneel and confess and accept Jesus anew in their lives. The Black pianist rolled out some heavy Southern gospel music as the men streamed up. The place felt like home as the familiar tunes caressed his soul. He helped out the chaplain, along with George and Tom, praying individually with the men as they came up, being careful not to make physical contact. Sending them back to the pews with words of peace. The guards in the back came up through the aisles now, to make sure no one started any funny business, but the prisoners were well-behaved for a change and seemingly as awestruck as Welby at the effect of his words. Welby kept pointing up to God, as the men, one after another, came up to thank him. One man slapped him on that back and said, "Great job."

A guard rushed over to intervene. Welby downplayed the slap. "He didn't mean nothin', just an affirmation, sir."

"You know the rules," the guard told the man. "You must leave. Back to your cell now."

"Jesus forgives and will bless you. Today is a new beginning," Welby told the man, while also praying a silent prayer that the guard would relent. "He's turning over a new leaf, sir. Can't he stay?"

To Welby's surprise, the guard agreed. "This is your warning. Next time, you're on lockdown."

The inmate quickly kneeled by Welby's side, bowing his head and murmured, "Thank you, Jesus," over and over.

Other men offered words of thanks. One told Welby, "Thank you, brother." Another said, "You understand." As the first line of men returned to their seats, more continued to come down. Several asked about signing up for the Sun Power House in Ohio. George took their names, and agreed to share their interest with the prison officials and the parole board.

Welby was incredibly happy. Today, he was living out his call. Time passed quickly. The altar call ended and the chaplain announced a final hymn of "All to Jesus I Surrender." The chaplain had a big smile on his face, too. Welby thanked God for inspiring the men. That's all he ever wanted to do, to help each of them begin to dream again, to believe they could turn over a new leaf, just as he did himself.

As the guards led the inmates back out of the chapel, Chaplain Brown thanked Welby for coming. "I hope you'll come back," he told him. "I've been here a while now, but I've never seen anything like this, not here, or any of the other prisons where I served. You've got a gift, Welby."

"You can say that again," Tom chimed in. "You were alive with the fire of the Spirit. God answered our prayers from out there in the parking lot, for sure."

"Yes, and Welby's hard work paid off," George added. "I know you put a lot of thought and time in what you said this afternoon. Thank you for taking your call seriously and working to deliver a great message. You do have a gift."

Welby blushed from all the praise and his face felt warm. "Thanks, guys. It felt like I was back home in the little church where I used to preach as a child. I could hear all those old people back then, talking back to me and egging me on. It made me realize that almost all of those men spent time in a church in their childhood, too. Did you hear them? They knew how to egg a preacher on."

"Yeah, man," George agreed. "Sounded just like back home, like when you preached at our church."

"It's got me to thinking," Welby continued. "If they all started out in church, how did they get where they are today? What's going wrong? Why aren't they law-abiding citizens? What happened?"

"It's not all their fault," George responded. "There's a lot going against a Black man in our society."

"Don't I know it." Welby hung his head. "We gotta change what's coming down."

Tom offered, "I agree, but that's not easy. No, that's not an easy thing at all."

The chaplain looked at his watch. "Did you say, George, you lined up a visit for Welby with his dad? You better be heading back to the main building before it's too late. They cut off visits at four and they'll need time to get him up."

"Oh, thanks." George looked at his watch. "We've got an hour. We better head out." He shook the chaplain's hand.

The chaplain gave Welby a hug. "Come back any time, brother. You are always welcome here."

Welby laughed. "After five years in this place, I really didn't want to come back. I know what you're saying, but you hear me?"

Pastor Brown chuckled. "I got you. Just saying we need people like you in here to give our men hope. You did an amazing job today."

"Give God the glory," Welby insisted.

"Well, you and God got it goin' on," the chaplain bantered back. He signaled the single guard left in the chapel. "Could you walk these fine men back to the main building and get Welby set up for a visit with his dad?"

"Sure thing," the guard responded, motioning to Welby, George, and Tom. "Come with me."

Once more, they walked across familiar grounds, heading back toward the visitation building. This time, Welby's thoughts focused on his father. He tried to remember something good about the man, but he couldn't conjure a single thing. On the other hand, he just preached to a room full of men probably as badass as his father. He remembered the look he exchanged with his dad in the chapel. As he considered his father as a new man, he had to smile. It sure would be nice to have a real father who wanted the best for him, one who could love him and actually celebrate his successes.

Reagan Pondering

Reagan enjoyed the beach, but her mind wandered to other things, like Welby at the prison and her father's strange visit and his connection with Moses Sun. She felt conflicted. In her childhood, art helped her escape. As the others frolicked along the water's edge, she sat back in a beach chair, playing with her cellphone. Skimming through photos from the past week, she searched for something to paint. When she returned to the FARM, she hoped to paint to memorialize this trip. Certainly, one of the marshes near the Pin Point Museum, where she'd enjoyed a stroll with Welby would be good. Maybe she could paint the Gullah woman who spoke at the plantation. She would also like to do a painting with gardens superimposed over plantations. Could she "sugarcoat" the evil, as Welby called it? She wanted to make a statement with her painting. Did she sound like Welby or what?

Reagan wondered about Welby at the prison. She really wanted to go along, or at least get a recording. But he said no cellphones were allowed, and no recordings either. That sort of thing would provide too much information to those on the outside who might try to help with escapes and uprisings, he said.

Her cellphone buzzed. She looked down in surprise and pushed the button. "Dad?"

"Wanted to let you know we arrived home safely. I won't be taking any more trips for a while, but I sure do hope you'll come to visit," he drawled. Although her father spent many years up north, he still slipped into a Southern accent when in Savannah. "Could you come next weekend? You mother and I have a party planned."

In another month, Reagan would complete her year at the FARM and go back to work. She wanted time to process things. Her life would never be the same, and besides, she was still in treatment. The FARM didn't permit them to travel, other than their group adventures. Her father knew that. She checked herself, before saying what she really was thinking. She got herself off the hook another way. "Oh, Daddy, I'm sorry, I can't come yet. You know I'm in treatment. We aren't allowed to travel for parties. They gave me a special privilege to have this cellphone to keep in touch with you, but coming back to Oceanside isn't in the cards."

"I need you, Reagan," her father insisted. "You're an important part of my recovery. Doctor's orders. Could you at least ask?"

"Your doctor told you that your drug-addicted daughter should leave her treatment to be by your side?" she quizzed. "Did you want Welby to come as well?"

"Now, now, now," her father cautioned. "Don't go overboard here, Reagan. You know and I know that your boy Welby is on parole. I'm surprised they even let him leave Ohio."

Reagan fumed. But then Abigail saved her with a call to join in a group selfie on the beach. "Dad, I gotta go. My group is calling me. I love you and I'll talk to you soon." She hung up in relief, happy to have an excuse to disconnect. All her life, she and her father had been so tight. Now she didn't mind the miles between them. She seriously wondered how she'd ever thought the whole world revolved around him.

Sallie and Jane were lining the women up on the beach. Reagan snapped a few photos of them all as she walked up to join in the photo moment. The other women from the FARM looked genuinely happy, and the MAMs seemed to be living it up as well. No alcohol or drugs were needed here to experience the abundant life, just friendship and God's creation. The wind whipped her hair as she stepped out of her sandals and headed toward the water. The cool February waves washed over her toes, and she laughed.

"Say cheese," Sallie yelled.

Together, they posed, on the edge of America, on the shores of the great ocean that once brought her ancestors, from Ireland and from Africa. Here, in this place, she felt the sands of time washing over her toes, transporting her spirit into the past, into the present and off into the future. As they packed up their fun and headed back to the van, Reagan continued pondering changes in her life. She offered a silent prayer of gratitude for all she'd learned. She also prayed for Welby in his speech at the prison. Her life belonged with him now. Her father needed to get with the program or he'd find his daughter drifting further and further from his side.

Welby Visits his dad

In a matter of minutes, Welby found himself seated at a table in a room full of prisoners and other outside visitors. He didn't like the place, but he remembered well the joy he'd felt when someone visited him during the five long years he called the pen home. Back in the main building now, the room reserved for visitors looked sterile and cold. Guards stood around the room, keeping watch over each and every conversation. The smell of sweat, cigarettes, and body odor created a stench in the room. Welby remembered it well. He could never figure out why it smelled so bad, but it just added to the frustration for him, especially when his favorite aunt came to visit. She never complained. She would spend the few minutes together, showering him with love and catching him up with all the comings and goings back home. He made a note to call her as soon as they returned to Ohio and he could use a phone. In fact, he wanted to make a regular practice of calling her, after all she had done for him.

The wall on the clock read 3:05. They timed the visits, cutting them off at thirty minutes, regardless of what might be going on. He closed his eyes, bowed his head and asked for a right spirit for this conversation. No sooner had he shut his eyes than a guard tapped him on his shoulder. "Marcus Welby Jones?" he asked. "Your inmate has arrived. Sylvester Jones? Is he yours?"

Welby opened his eyes and there he stood. His father, looking only a fraction of the man he remembered, greyed and thin, with lines creasing his face. "Yes, sir," he replied. Taking a deep breath, he looked deeply into his father's eyes as he shuffled into the chair across from Welby at the table. "Hello, Dad."

His dad's eyes looked grey and a little rheumy, but still held Welby's gaze. "Son," his father pushed out the brief reply, then he cleared his throat. Were those tears running down his cheeks. Was his dad crying? Welby had never known the man to cry. Could it be?

"Oh, Welby, thank you so much for seeing me." His father wiped the tears off his face. "You don't know how much this means to me." He picked up a tissue from the box on the table and dried his face. "I bet you didn't know I could cry, did you, Welby?" Then his dad laughed.

"I mostly specialized in being a badass, I know."

Welby couldn't believe it. The exact same name he'd used for his dad earlier in his own thoughts. He certainly was one mean dude who thought he had the right to hit everyone in the household, including his wife. Welby didn't know what to say, so he just looked at him, and tried to comprehend. Who was this man sitting before him, if not the father who mistreated him from day one?

"I'm sorry, Welby," his dad confessed. "I know I did you wrong. I was mean and unfair and violent. I want you to know I'm so sorry. You may never forgive me for what I did to you, but I just want you to know I'm sorry and I love you, son."

Now Welby felt tears running down his own face. He didn't want to cry, especially right here in front of his father, but the emotions that erupted deep in his chest from his father's apology made it difficult to shut the floodgates. His father handed him a tissue.

"I guess we're both crybabies today, Welby, and that's okay. It means our hearts are open and we're connecting here. So thank you for your tears, Welby. I didn't think you could possibly have it in you to care for your old man, after all I've done. But I can see you do care, and I thank you for that."

Welby sat there, flabbergasted, staring at his dad. He dried his tears, but more replaced them. At first, he thought maybe the cat got his dad's tongue, but now it looked like his own was all tied up. That didn't seem to matter to his father though, who kept right on talking.

"Boy, can you preach. What a message you served up back there in the chapel. Made me downright proud to be your daddy. I know I don't deserve the recognition for the man you are today, but, still, I'm proud of you, Welby. If I died today, I could die a happy man, knowing you turned out so well, despite all I put you through. Your mama would be so very, very proud of you, too, son."

Welby began to doubt his father's words. He'd heard too many confessions in the past after his dad screwed up. Living with an alcoholic was like that. You wanted to believe their apologies. You wanted to believe they could change. But when they went back to the bottle again and again, after a while, hope died and trust right along with it.

Welby's thoughts raced back to all the apologies he'd received from his dad in earlier years. Once an alcoholic, always an alcoholic, the saying goes. Although his father could be a very kind person while sober, he left that all behind when he tied one on. Welby would never forget his father's drunken rages. During those times, his father beat Welby, his half-siblings and his stepmother, which landed him in prison when he knocked her out of this world.

He remembered his dad's visit on his 5th birthday, when his mom was still alive. Back then, Welby didn't know what it meant to get drunk, but his dad got so angry, yelling at his mom. Then he took a baseball bat to the brand-new bicycle his auntie brought him. He battered the hell of that bike. Welby remembered crying and worrying that his dad might start hitting one of them next. As much as he hated losing his bike, he felt relieved when his dad left and didn't come back. Later, his dad apologized and sent money for a new bike, and Welby had hope back then. And when his dad invited him to come live with him after he got remarried, he also apologized for the past and said he was turning over a new leaf. That sure didn't happen. Nope, if anything, he became nastier than before, making the lives of his second wife, Welby and those other children a living hell. And still he would apologize after a drunken episode, but that never stopped the next one from coming around.

How do you believe someone like that can change? He felt sorry for the other children who were farmed out to foster care. Fortunately, Welby could go back to his aunt's and uncle's house. Welby's thoughts raced through the ugly scenes of screaming and crying and welts. The man sitting in front of him now seemed just a fraction of that evil man. But was he actually all new? Didn't he just preach that it could happen?

"Did you really change, Dad?" Welby asked. "You're saying all the right things, but I've heard this before. How do I know this is any different? I want to believe you, but tell me something new. What's different about this time?"

His father hung his head, his smile replaced with a frown. He closed his eyes. Could he be praying? Was his father now a man of prayer? Welby realized, even though he cried, his heart felt cold and hard when it came to his father.

His dad opened his eyes and began to talk. "I know this may be hard for you to believe, son, but I feel all new inside. You know what it's like being behind these walls. Shoot, you only served five years. I've been here ten and am not done yet. But I thank God every day for the prison ministry and the mentor I have from a nearby church. With his help, I've turned my life over to Jesus. God knows I made a mess of it by myself, but now I'm trying to let God lead. There's no way I can prove this to you, but maybe over time, you'll come around to see that, yes, I am a new man. Born again, washed clean at the feet of Jesus, living an abundant life even here on these sorry penitentiary grounds. I've learned they can lock up my body, but not my soul. My heart's free to soar. Welby, I'm a new man, I am." His father closed his eyes again and this time, he bowed his head.

Welby half-laughed and half-yelled, "What are you doing?" His father had never been a praying man, so what exactly was he up to with a bowed head and shut eyes?

A smile spread across his father's face, and he opened his eyes. "Just prayin' for you, Welby, that's all."

"Praying for me?" Did his dad think he needed the prayer? "Why me?" Even as Welby asked, he heard the anger in his voice. His dad needed the prayer much more than him.

"Oh, Welby, I gotta pray God will soften your heart toward me, that's all. I can't do it myself, I just gotta hope you'll forgive me eventually. I'm asking God to help you do that."

Because that was a little too much information for Welby to digest, he changed the subject. "What about your other children? Do they come visit you, Dad? What happened to all of them?"

"I pray for them, too, son. So far, none of them have stopped by. In fact, you're the first visitor I've had for a very, very long time. My brother, your Uncle Max, used to come, but he's in a rest home now. I do have addresses for the children. So far, they're not answering my letters either."

"Could I have their addresses? I'd like to write them, too," Welby said.

"Of course," his dad answered.

Welby began to consider that perhaps his dad really had changed. If everyone deserted him, perhaps he discovered he needed the Good Lord. Perhaps he got that foxhole religion in this hellhole of a prison. Regardless, Welby knew God wanted him to forgive and give his father a chance. Now Welby closed his eyes and bowed his head, praying silently, "God help me, God help me."

He felt a wave of love wash over him, and, suddenly, he knew he could do it. He opened his eyes and told his father, "I forgive you, Dad. All have sinned and fallen short. I have, you have, everybody does it. Yet God forgives and loves us all unconditionally. I have no right to withhold my forgiveness, because I've been forgiven, too. What goes around comes around."

"Thank you, son, thank you. You have no idea how much this means to me."

Welby looked at the clock. Only ten minutes had passed since his father interrupted his first prayer. The moment was huge, and Welby knew it, but the gravity of the situation got to Welby, so he changed the subject.

"Now, what's this about an inheritance you want to share?" Welby said. "I always thought we were dirt poor. That's what you always told me."

"Now, ain't that the truth?" his father agreed. "Yes, we's poor. You got that right, I wasn't lying about that. But turns out we had some ancestors none of us knew about, Welby. You know, the white kind?"

"What?" Welby yelled, without thinking. But as soon as the holler was out of his mouth, a guard stepped out of nowhere and pointed directly at Welby.

"You, keep it down, or you can leave, now," the guard told him.

"Yes, sir," Welby replied, remembering that he couldn't afford any missteps in this place. No way in hell would he jeopardize his freedom. "I'll keep it down. I'm sorry."

The guard nodded and asserted, "Next time, you're out."

Welby guessed getting kicked out would be better than being left behind, but he was not about to take any chances. "Now, back to our conversation. You said what?" he practically whispered as his dad leaned forward over the table to listen.

Then his father told him, "You heard me. The white man's my father's father."

"Yeah, well, I know I got some Irish blood in me, but that doesn't mean those Irish ancestors were any good to my people. It's probably more likely rape. Grand Ma Ma said something about white folks on my mother's side, but on your side, too?"

"Don't be so quick, Welby. I've been able to do a little research here and our pedigree all adds up. Do you want to know the story, or just share in the pot of gold?"

"What pot of gold?" Welby asked. "What pot of gold? Are you crazy?"

"I know, son, I know. I thought someone was pulling my leg when they finally tracked me down a year or so ago. I received a certified letter to me, Sylvester Jones, delivered right here in the penitentiary. Said my name was included in the last will and testament of one Matthew Jones of Wilmington, North Carolina, who passed away at the age of 103."

"Who was Matthew Jones?" Welby asked. "Was he related to you?"

"You know I was raised by a single mother, but my mother gave me my father's name. My father was killed in the Vietnam War. My mother had a drinking problem. Runs in our genes, son, so be careful. Seems my dad's parents wanted to help her, but she turned them away. My father split with them before he went off to war. She respected his decision, and stayed away from them. I remember back then, presents would show up on our doorstep on my birthday and Christmas. She gave them to me, without a card. I didn't think they were from her, but she never said. Except one time, a delivery man dropped off a present when she wasn't home. Inside was a card from Grandma Suzy and Grandpa Matthew. My mom was so mad when she got home. She didn't want nothin' to do with them and told me to throw away the card and forget them. So I didn't say no more about it, but it sure made me wonder."

"And Matthew Jones was white?"

"Far as I can tell, yes, son. Not many Black men got the kind of money he's got. And seems like I am his sole heir," his father explained.

Welby smiled. "Are you pulling my leg? How'd you find out about the man?" Welby knew from experience his dad could spin a good tale attached to an apology. Perhaps he'd cooked up this scheme as an attempt to woo Welby into staying close by.

"Well, I wrote back, assuring him that, yes, I'm Sylvester. I added what I knew about my mama and what I knew of my dad and his parents."

"And then what?"

"Well, then the attorney came to visit. When I said I haven't had any visitors for a very long time, I forgot about him. My grandfather's attorney did come to visit me."

"Wow, Dad, that's really something! That must've made your day." Welby humored his dad, though not buying the story. He could see his dad's smile fill out a little bit. Welby still thought it sounded too good to be true.

"It's good, but not if I can't use it or have anyone to share it with. Welby, I'm so glad you came here today. You know what it's like here. I haven't told a single soul about this. You're the first to hear the words out of my mouth. It makes me nervous even to be saying it out loud right now." His dad scanned the room to the left and then the right, focusing back on Welby. "I don't want no one hearing what I got to tell you, son."

Welby looked around, too, and was convinced no one paid them any attention, except perhaps the guards, but they were out of hearing range. "Dad, no one's listening. It's okay. They're too busy with their own visits. Tell me, what did this lawyer say?"

His dad's voice grew soft and quiet as he began to give Welby the details. "The whole damn estate is supposedly worth about ten million dollars. It's mainly real estate and mutual funds. Do you know what kind of interest ten million dollars makes? Hell, we could both live off the interest for the rest of our lives."

Welby let his mouth hang open. He again tried to figure out whether or not this could actually be true. He fact-checked his dad. "Why didn't you tell me before, in all those letters you wrote?"

"I couldn't risk it. You know what goes down in this place. I couldn't take the chance. But I've been trying long and hard to get you to me, right?'

Welby couldn't argue with that one, but the whole thing seemed entirely too crazy to believe. Ten million dollars? Why didn't the guy find them before? It's not too hard to track a person down, especially with all that money to help. If the attorney could find his dad in prison, couldn't his grandfather have found him a long time ago? It didn't add up, but Welby had an idea. "Okay, this seems very unreal, Dad," Welby said. "How 'bout I contact the attorney? I'm free. I could go to his office. I want to go to college and seminary. Could I use some of this money to support myself when I get out of the halfway house?"

Welby smiled. He'd called his dad's bluff. Now he'd have to 'fess up to the lies. But instead, his father's smile deepened and he seemed genuinely happy. "You're going back to school, Welby? That's the best thing I've heard in years. Of course, you can use the money. Your mama would be so happy. I'll need to give the attorney the word to go ahead. No reason you shouldn't start using that money now. You seem to have your head screwed on right. Maybe you can help your old man stay on the narrow path once I get out of this place, too. Life is short. I've spent too much of it locked up and being ugly. Tomorrow is a brand new day."

"I'd like that," Welby admitted. He wanted to believe that his dad could really turn over a new leaf when he got out. Say the story is true, as unlikely as it seemed, the money wouldn't hurt. Some people get destroyed by too much money, though. How many sad stories had he heard about people winning the lottery? But still, he wouldn't mind having all that money one bit. He could find ways to do good things with it. Maybe even Reagan's dad would come around, if he knew Welby had more than a pocket full of change.

Welby felt like he'd just got hit by a ton of bricks, absolutely stunned. Was his father telling the truth for a change? Could they really be rich men? They sure didn't look it. There was only one way to find out. "Okay, Dad, give me the guy's name and I'll give him a call."

Welby thought that would shake his dad out of his impossible tale, but instead, he asked, "Got a piece of paper and a pencil?"

"Of course not," Welby said. "You know they don't let you bring anything in this place. Pencils are weapons, pens are worse."

"Okay, how's your memory?" his dad asked.

"Not bad," Welby admitted. "Mom wanted me to be a doctor. My teachers told me I had the brain for it, but I didn't believe them."

"They were right. Then, remember this: Howard Pinkleton, Esquire, in Wilmington, North Carolina. I didn't write it down, neither. No way in hell I coulda forgot that name."

"How d'ya spell that?" Welby asked.

"You know, the color pink? P-i-n-k. Then there's l-e, and finally ton, t-o-n. You got it, boy?"

Welby nodded. "I'll tuck that away. When I get back home, I'll give him a call. I used to have a friend named Howard. I'll just see him all dressed up in pink, carrying a ton of bricks on his back. I got it, Dad. Howard Pinkleton of Wilmington. But will this guy believe me? Why would he give me the time of day?"

"Oh, it's no problem," his dad insisted. "I already assigned part of the fortune to you and your siblings. You got one million in your name just sitting there, making money. I gave your brother and sisters, Charlie, Bess, and Tabatha, a million each, also. Keeping six for myself, but that will be all of yours someday, too. I don't plan on spending any more than I need, although I plan to give some away. You're a millionaire, Welby."

What would it hurt to play along? At least until reality knocked him down, he could enjoy pretending to be rich for a while. "If I get ahold of my brother and sisters, can I let them know they're millionaires, too?" Now Welby felt oddly happy inside and a foolish grin formed across his face. Yes, this could be a lot of fun.

"Let me do that, son. I want to see how they're doing. The attorney will not dole out the money without assurance they're clean and on a good path. If they're on drugs or alcohol, they've gotta get clean first. I don't mind using the money as an incentive, but first, they need to do the work. Do you stay in touch with them?"

"Seriously, Dad, once they went into the foster care system, I didn't keep track. I was too caught up in my own life, glad to be off the hook as their big brother/caretaker. You put a lot on me, you know? But I do care about them. I'd like to see how they're doing. Maybe I can help them. I'm not as self-centered anymore. God called me to service and help the people struggling like me. I'd like to be a good brother."

"Great," his father said. "If any of them respond, I'll tell them to work with you then. Maybe they could come up to your group home there in Ohio with you?"

"Definitely!" Lights started blinking in Welby's heart. Yes, it would be a perfect place to help them start over, with the MAMs. "But maybe they already straightened up. Some foster families are all good."

"Right," his dad responded. "So glad you came by, son. Thank you. You don't know how much this means to me. And I'm counting down my days now, eleven months to go. Maybe I can come up there to the MAMs in Ohio, too."

Welby nodded. "Maybe so." He didn't know if he was ready to take his dad on. But a light bulb went off. "So you want to move into the Sun Power House? I'll be out by then, but you could stay there a year and get your head screwed on straight. You've been in here a long time. It would help you get re-oriented. They're good people, the MAMs."

The more Welby thought about it, the more he liked the idea. That would keep his dad close, but not as dependent on Welby for his re-entry into society. Could he get Reagan to agree to stay in River City, or nearby? If his dad really wanted to live in the Sun Power House, Welby realized he might actually be telling the truth. "It's a Christian program, you know."

His dad's face lit up and his smile spread from one ear to another. Welby got his answer before he said a word. "Would they take me?" his dad asked. "An old man with a record like mine?"

"That's what they're all about," Welby said. He thought it might be awkward, though, if his brother showed up and lived in the same house with his dad. No love lost between those two.

"Well, yes," his dad said, still smiling. "I'd be much obliged."

The guard came over and announced, "Time's up."

Welby nodded to the guard and then to his dad. "It was good to see you. I'll see if someone will take me by the lawyer's office before we leave Wilmington tomorrow then."

"I'm going to see if I can give him a call, but just explain you talked with me, if I don't get through. You know how the phones are here. Don't be a stranger," his dad said. "You can start answering my letters now. Come back and see me sometime?"

"Sure will," Welby said. "I sure will." As he stood to go, he added, "I love you, Dad." The words surprised him, but, in the moment, he felt the love and really believed his dad had turned over a new leaf. At least he sure hoped so.

His father, still smiling, replied, "Love you, too, son." The guard motioned to his dad, who got up and turned to Welby one last time. "Hope to hear from you soon."

Welby nodded and watched his old man shuffling away with a limp. He realized the years had not been kind to his father. He hoped his dad would still have some good time left when he got out. Then he left the visitation area to find George and Tom in the waiting room, ready to get back to Reagan and call it a day.

"How'd it go, man?" George asked as they walked out to the parking lot.

"Good," Welby said. "Better than I expected. I think my dad really turned over a new leaf in here. At first, I didn't think I could believe him, but I think I do. I really do."

Tom slapped him on the back. "What a day, Welby. First, you bowl over the inmates, getting them all dreaming again, then you find out your dad's a new man. Looks like the Good Lord listened to our prayers."

"You got that right," Welby agreed. "You know what, my dad says, we, I think, have an inheritance waiting for us. In fact, he gave me the name of an attorney in Wilmington to contact. Is there any chance I could go over there tomorrow before we head home?"

Tom asked. "What kind of an inheritance are we talking?"

Welby paused, then said, "You won't believe this. My dad says ten million dollars. I didn't believe it at first, either. That's part of why I want to go see his attorney."

George said, "That's quite a lot of change, Welby. Are you sure? Do you really believe that?"

"Well, I know. It sounds impossible, right. Ten million total, only a million   for   me." Welby laughed. "Only a million. Maybe it's not true, but the more I listened to my dad, the more he seemed to be telling the truth. I thought finding out the truth as soon as possible would be good."

"Well, then, I can understand wanting to check that out, but don't get your hopes up too high." George looked at Tom.

"We'll see what we can do," Tom said. "I know the MAMs hope to leave in the morning. Perhaps if you could get an early meeting, we could postpone it a couple hours. But I agree with George, don't get too happy about all this yet."

As George pulled the van out of the parking lot, Tom asked, "What's the name of the attorney? Let's call him now and see if he could fit you in early."

"Howard Pinkleton," Welby replied, pulling the name out of his memory.

A few minutes later, Tom announced, "Found him. Here's the number. I'll punch it in and you talk, okay, Welby?"

Welby nodded and Tom handed the phone to him. "Go ahead and make the appointment if he agrees. We'll deal with the MAMs. They can wait a few hours to get on the road."

Just when Welby thought the day couldn't get any better, it went ahead and did. A few minutes later, he handed the phone back to Tom. "He'll meet with me at eight in the morning. Can you believe it?"

"Good deal," Tom said.

George said, "I can understand you wanting to check that out. Well, hold on. I guess we'll be finding out tomorrow if you're a wealthy man."

Welby laughed. "I guess so, maybe so. Now, it's not all mine, but at least one million, he said, is earmarked for me."

"Only a million?" Tom quipped. "Poor boy."

Welby smiled. Perhaps it wasn't true. It could just be another one of his father's lies. But the attorney really existed and had wasted no time scheduling an appointment with him. Welby imagined that would be the sort of attention a client with ten million dollars might get. Time would surely tell.

CHAPTER TWENTY
IT'S A WRAP

Reagan gets a Surprise

The van cruised out of Wrightsville Beach at 4:30. Reagan longed to stay for the sunset, but the MAMs made other plans. Abigail took the mic as they crossed the bridge, heading back toward Wilmington. Reagan looked regretfully at the water, knowing it might be a long time before she made it back to the ocean again.

"Okay, listen up," Abigail told them. "We will be staying in the historic district tonight in Wilmington. We ordered dinner from a good Southern restaurant that gets high ratings for their soul food. After dinner, we will give you all some time to reflect and share what you've learned on this trip in a listening circle. So be thinking about that. When we get back to the house, take some time before dinner to write in your journals."

Reagan decided to get a head start and pulled her journal out of her bag. She wanted time for Welby when they got to the house, providing he made it back before dinner. As her thoughts meandered back through the last few days since they'd left Ohio, she realized it was a lot to process. What began as a fun tour and quality time with Welby turned into a nightmare with her parents, her father's heart attack, and then her own hospitalization.

She loved Welby. That, she knew for sure. Regardless of her father's disapproval, she believed in him. Reagan couldn't wait to hear about his prison talk. That's where God is, she thought. Welby's got the Spirit going on, for sure. Welby's got faith, he's got hope, and he's got love. That's what it's all about.

On the other hand, her father seemed terribly misguided and confused. How could he even call himself a Christian and set Welby up like that? Before this, she hadn't believed the Republican party really believed in white supremacy. She'd thought that was just something liberals said to bash the conservatives. Now she was beginning to wonder. Further, she even worried that she could continue being a Republican. How could the party of God follow practices that seemed unloving and downright evil? Sure, they said they wanted to protect unborn babies, but what about the rest of God's people, especially those with skin of color? Why were they trying to keep so many people from voting?

The trip had certainly raised more questions than it answered. She realized she actually looked forward to the listening circle, to hearing what the rest of them thought. Priscilla seemed to be questioning a lot as well. Once you get beyond simplistic black and white thinking, it gets complicated. And when you acknowledge that you yourself are both Black and white, things change. They must. It's just a question of how much and in what way. She wasn't even sure what to write, so she began with a prayer:

Dear God,

Help me understand this country where I live. What do you want me to do? How can I follow Jesus with my life? I don't understand how my parents could be racist. It doesn't make sense to me. They follow you, so why won't they give Welby a second chance? Don't you teach us to forgive? They forgive me, why not Welby?

He just had illegal drugs in his glove compartment. I stole drugs from the hospital. I was the one who should have gone to prison.

Help me make sense of this all. Republicans, Democrats, your love, my family, my relationship with Welby, guide me now. I need you!

Love, Reagan

Reagan wrote on. *Maybe all I can do is rely on God. I'm so angry. I probably need to give that over to God. I'm mad at my dad, but I can't tell him. I already caused his heart attack. Thank God for helping me save his life and get the surgery he needed. Basically, I'm a mess. If I could have some of those opioids again, I'd just feel fine. Looks like it's time to talk to my sponsor. But that would be hard, maybe George? Tonight?*

Now as we head back to Ohio tomorrow, it's time for me to finish up my year at the FARM and get ready to do art therapy. I want to paint some pictures from the trip and I also need to start applying for jobs. Where will I live? How will Welby and I keep our relationship going after we leave the MAMs' houses? So many questions.

I need to have a good sit-down with Welby about the future. Maybe tomorrow, we can talk on the way home? Where would we live? Is he okay living in Ohio or does he want to go back to North Carolina? If he's attending college and seminary, where will that be?

Reagan closed her journal and slipped it back into her satchel as Abigail announced, "We'll be arriving soon. Take your suitcases into the house. Seamus will give you room assignments. You've got about an hour to freshen up before dinner at six-thirty."

Reagan gathered her belongings, waiting not so patiently to arrive. Would Welby be back yet? She sure hoped so. She hoped for an hour to talk with him.

The van pulled into the driveway of a large brown house with a wraparound porch. "Okay, folks, we're here," Seamus said. He went to open the luggage compartment in the back.

Reagan hurried off, grabbed her rolling suitcase from Seamus and making it to the front door before anyone else. She tapped lightly and spied her reward through the glass door. The door opened slowly. Welby stepped out, embracing her in a bear hug.

"Great to see you, Reagan," Welby whispered into her ear. He let her go, but took hold of both of her hands. "You're looking so good, baby. Boy, do I have news. Let me help you get your suitcase up to your room first."

Reagan smiled, happy to find Welby there and wanting to talk, too. "How did it go?" she asked.

"Amazing, really amazing, actually," Welby said as he rolled her suitcase in. Welby pulled her heavy luggage up the stairs as if it was light as feather. Reagan knew it was not. He set it in her room and said, "Let's go."

Reagan claimed a bed, putting her smaller bag on a low bed, not wanting to get stuck with the high bunk with her broken arm. It wasn't the first time they'd had bunk beds. Someone else could do the climbing this time. She turned to Welby. "Okay, where now?"

"How 'bout the back porch? I checked it out earlier, there's a swing and we can get some privacy."

"Perfect," Reagan said. She followed Welby down the stairs, through the house and kitchen and out the back door. "Nice that it's warm enough to sit outside, likely to be much colder when we get back to Ohio."

"You got that right," Welby agreed. "Better enjoy this while we can."

He plopped down on the swing. Reagan sat close, enjoying his warmth. Welby wrapped his arm around her. She rested her head on his shoulder, feeling comfortable and loved. "This feels so good," she told him.

"Mm-hm," Welby replied.

"So, tell me about your talk at the prison," Reagan insisted. "How did it go?"

"Oh, man, what a day." Welby responded. "I didn't like being back there at all. Too many bad memories. They let me know up front I better not mess up, or they would bring me back. Scared me to death, Reagan. They don't usually let ex-cons come back in for five years, but they made an exception for me.

"Once we got to the chapel, I relaxed. The Reverend welcomed me with open arms. He said the inmates would hang on my every word because I was one of them. I didn't believe him, but he was right. You would not believe the energy in that place once I started talking. All their eyes were fixed on me, eating up my every word. At one point, I asked them to stand and say, 'I have a dream.' Every single man in that place got up on his feet. They chanted, the volume rising until a whole battalion of guards came in and the commander told us to quiet down.

"Crazy, crazy, crazy. I'm trying to get the men to turn over a new leaf and all the prison guards want to do is tell them to shut up. But not wanting to get in trouble. I told them to sit down.

"After I spoke, the chaplain issued an altar call and so many men came up, Reagan, you would not believe it. One slapped me on the back. A guard was there in a minute. The convict didn't mean nothing, but that's the way it is there, no physical contact allowed. But, overall, it was absolutely amazing, so much better than I ever could have imagined."

Reagan smiled, proud of him. "That's good, Welby. Sounds like you did an awesome job. That's really great."

Welby placed his hand on her chin, turning it toward him and covered his mouth with hers, beginning a gentle kiss.

Reagan felt her whole body responding as the kiss deepened into something more. But just when she yearned to take it inside, Welby broke away.

"Reagan, I love you," he said. "In a few months, we'll be out and I was wondering …" He got down off the swing and knelt before her and said, "Reagan, would you marry me?"

Reagan's mouth dropped open. On the one hand, this was exactly what she wanted. On the other hand, it seemed too soon. She knew her father would not approve. Maybe they should wait until they'd been out for a while. Yet despite some reservations, she knew deep within that she absolutely could not turn him down. This was Welby and, yes, she wanted to marry him. She knew that with her whole heart. Throwing caution to the wind, she said, "Yes! Yes, I'll marry you, Marcus Welby Jones! I would love to be your wife!"

Welby pulled her up into a strong hug. The energy of their connection surged all the way down to her toes. Time stood still as their bodies entwined, and she relished being alone, together. In Welby's arms, everything felt just right.

When they sat back down, Reagan still wanted to know more about the prison talk, but she also wondered when Welby wanted to get married, so she asked, "When?"

"When what?"

"When do you want to get married?"

"As soon as possible," Welby replied. "This platonic relationship may have been good to help us really get to know each other, but it's getting old fast. I'm all in, Reagan. I want to do this the right way. We can wait until marriage, but that can't be too much longer."

"Oh, okay." Reagan smiled. She shared Welby's sense of urgency. Living in the halfway houses definitely slowed them down physically. "As soon as we get out then? But how will we support ourselves? I need to get a job, you want to go to school. That takes money. I'm not sure my dad will come around. We may be on our own."

"Reagan, there's something else I want to tell you. I may have some money of my own, waiting in a bank in Wilmington. I need to go see my father's attorney before we leave tomorrow."

"What? Your father's attorney?"

"Well, according to my dad, he just inherited a pocket of change from his white grandfather he never knew. Ten million dollars, actually. He said he already assigned one of those millions over to me. It's hard to believe, because my dad used to be real good at lying. I can't be sure until I visit the attorney. But honestly, I think he may really be on the straight and narrow now. He says he's following Jesus and he's clean. He would like to come up to the Sun Power House when he's released next year. Can you believe it?"

"Oh, Welby, that's amazing. Wow!" Reagan couldn't quite believe her ears. "Your white grandfather? Did you know about him?"

"No, I didn't. My dad was raised by a single mom. I had no idea." Welby responded.

"Wow. That is big, Welby. That's so big."

"I know," Welby agreed. "And you said you would marry me before you knew. That makes me so happy, Reagan, that you could love me as a poor man. But again, it may not all be true. Let's wait until tomorrow to get excited, okay?"

Reagan nodded, laying her head on Welby's shoulder, just as the back door opened. George stepped out and called to them, "Hey, guys, dinner is served. Come on in!"

Closing Circle

Priscilla stepped up into the van, joining the MAMs and entourage to visit a labyrinth just a few minutes away at the Episcopal Church. After a delicious final Southern dinner that filled her stomach beyond comfort, she looked forward to stretching her legs, but first another van ride. The MAMs loved the labyrinth and often walked it in the barn at the FARM. Over time, she learned to enjoy the quiet path as a place to pray. God knew she needed prayer right now. Abigail told them to bring their journals along. Priscilla looked forward again to some time to reflect like she did at the labyrinth at Brookgreen. She wanted to write more about this trip.

When they arrived at the church and piled out, she asked Abigail,

"Is the labyrinth outside?"

"No, it's actually on the floor of the sanctuary," Abigail explained. "Just like the Chartres Cathedral in France. My friend attends this church. She's meeting us here to let us in."

Priscilla noticed a tall, thin woman walking up from behind Abigail. She placed her hands over Abigail's eyes and said, "Surprise!" Then she laughed and removed her hands as Abigail turned into a warm embrace.

"As I was saying," Abigail turned to Priscilla, "this is my friend, Ruth Turner. Ruth, meet Priscilla."

"Welcome, Priscilla," Ruth said. "Pleased to meet you. Let's go inside."

"Yes, " Abigail agreed. Seamus came up to them. "And this is Seamus, my Irish friend I told you about."

Ruth shook Seamus' hand. "Good to meet you. Welcome to Wilmington."

"Aye, the pleasure's all mine. Any friend of Abby is a friend of mine. So nice of you to meet us here and open your church for our wee little group." Seamus took Abigail's hand as they began to walk toward the church's entrance.

"My, not so little. You have a large group," Ruth observed.

"Well, quite a few," Abigail agreed. "We've got the six MAMs, then three from each of our group homes, along with Molly's spouse and brother-in-law who came along as chaperones, and then Seamus. We brought along all we could fit in one van to keep expenses down."

Inside, they gathered in the sanctuary. Ruth oriented them to the labyrinth, explaining it was three-fourth's the size of the Chartres Labyrinth, sandblasted into the sanctuary floor. "Do you want an orientation?" she asked.

"Hm," Abigail pondered. "Do you have a standard introduction? I think that would be good, just to remind everyone. And tell us about your labyrinth. Some are more familiar than others. Then turn it over to me, because we want them to listen at the labyrinth for their personal response to our trip. How about we give them an hour to walk and journal, then we'll have a sharing circle, and you're welcome to join us."

Priscilla took a seat near the labyrinth with the others as Ruth explained the history of the labyrinth and passed out directions on walking. Then Abigail took over. "This evening, we'd like you to take some time to reflect on our trip. As you walk into the labyrinth, consider what you learned and how that is affecting your perspective. In the center, consider the gifts you've received, give thanks and pray about them. As you walk out, think about how you'll incorporate this learning into your life. Those of you in the group homes, think about whether this trip was helpful to you in your recovery and re-entry. We have a grant to fund the trip. We need to do reports. We planned the trip with the hope that it would help you each personally. Maybe it did, maybe not, but reflect on that. If this sort of thing is helpful to you, perhaps others will want to do something similar."

"Okay, then, are you ready to begin?" Ruth asked Abigail.

"Yes, let's go for it," she responded.

"I'm going to open the labyrinth now with this chime," Ruth said. "I will also stand at the entrance and ring the chime over your head as you begin your walk."

"Open the labyrinth?" Molly asked. "We've never done this."

Jane said, "I thought I did that with you before. When I went to Labyrinth Facilitator training, Lauren Artress taught us to do that."

"Yes, it's a ritual to open the sacred space of the labyrinth. The labyrinth is always open in some ways, but this signals our special time of prayer begins. And when I dangle the chime in front of you, I'm saying a prayer for each of you and your walk."

"Okay," Molly said. "Different, but that makes sense."

Ruth began walking around the labyrinth, swinging the chime, which made a musical sound. When she finished circling the labyrinth, she took a thick stick and hit a large brass bowl sitting on a table near the labyrinth. Then she touched the screen of the nearby iPad and classical guitar music filled the sanctuary.

Priscilla wanted to write before she walked. She found the sacred place comforting after the experiences of the week and she sensed God's presence. The one constant in her life was her relationship with God. She could always count on Him in good times and bad. She began with simple words of thanks.

Thank you, God, for time to pray. Thank you for the MAMs and the adventures we share together. Thank you for teaching me about my ancestors. Thank you for giving me clarity about Moses Sun. Thank you for the kindness of my new relatives and the others we met.

What question should she ask during her labyrinth walk? Was this trip calling her to action? In the back of her mind, she sensed a nudge to become more active politically and to speak up against racism within her political party. She doubted she could ever become a Democrat, but she also didn't want her party to be the racist one. She settled on two questions. On the way in, she would consider what she learned on the trip. In the center, she would give thanks and ask God for marching orders. On the way out, she would consider how she would to respond to God's call.

All the others were already circling on the labyrinth when she finally approached the entrance. Ruth dangled her chime above her head as

Priscilla stood, ready to walk. Then Ruth moved away, giving Priscilla a smile.

Priscilla walked slowly, savoring the music and the community of friends walking, each on a singular journey, yet together during this time. In her mind, she considered the gifts of the trip as she walked in. She gave thanks for sightseeing, boat rides, gardens, educational tours, and especially meeting her friendly distant relatives. She gave thanks that Welby was exonerated, that Reagan's father seemed to be recuperating from his heart attack, and that Reagan seemed to be healing well from her tumble also. She gave thanks for the journal, which told her family story that came alive in a new way for her during this trip.

In the center of the labyrinth, she knelt down, expressing thanks to God for the whole trip. Then she asked, "What do you want me to do?"

Suddenly, a strong thought popped into her head which wasn't there before. "Love my people, on both sides of the aisle. Expand your circle of friends. Get to know more people of color. Speak up against injustice. I will show you the way."

Whew, Priscilla thought. That was clear and made perfect sense. She got to her feet, thinking she needed to go write it down before she forgot. But then she remembered she could use her cellphone, so she sat in the center and texted the message to herself. Only then did she again rise to walk out of the labyrinth. As she circled on the path, now she considered ways to focus on loving people in both parties. She also thought about wanting to expand her circle of friends to include more people like Molly. Perhaps they could invite some new people to join the MAMs? It bothered her that some people in her party seemed to want to keep Black people from voting. She could speak up about that, for sure.

The path of the labyrinth soothed and comforted her as she felt embraced in the arms of God, surrounded by a great cloud of witnesses, these good friends of hers. Her heart held hope for tomorrow and concrete ideas about how to respond as she completed her best labyrinth walk ever.

Once back at her seat, Priscilla rewrote the text message in her journal and added the thoughts about what she could do. Then she started praying for each member of the group as she waited for the forty-five minutes of silence to end. A deep sense of gladness flooded through her whole body.

A few minutes later, Ruth rang the bell, then walked around the labyrinth again, swinging her chime, explaining she was closing the labyrinth. Abigail directed everyone to a circle of chairs in the narthex. Seamus stood by a flipchart with a marker. She imagined he would record what they all had to say.

Abigail asked, "What did you hear at the labyrinth? What gifts did you receive on this trip and what did you learn? For the group home members, remember to add what you think about the value of this sort of trip for the grant."

Max, who Priscilla really hadn't seen or heard much during the whole trip, spoke up first. "Thank you, MAMs, for an all-expenses paid trip to my homeland. You rock. I received a free vacation and a peek into the life of my people, the Gullah ones. What else? I gained a respect for my heritage and, damn yes, I recommend this for all re-entry people. When you get locked up, you start to believe you're no good. When you believe that, you start to act no good. But when someone rolls out the red carpet for you, you start to feel real good, like maybe you are somebody after all. The millions of dollars they spend on our prison system could be better used helping people start over. Thank you, MAMs. I appreciate you."

Priscilla looked at Max. She didn't think about the prison system much, but she knew those who came out usually went back in. The other group home folks nodded in response.

Welby agreed. "You got that right, Max. With the MAMs, we get treated royally. They offer us a new beginning. This trip was wow, yes, so much. It started out pretty rough for me down there in Oceanside. But thank you all for circling around me and believing in me and seeing me through. That means a lot. I received the gift of learning more about my people, the Gullah.

"Today by itself might be the best day of my whole life, going back to that prison, where I spent five long years, to preach. Those guys hung on my every word. I got them on their feet, yelling, 'I have a dream.' Quite a few answered the altar call. God used me today, and that's not all. I talked to my dad for the first time in fifteen years. I believe he's turned over a new leaf, and that's really something. I hope he's telling the truth, but I do believe him this time."

"Okay, okay," Antonio affirmed.

Abigail then drew attention to Seamus' growing list of gifts from the trip. "Thanks to Max and Welby for sharing. Who else would like to tell us what you've received?"

"But I'm not done," Welby said, jumping back in to the discussion. "I can't thank you MAMs enough for bringing me on this trip. Like Max, I agree that this country would be a whole lot better off if they started helping the prisoners believe in themselves again, rather than locking them up and throwing away the key. To make our country better, we gotta work at all levels, and after a person's been broken, it takes a whole lot of effort to help put them back together. Learning about ancestors, developing a respect for history, meeting good people, traveling, all these things build a person up. More grants like ours would be a good thing."

"Thank you, Welby," Abigail said. "It's good to hear you and Max would recommend more of these trips. Who else would like to share?"

Tom raised his hand and Abigail gave him the nod. "Man, I agree with the guys, learning about your people is good stuff. I knew a little about the Gullah people, but now I know a lot more. It completes me in a deep way to hear how they maintained their culture, despite everything that happened. I also appreciate that they didn't fault my people for heading north to find opportunity.

"I've always laughed at Molly when she told me about you all circling around on that cloth of yours back home in the barn. But here today, I believe I heard God speaking. I won't laugh at Molly anymore. I apologize."

"Thanks for that," Molly acknowledged. "And what did God say?"

Tom looked down and paused. Then he looked straight at Molly. "You know I wasn't all too crazy about retiring. I did it to be with you after your close call with cancer. I'm glad I did, but now I think God's calling me to get involved in Black Lives Matter with the police in this country. Watching Welby get picked up for doing absolutely nothing besides being a Black man in Georgia affected me deep inside. This stuff must stop. I believe God wants me to work on it. Being a retired cop, I know what goes down. I believe I can make a difference. Not sure exactly what, but I'm going to work on it when I get home."

"Wow," Abigail said. "That's big, really big."

Priscilla decided to share her call. "I heard God calling at the labyrinth, too. God wants me to get out more and meet more of my people, my Black people, I mean. And to become more active as a Republican, speaking out against racism in my party. It's not right and it needs to stop."

"I don't think that's going to go over real well," Jane said. "We want everyone to get along, but you start labeling people racist and they'll shut you out."

"I know it's not going to be easy, but I need to speak up," Priscilla asserted.

"Good luck with that," Jane said. "I agree that maybe something should be done, but it's hard to figure out how to approach it in a way that will work."

"You want to help me?" Priscilla asked.

"Not sure I'm ready to take that on," Jane said.

"Think about it. I could use your help." Priscilla hoped Jane would come around. She decided to continue with her report. "I received so many gifts from this trip, especially meeting some of my distant relatives and learning about the Gullah people, my ancestors. At times, it was hard, and very strange, but I'm growing as a person. I'm so glad we made this trip. Thank you, Molly and Abigail, for making this happen."

"You're welcome," Abigail said. "I think it's been good for all of us, including me, for one. I don't have any Gullah ancestors, but I learned more about the history of this country. I developed a deep respect for the way the Gullah people maintained their language and culture over here. As an environmentalist, I also appreciated seeing first-hand what's happening to our coastal lands with more flooding and destructive hurricanes. As I observe how it's affecting the people of the Sea Islands, and even further inland, I can share that information as I work to educate about climate change. And then traveling with Seamus was very nice, too." Abigail smiled at him, and Priscilla saw him give her a wink.

"I suppose that be my cue to take a turn," Seamus said. "I thank ye all for giving me this opportunity to learn more about your country. I see the troubles of the Americans, yer problems with slavery and treating the Gullah people and their descendants as less than human. Our conflict over in Ireland be a little different, but the nastiness feels the same. There, the Unionists and the Nationalists fight each other and regard each other as less than human. We Quakers keep hoping that eventually each person will realize that everyone has a touch of the divine in them. I think that's why the Good Lord told us to love our enemies, don't ye?

"Abigail here's been the best part o' this trip for me, the gift from God that just keeps on giving. Before we go home tomorrow, I've got something I've been wantin' to say to me love." Seamus reached into his pocket and pulled out a little box. He walked over to Abigail and knelt down in front of her.

Abigail's mouth dropped open. She covered it with her hand as Seamus began.

"Abigail Wesley, from the moment I met ye on the Emerald Isle, yer smile and yer gentle spirit lodged in me heart. Ye brought me out of the shadow of grief. Ye help me laugh and enjoy life again, you do. Ye turn me day to night, and me night to day. Your love makes me heart sing. I want to spend the rest of my life loving ye. Abigail, will you marry me?"

Priscilla wondered how Abigail would respond. She remembered how terrible she felt when Moses Sun sprung the question on her. But Abigail didn't hesitate at all. She jumped up out of her chair and told Seamus very clearly and emphatically, "Yes!" To seal the deal, she swung her arms around him in a firm embrace, placing her lips on his while the MAMS broke out into a cheer.

Priscilla cheered along with her friends. She saw Reagan and Welby smiling and clapping, but the other group home folks seemed rather quiet. Artemis actually scowled. She wondered why they wouldn't celebrate with Abigail and Seamus.

When the cheering died down, Welby asked Seamus, "So what are you going to put up there on that sheet about this?"

"That be easy, I got the gift o' a wife!" Seamus left Abigail's side and went back to the flipchart. He added, Seamus gained a wife, then he put fiancé in parentheses. "We not be married yet, are we?"

Reagan spoke up and said, "Seamus, you're not the only one. A few hours ago, Marcus Welby Jones proposed to me. I have accepted his offer as well." Reagan's face shined. Welby's grin spread from ear to ear. "Welby's proposal was hands down the greatest gift of this trip for me, too," Reagan said.

But this time, no one clapped. An awkward silence ensued. George spoke first. "Are you sure you're ready for this? You haven't finished your time with us yet. Don't you think you might need some time outside before making a big decision like that?"

Reagan looked crestfallen and Welby appeared downright angry. Priscilla agreed with George, but, still, it was their life and they clearly loved each other. "Did you set a date?" she asked, trying to smooth it over.

Reagan said, "Obviously, we're not getting married tomorrow. We will wait until we get out and settled. George, you're right, we need to take our time, but long term, Welby is who I want and I couldn't be happier."

Welby looked somewhat relieved. He added, "Yes, George, we're not rushing into anything. It's a commitment for the future. Things happen, we could change our minds. But I, for one, believe that Reagan is the best thing that ever happened to me. I don't want to lose her. I've been praying about it. Today seemed like the right time."

"Welby, really? I thought better of you," Artemis said. "Why aren't you going after one of us? I thought this thing with Reagan was just a fling."

Zorastria nodded. "Brothers crossing the line is not a good thing. That can only lead to trouble. There's time for you to see the error of your ways."

Welby's frown returned. "Everybody needs to find their own person. The color of my skin doesn't dictate who I should and should not love. I don't agree with you. I know you want all us Black men for yourselves, but sometimes that's not how it goes down."

Priscilla scanned the circle for reactions. Abigail looked flustered and George kept shaking his head. Trying once again to help Welby and Reagan feel better, she told them, "I'll pray for you two, for sure. I hope God blesses you with a long life together."

Abigail broke in. "Let's see, where were we? Reagan? Anything else to share?"

Reagan looked at Abigail and said nothing. But then she told the group, "I'm so glad to unravel the truth of my family tree. It's hard to accept that my dad is racist, pure and simple. It's hard to forgive him for what he did to Welby. But I know Jesus calls me to love and forgive him. I just wish he would step up and be a good Christian himself. I thought he changed, but I'm not convinced. So, all I can do is pray for him. Like Priscilla, I need to talk to fellow Republicans about this issue of racism. It's not right. If we are going to continue to be the party of God, we need to get this right. We must love all people.

"I want to thank you, MAMs, for this trip. Powerful stuff and great for all of us in re-entry and recovery. It helps us face the truth of who we are, which is so important in recovery. Yes, I recommend this for others in re-entry and recovery."

Jane lifted her water bottle. "These announcements call for a toast! Hear, hear! To Abigail and Seamus, to Reagan and Welby, long live your love!"

Water bottles lifted around the circle. Priscilla turned to Katharine and clicked her metal water bottle against Katharine's. Everyone laughed and joy seemed palpable. What a different experience than she'd had the day before with Moses Sun.

Abigail interrupted the fun. "Let's finish up here, folks. We've had a long day. Anybody else want to share before we close? Even if you prefer not to share it out loud, I would like to ask each of the group home members to submit something in writing so we can use it for the grant."

Zorastria raised her hand, surprising Priscilla. She knew her background included prostitution and drug dealing. She also had a lip on her, but remained strangely quiet during most of the trip.

"What would you like to share, Zorastria?" Abigail asked.

"Well, you may not want my opinion, but I think we gotta go to Africa to really get to my roots. I'm not just some Gullah descendent. My people started out on another continent and that's where I belonged, until the white man stole me over here. My people bled and died on the Sea Islands, making fortunes for the white men. To me, this whole trip seemed like a sorry story about what went down and what keeps going down. Why you think I became a prostitute? Why you think so many Black people out there sellin' drugs? Why you think we got this divided country? The story's all here and it's not something to celebrate. I don't see the gift you're all talking about. Sure, I like a little vacation as much as the next person. But exposing my roots? No. I need to go to Africa for that."

That's one angry Black woman, Priscilla thought. The raw anger bothered her. She didn't like the way it made her feel. And she couldn't figure out anything to say or do to make it better.

Fortunately, Molly picked up the slack. "I got you, sister. You're right. We shouldn't be too quick to celebrate when the reality of racism still rules. Your anger is important. We all know history ain't right. Things need to change. But, Zorastria, I challenge you to take your anger and channel that into positive energy to bring change. It's not easy. We've got a long way to go. Welby's leading the way. We can follow him and each of us have a unique role to play.

"Our trip won't solve the race problem, but look at Priscilla and Reagan. Both of them are making plans to speak up. That's a start. This trip may be more worthwhile than we can see right now," Molly continued. "And Africa is our next destination. You're on the list to go, Zorastria. Next time the MAMs head across the Atlantic, we'll be flying to West Africa. You're absolutely right. We need to get all the way down to our roots in our homeland. I'm with you on that, sister."

"Can I say something?" Sallie asked.

"Sure," Abigail responded.

"I do think this whole thing of tracing our roots is important, for kids and for us all. We need to know where we came from. It helps us figure out where we want to go. Now, the Sea Islands were not home to my ancestors, but it does help me understand more of the American history we share together.

"There are many accomplishments of the Gullah people on this continent that should be acknowledged. I developed a new respect for their abilities as skilled craftsmen, builders, experienced rice farmers, and more. And I didn't realize how they kept their cultural values from Africa, along with their music and creative cooking skills. We learn a lot from them."

Katharine chimed in. "You're right. Before we came, we read about the Gullah in books, but now we know it firsthand. Like Priscilla and Reagan and Tom, I heard a call tonight. That labyrinth thin space can be powerful stuff." She laughed a little. "I hear a call to jump back into academia and help students grapple with racism. I taught religion for many years, but I regret I never taught about race and religion. I want to awaken students to positive action. I'm not sure exactly where I'm going with this. I need to pray and listen to God some more."

Seamus jotted down a few words to summarize Katharine's remarks.

Abigail raised her hands in the air. "Let's give thanks to the Lord, for He is good." She then turned to her friend. "Ruth, we want to thank you for opening your church to us this evening. What a powerful experience we've had with your labyrinth, reflecting on our trip and listening to God. Thank you so much. Would you be willing to lead us in a closing prayer?"

Ruth nodded. "Why don't we stand and hold hands."

Priscilla watched as everyone rose and linked hands. Soon, they formed a large circle together. Priscilla smiled at the deep sense of community they shared, feeling so grateful for all of them.

"Let us pray," Ruth began. "We give thanks for the MAMs and their friends, and for their trip to the Sea Islands. Thank you for the gifts and learning they received. Thank you for the love they found. We ask you, God, now to bless Seamus and Abigail, and also Welby and Reagan as they prepare to marry. May your love be ever present among them. We give thanks for the MAMS' vision to conduct a trip like this and we pray that other re-entry and recovery people will have opportunities to trace their roots because of the success of this project. We pray that you will help all of us continue to address the ugly head of racism in our country. Thank you for the calls that Tom and Priscilla, Reagan, and Katharine heard tonight. Please continue to speak to them as they seek your guidance for the work ahead. We pray for traveling mercies as they go home tomorrow. In the name of Jesus, we pray. Amen."

"We've had a long day, and we've got a long ride home tomorrow. Let's call it a night," Abigail said.

The group gathered their belongings and headed back to the van. Priscilla's heart glowed in the warmth of their fellowship. Her earlier confusion slipped away. She thanked God silently for her call and for her strong sense of community as they rode back to their rental house for the night. God would show her the way. He always did.

Welby Visits the Attorney

The next morning, Welby stepped out of the shower and toweled off. He slipped into a dress shirt and khakis, the best he'd brought, wanting to look sharp for the attorney. In the mirror, he gazed at the same old Welby. Nothing looked different, yet he sensed an inner shift, casting him in a new light. Back in Ireland, he took the call to be a new MLK with a grain of salt, wondering if he could ever pull that off. Yet he knew it wasn't just a Welby thing, but a God and Welby thing. They'd certainly pulled it off together yesterday at the prison. His thoughts spun on to forgiving his dad. Not in his wildest dreams did he expect an inheritance. Part of him still doubted. The answer would come soon.

Welby joined George and Reagan at the breakfast table. "Thanks for getting up early for me," he told them.

"The rest of the group thanks you, Welby. Your trip to the attorney gives them a little more time to sleep in and relax before we head home," George responded. "I'm glad the attorney could get you in first thing. We still have a long drive home today."

"Yeah, thanks, man, for agreeing to let me visit the attorney before we leave. I know it will make a late night getting back." Welby turned to Reagan. "Good morning, beautiful, the future Mrs. Reagan Jones. I like the sound of that."

"Whoa, Welby," George cautioned. "We talked this over last night. We'd like the two of you to go to a counselor when we get back. You need to think this through and see if you're ready to take this step."

"No problem," Welby said. "We can do counseling, right, Reagan? We don't have anything to hide."

Reagan looked a little disturbed, but nodded. "Right, if we've got to do it, we will, but I don't think we need it."

"Good," George said. "Let's get this show on the road. Let's load our suitcases into the van and be on our way." He turned to Reagan. "Reagan, you can go back to bed for a while."

"I want to go to the attorney with Welby. We're going to be married. This affects us both," she told George.

"I understand, but I think Welby needs to go alone. He can fill you in later."

Reagan sulked. "Why? What would it hurt for me to go?"

Welby knew Reagan was used to getting her own way and could be very persuasive and he agreed with her. "Why not?" he asked. "This is our future. We're getting married. Why can't she go?"

"Welby, this is your business. The attorney agreed to meet with you, not Reagan. You can tell her all about it when you get back. Let's go, Welby," George said, dismissing Reagan, as they stood to depart.

Welby shrugged and then gave Reagan a hug. "I'm sorry. I want you to come. I'll be back soon and tell you all about it."

Reagan didn't look happy, but he tried and that was the best he could do. As Welby climbed into the passenger seat in the van, he began to think about the meeting ahead. He honestly knew this could go either way. The fact that the attorney cleared his schedule to see them at eight o'clock seemed significant. Maybe things would come down in a good way, even though the whole thing also seemed surreal and unbelievable.

"What do you think, George?" Welby asked. "Am I really going to be a millionaire in a few minutes?"

"Do you believe everything your dad tells you? What do you

think?" George bounced it back to Welby.

"Honestly, my dad lied to me all my life. There's no reason to believe this is any different, but he seems different this time. The attorney agreed to see me at a drop of a hat, so maybe he's telling the truth. Could it be true?" Welby asked again.

"I reckon we're about to find out," George answered noncommittally. "Whether you get the money, or you don't, Welby, your future is bright. You'll find your way, with or without the money."

"But it sure will make things a lot easier," Welby stated.

"For sure," George agreed. "You got a good head on that neck of yours. I think you could handle the money. Some people can't. You've heard what happens to many lottery winners?"

"I know, I know. Hard to believe they end up dead. Man, I don't want that to happen to me."

"Just keep praying, going to meetings and trusting the Good Lord to guide you," George recommended. He turned into the parking lot by a small building.

Inside, a matronly receptionist greeted them warmly in the office. "Welcome. Are you Welby Jones?"

"Yes, ma'am." Welby nodded, surprised she knew his name.

"Good, we've been expecting you," she continued. "Can I see your ID? I need to take a picture of that." Welby pulled out his driver's license and also his social security card.

"Oh, good," she said. She took the cards, scanned them on the printer behind her and then handed them back to Welby. "Have a seat. Mr. Pinkleton will be with you in a moment."

The waiting room looked like something out of a high-end fashion magazine spread. Welby chose a white leather couch and stretched out his long legs. George chose a striped recliner, pulling the lever for the leg rest. "Don't get too comfortable," Welby teased.

"I figure I may be here a while, so I might as well make myself at home," George quipped. "I've never seen a waiting room with a recliner before."

Before Welby could reply, the receptionist stood. "Mr. Pinkleton will see you now."

Welby looked at George. "Here goes!"

The receptionist held open the door and motioned to him to enter. "First door on the left," she added.

Welby quickly walked through the door and down the corridor, but slowed as he entered the attorney's office. A large man with a full white moustache and beard awaited him behind a desk in the spacious room. He stood as Welby approached. Welby held out his hand as taught and introduced himself. "I'm Marcus Welby Jones, sir. I'm here for an appointment."

The attorney grasped Welby's hand, shaking it firmly. "Pleased to meet you, Welby. Thank you for coming. I got a call from your father late yesterday and cleared my schedule for you. You can have a seat."

Welby sat in chair in front of the desk, waiting for whatever would come.

"So, I imagine you have a few questions you may want to ask me, and I have some for you as well. But first, let me explain a few things, which might help you understand what's going on here.

"Mr. Matthew Jones, your great-grandfather, was my client for the past thirty years. When I first met him, he was already sixty years old, getting close to retirement. He ran a successful shipping operation, investing wisely over the years. I helped him with legal issues for his business, then he asked me to handle his estate. It might surprise you to know he actually followed his grandson and all of his great grandchildren. He gave me a file with your names and the addresses he had. He wasn't happy with the direction of your lives, but kept hoping one of you would turn around."

"Why didn't he help us, then, if he wanted us to get along better?" Welby asked.

"Well, he believed you each need to figure out life for yourself. He did find out about your entry in the Sun Power House up in Ohio shortly before he died. That made him very happy. Seems your aunt gave him reports from time to time on your whereabouts."

"Why didn't she tell me?"

"You'll have to take that up with her, son. Matthew probably swore her to secrecy, I imagine. Definitely a peculiar man, that one. But now, let's get on with this. Your great-grandfather wanted to leave his estate to his heirs, but he wasn't sure any of you were going to be in a position to handle the wealth. When he found out your father turned over a new leaf in prison, he decided to go ahead with setting up his estate with the hope that you would all come around.

"Your great-grandfather's will provides for one million dollars for each of the great-grandchildren once they fulfill the requirements, getting their lives in order, drug and alcohol-free. The remainder of the estate goes to your father. He felt considerable remorse about his treatment of your father. He wished that he and his wife had stepped in to take custody of your dad when it was clear his mother would not stop drinking. But this is the South. Skin color kept him from doing the right thing back then, a decision he lived to regret."

The words jarred Welby. He complained about Reagan's father being racist, now his own great-grandfather was, too? He wondered just what kind of hoops he might have to jump through to get the money. "Requirements?" Welby asked. "What are the requirements? Don't you usually just inherit the money?"

"Right," Mr. Pinkleton responded. "Usually, yes, but it's also common for wills to make certain stipulations. Matthew knew that alcoholism and drug addiction might affect his descendants. He didn't want to throw away the money on people who might use it for their addictions, so he stipulated the beneficiaries must be in recovery for at least a year, if they suffer from addiction."

The idea sunk in. Welby realized it might make sense. He'd watched his father drink his life away. God knows he would have squandered an inheritance back then, without a doubt. "So, blood tests? References? What do I need to do to prove I'm good?"

"Well, Matthew gave me some discretion in these matters. In your case, I would like a statement about your status from your group home counselor when you're ready to leave treatment. If you're still doing well, as I assume you will be, I will become your trustee for your first year out. Do you have any plans?"

"I want to get my bachelor's degree, then attend seminary. I'll be in school for a while."

"Becoming a man of the cloth?" Mr. Pinkleton smiled. "Your great-grandfather would love that." Welby smiled back as he continued. "Then, assuming you're good at the end of the year at the Sun Power House, I will give you enough money for housing, and living expenses, as well as pay for your tuition. After the first year, I'll re-evaluate the situation. If all is well, I'll turn the money over to you, with a financial advisor to assist you."

Welby couldn't quite believe his ears. "Really? One million dollars?"

"That may sound like a lot of money, Welby, but with inflation, it doesn't go far these days. I hope you won't spend it all. Get a job. Save as much as you can. It might be better in the long run to get a job while going to school so you can preserve your money for the future. You buy a house, and there goes big chunk right there." The attorney cleared his throat. "Do you have any other questions? I have another appointment at nine."

Welby thought quickly. "So are you giving my dad his money when he gets out of the pen? What if he backslides? What if none of us would have made it to the straight and narrow? What happens to all the money?"

"Well, first off, your dad has agreed to participate in Alcoholics Anonymous for the rest of his life. Like you, I'll give him money for expenses for the first year after he gets out, and then if he is managing well and staying sober, I'll release the rest of the money to him. There are specifications in the will that the money would be left to various charities if your siblings and your father were not able to make significant life changes. Anything else?"

"When I talked to my dad, I told him I'd contact my half-siblings. He said you know their whereabouts. Could you give me their contact information?"

Mr. Pinkleton hesitated, but then he spoke. "Welby, I find that very impressive of you. I know you got the raw deal in that family. However, you fared better than your siblings, once your father went to prison. I will give you the information, if you promise not to say a word about me and your great-grandfather. Can I trust you on this one?"

Welby thought about it. He could see the carrot of an inheritance motivating a person to get their life on the right track. Perhaps he could encourage each of the kids to turn over a new leaf. Would Mr. Pinkleton possibly trust him to help them get onto the straight and narrow? God knows he knew more than enough about how hard drug recovery could be. He had no idea how the foster home situations may have further damaged them. Maybe he should take some time to think about this. Later, he could come back to Mr. Pinkleton with a sound proposal.

"Cat got your tongue, Welby? It's time to wrap this up," Mr. Pinkleton interrupted his thoughts.

"Yes, sir, I mean, no, sir. I won't mention anything about you and the inheritance if I contact them. But with your blessing, I'd like to prepare a plan, a proposal of sorts, to possibly use the inheritance as a carrot to help motivate them to change, and maybe even to use some money if needed to help them get cleaned up. I need to think about this. I can email you my ideas after I get them together and see what you think. I won't do anything without your approval. For now, I promise not to mention the inheritance. If you would just give me the information about how to get ahold of them."

Mr. Pinkleton called in his secretary. "Mary, please make a copy of this paper for me and give it to Welby." Then he looked at Welby. "I would be more than happy to entertain your proposal. You have a good head on your shoulders. I believe you have their best interests at heart. I never quite agreed with the old man's tactics. A mentor can make a world of difference in a person's life. He took a risky gamble, hoping you would all come around on your own. I wanted him to take a more active role in your lives. I couldn't for the life of me figure out why in the hell he wouldn't make himself known, but he made his own decisions.

"Welby, I wish there were more young men in the world today like you. I must say, I'm mighty impressed. If anybody can help your brother and sisters turn around, it will be you. I'll be eager to hear your proposal. Shoot off an email to me as soon as you figure it all out." Then he rose and extended his hand to Welby. "Very good to meet you, son. Thank you so much for coming in. You've got a bright future. I look forward to working with you. Remember, I do have discretion. Fortunately, he trusted me with his estate. We'll be in touch."

Back in the waiting room, the secretary handed Welby the information about his siblings. Welby was elated as he walked back to the van with George.

"You look mighty happy, Welby," George commented. "Good news?" He opened the door for Welby, who climbed up into the passenger seat.

Once George got in the van, Welby answered. "Oh, man," he said, putting his face in his hands. "Who's going to believe all this stuff? I keep thinking I'm in some kind of dream and I'm going to wake up any time now. Oh wow, oh wow. When that little leprechaun gave me my marching orders in Ireland, I never in a million years could've imagined all of this. God is good. It's so much," Welby gushed.

"Good news, then?" George inquired again.

"Yes, the attorney confirmed what my dad told me. I'm a millionaire, George. He'll release money when I leave Sun Power for my support and tuition. After a year, if all goes well, he'll turn it all over to me."

George slapped Welby on the back. "Way to go, son. I'm proud of you. Remember, I knew you when you were poor like the rest of us." George laughed.

Welby laughed, too. "You're not poor, George."

"You're right. I've got what I need to get by, but I'm no millionaire."

As they headed back to the house, Welby let the good feelings roll. For today, he aimed to be happy and celebrate the goodness the Good Lord seemed to be sending his way.

CHAPTER TWENTY-ONE
HOME AGAIN

The MAMs Regroup

A month later, Priscillas joined the MAMs at Molly's house to debrief their trip. Jane sprung for a catered dinner of soul food. As they commenced their meeting around the Mabras' dining room table, Abigail led the discussion.

"Ladies, it's time to finalize our grant report and plan our third trip. Time is running out. I know it's a lot, but we've got to get our third trip in before the end of the year. The longer we wait, the more expensive it will be. Already, it's going to cost a pocket of change."

Jane said, "Come on, Abby, give us a break. Let's relax and celebrate tonight." She uncorked a bottle of wine. "Who wants something to drink?"

"Have you ever thought about how hypocritical we are?" Priscilla asked. "We run drug and alcohol treatment houses and then we drink wine at these meetings. We should be better role models." Although she could enjoy a glass of wine now and then, she didn't like the MAMs getting tipsy during a serious discussion. The debrief of their trip was no laughing matter. Would they make light of the whole thing?

"But we're not addicts," Jane argued. "We shouldn't drink in front of them, but privately, what's the harm?"

"I'll take some wine." Sallie laughed. "Hear! Hear! I'm with Jane, we need to celebrate before we launch into more work. We've done enough, Lord knows. We're just a book club. I thought book clubs were about having fun. Have we forgotten how to laugh?'

"Laughter is the nectar of the gods! I'll have some, too, Jane," Katharine said, holding up her glass to receive. "Let's plan a date night real soon. Sallie's right. All work and no play could send us to early graves. It's so easy to forget my biggest lesson of our archaeological expedition in search of Thecla: life is short. Let's go dancing."

Molly agreed. "Yes, and I need a little wine to deal with the reality of our trip. That was a lot. I'm still trying to take it all in." Jane filled her glass. Molly promptly sat back and started gulping it down.

"Okay, okay, give me some wine," Abigail acquiesced. "Is this all you want to do tonight?"

"First, let's enjoy this food," Sallie said. "Eating is our serious business. Thanks, Jane, for bringing in this spread. Ribs, collard greens, sweet potato pie, macaroni and cheese, oh, my!"

"May I offer a prayer?" Priscilla asked.

"Of course," Abigail responded.

"Let's hold hands," Priscilla directed. She noticed Jane raising her eyebrows, but she proceeded regardless. From the beginning, the MAMs were a spiritual group. She, for one, thought they should act like it and not skip honoring God before a meal. She closed her eyes and hoped they would follow suit. "Dear God, we thank you and Jane for this wonderful soul food dinner. As we gather to celebrate our trip to the Sea Islands, we give thanks for everything we learned and witnessed, for the distant relatives we met and the fun we had together. Bless Welby and Reagan and Abigail and Seamus as they plan their lives together. And also, please make our path clear as we consider the future. Thank you for a safe trip. We pray that you'll be with the Sun Power House and FARM residents this week. Bless each of them as they continue to heal from their addictions and rebuild their lives. Be with each of us and may this food nourish our bodies to do your will. In the name of Jesus, Amen."

"Amen," Sallie yelled.

"Thank you," Abigail told Priscilla. "That was very nice. Seamus and I are trying to decide how to join our lives. It's not very simple, you know. We both have houses and family, so for him to move here, or for me to move there, creates a rift we don't want. On the other hand, maintaining two houses and all the travel will become difficult as we get older. We are thinking we might sell our houses, and give our children money to add some additions, so we can live with them, but that can also be difficult. Please keep us in your prayers."

"Did you set a date for the wedding?" Sallie asked. "Do I get to be in it?"

Abigail laughed. "No, not yet. It's going to be a small affair. Again, with our families, it's hard to figure that out. We might have a ceremony here, and also in Ireland, but we'd like for our families to meet each other, so we're trying to coordinate their schedules right now, and it's expensive for whichever ones have to travel. For now, we're spending three months here, then three months there."

"I wish you'd just get married," Priscilla said. She knew she sounded judgmental, but she also thought Abigail and Seamus were old enough to know better.

"I know," Abigail responded. "I'd prefer that too, and we may just elope and have receptions with the children later. Speaking of weddings, what are we going to do about Reagan and Welby? Don't you think that's too soon for them to be engaged? We allowed them to break the rules after Ireland, and now look where we're at."

"Good question," Molly concurred. "We can't really tell them what to do, only control how they can be together until they're out of our programs. Remember, we're going to have them go to counseling; hopefully, that will help."

"Yes, that should help, Molly," Katharine said, then changed the subject. "What are we reading next?"

"Let's talk about that." Molly shook her head. "If we're getting ready to go to West Africa, I, for one, would suggest we start reading about Africa."

"Do you have any recommendations?" Katharine asked.

"I need to do some research. I have friends who took tours to West Africa. Maybe I can talk to one of them again. I used some of their information when we wrote the grant, but that's been a while."

"I certainly don't know where to begin," Abigail said. "It's such a large continent and I really wonder what our purpose is in this trip. Are we exploring roots or learning about the slave trade?"

"Both for me," Sally commented. "You know, the slave trade is so ugly."

Molly said, "I think it's okay to visit something about the slave trade, but, really, I think the goal should be understanding the homelands of our people. I want to revisit my DNA maps. We could get the others with African roots to come together for that. And you, Priscilla! I want to see where our African roots are, that will give us some direction. I believe my people came from the area that is now Ghana. We need to find some books about Ghana."

"I like that idea, too. I want to learn about the places of origin of my African ancestors," Priscilla agreed.

"Great idea," Abigail said. "I'll do some research on the DNA. Then we can find books on those countries and look for a tour that might incorporate several. In the meantime, Molly, didn't you say you have some pictures? If we're all done eating, can we regroup in the living room and look at your photos of the trip?"

"Yes," Molly exclaimed. "Let me get my laptop hooked up to the big screen while you finish up. Just take all the plates into the kitchen. I'll clean them up later."

The MAMs gathered around the big screen, watching their trip unfold before their eyes. From Savannah to Hilton Head, from Charleston to Cypress Gardens, Brookgreen Gardens to Wilmington, they relived their adventures and closed the evening out enjoying the memories of good times together. Priscilla marveled how well Molly had captured their travels. She continued to process the trip, a work in progress that would take time, but she thoroughly enjoyed the kaleidoscope of colors and photos of the journey that had certainly changed her life.

"Wonderful," Katharine exclaimed when the photos stopped scrolling. "You should share these with the FARM and Sun Power Houses sometime soon. What a great job. I love your photos, Molly."

"Thanks," Molly replied. "I love taking pictures and finding ways to share them with others. It's fun to keep experiences alive through the photos. I will make a YouTube video out of them and we can share the link when we do the grant report."

"I love reliving our journey," Priscilla told Molly. "This trip meant a lot to me. I learned so much about my ancestors and myself. Thank you, Molly."

"Can you do one from the Ireland trip, too?" Abigail asked.

"Great idea. Yes. I do have a lot of photos from Ireland. That's the thing about taking so many pictures, it takes time to process them. Sometimes I never get around to it. I will set a goal and work on that to have it ready to show you at our next book club meeting," Molly decided. "And now, I think it's time to call it a night."

"Do we have a book for next month? I know we agreed to explore the African DNA map, but we need something now for next month," Sallie said.

Then Katharine and Molly started searching on their phones. Katharine said, "Hey, here's a simple one with only a hundred and sixty pages: *History of West Africa: A Captivating Guide to West African History, Starting from Ancient Civilizations through the Medieval Period to the Present, 2022.* Only two ninety-nine on Kindle. Maybe that's a place to start?"

"Sounds good to me," Molly said. "Katharine, can you send us the link? And, Abigail, you're going to look for books connected to the DNA, right?"

Abigail said, "Yes, that's my plan."

"Good. Bring those suggestions next month," Molly said. "And thanks, ladies, for coming. If you want to take some leftovers from our meal, join me in the kitchen. However, don't feel obligated. I'm sure Tom and I can handle them ourselves."

Priscilla smiled. "You go right ahead. You offer your house to us every month. You deserve some rewards now and then." As she slipped into her coat and bid adieu, she felt downright happy. Happy to be friends with these wonderful women, happy to know the truth about her past, and happy to have a mission ahead as she worked to build bridges in her own political party.

Reagan dabbed a few finishing bright brushstrokes of orange on her painting of the sunrise, the view of the waterfront at her parents' home in Oceanside, Georgia. Then, she turned to admire the other works in her series, "Sea Island Journey," surprised at how much she enjoyed her own work. She loved the first ones she did of the plantation gardens. Along with the beauty of the place, she managed to include something in each photo which indicated their common history of serving as plantation grounds during slavery. Brookgreen Gardens, Boone Plantation house gardens, and Cypress Gardens came alive in her work. Her series on Savannah included the waterfront, but also the Pin Point museum and a depiction of the story of her ancestors in downtown Savannah. Yet to come were the scenes from Hilton Head and Charleston Gullah tours and collages for Priscilla, Molly, Reagan and Welby, and what each learned during the trip. The event would be a fundraiser for the FARM, but also an artistic launch for Reagan. Although she'd been painting for years, she never had her work displayed publicly in this way. When the MAMs first approached her about doing this art show at a local gallery, she readily agreed without thinking. Later, the monstrosity of the job dawned upon her, yet she persisted and really enjoyed the process and the opportunity.

She glanced at the clock and realized she needed to stop and clean up for the counseling appointment with Welby at Molly's church. The MAMs didn't approve entirely of their early engagement, but she had no second thoughts herself. They'd arranged this session after telling Reagan and Welby they needed to attend engagement counseling. She was skeptical it would help. Welby thought it might assist them in their future together. She supposed it couldn't hurt.

She took a quick shower, returned to her room to dress and went downstairs to wait for her ride. Her cellphone buzzed, and "Dad" scrolled across its screen. She barely communicated with him since the luncheon in Wilmington and she didn't want to talk to him now, but she knew she couldn't avoid him forever. She answered the call. "Hi, Dad, What's up?"

"Checking on my baby, how you doin', honey?"

"I'm good, Dad. How are you? You're the one recovering from a heart attack."

"You know me. Can't keep a good man down. I'm heading north for the springtime soon. Wondering if I could come take you out to eat when I get back," her father said.

"Oh, well." Reagan hesitated. "You know that's not really a part of our program. We don't go out to eat, we just eat in."

"Well, seems to me that we just had a meal together with all your people not too long ago at that restaurant in Wilmington. When did they change your rules? What's going on, honey? Do I need to talk to them for you?"

"On our trips, we do eat out, but not at home. But, hey, if you want to come visit, we've got a fundraiser coming up, my first art opening, my paintings about the trip. Could you come to that?"

"What's the date?"

"Three weeks from Saturday. I've got a boatload of work to do before then!" Reagan added.

"Well, I suppose I could put that on my calendar, if you promise to save some time for your old man that night. And Tyler wants to see you. I'll bring him along."

That stopped Reagan in her tracks. Tyler? Really? The Tyler who didn't want to have anything to do with her? Her father knew she was with Welby. Oh, yes, but he would do anything to stop her relationship with a Black man. "No, Dad, don't bring Tyler. I'm engaged. Welby and I are getting married!"

"You are what?" her father's voice blared into her ear.

"You heard me. I'm engaged to Welby. I'm very happy. I want you to be, too."

Her father mumbled something she couldn't understand and said he needed to talk to her mother. She didn't expect him to be happy, but she felt nervous about what he might say. She decided to sign off and not give him the chance. "Dad, I've got an appointment in a few minutes and I can't be late. I'll talk to you later." She hung up without even hearing a good-bye.

***

An hour later, Molly dropped Reagan off for the counseling appointment. Reagan revisited the conversation with her father as she walked into the church. Did he really want to fix her back up with Tyler? And had Tyler agreed? It was very weird. She knew her father absolutely did not accept her relationship with Welby. That was a problem, but more his problem than hers. If he couldn't allow her to make her own decisions, then he would have to suffer the consequences.

"Hi, beautiful," Welby welcomed her. "You're just in time. Pastor Jahnaka just paged us." Welby took Reagan's hand and pulled her toward the suite of offices off the large foyer. "We're going in here."

Together, they walked down a corridor and into a pleasant office. She looked out a window at the rolling fields behind the building. Verdant tropical plants graced the corner of the office. Living room furniture created a cozy setting. Pastor Jahnaka rose from her desk, welcoming them to her office and gestured for them to take a seat on the comfortable furniture. Welby and Reagan sat down on the small sofa, and the pastor sat across from them on a single chair.

"So, I understand you've been referred for premarital counseling," she began. "I usually schedule four sessions with couples, if you're willing. Today, we'll get to know each other. I'll give you some homework and we'll come back to discuss your answers. In the third session, we will discuss communication patterns and strategies. Then you'll return one more time so we can tie up loose ends, covering anything else you'd like to work on. How does that sound?"

Reagan responded first. "We don't think we really need this, but the group homes made us come. I guess that's okay."

"We're good," Welby explained. "They think we're rushing into this, but our eyes are wide open. We know what we want. We love each other."

"Okay, then," Pastor Jahnaka responded. "First, I want you to understand pre-marital counseling isn't a bad thing, it's just a good way to start what we hope will be a lifelong relationship. It's good to talk things out and have a sounding board. You want a strong foundation when the inevitable problems arrive. All marriages will have challenges. Being prepared will be a help. Tell me a little about yourselves and how you met."

Reagan launched into her story. "Well, you see, we're both in the MAMs' group homes. I came there last spring after going to rehab for a drug problem. In college, I suffered serious injuries after an accident with a drunk driver. I got hooked on opioids. I finished my degree and started a job as a nurse, but I needed my drugs. I started stealing them from the hospital. Fortunately, I went through rehab and the FARM house has been a great place for me to heal and get my life back together. I'm a nurse, but also an artist and I've had time to do a lot of painting this year. In fact, I'm having an art opening, which will be a fundraiser for the FARM and Sun Power House, in a few weeks. I've decided to become an art therapist when I get out."

"Okay," Pastor Jahnaka said. "And tell me about your relationship with Welby."

"Yeah, well," Reagan started slowly. "We're in separate homes, so we didn't really get to know each other very much until we went to Ireland last fall. I mean, we met and we talked some, but it wasn't until the trip that we started to really get to know one another. Well, wait a minute, we did play music together, before the trip. Welby plays the saxophone and the banjo and I play the fiddle. We played together at a fundraiser. That's when I really started to notice Welby." She smiled as she remembered that night.

"Oh, yeah," Welby reminisced with her. "But I noticed you from the beginning, Reagan, from the first time they got our group homes together. For me, it was love at first sight. Watching you fiddle, playing right along with you, I got hit hard." Welby laughed. "You got under my skin from the beginning, Reagan, before we went anywhere. Remember how I tried connecting with you that night they told us about our trip to Ireland?"

"I remember I swatted you good!" Reagan laughed. "It took me a while to come around. I mean, I'm a Republican, you're a Democrat, I'm white, you're Black. Our worlds never would have crossed if we didn't both screw up."

Pastor Jahnaka jotted something on her tablet and said, "There are several things you brought up that I'd like to explore later. First, you are both in recovery and that adds a dimension to a new relationship. Second, your political and racial differences bring you from different worlds. It does take a while to understand each other when your backgrounds are vastly different. When did you become attracted to Welby, Reagan?"

"Oh, well, I was always attracted to him, I just didn't want to be." Reagan smiled and looked at Welby, feeling awkward. "I mean, to be honest, I grew up in a racist family. Before the FARM, I never had friends of color. I would never consider dating a Black man where I grew up. It wasn't done. It took me a while to come around.

"I think for me, things started to open up in Ireland. Everything became new and different. We went on a silent retreat. I walked the labyrinth and Welby's great-grandmother started talking to me, like a ghost. Freaked me out, but once I realized Welby actually knew her and she wanted me to be Welby's friend, that really got me going. I mean, how could that happen? It was so cool."

"Can you explain what you mean? Welby's great-grandmother talked to you like a ghost?" Pastor Jahnaka asked. "That does sounds quite unusual." She smiled warmly, making Reagan feel validated, like maybe she just wanted to understand.

"Well, it was totally weird, yes. She was like a ghost. At first, I truly thought I was ready for the loony bin. Later, I painted a picture of her and Welby recognized her as his Grand Ma Ma, as he calls her. Turns out she'd been talking to him, too. Things ignited after that. I mean, a visit from the other side doesn't happen every day, if you know what I mean?" Reagan stopped talking, wondering what the lady thought. "Do you believe me?"

The counselor cleared her throat. "Stranger things have happened. I believe sometimes those who have passed on come back to visit. It's never happened to me personally, but certainly I've heard stories. I can see when Welby recognized her in your painting, it helped you believe what happened. That's quite a story, Reagan. I see how it affected you deeply."

"Thank you. And still later, when painting a picture of my life, I explained it to Welby, and he got it. He got me, like nobody, ever. Things just grew from there. Welby's amazing, the most amazing person I've ever met. And we both follow Jesus and we both want to make this world a better place. We want to help others who messed up like us. And you know, although I'm white and he's Black, we both have African and Irish DNA. So we're not so different after all."

Pastor Jahnaka nodded at Reagan. "Thank you, Reagan, for sharing that. It tells me a lot about the two of you. You've had very significant experiences together. Now, Welby, tell me a little about yourself and how you were first attracted to Reagan."

"Well, like I said, I was attracted to Reagan from the start. I mean, look at her. She's beautiful. After five years in the pen, the image of Reagan soothed my deprived soul. All my life, though, I kept away from white women. The sisters in North Carolina wouldn't give me the time of day if I kicked it with a white lady. But Reagan's one of a kind, one in a million. She's beautiful, talented, and smart. I don't know, how do you explain love?"

Reagan smiled at Welby and reached out for his hand. "That's so sweet, Welby."

The counselor smiled also. "Love can be hard to define, but I think you explained yourself very well, Welby. So tell me more about you."

"What do you want to know? I grew up in North Carolina. My dad was a loser, an alcoholic. He left my mom when I was young. I had some good years on the sea island with Mom and my Grand Ma Ma, but then my mom died. My dad picked me up, took me to live with him and his second wife in Raleigh. He wanted me for a free babysitter. When my dad killed my stepmom and went to jail, my stepsiblings went to foster care. Then I went to live with my aunt and uncle in Raleigh, which was good."

"So, you had some good times and bad times growing up. That must've been hard, losing your mom and feeling like your dad just wanted to use you."

"Yes, that's the story of my life. That made me hard inside, losing Mom and then living in Dad's messed-up life." Welby paused.

"But your aunt and uncle were good people. Sounds like you were in a better place after your dad went to prison." Pastor Jahnaka reflected what she'd heard. "What happened after that?"

Welby continued. "Well, I finished high school and found a good-paying job, driving trucks. But I got pulled over on the highway, driving while Black, you know? The officer found drugs in my glove compartment. They sent me to the pen for five years. You know how the law is for African Americans, right?" The pastor nodded and he continued.

"I pretty much gave up after that, five years of my life wasted. I didn't care about one thing in there, and even after I got out. But my auntie found the MAMs group home up in Ohio. I agreed to go, just to make her happy."

"Oh, I see," the counselor said. "That's how you got to Ohio. But you weren't very excited about coming here."

"Yes, but surprise! I discovered the MAMs and the Sun Power House are very cool. They got me a saxophone and a banjo to play. They taught me electrical skills, I learned how to install solar panels, and then they started taking us on trips. To Ireland! I never even left the country before, and there I was, exploring my Irish roots. Reagan's right, Grand Ma Ma showed up and showed out with her, but she also kept yelling at me to make something of myself. Maybe you heard there's magic in Ireland? It's so true. On that silent retreat where Reagan got a visit from Grand Ma Ma, I got visited by a leprechaun. I know, you probably think I'm crazy, but he told me to become a new Martin Luther King, Junior for today and that's what I hope to do. When I get out of Sun Power House, I'm going back to college and then to seminary. I believe God's calling me to make a difference for our people."

The pastor seemed puzzled. "So, Welby, a leprechaun talked to you? Do you believe in leprechauns?"

Welby grinned sheepishly. "I know, it's very weird. I would say no, I don't believe in leprechauns. They're mythical figures, part of Irish folklore, not real life. Yet, in Ireland, I saw one and he was talking directly to me. A leprechaun also talked to one of the ladies in our group. I can't explain it, really. I do believe, though, that God was talking to me that day. Strange as it may sound, that day changed my life. Following the call I got that day helps me find my path into the future."

"Isn't Welby amazing?" Reagan asked. "He even went back to the prison and spoke to inmates in the chapel. He told them they could be somebody, too! He's already living his call. Do you see why I love him so much?" Reagan put her arm around Welby.

"Okay," the pastor said. "I have to admit, your story is unique, but they say God speaks in mysterious ways." Then she laughed. "Thanks for giving me your background. So, you've known each other about nine months, but haven't spent much time together?"

"Well, yes. Generally, the group homes only get together once or twice a month. But the MAMs took us to Ireland and we just returned from the Sea Islands. We both went on those trips. After Ireland, the MAMs let us start to date a little. We know each other pretty well, I think," Reagan said.

"Have you met each other's families?" the pastor inquired.

"I've met Reagan's parents," Welby reported. "He came to a fundraiser the MAMs organized and we visited both of them in Oceanside, Georgia, on our trip."

"And how did that go?" Pastor Jahnaka asked.

"We've had some issues," Welby said, laughing nervously. "Yeah, I don't think Reagan's father is very happy with her choice."

"Reagan?" The pastor looked at her. "Is this going to be a problem?"

"My father embarrasses me. I thought he was a good Christian man until recently. Now I know he lied about our heritage and also tried to frame Welby. When I confronted him, he had a heart attack. He apologized and said he would do better, but he's not really coming around. He just tried to fix me up with my old boyfriend," Reagan said.

Welby's eyes widened and his mouth dropped open. "You didn't tell me about that," he complained.

"Yeah, well, he called just before I came over here. I'm not going to let him control me. He's been in charge of me all my life and I always respected his opinion, until now. I'm on my own now. If he doesn't come around, that's his problem," Reagan asserted.

"This could be a problem for you both. What if you get married and he's still not supporting your decision? You say he tried to frame Welby? Can you explain that?"

"When we were at my parents' house, an assistant police chief visited Dad to complain about me dating a Black man and offered to frame Welby. My dad went along with it. They picked up Welby on an alleged rape charge. Fortunately, I remembered the security system picks up what happens in the house and was able to get the video of their conversation before my dad could erase it."

"Wow, Reagan, Welby. That must've been really hard for you both."

"Tell me about it," Reagan said. "I was furious. I'm glad he pulled through, but I'm still upset."

"Yes, this is a lot, for you both," the pastor reflected. "Welby, you must be having a hard time with this."

"I don't like it," Welby admitted."I've tried to respect the man, but it's hard. He acts nice in front of my face. It's what he does when I turn my back that worries me."

"I'm not going to put up with his bad behavior," Reagan announced. "If he wants to be part of my life, he needs to stop being racist."

"One of the things you must accept is that Reagan's father may never change. Going into this marriage, be aware that his alienation could be permanent. Surely, you hope he'll come around, but if not, you need a game plan."

"I agree," Reagan said. "For me, it's about standing up to him and not letting him push me around. I'm going to be with Welby, whether or not he likes it. I love him and I hope he comes around, but I'm not going to condone his bad behavior. Only he can make the choice to do the right thing."

"I encourage you to think about that some more," the pastor said. "Can you live with it? How will it impact your family life, holidays and gatherings? Now, I'm giving you both these questions to consider before our next session. And if you have no other questions, I'll see you next week."

Reagan and Welby walked out of the office. Reagan paused in the hall. Facing Welby, she took both of his hands in hers and said, "I love you, Welby."

Welby leaned down and gave her a quick kiss, whispering, "Love you, too, baby."

Then they locked arms, walking together out of the church, where George waited to take them home. Reagan felt warm all over, happy to have found love with Welby. She couldn't wait until they could make their union official.

Seamus and Abigail Plan the Fundraiser and Tie the Knot

Abigail invited Seamus to stage the art opening for Reagan. After years as a tour guide in Ireland, he knew how to organize a party, an event, or almost anything. She also asked him to keep himself in the States a little longer. She didn't want to say good-bye just yet. As the planning unfolded, they both sensed something more.

They began with writing intentions for the art show. They both hoped to launch Reagan into the art scene. They also both wanted to raise awareness of the MAMs group homes and, along with that, some additional funds for the future. They wanted to invite the families of their group home members to share and celebrate the trips and to express the unity they all felt as they explored their roots.

When they talked about families, Seamus and Abigail also realized they wanted to invite their own. Seamus knew his kids wanted to come to the States. "I'm ready, Abigail," he admitted to her as they discussed possibilities.

"Ready for what?" she asked with a smile. She thought she knew exactly what he meant, but didn't want to assume she could read his mind. Could they be thinking the very same thing?

"I think it's time for you and me to make our connection permanent.

We could tag it on to the art show fundraiser, perhaps the next day? If we rent the venue for two days, instead of one, we might get a good deal. Let's do this right. What do you say? Are you ready, my dear?" Seamus put his hand on her arm with an expectant look on his face.

Abigail let out a breath she didn't realize she was holding. She wasn't completely comfortable with having Seamus live with her these past few weeks, because she worried what others might think. Her commitment to him was ironclad. "Yes! I'm ready, my love. Of course! That's a great idea. I've worried we're not setting the best example, living together before marriage, but it just seems so right. We haven't figured out everything about our future, but the one thing I know for sure is that I want to be with you."

Seamus embraced her and their lips locked. Abigail felt joy from the tip of her nose down to the bottom of her toes. She wondered, not for the first time, how she ever could get so lucky to find amazing love twice in one life.

The coming days blurred together as arrangements unfolded and flights were booked. The double-header slowly took shape. Ohio galleries expressed much interest in Reagan's work. Excitement built over the timely subject matter of race for the exhibit. The MAMs invited people working in recovery and re-entry in Ohio. They wanted to build networks with those doing the important work of helping people find new lives, rising from the ashes of their pasts. The MAMs' group homes and travels provided intrigue and interest, attracting quite a crowd. In fact, as the reservations flooded in, they changed the venue from the small gallery originally booked to a large banquet hall at Molly's church. Her nondenominational, predominantly African American church embraced the Sea Island trip theme with fervor.

While Reagan painted, Abigail and Seamus carefully continued to plan and extend invitations. The only blot on the event came in the form of a phone call from Reagan's dad, who threatened bad publicity. "Reagan didn't sign up for a match-making service," he barked into the phone to Abigail. He also complained about the art opening. "I've always encouraged Reagan's art, but she and I both knew it was an avocation, creating something pretty to decorate the walls. It isn't the purpose of her life."

Seamus didn't seem disturbed, convinced he would come around, but Abigail began to lose sleep over thoughts about what Reagan's father could do. However, the week before the event, Reagan's father announced that his doctor forbid his attendance, citing the dangers of the lingering coronavirus as he recovered from heart surgery. Abigail slept more peacefully as they forged full speed ahead with plans for the art opening and their wedding.

CHAPTER TWENTY-TWO
OPENING

Reagan Shares her Art

Welby took Reagan's hand, leading her into the large fellowship hall at Molly's church. After days of feverish painting and last-minute touching up, Reagan had completed her work, turning it all over to the MAMs the previous week. They promised to do her proud with help from professional gallery owners, members at the church. The MAMs invited Reagan to view the show with the group home residents and the MAMs an hour before opening to the public.

As she walked into the large room filled with her paintings, the MAMs and her friends from the FARM and Sun Power House spilled out from behind the displays and began to applaud. Tears spilled from Reagan's eyes as she acknowledged their praise. Overwhelmed with emotion, she scanned the room, feeling their love, as well as a deep gratitude for those who had crafted the exhibit.

"Thank you so much," she told them all. "Wow! What a great job, Molly!"

"Don't thank me," Molly quickly answered. "The real designers are coming later. We MAMs just helped them execute their plans."

"It's beautiful," Reagan said. "You told my story, our story. Wow!" She pulled Welby by the hand, beginning her personal journey through the paintings. "This is so cool," she exclaimed. "The Ireland journey! You grouped them together, so it tells a story."

"You're the storyteller, Reagan," Katharine commented. "They displayed your paintings chronologically, for the most part. It's great that you date all your paintings."

The group crowded behind Welby and Reagan as they began to peruse the exhibit. The first panel read simply The FARM, displaying Reagan's painting of the farmhouse. Her mind raced back to those early days out of rehab. She remembered her joy when the MAMs purchased watercolor and acrylic art supplies. She'd often escaped to her room to paint, still feeling so raw from the fallout of her addiction. The second panel announced Success Stories, and displayed the portraits Reagan created of FARM members who completed their first year and moved on to live their passions. She remembered attending the fundraiser to launch and celebrate the FARM graduates and later giving the paintings to each of the women. "How did you get all of them back?" she wondered out loud.

Molly laughed. "We're borrowing them, but they didn't argue. I think most of them are coming tonight. They also gave us permission to make prints. You'll see them on the walls at the FARM house soon."

Reagan placed her fingers over her mouth in surprise and continued to cry. "I'm going to have to do redo my makeup," she told Welby. "This is so, so much."

"I'm real proud of you," Welby said, patting her back and rubbing her shoulder with his free hand as he squeezed her other hand tight. "Cry all you want, baby. This is your happy day."

Next came the miniatures she sold at the Farmers' Market. These, she memorialized herself with her camera, not wanting to lose her work. When they planned the exhibit, she gave them to the MAMs to print and frame. The forty-some little paintings included mostly pictures of nature, things growing, blue skies, flowers and vegetables in the fields. Together, they created a mosaic of Earth's beauty, celebrating the magic of the FARM most of all.

When she'd first come to the group home, she hated getting her fingers dirty in the greenhouse and in the fields, but over time, she'd come to appreciate the manual labor and the goodness of cultivating earth. With the MAMs, she now realized that gardening and farming were important parts of her path toward healing. Somehow, gardening helped build inner wholeness as she watched the miracle of life unfolding through the growing season on the farm. Now, she simply said, "I love it! I love, love, love this. How did they do it? It looks like a patchwork quilt. It's a work of art all by itself!"

Artemis put her arm around Reagan. "You did good, sista. I remember selling these little pieces at the Farmers' Market. They went so fast, faster than the produce. We should've jacked up the price. They got these little masterpieces for five dollars. Highway robbery!"

Reagan laughed and told Artemis, "Thank you. Painting is like therapy for me. It provided an outlet for me in the early days on the FARM. I was happy that the people liked them. It wasn't about making money. That's not why I paint."

"Why do you paint, Reagan?" Antonio asked.

"It's my thing. Ever since I was little, I've loved making art. I made people smile. I could be creative and express what I saw. I don't know. It's a part of who I am."

"It's so important to live your passion," Abigail said. "We hope all of you have the courage to live your unique lives."

"Like my tattoo parlor?" Antonio asked. "That's my art."

"Will you give me one?" Artemis asked. "I want one right here," she added, smacking her butt.

Antonio laughed. "Sure, baby. Visit my parlor when we get out." He smacked his lips and Reagan noticed his eyes lingering on Artemis. He gave her a little spin, scoping out her backside. "Ah, yes. A prime spot for a little tattoo. Maybe the MAMs can give me a show, too."

"That would be fun," Artemis agreed. "They could invite your customers to come and display their decorated bodies!"

"Possibly," Antonio replied. "But I think we'd have to move it out of the church. My show would be X-rated."

Reagan appreciated their lightheartedness. Their bantering helped Reagan stop sobbing.

"Let's keep moving," Molly said. "The doors open in about a half hour."

Together, the group made their way through the rest of the exhibit. They relived the journey to the Emerald Isle, remembering the tourist sites of Newgrange, the Wicklow Mountains, Kinvarra, and the Dingle pub. Reagan's art captured the beauty of the gardens around the Blarney Castle, the sunrise cruise on the east coast, and the silent retreat at Brigid's Retreat Center.

Reagan found herself being transported back to those days in Ireland with Welby, when she'd painted the story of her life on silent retreat, remembering how Welby got it and how they grew so close during the that trip. She smiled at the picture of Grand Ma Ma visiting her on the labyrinth. The ghost turned out to be a member of Welby's family. More memories surfaced as she walked by her depictions of the Leprechaun Museum, Belfast, Brigid Retreat Center, the Giant's Causeway, Carrick-a-Rede Island Rope Bridge, and the Shalem Centre of Peace. Her heart felt full, reliving their journey. She squeezed Welby's hand.

"These are beautiful," Abigail commented. "Reagan, you did a lovely job."

"Aye, you did," Seamus agreed. "I think some Irish galleries might love to put some of these paintings up back in the home country. You paint us proud."

They moved on to the Sea Island panels as their more recent trip south came alive.

"These are so good," Priscilla said. "Can I get prints of all of these? I don't know if I can afford them, but I want them all."

"I think we can work something out, Priscilla." Reagan smiled. "I know the trip was as important to you as it was to me. This is all part of our heritage now."

"Certainly, if Reagan is willing, we can make them available to you at cost, Priscilla. But you might want to pick out your favorites," Abigail offered.

Reagan thought about the financial arrangement with the paintings. Half of the proceeds would go to the FARM, the other half into her savings account. She loved being able to support the MAMs after all they did for her. She only insisted on keeping the painting about her own life. The others, she didn't mind sharing, knowing she could retain a digital image and the print, if she ever wanted to display some in her own future home. As an artist, she created way too much to keep. Long ago, she'd discovered that she found more joy in giving the paintings away and letting others enjoy them in their homes. That she now could sell her art still baffled her.

"Oh, my gosh," Priscilla gushed. "Pinpoint, Savannah, Hilton Head, Brookgreen Gardens, Boone Plantation, Cypress Gardens. These are amazing, Reagan!"

Reagan blushed, even as she also admired her own work. Hung together, they created an explosion of color, celebrating the beauty of the South.

"Ooh, the Angel Oak," Molly said, focusing on the sprawling Charleston tree depicted with ghost-like creatures flying around and hanging from its branches. "This is spooky, but so cool. The spirits of the slaves, right? You make the legends visible. I love this, Reagan. I want this for my living room."

Reagan didn't want the evening to end. She wished she could linger at each painting, but she knew they needed to move on. The final panel announced Revelation in the Roots. Here were the new paintings that surfaced from her imagination late one night a couple weeks ago. She sought to capture the family trees of those with mixed roots. Specifically, her own, Priscilla's, Welby's, and Molly's. The paintings included background silhouettes of Ireland, select Southern states and Sea Islands, as well as the west coast of Africa. A portrait of the person, with shades of brown, green, and white on their faces, filled the center of each canvas. Other images of the known ancestors were scattered in the foreground. Grand Ma Ma figured prominently on Welby's painting.

"Oh, my God!" Priscilla said, stopping in front of her own story. "Reagan! This is beautiful!" She was looking at her own story, a slave quilt waving in the breeze, the plantation owner's son embracing his young slave lover, Annie, a cameo that faded into a portrait of a young woman, Moriya, created of their union. Mitchelville, a sketch of some of her newly found relatives rounded out the scene. "How did you do this?"

Priscilla embraced Reagan, hugging her so hard Reagan pulled away.

"Okay, now," Welby said. "Let's not get too excited here."

"Why not?" Priscilla said. "You should be the most excited of all, Welby. This is incredible."

Welby didn't respond. Reagan wondered what he was thinking. Perhaps he didn't like it because the painting included his sordid past and Grand Ma Ma with a pointed finger, obviously giving him another piece of her mind?

But then he asked, "How did you do all of this? You even included my marriage proposal. When did you even have the time?"

Reagan grinned smugly. "I've been staying up late. Do you like it? See, here we are, walking outside at Pin Point. Here you are, speaking at the prison. See your dad? He's not very clear because I don't know what he looks like, and there's your great-grandfather, money bags by his side. Again, in the shadows because I don't know what the man looked like."

Under the painting, the rap poem Welby wrote in Ireland hung, framed. "My poem," he exclaimed. "How did you get that?"

"You don't remember, do you? I photographed that in Ireland and it helped me paint your story. 'I am Black. I am Green. I am Gold,'" Reagan read aloud. "See your face? All three colors are there."

Molly said, "Reagan, I absolutely love your portrait of me. Thank you so much. Another one for my living room, although I think I want the original for this one. Did you notice the gallery owners priced your pieces? Mine's worth five hundred dollars."

"You know I made that for you, Molly, don't you? I would never dream of charging you for that, after all you've done for me. You, too, Priscilla. It's yours after the show."

Reagan's own self-portrait closed out the show, showing her Black and white roots, with her known and previously unknown ancestors. She stood now, reviewing the piece into which she'd poured her very soul. The culmination of her life at the FARM, the trips to Ireland and the Sea Islands, her rehab, and her love for Welby. She'd included it all. "This is me," she whispered to Welby. He pulled her into an embrace.

When he released her, the group began clapping again as Molly led them to the food tables. "You all might want to have a little food before the vultures descend. The doors are opening in five minutes."

Soon, the guests began streaming in, crowding around the exhibit. Everyone wanted to meet the artist. The evening seemed like a dream to Reagan as she greeted person after person, accepting their praise.

Mr. Hammond, her college art professor, shook her hand shortly after the door opened. "I've been authorized to purchase two of your paintings for our university gallery."

Reagan didn't even know they'd invited him. "How did you even find out about my opening?" she asked.

"Oh, this was very well publicized, Reagan. Whoever did the PR for tonight knew what they were doing. The Ohio art community is well-informed about things like this."

"Thank you for coming," she told him. "You taught me so much. Thank you for that."

Most of the guests she didn't recognize, but she greeted them politely and talked about the FARM as the night progressed. About an hour after the doors opened, Abigail went to the microphone to make an announcement. She thanked everyone for coming and then invited Reagan to speak. Reagan pulled her prepared speech out of her purse and made her way to the lectern.

"Thank you so much for coming," Reagan told the crowd. "You honor me with your presence this evening. I owe so much to the MAMs, the Magnificent and Marvelous Book Club, who opened a group home for people like me less than two years ago. The paintings tell the story of my past year that I've spent living at their FARM, the place for Farming and Restoring with the MAMs. They are fabulous women. They created a place where many of us can heal from our addictions. And an added bonus were the trips they took us on to explore our roots. On these panels, you'll see pictures of the farm where we live, some of the growing things there, as well as the paintings of places in Ireland and the American South we've visited in the past year.

"Sometimes, we are rather divided in America these days. Our politics pull us apart, racism has been very evident, but here with the MAMs, we are exploring our roots and learning we are all connected. My own roots include both Irish and African ancestors. Their stories are my stories, as is the case with several other of the MAMs and group home members. I didn't try to sugarcoat the past, but to expose the racism rampant in the South and the plantation system. On the other hand, I hope I celebrated our diversity and our mixed roots. I do believe we are all one." When Reagan stepped away from the lectern, those gathered began to applaud, and she blushed, returning to Welby's side.

A member of the Ohio Re-Entry Task Force gave the MAMs an award for outstanding programming for re-entry citizens. "We hope that your program will be replicated across our country. We applaud your innovative group homes and also your outstanding travel program for your residents in recovery," the man said.

As the night drew to a close, Reagan thought about her parents. They hadn't come and she hadn't expected them, but there was a part of her that held out hope they would show up. She longed for her dad to embrace Welby as the wonderful man he truly was.

A commotion drew her attention near the front door. "Reagan!

Reagan! Where are you?" She peered over the crowd, trying to figure out who called her name. It sounded strangely familiar. A pathway opened between them, as people pointed to Reagan. And then she saw them. Her brother, Dean, and her ex-fiancé, Tyler, staggered up to her, looking somewhat disheveled, like they'd stopped at a few bars on their way to the opening.

She didn't want them to make a scene and ruin a perfect night. Fortunately, Molly began to speak, giving her a few moments to compose herself.

"Thank you all for coming," Molly said. "We are so proud of Reagan Hunter Smith and we're glad you enjoyed the show. Before we close the evening, I'd like to ask Abigail and Seamus to come to the front with their families. Abigail, one of our beloved MAMs, fell in love with our tour guide on our trip to Ireland, and the love was reciprocated. In fact, their wedding will be celebrated with us tomorrow." Then she searched the crowd. "Reagan, could you come help me?"

Reagan happily left her brother and Tyler and went to gather the painting hidden in the corner of the room that she'd made especially for Abigail and Seamus. She then brought it up to the front of the room and unveiled it while Molly told the crowd, "And there's one final painting for this show that Reagan is revealing now, about the love story of Seamus and Abigail. Reagan created this for you in celebration of your marriage."

Reagan placed it on an easel and then joined Molly at the microphone. "Thank you, Abigail and Seamus, for your love and presence in my life. I tried to capture your love, the trips we've been on together, and the union of your lives happening tomorrow. Congratulations."

Reagan perused her work one last time, delighted that it would soon hang in their home as they began a new life together. In one corner, she'd included a little scene with the leprechaun who talked to Abigail in her living room, long before the trip to Ireland. In another corner, she painted a jolly Seamus driving their travel van. In the center of the painting, she placed a portrait of the happy couple, holding hands and gazing into one another's eyes. Circling around them were images from the trip to Ireland: Trinity College, the Dublin bridge, the Cliffs of Moher, the Dingle Pub, the Blarney Castle, singing together in the pub on the east coast, St. Brigid Retreat Center, Belfast, and the Shalem Centre of Peace. She knew their love story followed a similar path to her own with Welby. She could remember Welby in all those places, and imagined Seamus and Abigail would appreciate the place memories, as well.

Seamus spoke for both of them. "Thank ye, Reagan. Thank ye. We be most blessed by this painting and the presence of our families here tonight."

Molly then continued her closing remarks. "If you entered a bid for a painting, please go to the table in the rear of the hall to see if you were the high bid. If so, please pay for your purchases and take them with you tonight. We do want you to know that these are all original paintings, but we have made prints of Reagan's work and will also be selling them for fifty dollars each. You can order those before you leave, if you wish."

Reagan's brother and Tyler reappeared at Reagan's side. Dean opened his wallet. "Dad asked me to buy a couple of your paintings, Reagan. Which ones should I buy?"

"Well, I'm afraid most of them have already sold. See if the ocean view from their house is available. Here, I'll show you. You can go back and bid on it." Reagan didn't honestly know which of her paintings she would want displayed in her parents' home. "Why don't you get that one, bid it up. The rest are available as prints and will be on the MAMs website for purchase. Dad and Mom can pick out the ones they want there."

Then she turned to Tyler. "What are you doing here?"

"Reagan, I missed you. I'm sorry I let you go. I haven't found anybody like you." He held out his hand.

"What?" Reagan said. "I heard you didn't want to have anything to do with me. It would mess up your political aspirations. You called everything off. Now you've changed your mind?"

He got down on his knee. "Reagan, I love you. I've loved you ever since high school. I still want you to be my wife. Will you do me the honor?"

He held out a large diamond as the people in the hall gathered around them. Reagan stopped him in his tracks, holding up her hands. "No, Tyler, I will not marry you. You made yourself perfectly clear earlier and I have moved on."

Welby came and stood beside her and she introduced him. "I'd like you to meet my fiancé, Marcus Welby Jones." Tyler looked flustered and she didn't care. "I hope you have a good life, Tyler. Good luck with your political career." Reagan turned and walked away. She didn't want him to spoil her magnificent evening.

As the people started to leave, she held Welby's hand and they walked through the exhibit one more time, before the paintings that were sold were taken down. All in all, the opening surpassed anything she could have imagined.

West Africa, Here We Come

The weeks after the trip and art show sped by for Priscilla as she returned to work. She began to put feet on her plans to speak up in her local Republican party. She scheduled a presentation about their trip to the Sea Islands at her church, planning to invite Republican friends. She knew it was only a beginning, but more would come.

Then, when Abigail and Seamus returned from their honeymoon, the MAMs called a special meeting with the group home residents to discuss their next trip. "As you know," Molly began, "we have our re-entry grant to complete with a final trip to West Africa. With the growing season beginning again at the FARM, we have decided to postpone the trip until late August, and have received permission from the foundation to extend the grant. But this raises some issues for those of you completing your year at the group homes. You may be working in new jobs, enrolled in classes, and not be able to attend with us. Tonight, we want to tell you a little about what we have planned and then you'll each need to decide if you can free your schedules to participate. We will fill any open slots with new residents.

"The details of our trip are not finalized yet," Abigail continued, "but we're planning to go to Ghana. We will visit the Cape Coast Castle, a part of the slave trade. Also, those with African ancestors will receive their African names at a naming ceremony. I believe that all of you with African roots came from the area of West Africa, which is why we chose Ghana. We want you to learn about the history of West Africa, to meet some of the people and to learn as much as you can about the culture there."

Priscilla's heart warmed as she imagined going to Africa, now one of her own homelands. "I'm so excited!" she told the group. "I can't wait."

Molly continued. "Now, we will need to get yellow fever and typhoid vaccinations and apply for visas, which is a lengthy process. We need to know by next week who will go along."

"How long will the trip be?" Reagan asked.

"Plan on ten days," Abigail responded. "By the time we fly over and back, and spend a good week there, we will be gone about ten days."

After questions were answered and a brief slide show on Ghana, the meeting concluded with a buffet of African food. Priscilla enjoyed the experience, imagining her ancestors of earlier days.

Grand Ma Ma Weighs In

Revelations on the Sea Islands brought new family stories into the lives of Reagan, Priscilla, and Molly as they explored their ancestry. My boy, Welby, got a taste of that evil Southern hospitality that enslaved our people, kept them from full citizenship, and currently does everything they can to lock them up. If you really listened to this story, you know we haven't solved the problem of race in the good ole' USA.

People change slowly, one person at a time. I'm real proud of Welby and Reagan. They show us possibilities. Priscilla's coming around, as well. But Reagan's parents and Moses Sun are plumb stuck in the past.

Tell me why racism is so dang hard to kick? And why in God's name are they aiming to keep all talk of it out of the schools? What kind of education teaches lies? Why you think the white people got themselves worked up into a tizzy over all this? I'll let you in on a little secret, something the fat cats with the power try to keep under cover. Keeping people mad at each other helps those on the top. Then they do their magic behind your back, pretending to work for one side or the other, while really aiming to pad their own pockets. Our Bible says it well. "Be aware of the wolf in sheep's clothing." And that's all I got to say. But believe me, you all got some work to do. I did my time, now it's your turn.

EPILOGUE

The old man asked his driver to stop as they approached the beach. John looked out over the waters, thinking back to the times he came to this very place to check on the Sea Island plantation work for his father. After all these years, the natural beauty still dazzled him. "You can go on, now," he told the driver. Then they cruised over the bridge, now connecting the mainland to the island. More memories flooded through his aging mind.

An image of his young lover, Annie, surfaced on the landscape ahead. A surge of joy flooded through his entire body as he remembered the comfort of her arms. But his heart quickly dropped as the odious task of looking over his father's plantation came to mind.

The island now bore little resemblance to the sprawling plantation of former days. Little shacks scattered the landscape. Once makeshift houses for the slaves, now they were falling into ruin. They passed abandoned rice fields and entered a small town. He felt like a stranger in a strange land and just wanted to go home.

He couldn't shake the regret, lodged deep within. Even now, he wondered what happened to Annie and their daughter, Moriya. Once he helped Moriya escape into a new life up North, he cut her off. He couldn't risk letting her interfere with his political career and his happy family life. He never told his wife. He never checked up on Annie at all. He knew many of their freed slaves settled in Mitchelville after the war. He assumed she might be there as well.

I'm sorry, God. Forgive me, he pleaded silently. A thought came to mind. Could he atone for his wrongs if he could find his daughter and her mother? Those early years haunted him yet. He'd pushed them back into the shadows, working hard to become a good husband and father, businessman and a congressman. Who was he trying to fool? Nothing could erase his mistakes and the suffering he caused. "We can go now," he told the driver. "Let's go on back home."

The sun continued to sparkle over the water, while the sins of the plantation cast long shadows over the land. Absolution would not come.

BOOKS AND FILM REFERENCED IN THIS BOOK

<u>Books</u>

Alexander, Michelle. *The New Jim Crow: Mass Incarceration in the Age of Colorblindness.* New Press, 2012.

Branch, Muriel Miller. *The Water Brought Us: The Story of the Gullah-Speaking People.* Dutton Press, 1995.

Brown, Alphonso. *A Gullah Guide to Charleston: Walking Through Black History.* The History Press, 2009.

Cooper, Melissa L. *Making Gullah: A History of Sapelo Islanders, Race and the American Imagination.* The University of North Carolina Press; Illustrated edition, 2017.

Cross, Wilbur. *Gullah Culture in America*. Praeger, 2007.

Daise, Ronald. *Gullah Branches: West African Roots*. Sandlapper Publishing Company, 2007.

Fant, Jennie Holton, *Sojourns in Charleston, South Carolina, 1865-1947, From the Ruins of War to the Rise of Tourism*. University of South Carolina Press, 2019.

Haley, John. *A Guide to Wilmington's African-American Heritage.* City of Wilmington, North Carolina, 2014.

Holmes, Barbara. *Joy Unspeakable: The Contemplative Practices of the Black Church.* Fortress Press: 2004.

Naylor, Gloria. *Mama Day*. Ticknor and Fields, 1989.

Pinckney, Roger. *Blue Roots: African American Folk Medicine of the Gullah People.*

Stephenson, Bryan. *Just Mercy: A Story of Justice and Redemption.* One World, 2014.

Film

Daughters of Dust, Julie Dash. Kino International, 1991.

About the Author

 Nancy Flinchbaugh is an award-winning author who writes for change, for peace, justice, and the Earth. She wrote this book as she hopes for beloved community, as she grapples with racism and tangled roots in America.

Her other books include: the MAMs Book Club series *Revelation in the Cave* (2012), *Revelation at the Labyrinth* (eLectio Publishing, 2017), and *Revelation in the Roots: Emerald Isle* (All Things That Matter Press, 2022), and *Mariah of the Wind* (All Things That Matter Press, 2023). In addition, she has written a memoir, *Letters from the Earth* (Higher Ground Books and Media, 2018), and *Awakening: A Contemplative Primer on Learning to Sit* (Higher Ground Books and Media, 2020).

She enjoys nature, gardening, bicycling, traveling, leading contemplative experiences, community building, and writing books with purpose. Nancy is a member of First Baptist church and mother of two wonderful sons, Luke and Jacob. She lives in Springfield, Ohio, empty nesting with her husband, Steve.

Learn more about her work at nancyflinchbaugh.com. Connect with her on Facebook at Nancy Flinchbaugh, Author, and YouTube@nancyflinchbaugh.